The Nanny Outside the Gates

BOOKS BY SHARI J. RYAN

The Bookseller of Dachau

The Doctor's Daughter

The Lieutenant's Girl

The Maid's Secret

The Stolen Twins

The Homemaker

The Glovemaker's Daughter

The Perfect Nanny

The Nurse Behind the Gates

My Husband's Past

The Family Behind the Walls

The Singer Behind the Wire

LAST WORDS

The Girl with the Diary

The Prison Child

The Soldier's Letters

The Nanny Outside the Gates

SHARI J. RYAN

Bookouture

Published by Bookouture in 2025

An imprint of Storyfire Ltd.
Carmelite House
50 Victoria Embankment
London EC4Y 0DZ

www.bookouture.com

The authorised representative in the EEA is Hachette Ireland
8 Castlecourt Centre
Dublin 15 D15 XTP3
Ireland
(email: info@hbgi.ie)

ISBN: 978-1-80550-164-0
eBook ISBN: 978-1-80550-163-3

To those who find their life's purpose between the pages of a book...

PROLOGUE
HALINA

August 1943
Oświęcim, Poland

The baby's desperate cry travels on a gust of wind, whipping around me as I forge through the darkness along the narrow path, running as fast as I dare. The thicket of trees presses in on me, their low-hanging branches like clawed arms with gnarly fingers catching on the fabric of my uniform. The ground is warped with bowing roots, threatening to trip me with every step, and the night tightens around me as I press on, only focusing on moving forward.

For a moment I stop, just to catch my breath, bending forward, hands on my knees, ears straining for the baby's next cry. Except, the next gust of wind travels alone. I gasp for air, my lungs burning, my pulse thrumming. I can't afford to stop.

My legs grow heavier as I trudge on, the trees thinning until a sliver of moonlight spills across the ground, exaggerating every shadow, but guiding me toward our meeting spot. Broken twigs and damp matted leaves litter the dirt, and the air clings to the scent of late summer rain.

A whimper ripples through the air and my breath stutters as a piercing cry follows, drawing me to the next tree where Gavriel waits, shrouded in his loose-fitted clothing, gently rocking the sweet, innocent baby girl in his arms.

"Shh," I whisper through my panting, touching her chest, trying to calm her down. When she hears my voice up close, her cries falter as she grasps onto a strand of my hair between her tiny fingers. Her tired giggle bounces between the trees, but her delight will be short-lived.

"We have to go," Gavriel says, his scratchy whisper catching in his throat.

"Here, I'll take her," I say, reaching my arms out.

"Not yet. I've already had a minute to catch my breath. You haven't."

Behind us, raging shouts fire out in the distance and dogs are barking. They know.

I follow Gavriel through the clearing and onto another uneven dirt path as the little baby in his arms starts up a relentless wailing. Is she hungry? Hurt? Tired? Or does she sense the danger we'll face if we don't make it out of the woods quickly?

The trees end abruptly, spitting us out onto the road, our breaths heavy with exertion and fear. My foot presses into the gravel, and I hesitate...just for a second. Gavriel doesn't. He pushes forward into the sweep of spotlights.

Just beyond the trees to our right, the barbed wire surrounding Auschwitz hums with electricity, a sound I'm familiar with. The existence is a warning of the grave consequences we'll face if we're caught.

"Stay under the branches to the side of the road," Gavriel says, still charging forward.

To our right, the barbed-wire fence enclosing Auschwitz cuts across the horizon like a jagged scar. We're not inside the death camp itself, but we're close enough to make out the faint cries from within. Still, we're trapped within German seized land, an SS-controlled zone that clings to the camp's edge.

The checkpoint ahead isn't an exit from Auschwitz proper, but from the so-called "Area of Interest," a tightly patrolled forty-square-kilometer restricted zone meant to protect the secrets of SS homes, camp-run factories, and the regime's lethal order. Beyond it, where I come from, Polish civilians still scurry about. If we can just make it past this checkpoint, we might find somewhere safer than here.

This was the first gate I crossed when I was brought here, where I let go of the hope of ever seeing the Vistula River again. Nothing says "the end" like an SS guard with a rifle slung under his arm. Gavriel slows then stops. I nearly bump into him before he turns to face me, his gaze catching mine in the dark. "Here," he says, his voice low and raspy. "It's best if you take her now."

As I take the sweet baby girl into my arms, her cries turn into more of a weak whimper, and as we walk, she finally takes a deep breath and sighs, falling quiet. I keep my eyes on the road, avoiding the deep, jagged holes, making sure I don't trip. There's too much to fear all at once.

"What if this doesn't work?" I don't expect him to answer. The question is weighing heavily on us both.

But he stares into my eyes. "We can't think that way. It's our only option—it will work."

Each step closer to the freedom lying beyond this last blockade is endless, especially now that the guard's flashlight is gliding our way.

The damp rubble beneath my feet crackles and pops, and the fog hanging in the air begins to suffocate me. My heart pounds painfully. "Papers," the guard demands. "Where are you coming from and what is your destination?"

We stop just in front of him, his eyes concealed by the rim

of his cap. "We've been on the compound visiting family, the Schäfers—you must know them. We were to attend their dinner party tonight, but our baby's illness has taken a turn for the worse. She needs a doctor. She's very sick. If we don't get her there—"

"Papers," he snaps, interrupting me.

My throat tightens and my focus falls to the rusty gate, framed by sandbags and stacked wooden crates. A smeared red streak near the latch...is that paint or blood?

"There's no time for papers," Gavriel says, his German accent impeccable. "Our daughter...she won't survive another hour. She needs help right away."

No one comes and goes easily from the occupied villages surrounding Auschwitz. The entire area is heavily barricaded by guards, even though the only people who live within this "restricted zone" are working members of the Reich, domestic servants, and beyond them, the prisoners.

This little girl so obviously senses every emotion surrounding her, explaining the returning of her piercing cry. I hold her tighter but don't rock her in my arms like I normally would. I don't hush her either. It's important that she continues to cry now.

"What is the baby ill with?" the guard asks with haste, shining his flashlight onto her sensitive eyes, lingering on her flushed skin. He stumbles back a step. "Typhus," he utters, as if the word itself is infectious.

All the guards are afraid of this disease. As they should be.

"There's a rash—on her belly. The fever...spiked just an hour ago. She's already had one seizure. We're sure it's typhus," Gavriel explains.

I gasp a stuttered breath as a sob relents. "You must understand," I cry out. "Feel her head—how hot she is..." I hold her out toward him, my arms shaking.

He won't touch her. The risk of typhus isn't worth it to him. *Please God, keep us safe right now.*

The guard takes another step backward. "Go on," he snaps, tearing a handkerchief from his pocket to press against his nose. "If you return without a doctor's note..." He doesn't finish his statement, but the implication is clear.

His grip tightens on the gate lever. He's letting us go. But then his jaw clenches, and as if someone has whispered a warning in his ear, he appears to reconsider. The flashlight angles toward our faces, blinding us. "Show me your forearms."

"Wh—what do you mean?" I ask. "Why must you see our arms?" My acting isn't believable—nor is my naivete.

He's looking for tattooed numbers from Auschwitz. The tattooed numbers all the prisoners within the barbed-wire fences have...The tattooed numbers we shouldn't have if we're truly just visiting family here on the compound.

"Show me, or you don't pass." The ground disappears beneath my feet and my vision blurs.

It's over.

This is the end for all of us.

ONE
GAVRIEL

Three Months Earlier—May 1943

I lay each brick slowly, pressing it into the wet mortar, knowing it will outlive me. I'm twenty-three, and already I know that these walls, when finished, will stand long after the last scream blurs into ash.

The long rectangular structure, shallow and partly underground, is unmistakable. I recognized it once the foundation was set. Same width. Same slope. The dimensions match the crematorium just south of here—the one where the chimney never stops sputtering and smoke drifts up until it becomes one with the sky.

There, the line of unsuspecting and innocent people never ends. They only move in one direction.

They go in.

They don't come out.

Burning ash fills our noses and it sticks to us long after we're done working, reminding us of what's around us and what's waiting for us.

The air at this end of the camp is dry with soot and the dust of limestone. Mortar gums up my throat and feels gritty between my teeth. I focus on the metallic scrape of the trowel and dull thud of stone, a familiar companion.

Pa wouldn't recognize me now. Just skin, muscle, and bone. No fat anywhere. My hair's been shaved to avoid lice, but I'm left with sunburns. I've never had that issue before, not with a thick head of dark hair.

Sometimes, I catch my reflection in puddles. The sight is jarring. I tell myself the water distorts features, but...the face looking back, the hollow cheeks, and eyes too deep. It's me. I feel it. Even my hands used to be calloused and ready to work. Now, they split open too easily, always raw and bloody.

Pa may not be here to see what's become of me, but at least I can still hear his words with every brick I lay. "Don't force it, Gavriel. Let it settle into the mortar. Let it become a solid." He said if we build slowly with a critical mind, the walls will shelter, comfort, and last for generations of families. Not here. Families are a distant thought here.

Back in the suburbs outside of Krakow when I built walls alongside my brothers and Pa, I would imagine the people who would eventually live inside them: A young couple sharing their first home together, a baker preparing to become well-known for his fresh bread, or a schoolhouse that would keep the youngest generations educated and safe.

Before September 1939 and the invasion when the Reich took everything from us, we'd be up every morning before dawn. Nails in my pockets and sawdust stuck to the scruff of my chin. Every day felt like a new adventure.

Days blurred together until Friday. Shabbat. Ma's table would be set like nothing else mattered. Wine filled our glasses, bread steamed from the wicker basket, and Hebrew prayers were sung with passion.

"*Music to my ears*," Ma would say, gleaming with pride. "*Feeding my hungry family of men is my life's purpose—until one of you gives me grandchildren, of course.*" As the oldest son, she'd look right at me, then she'd say it again, so I knew she was serious. I would then bite my tongue until she concluded her thoughts with: "Regardless, I am a blessed Jewish woman."

We believed every word. Because we were a blessed Jewish family.

Our family had been building homes since my great-great-grandfather laid his first foundation with his bare hands. Pa always had a dream of his three sons taking over the business someday, but Jozek, my younger brother, has plans to become a doctor, and Natan, the youngest, wants to be a world-renowned journalist who writes about the corners of the earth no one has discovered. Me, though, I'm like my pa. I always knew I'd step up to the position someday. I just had to earn my way there first.

We prayed the war wouldn't last long. That forced labor would be the worst of it. It wasn't. A year and a half later, in March 1941, they tore us from our home and locked us inside the Krakow ghetto.

More labor awaited, but not the kind that builds anything. Just sweeping and shoveling streets. Tedious and relentless work. We dreamed of the next time we'd be allowed to build something again. Ma told me to be grateful. She said what we had was enough. I should have listened better.

Now I'm building again, but for cold-blooded killers, not families. The family business is long gone, along with my family who I was stripped from in the ghetto six weeks ago, brought to Auschwitz's tall black gates that read: "Work Will Set You Free."

Despite my anguish over being separated from my family, I consider myself lucky for being assigned to masonry work here. But everything we're told at Auschwitz is a lie.

We will all work until we die. Even Pa's promise that hard work is the ticket to a good life seems impossible here.

"The sun is going to fry us up here today," Adam says,

handing me the next brick. His hands are raw, knuckles bloody. If I look anything like he does right now, then we both have black streaks of sweat carving trails through the ash stuck to our faces. The mortar is drying up too quickly and there isn't a spot of shade on this wooden scaffold that groans with every shift of our weight.

Adam doesn't have masonry experience, but he was a farmer. He's been quick to learn, has steady hands and is sharper than he lets on.

I'm a few years older than him, and he reminds me of Jozek. Same way of moving, same quiet strength. And his sense of humor—dry and unpredictable—is just like Natan. He reminds me of my brothers in more ways than I'd like to admit, and somehow that helps. He's filled part of the painful void I was forced to leave behind.

It's a gift to have a dependable friend in this place, and quite rare. Plus, we work well together. He has the bricks coated in mortar, ready and waiting for me. I scrape off the excess, place it, then level the row. It's become a mechanical rhythm for us.

There's only one difference between us. He's a dreamer, and I'm too honest with myself. But I need him. Just like I needed my brothers. We were always dependable, and a team, even when arguing over stupid things. I try to be that to Adam now, and he does the same for me.

I guess we balance each other, which gives us each a sense of purpose to make it through another day.

"You know," I say, squinting toward the clear sky, "we should have made a weak spot somewhere so the whole thing collapses in a week."

Adam scratches his eyebrow, a faint smirk creases along the dirt smudges. "We'd get two minutes of celebration before they made us rebuild it. Twice the bricks, half the mortar."

He has a point. "You're right. They'd want us to build a bigger, more reliable chimney of death," I say, nodding toward the other crematorium building. But would it even matter? Would the setback save anyone? Or slow the inevitable?

Adam stares toward the other crematorium, his jaw shifting side to side. "That's not what this building is. You can't believe every rumor that goes around—I keep telling you, my friend."

"But you can see it's the same layout. Same design."

He shakes his head, his mouth pinched shut as if he's holding in more than words. "It's different. You'll see. It'll be another kitchen or something."

"Another kitchen for who?" I ask. "They don't feed us Jews as it is." The truth and reality are so ridiculous that I chuckle. "Don't you remember when you thought the sauna was for relaxation rather than a delousing station?"

"Point taken. Point taken," he mutters. "Then a barbershop. Now, that's something you can't argue. The guards are always eager to shave every hair off our heads. They probably just need more space to do that."

I let his dry joke land between us. "Maybe you're right." I can't tell if I'm watching out for him or allowing him to watch out for me. There's no real method of protecting anyone here, but we're in this together no matter how we end up.

The mortar has gotten too thick. "We need to add water," I say, tapping the trowel against the rim of the bucket.

"I'll grab it," Adam says, already climbing down the rungs.

While he's gone, I push the last few bricks closer and stir up what's left of the mix. The wooden handle of the trowel shakes in my grip, the metal neck threatening to snap. But it holds. I smear on a wad of compound, line the brick, and guide it into place. My makeshift plumb-bob swings once, twice, then stills. And on to the next.

When Adam returns, he's flushed, the whites of his eyes reddening as he winces from something. He scans the scaffold plank from one side to the other. "Load up the next stack," he hollers down to the man below, his breath ragged.

"Want me to get the pulley this time?" I ask. If we don't finish up soon, one of us is going to drop.

"I got it," he says, setting the bucket of water down. "This should be the last load."

I scrape the extra mortar from the edge and take a step back, staring down at the chimney's rectangular column. I glance through the trees toward the identical structure across the way and shame simmers in my gut. I built this chimney. I ensured that each brick was lined up to perfection and the sturdiness could never be in question. The smoke will rise high into the clouds, bringing fragments of innocent people to heaven. Pa would be so proud of the craftsmanship...until he found out what this chimney is being used for.

I lift the hem of my jacket and dry the sweat off my face, noticing an SS officer standing between a couple of guards. They're staring up at the chimney, pointing and chatting. Did I work too fast or too slow? Did I forget something? I return my focus to the brick pattern, studying it for inconsistencies, but finding none.

A whistle slings through the air, recapturing my attention. "You there, brick-boy, come," the watching SS officer shouts up to me. Me. He's talking to me, just me. I curl my hand around my throat, where my pulse hammers. I grip the ladder's side and take another glance down at the officer, wondering if he's laughing because I'm sure he can sense the fear from where he's standing. He's still, just staring with his arms folded across his chest.

He told me to come. As if I'm a dog.

I scale down the ladder and make my way over to the officer, trying to hold my posture straight as my stare falls to the ground. My fingers twitch by my sides, coated in mortar dust and sweat. The moment I stop working, the pain and hunger set in. I clench my fists to steady myself.

I step up to the man, nearly a head shorter than me, and wait for him to speak.

"You have experience with masonry, yes?"

"Yes." My response is muffled by a passing laborer pulling a wagon over dirt-riddled rocks. The clatter is so loud it sounds like a metal rubbish bin rolling down a hill. I can't help but stare at the pile of cans the man is transporting. Each of them is stamped with a single label: Zyklon-B.

There it is.

The poison they use to kill people.

The ultimate proof.

Even Adam reacts to the sight. From the corner of my eye, I notice him stiffen, staring at the cans.

The officer clears his throat as the wagon stops to the side of the building. "Your attention to detail is—" he says with a hard blink before continuing. "Your skills are needed elsewhere." They would never pay a Jew a compliment, and I don't want one from him or any of the other beasts. "Come."

No one in the vicinity speaks. No one moves. They just watch me go—like they've already decided I won't be coming back.

TWO

HALINA

July 15, 1943

Eva darts out the church doors and makes a beeline for the clearing in the woods. "Eva, come back here," I shout, already breaking into a run.

Her little feet smack the dirt road, shoes too tattered to soften the clamber. Dirt clouds up behind her like smoke. She bolts forward with the worry-free confidence only a child can have, arms pumping, curls flying in the wind. It's as if the forest is hers to claim. She doesn't even hesitate at the split that breaks into several directions, just continues down the one where several low weather-worn branches arch toward the ground. Every weaving motion is methodical, like this attempt to flee was pre-planned. I'm sure it was.

This seven-year-old little girl is going to give me gray hair, but she reminds me of her at the same age. This must be my retribution.

Eva's heading straight for the bridge, the connecting seam between what's left of civility on our side of the Vistula, and the Reich-occupied restricted zone on the other.

What was once Polish-owned is now property of the Reich. The people of Poland should have the right to cross whichever road we please here, but that's a war we won't win.

At twenty-two years old, I'm more staff than ward now. Julia took me in when I was left on the church as a newborn, an orphan, and I've lived here ever since. It's barely a church anymore, more of an aged sanctuary being utilized as a shelter. That's just the façade though. Julia and the other housemothers keep the inside warm, clean, and as close to home as anything I've known.

No one in their right mind would choose to live beside Reich soldiers, but we weren't given a choice. Nearly four years ago, they forced all Polish citizens out of the forty-square-mile area of land surrounding Oświęcim and its nearby villages, sealing it off like a fortress and declaring it a "restricted zone." It's off limits to anyone not branded by the Reich.

The orphanage sits less than fifteen minutes from the nearest checkpoint of the SS settlement area, and thirty minutes from the front gates of Auschwitz—the former Army barracks turned prison labor camp for war criminals. But no Polish citizen truly knows what happens behind those forbidden barriers—or the road that leads to the smokestack—unless they've been taken inside.

In winter when the trees are bare, gunshots echo between frozen embankments. In summer, when the air is thick and sticky, the stench of smoke weaves through the branches.

"Eva!" I shout, this time through a harsh whisper, winded as my lungs threaten to splinter my ribs. I don't know how this little girl is so much faster than me. "Stop running! Let's talk about why you're upset. I can help!" I don't know how I managed to let her slip past me. I'm better than that. I must have been distracted—something I'm not allowed to be when taking care of children. How could I have let this happen?

She doesn't bother to look over her shoulder toward me. Just keeps on running, taking all the correct turns between the maze of trees as if she knows exactly where she's trying to go—where she's not supposed to go. Most people would get themselves lost trying to get in or out if they didn't have directions. Not her, though. Nope. She doesn't understand the danger that looms in the distance.

The humid air catches in my lungs as I continue after her, finally gaining more speed, or she's becoming tired. I catch her by the wrist just as she sets foot on the road, just footsteps from the bridge, and a two-minute walk from a German checkpoint.

"No!" Eva screams. "Let me go!"

"Eva, you know the rules, and you know exactly where that bridge will take you," I scold her, breathlessly, painfully, understanding the exact reason why she's trying to run away.

"Because," she says with a heavy groan. "The bridge goes to the bad place—the one that makes people disappear." After a roll of her young, naïve eyes, I tug her backward a few steps onto a patch of grass with sprouting weeds and dandelions.

"We need to go back to the orphanage. We can't be out here. Let's go back so we can talk about what's upsetting you." I lower to my knees to get a better grip on her, taking her small hands within mine. "Come along—there's no sense in calling attention to ourselves here. We don't want any trouble with those soldiers. You know they're always over here, looking for more Polish people to kick out of their homes."

"Well, I want to go back to my home," she says, stomping her foot and crossing her arms over her chest. Her short blonde hair swishes along her pink cheeks.

She's been at the orphanage a few years, brought here not long after her parents were killed, along with thousands of civilians in Warsaw during the invasion.

She was too young to understand what she survived, or the meaning of death. So now she carries hope that her parents are still at home waiting for her.

No matter how many times we explain that they're gone, she doesn't listen. She's just a child, protected by her imagination.

We could all learn a thing or two from her.

"The church we live in is your home, Eva," I remind her.

"You're not Mama or Papa."

"I know, but I still love you very much and want you to be safe." I release one of her hands and poke the tip of her nose with my finger.

Her big hazelnut eyes widen as she stares back at me, and I'm not sure what has spooked her. A low rumble of an engine simmers in the near distance, followed by the crunching of rocks beneath tires. The squeal of brakes follows. With a cautious glance over my right shoulder, I spot an expensive black vehicle pulling over to the side of the road.

"Eva, look at me," I say, squeezing her hands. "Go back now. Don't stop running until you are back inside. Do you understand?"

With just one nod, she turns away from me and takes off, back in the right direction this time. Her ragged shoes slap heavily against the dirt as she becomes a blur between the trees. I should go after her, but I don't like the look of this car, and I don't want this person following us.

I drop my hands into the pockets of my skirt and stare across the road, waiting for the car to pass. But it doesn't. A door creaks open. My pulse thuds in my ears, so loud I can hear each beat. A man steps out, his uniform crisp, the lightning-bolt runes sharp on his collar tab, and a red band tainted by a swastika.

He walks slowly, never taking his eyes off me. What could he want? I'm outside the "restricted zone" and I haven't done anything.

He stops before me, his silence speaking for him as he rests his hand on his belt. "What are you doing this close to the checkpoint?" He stares down at me from beneath the rim of his peaked visor cap.

I take a breath and swallow the lump rising in my throat. We speak Polish, but when the German Reich stormed in, they demanded we speak their language. At first, I refused. I wouldn't follow their bullish commands. Then I realized they were speaking German because they can't speak Polish.

That's when I realized that if I wanted to survive this war, I needed to know their language better than they knew mine. After three years of just me and a worn-out textbook, I'm nearly confident in my practice. Though I've never had to use it. Not like this.

For a moment, the foreign words stick to my tongue. "I—I'm taking care of a little girl. She wandered off. I was just bringing her back."

He peers past me through the trees, and I follow his stare, finding no sight of Eva. I hope she made it back inside.

"You're out here begging?"

"No, that—that's...not true. I wasn't begging."

"You're loitering like a street rat. Waiting for someone to toss you money or food, yes?" He steps in toward me, coming too close for comfort. "Unless, perhaps, you're a simple thief?"

"No, never—" I curl my fingers into fists, pressing them into the sides of my legs. "I was helping the little girl. That's all."

The officer breathes heavily through his nose and recoils as if he's gotten a whiff of something rancid. "You look like a Jew."

A shiver runs down my spine, colliding with the droplets of sweat, now fearing this awful man more than before. I'm stronger than his fear tactics. I'm stronger than him.

"I'm not Jewish," I say, my words shooting out of me like a protective shield. Anyone who isn't Jewish has seen how the SS treat them, and we fear for them more than ourselves.

He tilts his head to the side as if inspecting me from a different angle. "Where are your papers?"

"Back at the house I work at. Like I said, I was trying to stop the little girl I care for from running off."

He rolls back onto his heels and eyes me up and down, not in the way men sometimes do, but as if I'm being evaluated—like produce in a store.

"You take care of children?" he asks.

"Yes." I think my last statement was enough of an answer to his question.

"The timing is stunning," he says, scratching his manicured fingernails along his chin. "I promised my wife I'd find someone like you today: a young Pole, working-class age, able-bodied, and capable of speaking German. We need a caretaker for our children—the last one just...parted ways with us."

"I already have a job," I remind him for the third time. "And I should get back to work—make sure the little girl found her way back."

The man shakes his head and snickers before all hints of emotion leave his angular face. "I don't have time to go searching for another caretaker today. You understand this, yes?" He doesn't let me respond before continuing. "Good. Good. You have two choices..." He speaks casually, as if he hasn't already begun to threaten me. "You will come with me and serve in my home and tend to my children."

I clench my hands into fists by my sides, my nails piercing the flesh of my palms. "I—I already said—"

"And the second choice is, I arrest you for loitering, begging, and withholding papers. You go to the prison labor camp. This should be an easy answer." He shrugs, then grins, making it known I have just as little power as every other natural-born citizen in this country.

The word *prison* replays in my head. Prison must mean Auschwitz.

There are many rumors about Auschwitz, most of which I hope aren't true.

I can either look after Nazi-born children or surrender to imprisonment in Auschwitz. These aren't options.

Any child raised by a Nazi has already been taught to hate. Taught that they're a superior race, and that others are disposable. I'm sure he'll expect me to support the beliefs and mindset of the regime.

I won't.

I'll do the opposite. In silence and with caution, I'll be the crack in their solid foundation. I'll unteach what's been forced into them. Maybe I could stop just one child from becoming this man standing in front of me. From becoming a monster.

The Reich has already stolen the freedom I never really had. I won't let them steal my beliefs.

If I have to avoid prison by serving this Nazi family, it will be on my terms.

"I'll serve." But if he thinks I'll be grateful, he's wrong.

"Come along then," he says, jutting his head toward his car.

I look to my side, where the labyrinth of trees spills out onto the road—where I sent Eva just before the officer approached me. "I need to gather my belongings and papers." I must make sure Eva made it back to the orphanage too. And Julia—I need to tell her what's happening. I might not have parents, and she's no longer considered my housemother as I've been working for her, but she's been the closest thing I have.

This man isn't going to let me go anywhere. I can see it in his narrowing eyes.

"Fine. Lead the way."

What have I done?

This is why the church-turned-orphanage still looks abandoned on the outside. With overgrown brush and nestled tightly between trees that have survived every known war in this country, we've been left alone.

I take hesitant steps forward, thinking of a way to stop him from following me, but he's on my heels. I stop and turn around. "It can be a long walk, and it's muddy from last night's rain."

"How long of a walk?" he asks, his patience questionable by his complacent tone.

"I could run." He won't run with me, not with his shiny boots.

He holds up his wrist to look at the time. "You have five minutes. If you aren't back here then, I'll find you, and you won't have a second option."

I can't believe he's letting me go. Without a moment to spare, I race through the trees, as fast as Eva did earlier. I avoid the mud and bang on the locked front door.

Julia opens the door a crack then releases the thick latch to pull me inside and into her chest. Her embrace holds a trace of lavender soap and flour, a scent that I had become too used to and stopped noticing. It now hits me like it might be the last time I ever smell something so nice. "Dear God, I thought they took you. Eva said a man in uniform came for you."

"Yes, and I have to go with the officer who found me. He said I'd serve him—his children."

"In their home?" she snaps. "Halina, you know what that means. You realize you won't just be cleaning floors, don't you? And those children...they aren't just common children. They're—why, they're bred Naz—"

"I know who they are," I say, stopping Julia from speaking in a way she likely won't forgive herself for later.

Bile burns up my throat, knowing I don't have a choice, and she doesn't realize that yet.

"You'll be inside of their territory—that God awful 'restricted zone' they've claimed," she says, pointing in the direction of the bridge—the guarded checkpoint. "You will see things you can't unsee, and you won't be able to—" She clutches her hand around her aging neck. "You won't be able to get back to this side. Civilians don't go in or out of there for a reason. You know this."

A chill runs down my hot back and my chin shivers. "I don't have a choice." Not about going with that officer, but what I do when I get there. I can teach these children of the Reich the truth. Show them who they're being shaped to become. I can be a quiet act of resistance from the inside. One *they* brought into their home. It might not make a big difference, but it's something.

"No. No, absolutely not. Where is he, Halina? Where is this soldier? I'll have a word with that—with that…" She steps to the side, reaching for the front door. Her face is red, her temples pulsating around her protruding veins.

I grab her arm. "You can't—he'll take you away. The children here—they need you. And this man is a high-ranking officer. If I don't return, he'll come find me here then take me to prison for loitering, begging, and not having papers on me. That's what he said. You know these people hold on to their word as if it's made of gold."

Tears stream down Julia's cheeks as she cups her hand over her mouth.

"How will you survive there? What if those children are unmanageable?" Her words become a whisper, "They've undoubtedly been brainwashed…"

I can't answer her. Not with any sort of reassurance. I'm terrified of what lies ahead or who I'll have to become to survive. But if I can make a difference, even just a small one, it will mean I've done something. Make an impact and have a purpose in life like she's had on me. Even if no one else ever knows it.

I race upstairs to the small bedroom I've called mine for the last four years, since transitioning from a child orphan to an adult worker.

Dropping to my knees, I pull my borrowed suitcase out

from beneath the low bed. I tuck in my shabby brown teddy bear and the worn folktale book—its cover etched with a hand-drawn dog standing among a set of trees. These are the only thing my parents left me—a smidgen of comfort and the only story to my life.

The few other small belongings and identification papers fit into a small satchel that I sling over my shoulder. I grab the suitcase and hurry back down the stairs, right into Julia's waiting arms.

"Write to me. Promise me, Halina. Promise me."

"I will—I'll write you. I'll be careful. I'll follow the rules, and do what I'm asked, and—" my tongue catches in my throat and I tug at the collar of my dress as if it will give me more air to breathe. "I'll survive. That's what I do. That's what all of us here have done, day after day. It's the only thing left that we're allowed to do."

Julia cups my face in her hands, kisses my forehead, then tucks the loose strands from my braid behind my ears.

She used to fiddle with my hair when I was small, usually when I had a fever. While curled up beside her, she'd dream aloud about my future, whispering all the wonderful things I was meant to see. Back then, they were just words. Now I wish I had believed them.

"God brought us together, and together we shall be, my sweet girl. Always. I love you." She wraps her arms around me, an embrace that hurts inside. It hurts so much. My heart. My stomach. And all I can do is clutch the handle of my suitcase until my knuckles ache.

The only words that come to me are cold and hollow. Not enough. "Thank you for taking me in and keeping me."

A breath catches in my lungs as I rush back out the door, each step heavier now as I carry my life within my hands—my small, invaluable life.

The officer has his eyes set on his watch as I turn the corner.

He raises his brows, as if impressed, but he doesn't say another word as he leads me to his car.

"Papers?" He presses again before saying another word.

I pull the folded documents from my satchel and hand them to him, wondering how closely he'll look through them.

A quick scan doesn't raise an eyebrow, but he slips them into his pocket rather than handing them back.

Cigars, nicotine, and leather, a pungent mixture that fills my nose. We drive in silence across the first half of the bridge up to the barred entrance of the Reich's stolen domain. The officer is chummy with the checkpoint guard, laughing and muttering in German slang about the weather and completing the interaction with simply telling the guard that I'm with him, as in property.

We continue over the remainder of the bridge, the guard towers of Auschwitz coming into focus the further we drive into the "restricted zone." For a moment I consider if everything he said was a lie. There aren't truly two options, and he's bringing me to Auschwitz. It's because I was too close to the boundaries. I must know more than I should. Now, I'm on the inside and the gate has been sealed behind us.

The thought of Julia's embrace and my stiff response is already tearing me to shreds. She held me like a mother...the person who has always kept me safe, who would risk her own life for me. And I just stood there. Frozen. She deserved more from me. I should have told her I loved her. God, I do.

Those words feel foreign on my tongue and in my heart, like I shouldn't speak of something I know nothing about.

My pulse stutters as he takes a sharp turn away from the towers, and away from the barbed-wire fence that's close enough to make out. *He's not taking me to Auschwitz. Yet.*

We end up on a road surrounded by fields of overgrown grass, some as high as wheat, leaving only the tops of a tree line. The barren landscape fills me with dread, as if I'll be dropped in the middle of nowhere, with no way to return to civilization.

Clouds roll toward us like foreshadowing in a scary story, and my reflection in the car window sharpens. When did I become this person? My sun-streaked chestnut hair pulled back tightly, a sharp expression of dread mixed with bravery, a straight line across my lips rather than a soft natural smile. I can't see my eyes, but they're heavy and tired. I'm not the young girl who used to help Julia bring smiles to children's faces.

Now I'll have to protect the light in children who've been raised by darkness—even if I've lost mine.

My breathing grows heavier, and I think he's noticed as he's glanced over a few times now. The open space tightens quickly as a wooded area unfolds over a shallow hill.

He turns down a narrow side street with old houses, broken fences, shattered cobblestone. More desolation.

Two more streets pass, just as bleak, before we turn onto a well-groomed road with larger, modern houses. Tall oaks for privacy—because we're minutes from Auschwitz.

The car comes to a slow halt in front of a two-story house. "Wait here," he says.

THREE

GAVRIEL

July 15, 1943

The relentless rainstorm from late last night flooded the dirt roads between the rows of wooden stables we call barracks. The sky hangs low with heavy cloud cover, and the spotlights are still on—scanning, flickering—highlighting the swarm of trilling insects overhead.

The mud is like tar, sticky like hands clinging to the soles of my warped boots, threatening to drag me under with each step. Guards linger at every intersecting corner, rifles slung low, angry dogs at their sides, watching as we limp from point A to B while hungry, exhausted, and barely alive. There's no choice but to keep up with the man in front of me. One misstep or being too slow could result in a consequence, depending on who sees it happen.

I begin each morning already sore, muscles as stiff as steel from the previous day's labor, waiting in one of two short lines at the front entrance of the labor barracks for an SS escort to bring us to our job site.

The path through the woods is worse. Fallen pine needles

mask the slickness beneath, each step a hazard. By the time we reach Pelizy Road, I'm already drained. The houses here mock us with their affluence. Two-story whitewashed structures with red-tiled roofs, framed in polished walnut and trimmed emerald hedges.

Six of us prisoners are assigned to these homes. I work at the Schäfer house because Officer Schäfer is the one who took notice of my handiwork when building a crematorium. Adam, my only friend left in this world, tends to the garden and landscape out back, keeping the flowers alive better than we're being kept alive. Kasia scrubs and cooks inside. And I sweat in the attic, building a storage room for the Frau's nonsense. An attic for valuables when most of Poland has nothing.

The kapo Oskar is short, shaped like a bulldog and always scowling, and all he does is hover all day. He rotates between houses throughout the day, but when he's not around, the female kapo acts on his behalf and is just as cruel.

From the skeletal frame of rafters and beams, I hear the sound of crackling rubble and the sputter of Officer Schäfer's car. Since I've been assigned to work here, he hasn't been home at this hour. I shield my hand over my eyes to block out the sun, watching him step out of his car with haste. His boots clap against the stone pavers, curt, urgent steps. The front door slams, and I wipe the sweat from my brow.

On the street, a boy, maybe nine or ten, studies Schäfer's dark car. His hair is too light, but his posture and curiosity...He looks like Natan at that age.

My youngest brother and the spark in our family—Ma thought Natan could do no wrong. Pa always kept one eye on him. Mischief was his mission, but no one made us laugh like Natan. Every dinner, we ended up clutching our stomachs, laughing at a story or joke Natan had saved up.

Even the last night in the ghetto, it felt like nothing could touch us.

Until something did.

* * *

"I saw a chicken today," Natan says with a mouthful of bread.

"Where?" Ma asks, smiling.

"It was running wild right through the square like it knew it had ended up in the ghetto. Next thing I know, half the people on the block were chasing it."

"Oh really, and who won this chase?" Pa asks, an eyebrow raised.

Natan waits a moment, his grin unfurling devilishly. "The hen. It was a real peep show!"

I nearly choke on my bread as laughter bursts out of us all. Jozek claps his hand down against the table, the ceramic mugs clattering against our plates. A ruckus. That's what we are.

Pa moves to the window and pulls back the lace drapes Ma hung to remind us of home. A darkness pools over Pa's face as he waves a hand at us. "Quiet down," he says.

As the aftershock snickers from Natan, Jozek, and me die down, a rumble of marching boots and shouts echoes between the tenement walls. The two families we live with pour into the central room we share, the only space with a small table for meals. I glance at my brothers, both pale with wide eyes.

Natan is shivering with fear.

Marching boots thunder outside. Coming closer by the second. "Grab your suitcase," Ma whispers.

The knock comes with fury.

"Papers. Have your papers out," Pa tells everyone, preparing to face the evil lurking behind the thin slab of wood.

"Move. Let's go. Let's go. Let's go," a Gestapo shouts from outside. We shuffle out of the tenement, onto the exterior balcony overlooking the stone courtyard. Ma goes first, then Natan, Jozek, and me before Pa. A Gestapo yanks my identifica-

tion from my hand and shoves me in the opposite direction of my family.

"No, no, that's my son. Please, don't separate us," Pa pleads from behind me.

"Your son. He's a grown man. Shut up, move." The shouts continue as I'm pushed to keep walking. I'm twenty-three. Jozek, seventeen, and Natan fifteen. Is that why I've been separated from them?

I glance over my shoulder before turning a corner, finding my family doing the same as people are shoving in against their backs. I shout the words, "I love you. I'll find you. I promise."

* * *

I've never broken a promise to them, and I still whisper those words when no one's listening.

A voice below pulls my mind back to the roofless attic.

"All that matters is whether she's capable of caring for our children. Is she or not?" Frau Schäfer snaps, her words sharp and cold.

"How should I know without seeing her with them, Ada? I spotted her on the side of the road as she was reasoning with a young child she was desperately trying to protect from me. She confirmed her current role was, in fact, taking care of a child. Therefore, I can only tell you it appears she has experience," he replies. "I'll look into the missing information on her papers, but I won't have it immediately."

"She'll do, then. Just fill in the missing information yourself, Heinrich. If she's not a good fit, we'll find another replacement," she says, as if there are women lining up outside of their house to take this unpaid position. There aren't.

A shrill whistle zings between the rafters from the front door below.

"Come!" Schäfer barks.

A young woman steps out of his car. White apron. She's not an Auschwitz prisoner. She's one of the others. A domestic servant. Her posture stiff with a hint of confidence. She pauses, just for a second. Her hands tighten around her suitcase.

Frau Schäfer relents an exaggerated sigh, inflected with disappointment. "It's only a mere few steps, dear," she draws out her words into performative mockery. "Surely, it can't be that difficult."

The young woman flinches when Frau Schäfer mocks her. But she moves anyway.

Something wavers within her, a shift in thought. I don't think it's fear, but rather, something unbreakable. I turn away from the front opening, telling myself the encounter below is none of my concern. The silence that follows the woman's entry doesn't feel like peace. More like a warning. That poor woman just became another functionary of this home. Another soul they'll try to erase.

FOUR

HALINA

The maroon Baroque door towers above me with whittled embellishments, curling like vines around the edges. It's the kind of door that might swallow a person up and never spit them back out. I force my feet forward, one step, then another over a stone threshold and into a breath of cool air that cloaks me like damp linen. The sunlight fades behind me and I debate whether I'll ever see it again.

Frau Schäfer, the officer's wife, stands as if sculpted, poised with golden curls pressed against the collar of her olive-green dress. Pearl earrings frame her pale complexion, but her eyes—they're dark, shadowed beneath thick lashes. Her lip curls—just a smidge—as she sweeps a hand over the slight swell of her belly. A reflex, or a warning. She watches me with cat-like eyes as if I'm a common thief who wandered into her home.

"Children," she says, her voice smooth but stern, "come meet your new nanny."

A succession of hammering or banging fills the quiet as two young girls step out of an adjoining room just beyond the officer and Frau Schäfer. Both spitting images of their mother except for their chocolate brown hair, neatly braided down their backs.

The older of the two girls holds an infant in her arms and steps forward first as they walk past their parents and up to my toes. When the hammering ends, the girl takes the moment to speak. "We're pleased to meet you," she says. "My name is Isla. I'm ten. This is my sister, Marlene." The younger daughter steps up to her sister's side, her expression shy. "Marlene's five. And this is our baby sister, Flora." Isla tugs the blanket down from Flora's chin as if presenting her. "She's ten months old."

While inspecting each of them, I catch the reflection of the chandelier against the polished floors.

The hammering begins again. The walls rattle, the floors vibrate. The children seem unaffected though. Even the baby stares up at the shimmering crystals dangling over her head. She must be entranced by the sparkles.

These children don't appear to be miniature versions of evil yet. Maybe it's not too late for them after all. Though the sight of Flora's stillness has a hold on me. Her body is limp in Isla's arms, her expression vacant.

"Very well. Now that you've all met, I must return to work. If any problems arise, ring Administration," Officer Schäfer shouts above the racket of banging.

He straightens his cap, nods his head at the girls and walks out the door without so much as a goodbye. Despite the cold exchange, Frau Schäfer's tight-lipped smile doesn't speak of an issue. His sudden movement stirs up an overpowering aroma of a powdery-rose perfume.

"Follow me. I'll show you around," she says, curling her finger toward the adjoining room the girls came from. "It won't be long until the girls are heading to school once the summer break ends, but for now, they'll need to be kept occupied."

Her heels stomp on the hardwood floors in contrast and off beat from the hammering above us. We walk into what appears to be the formal sitting room. We pass an ornate mirror with golden trim where I catch a glimpse of myself as we pass by. My braid is fraying at the edges, singular strands sticking to my damp temples. My apron has a yellow-tint I didn't notice before, and the fabric of my dress has a burgundy hue rather than the flat black I've always seen. My pale complexion and cracked lips are the only familiar features I notice.

It's clear, I don't belong here, surrounded by all this luxurious furniture and expensive wooden side tables. My focus latches onto the brick wall above the fireplace, a large, framed piece of a black eagle clutching a swastika inside a wreath. The eagle eyes stare back at me with venom as if it might swoop off the wall and gauge my eyes out.

"This is the formal sitting room. Family and guests only. There won't be a need for you in here," Frau Schäfer says, her final words ending in venom as she was speaking over the upstairs thudding that paused suddenly.

"We had another nanny before you," Marlene says, her words a mere whisper. "But she didn't listen. Isn't that right, Mama?"

Frau Schäfer grips Marlene's shoulder, silently telling her to be quiet.

I shouldn't be jolted to find out this information.

She circles around the room, walking back into the hallway, toward the front door. We pass a narrow door on the left, and a muffled whimper, so faint it might have been a creaking floorboard, grasps my attention. It wasn't the floor, I know it. I stop and tilt my ear toward the door. A scratch, or a sniffle. Then nothing.

"Come," Frau Schäfer snaps, smoothing her hands down the side of her dress as she turns for the stairwell. "It would be wise of you to do only as you're told. Do not take liberties. This is our home, not yours. You are merely staying here as part of your servitude." Servitude. A servant.

"Of—of course, Frau Schäfer," I reply, peering back once more toward the door before following them up to the next floor. "What will the pay be for this position? Your husband didn't mention."

Frau Schäfer rumbles a laugh, cupping her hand around her swollen abdomen. "My...husband..." she speaks slowly as if I can't keep up, "is an SS-Sturmbannführer, a major, and the top rank in his position as the Director of Camp Labor Services." She huffs and turns her nose up at me. "You should be honored to be working in this household, never mind worrying about being paid."

Anger boils through me as she releases a sigh. I won't respond. Not because I agree, but because I know some people...people with a sense of authority mistake silence for obedience. That might become useful to me here.

At the top of the stairs, there is a bedroom with two beds framing a center window and floral wallpaper. "And this is Isla and Marlene's bedroom." She pushes open the door across the hall next. "This is Flora's nursery."

Is she going to mention anything about the baby so obviously growing in her belly? Maybe she did and her words were lost among all the hammering. It's rude to ask a woman about her assumed pregnancy but I would think she'd tell me there will soon be a fourth.

The thuds grow in volume and ricochet between the hallway walls. Only now does Frau Schäfer press her hands against her ears before releasing a hand to open a closet door at the end of the short hallway. "Your bedroom is in the attic, to the left. There is a list of house rules and household responsibilities on the writing desk. Bring your belongings upstairs, read through the list, and report back downstairs. Make it quick. This racket is giving me another headache."

Some of the housemothers who came and left the orphanage acted similarly to Frau Schäfer. Their cold demeanors made me wonder what reason they had to be watching over abandoned or parentless children. I learned to ignore their attitude and instead focus solely on the directions they were giving. The older I grew, the more I realized the women acting out in such a cruel manner toward children were often abandoned or neglected themselves.

Thud, thud, thud, thud...Each thud grows louder and louder as I ascend the narrow stairwell, my slender frame barely fitting between the walls. At the top, I find the right-side wide open, exposed to the outdoors but framed by wooden beams crisscrossing like stitches. No walls. No roof.

The banging ceases again, and a man steps between two large beams. A hammer gripped in his bruised, scratched hand. The ashen blue and white striped uniform startles me.

Is he a prisoner? A criminal? In any case, he's certainly responsible for all the racket. With short, shaven dark hair, red cheeks, and sweat dripping down his sun-darkened complexion, the late-morning light pins him in a spotlight. He must be melting without shade.

The young man, maybe just a couple years older than me, looks as if he's lived an entire lifetime. And yet, he smiles. It's bittersweet but holds charm. The expression tugs at the corners of his lips and presses up into his eyes—teardrop-shaped with swirls of various brown hues that catch in the light like gold dust. My breath sticks to my throat and something within my chest tumbles, like a collapsing house of cards. *Could he be dangerous?*

With a quick wave, he whispers, "Good luck," as a scrap of newspaper drifts from his fingertips to the floor within reach. My eyes lock on it, just for a short second. My hand twitches with an urge to reach for it. A headline in bold ink peeks from the curled edge, but I'm not sure what it says. Is it something I need to know? I glance back up at the man, trying to read the answer within his mysterious eyes.

I don't know him. I shouldn't care. But his two simple words weren't mocking. They were wrapped in hope. Why offer some-thing so fragile to a stranger?

"There is to be no conversing between a servant and prison-ers," Frau Schäfer says, her monotone voice yapping up the stairwell.

A prisoner. For what?

My arms stiffen by my sides, my grip tightens against my belongings, and I shift my direction, as if physically forced, and move toward the room on the left. The man's words weigh on my shoulders, questioning if I can hold on to them, keep them for a while.

The tarnished doorknob wobbles in my hand, sticking when turned to the right. After a few jiggles and a shove, the door creaks open, a warning as if I shouldn't enter.

Dust rises in a cloud, catching in the light that threads between the two tree branches outside the small square window ahead.

The room is small and cramped. Yellow-striped paper lines the short walls beneath a low sloped ceiling tucked into the roofline. To the left side of the window, a rusting metal-framed bed leans against the wall. The far posts scrape the ceiling, and a rumpled cream quilt drapes the thin mattress and pillow.

To the right of the window is a small wooden desk, leaning crookedly into the corner with a backless stool tucked beneath. A tinge of mildew and sweat cloaks me like a blanket as I step inside the constricted space, and as a form of welcoming, the warped floorboards complain with an exhale.

I bow my head forward while stepping up to the side of the bed, careful to avoid a collision with the ceiling, then sweep the fallen debris, along with a layer of wiry hairs that are too short and bristled to belong to a person, from the bed quilt's creases. With the swift movement from my hand, another stench, some-thing rotten, strikes my nostrils and gnaws at my stomach. Then

I notice the mattress is still molded to someone else's body shape.

Julia would have found this room appalling but wouldn't have said so out loud. She would have clucked her tongue at the mildew and thrust open the windows. She'd spin around in search for something beautiful, even if just a patch of sunlight forming an unlikely shape on a warped piece of wood. She would tell me it's something special, meant just for me, even in a place like this.

I didn't hug her back.

FIVE

HALINA

With my suitcase and satchel settled on the floor beside the bed, I take a quick moment—the only quick moment I'm allowed, to sit along the edge, the lumpy wool flattening into matted knots as I sink. I spot the mentioned booklet of rules and responsibilities on top of the writing desk. From here, I can easily make out the words:

SERVANTS ORDERS

I reach toward the desk to take the booklet as anger sears through me. Why should I be a servant? I dare not ask again if they plan to pay me, not when the other option would be prison. Still, I've done nothing wrong. I wasn't loitering, and I wasn't begging. I assume the man with the hammer is a prisoner—the blue and white stripes on his uniform says so. How many others are there?

The thin, gray covered booklet is several pages, bound by woven thread along the left edge. Above the bold title is an embossed emblem of the Imperial Eagle holding a wreath, framing a swastika—a branded version of their artwork from downstairs.

The Nazis are nothing new to Poland. They've been pushing the Polish out, taking over, and claiming this country as theirs since September 1939. It's been almost three years, but I could be convinced it's been a decade. After spending my entire life in the orphanage, I had plans to venture out into the world and start from scratch somewhere. But then when I turned eighteen, I came to realize how difficult it would be to start anything from scratch without a single coin to my name.

My plans changed and Julia offered me a job, allowing me to work for the orphanage for a year, save up some money, then set out to make a life for myself. The war had other plans for me, though. Instead, I've been living under German law, told to fear the world beyond the walls I lived between.

I open the booklet to the first page, finding faded fingerprints along the edge of the hand-scripted text.

Servant Name: ~~**Paulette Sawla**~~

List of Servant Rules and Responsibilities:

Servants must rise by five a.m. each morning then report to the kitchen.
Personal belongings must be kept out of sight.
No conversation between servants and prisoners.
Servants shall not leave property without consent from the officer or his wife.
Failure to comply with rules and responsibilities will result in removal.

Removal?

Servant meals are to be eaten within living quarters, out of sight from the family.
Do not enter the officer's study, nor his and his wife's bedroom.
Do not question orders.
Anything seen or heard within the household is to be kept confidential or consequences will be enforced.
A servant may be removed from your position at any given time, without warning.
A servant is here to work, not think.

I study the name at the top of the page and trace my finger over the letters, trying to make out the name beneath the scratched-out lines. What did they do to the last person?

I flip the page, the booklet weighing heavily in my hands as I find a detailed daily schedule for the children beginning at six a.m. sharp, breakfast waiting for them in the dining room downstairs. We followed a schedule in the orphanage, both as a child and a caretaker, but nothing like what I'm reading here.

The bedroom door creaks open and my stomach knots. I peer up from the booklet in my lap, finding the man from earlier, the one with a hammer in a prisoner uniform. His hands, now empty, grip the top of the doorframe. The question of whether he's dangerous returns...

He glances back down the stairwell before straightening his posture. "May I?" he asks, his voice eager and unguarded.

"Uh—well..." I know better.

But the look in his eyes doesn't give me a sense of danger. More like...an ally of sorts.

I peer down at the booklet again, biding my time as I think of a response and thumb back to the first page.

"No conversation between servants and prisoners," I enunciate, quietly.

"We already broke that rule," the man says with a whisper

of defiance, or perhaps, mischief. He arches his dark eyebrows, and the corners of his lips lift into a knowing smirk as he steps inside and gently nudges the door back into the frame without latching it shut.

"I've hardly been here an hour."

"I'm sure that's a new record," he utters hoarsely, and I catch a hint of humor dancing within his eyes. "I apologize in advance for all the hammering. It will be frequent but not constant."

I stepped into this house. He owes me no apology.

"I understand..." A short pause isn't long enough before quietly spitting out my next question. "So, if you're a prisoner... what did you do?" I stare directly into his soulful eyes, searching for an answer before he has a chance to respond.

His smile falters with something that looks like shame. His gaze follows. "I'm just a Jew," he says, pointing to the Star-of-David embroidered on his arm band. He professes his religion as a crime. *Not to me, but to the Reich.* He turns his arm over, pulls up his sleeve, and reveals an inked number emblazoned along his flesh.

"Oh my—" I say through a shiver.

The sight steals the breath from my lungs, having never witnessed a person being stamped like livestock. My stomach clenches and my chest aches as a new form of horror reveals itself. "No criminal act is necessary to become a prisoner of Auschwitz. Though, they consider all Jews to be criminals, I suppose."

"You were sent to live in the Auschwitz prison just because you're Jewish?" I know that's what he's saying, but I can't wrap my mind around the idea.

He presses his lips into a straight line and nods. "Yes, but I'm escorted out of there every morning to work here. Then I return each night." He speaks of his days as if they're ordinary. As if he's accepted this unfair punishment.

He studies me for a moment, noticing my dress, apron, and long bronze braids dangling over my shoulder. "What about you? Where have you come from?"

"I was a caregiver at an orphanage. One of the little girls tried to run away this morning and I caught her just beyond the 'restricted zone.' Bad timing to be spotted on the side of the road by an officer. I'm just thankful the little girl made it back safely."

The man's jaw tightens, stiffening the defined features of his face. "Officer Schäfer grabbed you?"

Should I have had more of an option? It doesn't seem as though anyone has choices when it comes to the Reich. Especially the Jewish people. I shrug. "It was either this, or he threatened to arrest me for loitering. Begging on the street, he said."

He shakes his shaved head, and rubs the back of his sunburned neck before letting out a disheartened breath. "Whatever you do, hold on to this role here in the house." His gold-flecked eyes strain and his forehead creases with concern. "You don't want to become a prisoner."

My blood turns cold and chills shiver between my shoulders. "Of course," I say, though his concern becomes my dread.

He takes a hesitant step closer toward me like he's crossing a forbidden line. Though, the ceiling slope keeps him from moving in too far. He tilts his head, gauging the space.

Sun spills across his face, highlighting a cluster of freckles on his cheeks and the bridge of his nose. In another world, he might look sun-kissed from a day at the lake.

"It's a good thing you're petite," he says pressing his hand to the ceiling above his head. The cuts along his knuckles, some fresh, others scabbed, capture my attention. *Poor thing.*

"Well, I suppose my shorter height will come in handy here." I didn't consider how much worse this room would be if I was a head taller. "Any other tips?"

"I've only been here a month-and-a-half, not long. But

Marlene, the middle child, tells her mother everything. Be careful what you say." His wide stare is filled with sincerity.

The thought of the children turning against me hadn't crossed my mind yet, but I know better than to assume a child's loyalty, especially given the family she's being raised under.

"No child that age can be trusted with a secret," I say, matching his whisper.

I learned that lesson at a young age before I understood what trust even meant. Secrets were like treasures, high in worth for selfish gain.

"And the baby—" he says, looking over his shoulder despite the door being nearly shut. The quiet lingers for several long seconds before he speaks again. "There's something wrong. I don't think they know, or maybe they do and don't care. But the poor thing cries day and night unless—"

"Unless what?"

He takes in a hesitant breath and holds it for a long second. "Sometimes...they put bourbon into her bottle. To quiet her."

The breath escapes my lungs and I bring my hands up to my neck, choked. "That can't be. Who could—" I don't need an answer. I know *who* could do something so awful. But would they? To their own blood? Perhaps it's a rumor that's spun out of context. How could he be so sure when he's up here all day? Though that might explain the limpness and disconnected stare. How has no one protected this poor baby?

The rulebook rests heavier in my lap.

"They hide things well," he says.

"Anything else?" I ask, my hushed words sticking to my throat.

"There's a lot more," he says delicately, "But for now, don't make eye-contact with Officer Schäfer. And you should know... they don't give second chances."

"A second chance for what?"

"Just—just be careful around them."

He reaches into his pocket then pulls out a scrap of news-paper and presses it into my hand. "Take this."

"What is—"

"I'm Gavriel," he says, just as heavy footsteps clomp down-stairs, sharp heels chopping louder and louder against the wooden floors.

I clutch the scrap of paper and hesitate before finding my voice to respond. "Halina," I reply.

He slips through the door, disappearing into shadows within the construction.

I unfold the newspaper in my hand. A clipped German headline on one side, but on the back, a message is scrawled in pencil:

You can trust me.

I've heard these words before.

A nun once told me my parents loved me—something a young child would want to know. But my parents left me without a reason. That isn't love.

Then, there was once a friend who said she'd keep a secret safe. She didn't.

Even Julia, who always promised me *"God brought us together and together we shall be,"* couldn't stop the evil from taking me away.

Trust is poison laced inside the ripest berry, just within reach...when hunger hurts the most.

I tuck the scrap of newspaper into my apron pocket and press the rule book against my ribs as if it will protect me.

One rule already has already been broken.

For a stranger who seems to have far more to risk than me.

As I make it up to the bedroom floor, another faint sound—a

whimper, or a whine circles me before the sound is swallowed up by the low hum of chatter coming from the main floor below. My nerves buzz on alert, but I clench my eyes and push back on the fears sneaking into my mind.

It must be a cat, locked up or stuck somewhere. What else could it be?

SIX

HALINA

Frau Schäfer only gave me a partial tour of the house before sending me up to the eves to drop my suitcase before returning downstairs. She's left me to seek out the kitchen on my own.

Where the curled and embellished banister tapers at the bottom step, I spot a washroom to the right of the front door. I hadn't noticed it when I first entered the house. The door is cracked open just enough to see a white porcelain pedestal sink.

Continuing away from the entryway foyer, I spot two closed doors to my left, and the now familiar family room on my right. Then there's an arched opening to my left which offers a glimpse of their dining room, but the table is covered with stacks of paper. A multi-purpose room, I suppose.

Finally, I come to the kitchen's arched opening on the right, a larger space than I imagined. A cast iron stove dominates the left wall, copper pans gleaming above, hanging from a rod along white tile that matches the counters. Beside it stands a cream-colored refrigerator on thick metal legs, its rounded edges and chrome trim glistening in the sun. I've only ever used an icebox, nothing like this.

Pale green cupboards stretch floor to the ceiling, framing a window above a deep porcelain sink. A floral valance hangs like a lavish final touch. In the center, a rectangular table fills the space with a silent authority. At the far end, Frau Schäfer sits with ridged posture, writing in a journal with intense focus. Behind her, another grand archway frames a smaller room.

Isla and Marlene sit quietly within the glow of sunshine, one with a book, the other with paper and crayons. The baby is in a wooden cradle to the side of Isla.

A woman in a blue and white striped smock steps into the kitchen from behind me and makes her way over to the stove, retrieving a soup pot from the rack above. The clink and clatter send a jolt through my shoulders. Then a floorboard to my far-left creaks, pulling my attention to another woman, standing as if a statue in the corner. She's also in a blue and white striped smock, but instead of working, she's staring at the woman cooking.

Frau Schäfer closes her journal and drops her pencil on the table. "Well don't just stand there like—" she motions a gesture with her hand toward the woman in the corner. "Her."

"Yes, Frau Schäfer. I know the children should be engaged in reading and writing until their lunch is set on the table," I repeat the line written in the schedule. "Come along, children. Let's get to work."

Frau Schäfer raises a brow then folds her hands on top of the journal. "I have some correspondence to tend to in the other room. I trust you're capable of taking it from here." She stands from her seat, one hand holding the journal and pencil to her chest, the other curved below her belly.

"How far along are you?" A daring question, I'm sure.

She glares at me for a long moment, and I regret letting my thoughts slip out.

Gavriel warned me to avoid eye contact with Officer Schäfer, but it might be best to do so with Frau Schäfer too.

"Four months or so," she mutters, not with the joy and glow of most mothers excited to welcome a child into the world.

"How wonderful," I say, forcing more cheer than she.

"Yes, quite..." she says, leaving the room on that flat note.

Before engaging with the girls, I glance toward the cradle. Flora lies awake, staring at the ceiling. I kneel beside her and take her tiny hand in mind. "Hello, sweet girl." She doesn't flinch. Doesn't blink. Even when I wave my hand in front of her face, her eyes don't follow. "You're so quiet and content," I murmur, stroking her smooth cheek. For ten months old, something isn't right. I can't be the only one who sees it.

Yet not a word about her from Frau Schäfer.

"Well—um—um—Mama says..." Marlene scans the kitchen then glances at Isla as if looking for permission to say whatever is caught on her tongue.

"What does she say?" I urge.

"She says that...good babies are quiet babies," Marlene whispers. "But Flora is—is, uh—"

"Unusual," Isla adds. "She has a defect."

"A defect?" I repeat.

"Her nerves don't work right," Isla continues. "No one knows for sure."

If no one knows for sure, it's quite a big assumption. There must be more of explanation, but why not inform me so I can help?

"Is that so?" I scoot to the side, finding her scribbling out a drawing.

Marlene shrugs her shoulders and crumples up the drawing.

"Why did you do that? That was a lovely drawing," I say.

She sweeps a thin strand of baby hairs to the side of her face and looks over at her sister again. "I—I'm supposed to be doing my letters. But I already know them all."

"If you know your letters, I'm sure it's all right to continue your drawing," I tell her, patting my hand on the top of her silky hair. She flinches at my touch and stares up at me as if I've broken a rule.

"No, no. If Papa doesn't see my practice letters when he comes home, he'll—"

I stare at her little face, her eyes squinting as she searches for words.

"He'll be disappointed?" I ask.

"No," Isla says. "There's no such thing as disappointment. There's right and wrong."

"To be fair, that's not quite correct. You can be both right and wrong at the same time, and there's a place in the middle for mistakes or misunderstandings."

"Papa would disagree," she says with a bored sigh.

Your papa is a cruel man. The words fester in my throat but stay there. What good would a response do? These girls don't know any different. They've been raised in a world where obedience is the only option. Though, I've watched the effect of enforced obedience throughout my life, and some children learn only how to rebel.

I lean back, away from the cradle, watching Isla read. Her eyes aren't following lines though. She's just staring at the words. "What book are you reading, Isla?" I ask.

She peers over the soft edges then stiffens before gazing up at me. "*Der Giftpilz*," she says.

I toy with the German words in my head, trying to make sense of the title: *The Poisonous Mushroom*.

"What is the book about?" I ask.

Isla thumbs through a few pages to an illustration of a little boy handing an older woman something in the woods. "It's about spotting differences between a poisonous mushroom and one safe to eat because it can be hard to tell the difference."

"Ah, I see. That makes sense."

"Mushrooms are like Jews and non-Jews. It's hard to tell them apart, but—"

"Oh goodness," I say, interrupting her before my exasperation slips out in another way. I press my hand to my mouth, stunned by the vulgarity of it.

Nothing should surprise me after three years in an occupied country, but she's ten. And she's already learned to treat hatred like intellect. That book isn't a warning, it's a weapon.

If Julia ever caught wind of this book, she'd press it into a priest's hands, with tears in her eyes, and ask how something so vile could exist in God's world. I want to scream then rip the pages out and do the same to this book as the Germans have done to the books of Jewish authors. This should burn. Not the others. Instead, I smile and breathe through my rage before speaking.

"Isla, I think the real lesson here is that we're all different. That's how God made us. You can't always see who's good or bad, but if you listen closely, to how someone speaks and what they say, you'll learn far more than your eyes ever could. Could you imagine if we were all the same? How boring that would be?" I chuckle softly, adding a smile I hope will help her understand.

One of the women in the kitchen clears her throat, seemingly calling for my attention. The woman still standing as if she's a guard in the corner stares back at me, shaking her head, her lips pursed and nostrils flaring.

I push myself up from the ground and make my way through the kitchen, up to the woman in what I now know to be an Auschwitz uniform. "Are you not appalled by what that child is reading?" I whisper to her in Polish, curious if she speaks the native language.

She huffs a laugh and narrows her eyes. "You're ungrateful for your privilege," she replies in Polish.

Privilege. I've never been accused of that before. Not as a

baby left behind on the stone steps of a church. Not as a domestic servant. And not as a Polish woman prohibited to experience even a breath of freedom.

Then, my thoughts simmer rather quickly as I notice the embroidered Star-of-David on her armband beneath the German word, KAPO. Kapo means overseer. I glance back at the woman now dishing out food from a pan onto plates, spotting another Star-of-David badge on her chest.

Maybe she's right. Compared to them, the hunger in their eyes, the sag in their shoulders, the dirt-covered uniforms, I should consider myself lucky.

"I have no concern with reporting you to Frau Schäfer," the kapo woman says, her voice rising in volume.

I don't understand. Both women appear to be Jewish, but one is in charge of the other? I was defending Jewish people in my comment about the book being appalling, so why the angry response?

Without another word, I make my way back to the children's sides, still baffled. *No conversations between servants and prisoners*, I remind myself. She might abide by the rules. Both of them, I suppose.

I must shake the thought out of my head and refocus my attention on the girls. The clock in the kitchen catches my attention. Noon is in just fifteen minutes. "Girls, your lunch should be ready soon," I say, according to the booklet. "Why don't you both go wash your hands."

Isla drops the book to the floor and Marlene drops her crayon and jumps up to her feet. I make my way back to the cradle, finding baby Flora still awake and staring up at the exposed wooden beams above her head.

"Are you hungry too, sweetheart?" I coo at her before flipping through the booklet to the instructions on preparing her bottle.

The woman who cooked the older girls' lunch is placing the plates down on the table. She moves to one of the cupboards and retrieves two glasses then a pitcher of water from the refrigerator.

I'm studying the two tall cupboards on either side of the stove, debating where I might find a pot to boil water. I'm not sure if the two women will remain in the kitchen while the girls eat or if they'll go somewhere else. I don't want to end up in another confrontation with the kapo.

The booklet dangles by my side as I stride into the kitchen and head for the nearest cupboard. The kapo's stare burns into me as I open the bottom doors.

I find a small pot, grab it, fill it at the sink and bring it to the stove. Behind a glass-paneled cupboard, amber-colored baby bottles catch my eye. The canister of powdered milk sits on the shelf below.

While the water heats, I set out a bottle, remove the nipple, and reopen the instruction booklet:

~ *Lastly, add three drops of chamomile*

I've heard of this antidote. There had been a couple of babies at the orphanage with digestion troubles and the house-mothers were advised to use a couple drops of chamomile. I flip through a few more pages, searching for information on what finger foods Flora is allowed. At ten months, she should be able to eat something simple alongside her sisters. But there's nothing to be said.

I place the booklet down on the wooden table and search for the bottle of the calming herb, finding it just behind the powdered milk.

The girls return from washing up and jump into their seats at the table, wasting no time before digging into their slices of fried ham, buttered toast, and steamed tomatoes.

"Does your baby sister get a helping of toast too?" I ask Isla and Marlene.

"No, she only drinks her bottle," Isla says, her brows furrowing with annoyance.

Odd.

Once the water is heated, I pour it into the bottle, add the powdered milk and remove the dropper from the bottle of chamomile. A pungent odor of spice...and molasses or burnt sugar from the bottle strikes me like a splash of cold water. I lift the small bottle up to my nose and jerk my head away. That isn't chamomile. That's—

I blink, my mind turning over at high speed.

Gavriel...he was right.

I don't want him to be. I didn't want to believe what he said, or trust him, not so easily at least. But he was telling the truth, and I almost brushed it off. I could have poisoned this poor sweet girl because I didn't want to believe someone who was clearly looking out for me.

I swish the powder around until it dissolves in the water and screw the nipple-top back in place. After testing the temperature on my wrist, I make my way back to the cradle, finding her still staring in the same direction. I place the bottle down on the wooden chair next to me and scoop Flora into my arms. Her lips quiver as she sets her focus on my face. She's looking at me though. She wouldn't do that earlier when I arrived. "It's all right, sweetheart. I have your lunch too." I notice there isn't a highchair at the table for her either.

I set the bottle down on the kitchen table and pull out a chair to join Isla and Marlene as they eat. With Flora propped up in my arms, I offer her the bottle. She doesn't fuss, just takes the warm milk contently, her little hands pressed around the sides of the glass.

"Why is the milk so yellow today?" Marlene asks.

"Yellow?" I study the bottle, realizing she thinks it's a different color because of the amber glass.

"It's just the color of the glass, making the milk look like a warmer color," I tell her.

"Usually, the milk is the same color as the glass," she says.

"Could be the sun shining in through the window," I offer as an explanation I'm not sure I believe.

Marlene takes slow bites of her toast while staring at Flora as she sucks down the milk. "Mama says good babies don't cry. Flora is a good baby now that the last nanny went away."

If silence defines the good in a person, what does that mean for me? I've stayed quiet when warned and bitten my tongue when I've wanted to speak out. Being quiet has done nothing for me. And it won't do anything for Flora. She's too small to speak up for herself. To defend herself. And I was brought here for a reason, one that makes little sense, but one that might make a difference in this little girl's life.

My stomach tightens as I shift my weight around on the chair to get more comfortable. "Wh-what happened to your last nanny?" I ask, keeping my question quiet.

Marlene shrugs and takes another bite of her toast. "She just left. Mama wanted Flora to start sleeping again."

Her words hit me like a sack of stones, and I peer back at the counter toward the bottle of chamomile. Flora pulls the bottle out of her mouth and thrusts it against my collarbone just before releasing a shrill cry. Her body flails as if she's in pain and her cheeks burn into a crimson hue. Isla and Marlene's eyes grow wide, and they stop chewing the food in their mouths, both gawking at me as if I've done something very wrong...

SEVEN
GAVRIEL

July 19, 1943

With a quick glance at the crosshatching of framed beams, I can see I'm making progress, but at a much slower pace than I was once capable of. But there's only one of me.

The family doesn't seem bothered by the hammering, not even the baby. I'd figure she'd cry at the sound more often, but I guess not.

Then there's the new nanny, Halina...she didn't sign up for this. These aren't her children to love, and shouting over all my racket all day must be driving her mad.

Still, she's here. The last one only lasted a few days. The one before that, less than a week. Halina's on day four. She said she has experience with children from the orphanage, so maybe she'll survive Frau Schäfer's moods and endless headaches too.

Rain clouds form in the distance, giving me just enough time to secure the tarp over the framing. A gust blasts through the open rafters, ripping the tarp from my grip and slapping it against my face with a storm of dust. I stumble and kick my heel into a pile of timber, causing two beams to tumble hard onto the floorboards.

I catch myself against a support beam then lunge for the rope before the tarp flies off entirely. My breath sticks to my throat as I tighten my grip, my knuckles whiten and split at the freshly closed gashes. Mistakes aren't tolerated. I work too hard to avoid them.

I've worked plenty of construction jobs throughout my life, but never alone. I don't know if they realize this isn't a one-person task...or if they just don't care.

Probably the latter.

The last rafters will go in over the next few days, then I can move onto the roof decking—solid cover instead of a tarp that traps heat and barely keeps out the rain.

The floor beneath me shivers as heavy steps trudge up the stairwell. Must be Oskar making his rounds. He steps in through the doorless entryway in his matching uniform, a clipboard in hand, and a scowl he can't seem to erase. "What is your progress?"

I stare at him, wondering why he can't take his eyes off his notes to look up and figure it out himself. "Still working on the rafters," I say, pointing to the unfinished back right side.

"You should be finished with the rafters," he says.

I fold my arms across my chest, feeling a pull in my shoulders and a heaviness weighing on my knees. "The timber was just delivered a week ago. I didn't have all the necessary tools until three days ago. With proper tools and materials, a person working alone should be able to install three or four rafters a day. I've gotten a maximum of five up in the hours I'm here, even on the days I had to come up with makeshift supports. Do you have a suggestion on a way to save time? I'm sure you're aware that poor quality and skipped steps could cause the house to collapse beneath us."

I'm starving, tired, sore, and weak too, but no one cares

about that. Especially not a privileged kapo who receives extra daily rations for marching around with a clipboard in his hand.

Oskar takes a slow step forward, drumming his fingers along the brim of the clipboard. "Are you questioning me?" he growls.

I should have kept my mouth shut. My throat closes around another response in defense—instinct, but I keep it buried within me.

He grabs my wrist, digging his fingernails into my flesh, and bares his teeth at me. I was terrified of this man when I first arrived at this house in May. Now, I see him as a coward, but a coward who can still have me killed before I have the chance to fall asleep tonight. He holds the power, not me. We're all afraid to die, or to make a wrong move. Even him. He just doesn't want the rest of us to know he's no better than us. But I see it.

"Thirty minutes," he hisses. "Be out front and ready to leave."

The calluses on my hands burn against the railing as I head down the steep stairs as a heart-wrenching cry bounces between the walls, growing louder the closer I get to the baby's nursery. I glance into the room, finding her in Halina's arms, thrashing her tiny arms, fists clenched, and her face red as a tomato.

A smashing crack echoes from within the room, a fist against a wall or furniture. "I said, quiet her!" Frau Schäfer shouts. She must be sitting in the rocking chair in the far corner of the room just watching Halina struggle. "You have no idea what this is doing to my head. How many times a day do I have to tell you I suffer from horrific headaches?"

I hesitate in the hallway as I catch sight of Halina, her high-set rosy cheekbones and soft expression along her porcelain skin. Her tawny hooded eyes, fringed with long lashes, carry a silent plea for help as she spots me. I don't know how she's gone four days like this but the look in her eyes tonight, it's different from the last time I saw her. It's as if her armor has cracked.

If I could help her, I would, but she's not mine to protect.

But someone should. I'd step right in front of her and tell that awful woman she's an unfit mother and doesn't deserve the affluence she claims as if earned. I'd take the baby from Halina's arms and tell her to take a break.

Halina curls the baby into her chest a little tighter, the infant swatting at Halina's tensed collarbone. Hair has fallen loose from her braid, the struggle clearly wearing her out. She breaks her pleading gaze from mine and returns her attention across the room. "I followed your instructions," Halina tells Frau Schäfer.

I head down the main stairwell, wishing I could have given her better advice in the few short moments we exchanged words. There's no proper way to prepare someone for what they'll experience here.

Outside, to the right of the house, in a dirt pit road. Half of the other prisoners have already formed two lines, one for men and the other for women. Two other houses on the short street are occupied by SS officers as well and require a set of prisoners to aid them with various tasks. Some of us are shared between houses depending on the work—like Adam.

Oskar, and Sylvia, the kapo responsible for the women prisoners, stare at us in our respective lines, clipboards in position, waiting for just one of us to arrive a second too late. Adam and I have concluded that they must be rewarded for every infraction they report. Something must be benefiting them to enjoy ratting us out as much as they do.

A middle-aged man is the last to arrive. He reminds me of Pa, still shows a sense of strength, but must be fighting through each day with every bit of strength he has left inside of him. He looks like Pa too, with his sad eyes and dimpled chin. He was assigned work on this street a week after I was. He's been brought here to chop wood for a winter stockpile for all three houses.

If Pa were with me, I wonder if he'd be working here too?

I'm glad my family isn't here, and I hope they've still been spared. Each morning, I question the likelihood of if it will be the day I find out about my family, or news the war is ending, or —the Jews are being set free, but no one hears good news here. Or any news at all, for that matter.

Oskar steadies his stare on his watch, waiting for the older man to step into line one second too late. The man tries to hurry his step, but stumbles on a knotted root. He manages to catch his bearings and slips into the line, but I can't avoid the thought running through my head. He won't last much longer. He's just on time, but Oskar steps forward anyway and backhands him, a biting clap that makes the man's cheek split. Blood trickles. "I'll let your tardiness slide today," Oskar says while jotting down a note on his paper.

The middle-aged man doesn't make a sound, just straightens his shoulders and prepares to keep going.

I clench my fists, my heart pounding with rage. I swallow hard and Adam nudges me in the back. "Don't do it," he whispers.

Together, we shuffle forward between the trees, careful not to trip on our own feet in the growing darkness, waiting for the glow of watchtower lights to guide us toward the front gates.

An SS Officer stands just ahead, clipboard in hand, his shadow stretching across the dirt and gravel. He waves forward the two kapos with a stiff hand gesture, then collects their reports. He scans each of our numbers as we pass by, slow, with a threatening purpose.

The center square is crowded with new arrivals, their dirt-smudged faces are sunburned and, glistening with sweat. Each one of them, still unsuspecting of what lies ahead while a suitcase dangles from their white-knuckled grips. Mothers cling to their children while the elderly waver from toe to heel. And I hate that I search each person, praying I don't spot my brothers or parents among these crowds. "This is hell," I say.

"At least they don't know yet," Adam whispers.

No one ever knows until it's too late. Not until the screaming begins. By then, it's too late to do anything but plead for the end.

The door to the barrack swings open before we reach it. Two kapos step out, dragging a body by its a lifeless pale wrist as if it's nothing but a wet sack of sand.

I don't look. I can't.

But the sound—bones scraping over dirt and stone paints the image anyway.

I've seen too many people like him. I'm afraid I'll recognize him. Afraid I'll start guessing how he died? Was he in his mid-twenties like me? Tortured? Sick with something we'll all catch next? Maybe he just gave out. Maybe his body stopped fighting. Then it hits me, someone could be the thinking the same thing about Pa or my brothers at this very moment. And I can't let myself go there.

Stepping inside the barrack, the familiar odor of death lingers in the air, a sour stench of a person who has been lying dead, unnoticed for too long in the sweltering heat of this enclosure today.

"Another one gone," Adam says as he closes the door behind us. "What do you think he did?"

Adam thinks people are only killed here if they break rules or try to escape. He thinks the infirmary helps prisoners and convinces himself they've been sent to a different barrack after they're well again.

There's no blood.

He was sick.

"I don't think he did anything wrong," I respond, letting Adam piece the rest together how he sees fit.

Coughs and groans smother the silence, but the piercing wail of a baby is the only sound swimming through my head, and the look in Halina's eyes, raw with desperation, as she sinks deeper into the cruel reality of the life's she's been forced into.

EIGHT

HALINA

July 19, 1943

A train in the distance cries out for help as I retreat from my duties of the fourth day in this house after finally getting Flora to sleep. All I can say is I've at least figured out which of the attic stairs distort beneath my feet, threatening to snap with a growling moan. Every third step, I skip. So long as the train doesn't wake the baby, she'll stay asleep.

The moment I shut myself into the—my—dim moonlit attic bedroom, I slide down against the back of the door, still defeated and overwhelmed. "It hasn't even been a week," I utter, trying to reassure myself that I'll get used to this trapped new life. I'm not sure any amount of convincing will work.

Frau Schäfer insisted on making Flora's bottles ever since I prepared one my first day here. That changed this afternoon because she was too distracted. She regretted it quickly. I forgot to add the three drops of so-called-chamomile. Maybe it isn't my place to question how they raise their children. I'm here to follow orders.

I'm also here to do what I can to keep these children from

becoming the next generation of cruelty. No good comes from poisoning a baby. I won't be a part of that. If they can lace their infant's milk without guilt, what hope is left for any of them? They deserve more. A chance to be good.

Despite that, Frau Schäfer hasn't even mentioned what she suspects might be wrong with Flora. I wonder how long they've been giving this poor thing bourbon in her bottle? She could be dependent on it now. Maybe that's why she's been crying so hard. Which came first? The issue with her nerves causing pain and tears, or the bourbon? I've seen enough cruelty to children in the orphanage throughout my life, but for a woman carrying her fourth child, she doesn't appear fit to have the first three.

With the door closed, the heat swells quickly and I pull myself up to see if I can crack the window above my bed. The hinges are rusty, but I manage to shove it open enough for the air to move. I fold the quilt back, and slouch into the lumpy bed. The branches scrape against the windowpane, the hum of a conversation carries through the floorboards, and a dog is barking down the street. I've yet to notice a bird chirp or even a buzzing bee, and never a gentle breeze. Even nature hates it here.

I curl up on my side, my face pressing against the thin pillow, taking in a potent odor of oil and sweat. A scamper of tiny claws grasps my attention—a gray mouse makes its way from one hole along the floor to another. I would be hiding too if I could.

My unblinking stare catches on my small suitcase and I take it back to the bed with me. The clasps clack as I lift the top. The scent of lavender from a dry flower left in the pocket comforts me as I pull out my stuffed bear and folktale book.

The book has always been a mystery to me. I've lain awake through many long nights wondering about its intended purpose. Why leave me with that? To read for joy, or find a meaning?

On the other hand, the stuffed bear has brought me unconditional comfort. I slept with it pinched beneath my arm every night until I was twelve. But after I failed to find any information about my parents, I decided I didn't need the bear's comfort anymore. It joined the folktale book in my lone suitcase beneath my bed, banished along with the childish fantasies that I would someday find my parents again.

* * *

"It's time," I whisper to Lulek, my trusty stuffed bear. I snatch my folktale book from beneath my mattress and roll off the bed, careful not to make a sound. The other girls in the eleven-to-twelve-year-old room will wake up and ask questions. None of us manage to keep many of our thoughts to ourselves here, but I didn't want anyone to know about my plan.

I tiptoe around each creaking board as I make my way down the narrow stairwell and around the side of the building toward the main door we go in and out of. A lantern flickers against the chalkboard, still showing Monday's routine even though it's Wednesday. Next to the chalkboard are a line of coat hooks, each with name tags pinned above. I've always had the third hook from the right. I take my coat and scarf and quickly drape them over my shoulders. The door is in sight, and so is my chance to slip outside.

The lock grinds unless I lift the panel just right...something I've nearly perfected. Outside, the air is bitter. Winter still has a grip on us. It might never let us go.

My feet crunch against the icy snow, the crackle booming between the trees. This is why my attempts never work. Something always gives me away.

Still, I make it into the woods and begin counting my steps so I don't get lost. I should make it to the library by morning.

My body shivers, the cold eating right through my coat and scarf, making it hard to move my legs. I have to keep going. It's the only way I might learn something about my parents, or where they might be. The dream is within reach. I'll never give up trying to find something.

"Halina!" My name weaves between the trees. How could she have known I left? I didn't make a sound. She's been asleep for hours. I've been walking for what feels like half the night. "Halina Wojic, I know you are out here, young lady."

Despite Julia calling my name, I press forward. How can I tell her she's wrong about my parents when she says she has all the information available? I force my legs to move faster, gritting against the struggle and heaviness of each stride along the sinking snow.

Her hand grasps my arm, stopping me from making it to the exit of the woods. She's breathing so hard, I could pull away. But I wouldn't do that to her. I would've come back tomorrow, hopefully before she noticed I was gone...

"Halina, what on earth has gotten into you?" she asks, gasping for more air. "This is the fourth time this month. I'm not a spring chicken. I can't keep chasing you." I should apologize, but words don't find my tongue. "Is this about that foolish library again?"

"It isn't foolish," I reply. "Sister Mary was talking about a person finding a long-lost family member with the records located there. That means there's a chance I might find mine."

Julia groans. "Sister Mary believes every thread of gossip she hears in the market square and usually misses the first half of the conversation."

"Please. If I don't try to find them, I'll always be wondering. I'll never give up trying to find something."

"This age is going to be the death of me," she grumbles. "Twelve and we know everything known to man." Julia loosens her grip and slides her hand down to mine. "I will take you to the library myself tomorrow." She pulls me into her side and wraps *me in her warmth, an instant relief. "I told you I will always do whatever possible to help you find your parents..." She isn't finished with her statement, and I know what comes next. "Sweetheart." Julia takes my cold hand into hers and wraps her other hand around them as we walk back toward the church. "People aren't always who we wish them to be, and that doesn't mean your parents don't love you or didn't love you. It means they knew you would have a better life without them, and that's what they wanted for you."*

"How could you know that if you don't know anything about them?" Maybe she does know something. Maybe she doesn't want me to know what that is. Maybe my parents are horrid people and knowing that would steal every bit of my hope.

"I've been doing this a very long time—my whole life, really. I didn't ask for you to be placed on my doorstep as an infant, but I took one look at you and knew we were meant to be together. I would give you what someone else couldn't. I would keep you warm, fed, and clothed. I'd take care of you for however long you need. You ended up with me for a reason and I don't question fate."

"I would never leave you," I tell her. "I just—"

"I know, sweet girl. I know. I have written to the registry offices in every city of our country, requested help from the Parish Priest, and have repeated the process once a year since you arrived, but nothing with your surname has ever come back. All I've ever had is the scrap of paper that was pinned to your blanket with your name and birthday. That's all there has ever been."

"I'm sorry for upsetting you." It's my parents who I'm truly upset with. How could they just leave me with no trace of information about who I am or where I came from?

* * *

I set the folktale book on the worn square nightstand next to the small table clock then tuck the bear into my chest and press my nose to the side of its head for another inhale of faint lavender—the faint scent of Julia's hugs.

I close my eyes, pleading for sleep, imagining Julia's soft fingers stroking the side of my cheek. She always made me feel better. Always. I wish she could help me forget about this horrific week, but the sound of footsteps against the stairs holds me stiff. The wooden boards on the other side of the wall creak several times, leaving me to wonder if Frau Schäfer or Officer Schäfer have come up here for something.

Stillness follows the last creak.

Is it him? Her? Or someone worse?

NINE

HALINA

July 20, 1943

With a sharp gasp, I jerk upright in bed, the thin quilt tangled around my legs. A rumble of thunder stutters in the distance. Maybe that's what woke me up. My chest heaves. Sweat sticks to my back in the stale, humid air. The attic walls blur in the dim dawn light—faded yellow stripes turned gray. The air is thicker now, laced with must and the leftover stench of Officer Schäfer's cigarette smoke from last night. My fingers clutch the worn stitching of my stuffed bear, my nails poking through the small holes as if it might protect me.

Each morning before I open my eyes, I pray the prior days have been a nightmare. That I'll wake up in my tiny bedroom at the orphanage.

But I don't.

I'm still in their attic.

Trapped.

The sound comes again—masculine shouts, rough and berating, ripping through the walls. A shriek follows, the sound I've become familiar with in the past day, Flora's painful cry.

Rushed and panicked footsteps pound against the floors below as frantic squeals from the two older girls join the commotion. I can't make out what's happening.

My breath shudders as I kick my legs off the side of the bed. Did I sleep too late? It's still dark. I scramble for the old clock on the nightstand, my fingers fumbling against the scratched brass. 4:45 a.m. Too early for everyone in the house to be awake. It's too early for what I'm listening to. The wave of relief that I'm not late is short-lived as another shout rumbles through the house.

I reach for the doorknob but a crash of wood startles me backward. A chair splitting? A table falling to its side? My throat is dry, each breath burning as if I've swallowed fire. The girls are screaming. They need help. I force my feet forward, gripping the railing tightly to navigate the old stairs. My heart thuds against my ribcage as the shouts and screams grow louder —they're not coming from the bedrooms. They're from down below. I press myself against the wall as I near the bottom of the stairs, then peek around the corner, just enough to see.

Officer Schäfer stands barefoot in the hallway, his uniform disheveled, his shirt untucked, belt loose, and hair matted to his head. More unsettling is his face—beet red, veins bulging at his temples. His fists flex and curl at his sides as if he's trying to contain his rage but clearly failing.

"What do I have to do to make you understand, Ada?" he snarls, his voice full of venom.

Ada. Frau Schäfer never offered up her first name, and neither did he when he barely introduced me yesterday morning. A first name sounds too informal for him.

"She needs a doctor," Ada says, her voice controlled, but also trembling.

"You know, your desperation and ignorance are going to cost us our daughter's life. And to be frank, I'm sick and tired of having the same conversation with you night after night," he seethes. He steps in toward the kitchen—toward Ada. "As I've said before, Ada, if word gets out that Flora is unfit and unusual, our so-called perfect Aryan child will be seen as a threat to the 'racial hygiene' of the nation. Is that what you want?"

"Don't call her unfit or unusual," Ada interrupts, her words cunning, but desperate. "Flora's delay and nerve pain might be treatable, but how could we ever know?"

"And if it's not? If it's proven to be a type of defective heredity, then what? What will that mean for you both?" he grunts. "How would that make me look? Do you think anything through, at all? Goddammit, Ada!"

"What am I supposed to do? Just sit here and watch our baby suffer in pain?" Ada cries out.

Officer Schäfer releases a laugh with a cutting edge to it. "You're supposed to be a better mother. An ideal mother. One who knows how to console her child."

"We—we—what about if we can find a non-German doctor?" she suggests, ignoring his last insult, her staggering.

"And where do you think you're going to find one of those right now? They've all been sent out to Hamburg to tend to the victims of the British and American firebomb attacks. How selfish can you honestly be right now?"

"Selfish?" Ada repeats. "You told me to keep her quiet so people don't ask questions, and left me with no options. It must be easy for someone like you to condone poisoning a baby while you flood your veins with those God awful 'storm pills' and nightly bottles of liquor just so you can block out the pain of being a monster." Ada's words bleed with resentment, leaving me in shock. "So tell me, Heinrich, what exactly do you want from me?"

He jerks his back, shocked by her insult. "Did you ever consider that I'm taking those Pervitin pills just to stay in a marriage with you?" He points his finger at her. "You know what I want, Ada? A decent wife. Wouldn't that be grand? Huh?"

Ada steps out from behind the dividing wall between the kitchen and family room. She's still in her nightgown, her gold curls now a rat's nest. With shaking hands, she reaches out for her husband's chest. "I'm sorry, darling. It's the pregnancy moods. They come and go, and—I'll do better. I will. You'll see," she says, her response coming as if she's said it many times before.

He shakes his head and shoves her hand away. "When will I see? How long do I have to wait, Ada? Just prove it already, won't you?"

"Papa," Isla cries out from the kitchen. She must have been hiding behind her mother. "Don't hurt Mama again! You could hurt the baby!"

Officer Schäfer lunges into the kitchen and I take in an unruly breath, holding it—*please don't touch that little girl...*"I wouldn't lay a hand on our baby, Isla. Your mother, on the hand...Well, I wouldn't have to keep teaching her a lesson if she'd just learn to obey." His words whip and crack through the air. "Let this be a lesson to both of you girls."

"Papa, no," Marlene utters between hysterical sniffles.

"Never argue with the man of the house," he hisses. "Never!"

The word echoes through the hall and into my bones.

I spin back toward the attic, each step deliberate, toes skimming the wood to avoid the creaking boards. Almost there. Just a few more steps...

"What do you think you're doing?" A voice I don't recognize, deep and rusty, his German words spoken with a Polish accent.

I freeze, clutching the banister as the shadow of a figure rises behind me, then slowly turn to face him. A kapo, his armband stitched with a star beneath his branded title. I've seen him before, hovering over the prisoners as if he's proud to do so.

"I work here," I say, trying to sound composed, though my voice wavers. My skin prickles.

"You're not due to report downstairs for another hour. You were spying on the officer and his wife, weren't you?" His accusation seeps through his gritted jaw. "I'm due to inspect the construction, but instead, I find you moseying around an opportune time."

"I wasn't—" I swallow hard and warn myself not to repeat his words. If someone in this house didn't hear him at first, they could hear me.

"Then what? What is it you were doing?"

I want to tell him I don't owe him an answer or explanation, and I could point out that he's the one in a striped uniform. But I'm not a fool. Authority is the result of loyalty...a secret teller. A traitor.

"I was using the washroom."

"Liar!" he grunts, pointing his finger at me. "You aren't permitted to use the washroom on this floor. You think you're special? Like the others before you? You think because you're not wearing stripes, you can do as you please?" His voice strains with each word as if he's losing his steam. This isn't discipline, it's resentment.

"No. That isn't the case," I say, complicit to his unnecessary rage.

"Sure," he quips. "Come." The one word snaps between us. "We'll see what the officer has to say about your little spying habit." He takes two steps up the stairs.

"Leave her alone, Oskar."

Gavriel's voice slices through the air like a switch of a match. With haste, then silence.

My pulse thumps, and my stomach turns sour.

"Who are you to tell me what to do, fool?" Oskar whips

toward Gavriel and backhands him across the face, a crack so sharp and loud it echoes between the walls.

I flinch, my trembling hands clutching the sudden ache in my chest. This is my fault. I was spying.

"I—I was doing as he says," I stammer, desperate to undo what's been done. "I forgot my apron. I was going back for it before continuing my tasks."

Oskar sneers at me, his eyes narrow with a cold stare as if he can extract a truth he prefers.

"You're late!" he shouts at Gavriel instead, then drives his shoulder into his side in passing, sending Gavriel into the wall with an unforgiving thud.

Gavriel doesn't flinch. He doesn't blink. He straightens his shoulders and starts up the steps. Something fragile cracks inside of me as I watch Gavriel amble up the stairs, fresh blood dripping down his cheekbone from the blunt force.

"You shouldn't have..." I whisper.

He glances at me as he passes, and for a brief second, I think he might smile, but he doesn't.

"It's better me than you."

He disappears into the unfinished workspace, leaving me with guilt, despair and a pit in my hollow stomach.

No one has ever stood up for me before. Not like that. I should thank him. Apologize. Or...I should keep quiet and hold on to the words that always seem to search for a way out but never quite find the way.

Gratitude could cost me more than trust.

TEN

GAVRIEL

July 21, 1943

The deep metallic boom of the gong vibrates through the walls of the barrack, startling me awake as it does every morning. The lights crack on and every man in every tier of bunks around me strains to peek out of their tired eyes. Whoever is still alive, still breathing, pulls themself to the edge of the mattress then slithers and clambers out of their sleeping hole.

When the shock of the gong's reverberation simmers, the flesh of my cheekbone burns with a sting from yesterday's slap. There's no mirror anywhere, but the ache of a bruise has spread across most of my cheek overnight. Oskar hit me hard, but it's not the pain that's afflicting me, it's the reason it happened.

I was defending someone. I knew better, but the action—the words—came instinctively to protect her. Then the look on Halina's face, a mix of disbelief and shock, telling me I shouldn't have done what I did...I couldn't understand how she thought I could watch that happen to her instead. I'm still baffled.

Our paths crossed once more yesterday after the altercation, but she only gave me a brief glance. Not an unkind look, but one with caution. Or maybe, she doesn't know what to say. I don't either, but I do want to ask her if she's all right.

What I want doesn't matter though.

Ache, grief, and hunger are all just feelings I've learned to bury so I can keep moving. Keep working.

I haven't had bread in two days due to missing prisoners at evening roll call, a punishment we all pay. My stomach gnaws at itself from starvation. But hunger, like everything else here, can only be ignored. Time, too. It loops and stutters like a broken clock. The same day on repeat, leaving me to wonder how long I've been surviving like this.

All I know is, it's been long enough to question whether I'll make it through another twelve-hour shift. A weakness is taking over, and it's one I can't fight against. I think that may be the point though. If we drop dead of natural causes, it saves the guards from having to gas us to death.

As most mornings while trudging toward the main gates for labor escort, the flies swarm, treating us like walking rubbish. The bugs are the worst as we pass the rectangle shaped man-made ditch. It's become a swampy terrain covered with a film of sludge with pieces of blue and white striped fabric floating along the top.

No one says it out loud, but I'm sure there are piles of bodies decomposing in there. I hate wondering if I'll land in a muddy hole, or be turned to ash. Which I'd prefer.

Oskar stops short before exiting the wooded path onto the officers' residential road. "Wait here," he demands, holding his hands up. He turns around and takes another look out at the street.

We're quiet, allowing the commotion of hushed shouts to filter through the trees. A striking slap of skin to skin reaching us tells me why we're standing here. Another morning altercation between Officer Schäfer and his wife. Then a car door slams, the engine roars, and gravel catches beneath the tires. All rumblings fade into the distance, and we're released from our hold between the trees and sent to our assigned houses.

From the time Hitler's army invaded Poland, I wondered what type of life the members of the Nazi regime were living. My mind has painted pictures of them laughing over torturing innocent people. They must sit at their dinner table with their families, calling the Jews a threat. I've seen how quickly belief becomes a weapon, and how easy it is to teach cruelty as a duty to their kind.

People aren't born monsters, but they can be weak enough to become them, I suppose.

The back door of the Schäfer house is unlocked for us, the arriving prisoners. I walk in to a faint aroma of cooked sausage and spices filling the air. The mouth-watering scent stabs at my barren stomach. No one is even eating at the moment.

Neither Frau Schäfer nor her daughters are anywhere in sight as I make my way up the first flight of stairs, then the narrow set to the attic where piles of lumber never seem to dwindle.

Halina's door is closed too. She's usually knee deep in the children's breakfast routine by now. I stare the door for a long moment, wondering if it will tell me if everything is all right.

It does as a quiet whimper escapes from the cracks of the closed door.

Then another whimper...

And a shuddered breath.

"It's all right, there, there," Halina whispers.

"Papa doesn't love us...And when the baby comes, we'll be more invisible."

My thoughts trickle back to yesterday morning. Maybe she didn't want me to defend her. She might have thought I'd made things worse. But I can't stop thinking about that look in her eyes, the unresolved silence. All I can do is wonder who she is beneath the shield she holds on to. She's nothing like the last nannies. That much I know.

I hesitate before pressing open Halina's door to poke my head inside. Isla and Marlene are sitting on Halina's bed, their legs crisscrossed like pretzels. Tears streaming down their rosy cheeks as they stare at Halina with desperate hope. It's as if they're silently pleading that she has the means to mend their broken hearts.

I think I know why they look at her that way...

I've had to stop myself from doing the same.

They've come to trust her quickly. It's because of the way she looks at them. Something in her eyes says she still believes in their innocence, and that they're worthy of her time. That they're worth saving. Her kindness—it's as if she sees the world like everyone is equal and everyone deserves a chance, even a second or a third one.

Maybe that means I have a chance too.

Halina has pushed the terror she felt at being forced here to the side, and stepped over it to tend to her work. I haven't seen that type of bravery in anyone since...before my family and I were pushed out of our home and sent to the ghetto. That day, we all put on a brave face, but I had never felt so scared.

"It will be all right. Mamas and Papas argue over what they love the most," Halina says, her words encouraging, but also a bit hollow. No child should have to witness what these children have been. Flora is in her arms, staring up at the ceiling in silence. Frau Schäfer must have gotten to her early morning bottle before Halina.

Isla and Marlene gasp when they spot me, and I hold my finger up to my lips like I've done the few times I've shared quiet little stories with them. I'm not allowed to speak to them, under any circumstances, but they don't understand why, and I don't want them to be afraid of me.

To pass the time while my brothers and I were younger and

helping Pa at a job, he would tell us Polish folktales. Being the oldest of the three, I must have heard each story at least three times. I seem to remember them all.

"I'm not supposed to talk," I whisper, "but—do you know the old Polish folktale about why dogs chase cats and cats chase mice?"

They shake their heads and stare at me curiously.

Halina twists around in her seat, surprise softening her expression. Her striking gaze meets mine, and light flickers through the moss green and gold threaded in her hazel eyes. Something sparks within my chest. I tell myself it means nothing, but I feel it all the same.

* * *

"You're a Jew," Stacia said, her words spewing with hate. She had once laughed at my jokes, held my hand, and kissed me under the stars. But now that I'm being forced to wear an armband marked with the Star of David, she recoils. "You're a traitor to Poland, Gavriel." We've been dating for months and known each other for years, but something must have just snapped inside of her. It's clear she sees me as something less than human now.

I reach my arm around her like I've done a hundred times before, wanting to talk through her sudden anger and ask what happened. But she pushes me as if I'm vermin. Even her friends are watching and giggling, some silently, others out loud.

She's always been so kind. Until today. The girl I knew is gone and in her place is...hatred.

* * *

No one had ever made me want to scream or want to shed my skin like Stacia did. Not after learning how quickly love can decay into rot and hate—how a girl who once held my hand could suddenly see me as if I were a part of the festering mold that was said to take over the world.

I had been sure since I'd never want to give my heart or trust to another woman again.

I'll always be a Jew—revolting as so many seem to see.

"What's the story about?" Marlene nudges me out of my lost thought.

"Ah, right," I say recentering my focus on the folktale. "Well, you see, the dogs were always being bothered by people so they went to the king and asked him to sign a paper declaring that no person or animal shall ever bother another dog. The king signed the paper and gave it to the dogs to hold. Needing to keep the paper safe, the dogs asked the cats if they could hide it in one of their special small hiding places, the cats helped them and hid the paper. When the dog asked the cat for the paper back, the cat went to find the paper and realized the mice had eaten it. When the dogs found out, they were very angry with the cats, and the cats were furious with the mice, and so began the never-ending chase."

The little girls giggle into their little hands, and Halina grins. "What a storyteller you are," she says, her voice teasing, cheeks blushing...just enough to make my pulse race.

"It's not mine, but it matters."

There is a deeper meaning—one I didn't understand until everything in my life began to fall apart.

The dogs, cats, and mice weren't enemies at first. They trusted each other and tried to help. But after one misstep and one missing piece, everyone searched for someone to blame.

The blame turned into fear and then became a division.

Just like Stacia treated me, and like irrational hatred growing this war, not one cause or reason is based on truth. It's only about who gets blamed in the end.

I used to think this story was just that. A story. But now, it seems like a message that was stored away inside of me. Something I would eventually come to understand when looking for an answer I can't find.

My stomach unleashes a fierce growl, one that sounds like my body is eating itself.

Halina's gaze drops to my stomach as if she can see how empty it is. Her brows furrow as she peers back up. "You're starving..." she says, her voice cracking. The concern on her face is so pure, and—it is real, I believe it's real, but I don't know what to do with it. No one has looked at me with anything but disgust for years. Certainly not with the faintest hint of care or concern.

"I'm all right," I say, pressing my finger back against my lip before scooting from the room.

She opens her mouth as if she's going to say something but stops herself. Her gaze locks with mine, and pressure spouts through my chest. I think she might have the ability to speak without words. I feel lit. It's not fear, or pity. It's just something real, a bond, or an understanding. The look in her eyes holds me still for a half second longer than I should have stayed.

The stomp of heavy feet along the floor below sends me moving across the hall quickly before anyone can see I was in Halina's room.

I grab a piece of timber, the hammer and nails, making sure I'm busy if someone comes up here. I stretch my neck out to catch a glimpse between the rafters, particularly in search of Officer Schäfer's black car, but no one has pulled up in front of the house. The street is bare of vehicles.

I know the sound of Frau Schäfer's heavy steps, and it isn't her. Whoever it is, is coming up here. A recurring moment that makes me hold my breath for far too long.

"It's just me..." A whisper snakes into the open space. "I was kicked out of the garden, told to make myself useful elsewhere," Adam says, stepping over a pile of lumber.

"Frau Schäfer said that?" I ask, taken aback by her sudden

willingness to exploit her authority over an Auschwitz prisoner. She barely acknowledges our existence, never mind speaking to one of us. Any complaint she might have will be logged on paper and handed to her husband at the end of the day.

"She's hosting a luncheon," Adam says.

Frau Schäfer isn't the kind of woman to host a luncheon, not without an order to do so. She's austere and aloof and hasn't made as much effort to mingle with the neighboring SS wives as she should, not in the time I've been here, or that I've noticed. Perhaps she wants to show off the beautiful new nanny she's managed to capture.

"Well, I'll certainly take the help," I tell Adam. The thought of just an hour or two of a second pair of hands is a gift.

"Maybe we can get those rafters finished up today," he says, a growl in his stomach speaking louder than his words—a reminder that we need to figure out how to stay upright, running on empty stomachs.

Within a couple of hours, moving along without rest, we've accomplished quite a bit more than anticipated for the entire day. We take a moment to lean against the brick chimney wall in the center of the room, both of us struggling to catch our breath.

Adam steps away from the chimney and peers out an opening to the backyard. "They're being served finger sandwiches and tea."

"And the air has been flavored with sausage since I stepped inside this morning. No one was even cooking in the kitchen yet. Truth be told, I wouldn't put it past Frau Schäfer to make a potpourri out of dried sausage, just to torture us more. She probably hid satchels in the vents," I say.

"Or maybe she rubbed one on the windowsill," Adam says. "A baited trap for her so-called guests."

"Maybe that's why Officer Schäfer was so angry with her

this morning," I snicker. Although I don't think that man needs a reason.

"Shh," Adam says, holding his finger up at me as he studies the scene out in the backyard.

With careful steps, I walk up behind him, curious to see what he's found or listening to. A gaggle of women sit around the picnic table while their children play in the back end of the yard, alongside their nannies.

"The new servant," a woman says, peering in the direction of the children. "Where did she come from?"

The wind breathes a long exhale before there's a response. "She's Polish, and a former caregiver. Heinrich made the arrangement. I have to say, my husband has a thing about finding the best help available," Frau Schäfer says. She rubs her hands around her swollen belly. "I'm going to need all the help I can get soon."

"You said that before the last nanny didn't work out," another woman sings before scoffing.

"And the one before that," another says.

"And the one before that," a third adds before they all share a haughty laugh.

"We all have lapses in judgment, I suppose," Frau Schäfer continues. "The best of help—well, it's hard to find decent help."

"From the sound of the crickets chirping and birds singing, it appears this woman has figured out how to keep your little Flora from squealing up a storm. Not even you have had much luck with that." The hens all cluck and titter at Frau Schäfer's expense.

"Yes, well, as I said, Heinrich found the best of what's available. Of course, only time will tell. I just hope that happens before I give birth." Another roll of artificial laughter breezes through the air.

"Forget the nursery. You're going to need an entire barrack just for the caregivers you discard to Auschwitz."

Adam and I share a look, shaking our heads with disgust. We've made a habit of this...listening just long enough to remember why we don't belong here. I'm convinced his silence in these moments line up with my thoughts. "A barrack full of nannies who refuse to poison an innocent baby."

"And just to keep her from crying," Adam adds, staring aimlessly past me.

Despite nearing a week of being here, I'm not sure Halina fully understands what she's been forced into, but she needs to know. There's still that spark of hope in her eyes, something so rare to find within this fortified town. And the way she looks at those little girls, the quiet devotion...It's a form of empathy most people lost over the recent years.

It doesn't matter though. If she isn't careful, that compassion could mask the truth of where she is and what she's here for.

And if it does, she'll disappear just as quickly as the last.

ELEVEN

HALINA

Two slamming doors and a car engine in disrepair weren't even the cause of today's early wake-up call. It was the now familiar sound of a verbal lashing that led up to Officer Schäfer's heavy steps marching out the front door, followed by Frau Schäfer returning to her bedroom. A repeat of yesterday morning. I wonder if she goes back to sleep.

The girls certainly don't. Again, they found their way up to the attic and into my room where we've been sitting on my lumpy bed for over an hour while they talk and I listen, except for Gavriel's intermission, and a folktale story we all enjoyed.

The explosive shouts terrify even me, never mind how much they must scare the girls. Maybe the Schäfers don't care what they're doing to their daughters. Either way, I'll keep acting as if I've neither heard nor seen anything. It might be the only way I survive here long enough to protect them.

In little whispered voices, they told me their mother would be busy for the next hour and breakfast wouldn't be ready for them until then. And their father, "He acts like a hungry lion sometimes and no one knows why." The brief words were filled with sorrow and fear that painted a clear picture: they're convinced their father despises them.

At the hour mark, and not a moment sooner, I lead the girls downstairs to the kitchen, finding a bottle prepared for Flora, waiting on the kitchen counter, and breakfast set out on the table by the same prisoner who was here yesterday. There's also a note in the center of the kitchen table:

There will be a luncheon at noon.
Have the children dressed properly for the occasion.
–Frau Schäfer

The hours of finding ways to entertain the children have already dragged. Neither of them like board games, jacks, or dominoes. Isla prefers to read alone, and Marlene likes to talk and draw pictures with a black crayon. Neither of them likes to change their clothes, but we managed to find day dresses they eventually agreed to wear.

Just before noon, Frau Schäfer makes her first appearance for the day, strolling in as if she's royalty, her arms out, but hands delicately wavering, her wrists and fingers dripping with jewels.

The scent of hairspray and rose oil follow her through the kitchen where we're greeted with a surprising smile, bright eyes that speak of cheer, and large curls framing her powdered face. She looks as if she's ready for a night at a ball, but with a casual navy polka-dotted dress.

"Are we ready?" she asks, her voice taut with sophistication. Frau Schäfer presses her hands into the small of her back, stretching out the ache she appears to have.

"Are you all right?" I ask, wanting to bite through my tongue.

"Oh yes, just pregnancy growing pains." She sighs.

"We're ready, Mama," Isla says, curtsying with a smile mirroring her mother's.

"Good. Come along," she says, waiting for Marlene to follow Isla.

Without any further ado, she escorts us out the back door to a landscaped garden, blooming with a variety of flowers, several women sitting around a cloth-laden picnic table, surrounded by trimmed grass.

In the back of the yard are outdoor toys—a ball, wooden rocking horse, and a sandbox, all somewhat hidden behind thick over-hanging branches from a tree on the other side of the fence. "Halina," Frau Schäfer says, the tone holding me back from following the children off the patio. "You will be expected to socialize the children with the others on the street," she drones in a quiet breath. "However, I will remind you—do not speak of anything you hear or see within our household. Our lives will remain private."

This might be an opportunity to learn more about the arrangement between caregiver and family, see how the other children behave, and perhaps pick up on something about Flora's condition. All I can wonder is if we're all living the same way?

"Of course," I say, my gaze catching on the large number of children already playing together.

I join two additional young women, and seven young children. I lean in toward the nearest woman, hoping the sound of my voice won't carry far. "Are we allowed to speak?" They look to be around the same age as me, a bit fragile, but versed in caring for children.

"Yes, so long as we aren't heard."

"Correct," the other says. "I'm Rosalie." Rosalie has a sullen look behind her dark eyes, and a dullness to her auburn hair, fixed in neat braid, causing me to check the falling strands of my braid. Her straight-edged posture could be tested with a stack of books on her head, even while sitting on a thin blanket in the grass.

"I'm Celina." With short dark hair pulled back into a coiled knot and large, deep blue eyes that catch the sunlight, she has an essence of more spirit than Rosalie.

Both women are dressed in simple black dresses with white aprons like me, tattered and fraying along the seams. Despite their complacent demeanor, I see something lurking within both pairs of eyes, something I recognize from the orphaned children who gave up hope that someone was coming for them. Like me.

The children are playing in a small wooden sandbox, apart from Isla and a boy about the same age, both of whom are reading beneath an overhanging tree branch. Flora is the youngest by maybe a year. The other two nannies give her a long look as if seeking an unspoken answer.

"How are you adjusting?" Celina asks, shifting her gaze to me.

I smile, for show. "Not well. I'm not exactly here of my own free will. But it could be worse, I suppose. It was either working here or being arrested."

Neither seem surprised at my response. Did they arrive here the same way as me? Almost chosen at random or found to mark off one simple checkbox on a short list.

Celina fidgets with a wooden block that was left behind by one of the children and stares past me while responding. "I wouldn't classify this position as exactly the opposite of being arrested. This is the in-between, the 'restricted zone,' a place where we aren't prisoners, but we aren't free. We're objects with only a first name," she says with a tremble in her voice.

Rosalie glimpses over her shoulder, pretending to stretch out a kink in her neck. "Each house has different rules here. At the moment, we're the only three nannies on the street, but others come and go from the other houses. At least, they have in the past. Some of the officers will beat their nanny," Rosalie says, sweeping her hand over the smooth strands of her hair, revealing four oval shaped bruises side by side along the side of her forearm. My throat constricts as if a hand is squeezing around my neck. "Others act as if you're a guest in their home, but most of them just want you to smile, keep quiet, and forget any form of proof of the rest."

"I see," I say, breathless from the invisible chokehold. "I thought...this caretaker position would be safer than the prison camp."

"It is," Rosalie says. "There are no selections here. You'll live as long as you don't step out of line."

"Selections?" I repeat.

She touches her hand to her throat, almost as if straining to speak. "Each day, the officers walk between rows of people, stare them in the eye as if their fate will speak for them, and decide whether it will be the day they live or die."

"We've both overheard the stories," Celina adds in a hush.

They pick and choose who lives and dies as if playing God? "That's inhumane," I say, stating the obvious as I wave my hand like a fan in front of my face. The sun has suddenly decided to bear all its heat on me at once, or maybe it's another dose of real-ization.

"You should know—" Rosalie begins but clears a hush from her throat. "The other nannies who have worked in the house you're in have all been released within a week or two." She smoothes out the sun-faded fabric of her dress across her bent legs. "It's imperative you follow the rules in the booklet. All of them precisely." She must know our booklets are the same, but they could be different. Not that the outcome of disobeying the rules would be different.

Do they know about the chamomile drops, tainted with bourbon? Is this a common practice between the SS households? The other children seem aware of their surroundings and engaged in their play.

"There are a lot of rules, and some—odd ones regarding the baby," I whisper. Odd is putting it mildly.

"She's just a windy baby with some minor delays. There's little that can be done to help her," Celina adds.

"She isn't just a windy baby. There's something more going on, but whatever it is, there's less that should be done to fix her," Rosalie says. "However, you're in an impossible situation and must remember she isn't your child to protect. Therefore, all you can do is maintain your position by doing what you're told."

Who else will protect them? Their mother and father aren't doing much of that. Someone could have easily said that about me when I was left on the church stoop as an infant too, but Julia took me in and treated me as her own. She protected me. For as long as she could.

Rosalie's eyes don't meet mine. Her stare is heavy, as if she's looking past me. "I assume the last nannies had morals and resisted the instructions in the booklet." I'm not sure I need someone to answer me.

"We've all been forced to give up our morals upon entering the doors of the houses on this street," Celina says, her last word fading into silence as the youngest of the children runs toward her with a rock in his hand.

All of them look as if they could be siblings with their light blonde hair and sky-blue eyes, fair complexion, but rosy cheeks. The only two children without blonde hair are Isla and Marlene. Even Flora fits in with the others.

"Oh goodness, what is this, Halbert?" Celina asks, her tone changing to sweet, innocent, and a higher pitch.

"Rock," the young boy says. He must be somewhere between one and two years old.

"Are you sure?" Celina questions him. "I thought—well, it looks like a cow to me."

"Moo," the little boy squeals. "More cows." He returns to the other side of the sandbox in search of more rocks.

"How long have the two of you—"

"About a year," Rosalie answers. "The family I worked for was deported. When the SS raided their home, they took me too, as if I was some kind of loot. That's when I became a source of free labor."

"Six months," Celina follows. "I was found in a rather unusual place," she says, peeking out of the corner of her eyes toward the table of SS wives. "I had been staying at a convent—as a novice, hoping to be accepted into their order." Celina's voice softens. "The Mother Superior decided to release me from my commitment, telling me it was best for both the convent and me given my lack of knowledge...and true calling. She suggested I visit a family who often donated to the church and needed help with their children. However, before I could even leave the grounds, an officer overheard and claimed me for his family."

"Their way of captivity seems to be a common practice among the high-level SS officers," Rosalie adds.

"In any case," Celina says, abruptly changing the subject. "Usually, the lunches are hosted at the houses we tend to, but it was a last-minute surprise invitation from Frau Schäfer today."

"It was a surprise to me as well."

"It takes time to adjust, but you'll find a way."

I twist my neck, peeking over my shoulder at the picnic table of wives, watching as one of them shoves the tray of finger sandwiches to the side of the table. The kitchen prisoner steps outside and takes the tray of food from the women, bringing it back into the house. I would have eaten the entire platter if it was sitting in front of me.

A flash of motion catches my eye from two levels above the women, Gavriel spying out between the framework of the roof. Was he watching when the sandwiches were taken away too?

"They chat among each other, mostly about us, and make up lies about their husbands—each in competition with who has it better," Rosalie says. "The irony of how little they know about living a wealthy lifestyle is laughable. I previously worked for a family with more money than the next four generations would know what to do with, but the German army kicked them out of their house. Not even their money could save them from losing everything."

Marlene stands up from within the sandbox and brushes herself off, then jolts in my direction.

"I need to use the toilet," she whispers.

I'm not sure if I should allow her to go in by herself or—

"Here, I'll hold the little darling for you while you take her," Rosalie offers. "Go on. This happens often."

I should trust her. She's like me. We're in the same situation, I assume.

With concern rushing through me, I check over my shoulder, finding the wives deep in conversation, their necks stretched toward each other to whisper whatever it is they're sharing. I place Flora in Rosalie's open arms and push myself up to my feet before taking Marlene's hand. While crossing the open green space in the yard, the back door opens, the kitchen prisoner carting out trays of food. I thought they had already eaten.

I rush Marlene along, offering to hold the door open for the young woman. "That isn't necessary," Frau Schäfer calls over to me. I'm not sure if she's talking about bringing Marlene in to use the toilet or for holding the door.

Marlene slips her hand from mine and hurries for the stairwell. As I fall behind and pass the vacant kitchen, I spot the tray of leftover finger foods. My pulse drums within my ears as I peer toward the back door, ensuring I'm alone.

With little time to spare, I grasp several of the sandwiches, still leaving a couple dozen behind, and shovel them into my apron pocket.

I flee to the stairs, breathlessly making it to the second floor, finding the door to the toilet room closed. "Are you all right, Marlene?" I ask, my breath sounding more ragged than it should.

She's quiet for a moment before responding. "Yes, my tummy hurts."

"Can I get anything for you?"

A quiet grunt follows. "No."

I'm sure she'd like some privacy, which doesn't appear to be an option in this house.

"I'll wait down the hall for you. Take your time," I tell her.

I take a hard turn up the attic stairwell, hopping on my toes to avoid any unnecessary creaks before ducking into the construction area.

"What are you doing up here?" I saw this man tending to the garden yesterday.

"I—uh."

Gavriel steps out from an enclave to my far right. "Halina?"

"I don't have much time, but I have something for you..." I whisper, my breath unsteady as I reach into the pocket of my apron. My fingers close around the small bundle and pull it out carefully before unwrapping the cloth covering.

Gavriel's eyes lock on the sandwiches, and his chest falls forward. His expression shifts from curiosity to desperation—a hunger, or maybe comfort. His hands rise beneath mine, trembling a bit. I ease them into his grasp, my knuckles brush against his skin, coarse, dry, labor-worn. The brief touch lingers longer than it should, and he doesn't pull away.

Neither do I.

Our gazes collide, his studying hard, like he's just found what he's been searching for, and mine, realizing this might be more than a helpful gesture for a stranger.

There's something about Gavriel that draws me in, and my heart swells with compassion for his brutal situation. He holds the sandwiches to his chest as if they're his next breath, and I wonder how long it's been since someone's given him anything that hasn't come with a consequence in return.

"Don't get yourself in trouble," his words quiet, his gaze still locked with mine. "We aren't worth the risk."

He says it like a fact, like he believes it. And the way he's looking at me, as if I shouldn't be doing something to help... rattles me. He can't possibly mean what he's saying. I don't believe it, not with the pain I see within his golden-brown eyes. Pain wrapped in warmth and tenderness—I can almost feel it. So unexpected and unfamiliar, but also, real.

"Yes, we are," Adam cuts in before I can reply. "What he means to say is, thank you. Thank you very much." He retreats to the other side of the room and crouches, unwrapping one of the sandwiches as if it's a rare piece of treasure.

"Of course," I say to the other man before returning my attention to Gavriel as confusion spirals through me. "Why would you say that?" I ask, the question sharper than intended. "That you're not worth the risk?"

Gavriel studies me inquisitively as if I just asked him an impossible question. His head falls slightly to the side. "Because...we're Jews, Halina."

My breath catches. It's because of what he said, it's the pain in which he speaks. I reach for his hand without thinking, pressing my palm into his. His skin is rough, overworked, and warm. "I don't see you as less," I whisper. "You matter. You deserve more than this."

His eyes lift, deliberately seeking mine. "You aren't just like me," he whispers. "You're far more beautiful."

My cheeks burn and I take my hand away from his, holding it against my chest as if I've I touched something without asking first.

Flustered, I make a show of glancing around at the progress of the construction, and all that's been accomplished in the short time I've been here, then brush my fingertips that are still tingling from his touch, along the nearest beam. "You're pretty good at this."

"At—" he questions, gazing at me with a thought I wish I could read.

"The construction—the—the craftsmanship."

"Oh, the attic," he says with a chuckle. "Well, I better be." He brushes the back of his sleeve across his dewy forehead. "I was supposed to take over my family's company—construction, in Krakow. There's an entire neighborhood of houses on the outside of the city with my initials carved into a beam."

A smile presses onto my lips, imagining a colorful row of family homes with children playing on the street as their parents watch with loving smiles from their front stoops. "You were building perfect lives for happy families," I say. "You must miss it."

Gavriel drops his gaze, and he screws his lips to the side. "Every nail I hammer, I remember what I should be doing with my time, and who I should be doing it for..."

His words fall heavily on my chest. We all come from different paths, yet the pain...it's so relatable. "I must go."

Flustered and a bit dizzy from the emptiness in my stomach, I travel back down the steps, finding the door to the toilet room still closed. My pulse flickers like sparks as I wait for Marlene. I wipe my hands on my apron, repeatedly, feeling the evidence on each finger.

A whimper whines from the floor vent next to me, reminding me of the sounds I heard when I first arrived—the ones I convinced myself to belong to a cat—a cat they clearly don't have.

Marlene finally steps out of the toilet room with her arms crossing her stomach.

"Do you feel better?" I ask.

"A bit."

We walk side by side back down the main stairwell, both of us quiet, though my mind is anything but. "Did you hear something just now?"

She shakes her head. "No, but Papa says our pipes whine like old women."

A cold chill strikes my nerves, leaving me to wonder what the noises could have been from.

"I see. Well, lucky for you, you have two sisters, and another baby sibling on the way. Isn't that right? You'll always have someone to play with."

"I suppose," she says, stepping into the foyer from the bottom step. "I don't quite want a brother, and Mama doesn't know if the baby is a boy or a girl. And Flora, she doesn't do much except cry. Isla is too old to play with stupid toys." Her accent on the word stupid leads me to believe this is a conversation she and her sister have had before.

"Well, at least there are plenty of other children on the street to play with, right?"

Marlene forces a tight-lipped smile as we reach the back door. "Yes," she says. "But no one ever stays for long."

TWELVE
GAVRIEL

We're all starving. But it's a different kind of pain to watch another person eat as if they haven't in months. The desperation in Adam's eyes, the drool foaming at the corners of his mouth, the lump in his throat...He's crouched, shoveling bites into his mouth, his cheeks full like a chipmunk's. What are we living through? The sight claws at my heart.

For a moment, I see Natan instead of Adam. The thought burns through my veins. I know I must look the same way to him, but it's inhumane to feel and watch.

"That woman is an angel," Adam says, crumbs flying out from between his lips.

"Yeah, she's something else," I say, savoring the smoky taste as the nerves of my tongue coil. We've eaten stale bread and coffee grinds together too many times to count. We've also starved in silence, side by side. This is the first time I've seen Adam smile over a mouthful of bread.

A bite of bread catches in my dry throat, and I can't swallow it fast enough. Each morsel falls heavily to the pit of my stomach, an instant satisfaction I had nearly forgotten existed.

Adam's already reaching for another sandwich while I'm trying to pace myself.

"My mom and younger sister used to make sandwiches like these. I'd always poke fun and tell them they were making a picnic for mice with how small they were," he utters through a mouthful.

"I'm sure they appreciated that," I snicker.

It's the first time in weeks I've laughed without guilt, and Adam's the funniest friend—

The funniest friend I know...now, at least.

I haven't felt a laugh deep in my gut since the last time I was with my brothers.

"Not really. My sister had an eye for nailing targets and— we'll just say I frequently ran from the kitchen with mustard in one eye and something pickled in the other." He laughs for a short moment then sighs. "I hope they're doing all right."

"I'm sure your sister found someone else to throw pickles at while you're gone," I tell him, trying to use the same hope he depends on.

There were eight sandwiches in total and we're both staring at the last four like starved lions. We each take another. He shoves his into his mouth and moves back to the pile of lumber, grabbing another plank.

It's been so long, living on rations, it's hard to remember the last time I had a meal that filled my stomach so much. I know to eat slowly, and not to overeat. It's the easiest way to purge every morsel after, only to be left with an empty stomach burning with acidity.

"Give me a minute," I tell Adam, slouching against the beam I've been leaning against, and roll my head back, staring through a gap in the rafters. The glare of the hot sun slips through and blinds me for a moment.

I curl my fingers into my fist, recalling the touch of Halina's fingers brushing against mine—a touch I shouldn't have had a second thought about. It can't matter. Yet, it does. It's a connection. She isn't just another servant in this house. There's something magnetic about her.

I used to complain about the lack of quiet in my life, having two loud brothers, and energetic parents. I kept up, but the moments I wanted to lose myself in thought, someone would interrupt. I didn't know what I was wishing for until we were separated from each other after leaving Krakow. I never want to experience a moment of silence again. I want the air to be filled with joyful sounds, laughter, and love. Her spirit has given me a thread of hope that there's more than cries of pain left to be heard.

Though...she also seems a bit too brave.

She could end up like the others, who weren't sent away due to their courage, but lack of discipline. With each interaction I have with Halina, my concern for her well-being deepens. Maybe it's because I know too much and have seen the worst of what these people are responsible for.

Without the setting of Auschwitz behind me, murder might sound more like a threat, but it's a simple solution for the Reich.

They're called thugs, heartless and cruel people, but within the perimeter of this SS "restricted zone," there's something that exists within the guards and officers—something too dark for anyone to understand.

Humans don't kill other humans by instinct. There's something else that causes a man to pull a trigger without hesitation, and I'm not sure I'll ever know what that is.

"If the other two nannies don't warn her, she might not last here. And if they do, there's no saying she'll listen," I tell Adam as if he's a part of the thoughts running through my head.

"Yeah, hopefully," he says, getting restless, with the plank gripped between his hands, the bottom resting in an angle against the ground.

A creak in the floor grabs my attention. Adam and I share a questioning stare as my blood runs cold.

"Is someone coming?" I whisper, pulling in a breath to hold so I can listen for whatever sound might follow.

Another creak, this time a more defined footstep—the sound wrapping around my neck like a noose.

Adam and I lower our stares to the two remaining sandwiches and each take one, shoving it into our mouths and chewing as hard and fast as possible in case someone is coming back up here to check on us.

I grab the other end of the wooden panel, one of the final rafters to get into place. Adam follows, hiding the evidence of the short break and mouthwatering meal.

I climb up the scaffold and press the panel in place and grab a nail out of my front pocket, then the hammer hanging from a makeshift rope belt around my waist. By the time I have my end secured, I realize no one has come upstairs.

Maybe Halina was bringing us more food, but someone got in her way.

"That woman is going to get herself killed," I mumble.

THIRTEEN

HALINA

July 27, 1943

Flora is already asleep in her nursery across the hall, likely because Frau Schäfer beat me to making up her evening bottle. In here though, Isla is in her bed, propped up against her pillow, sheets tucking her taut. With neatly woven braids slung over her shoulders and a book spread open on her lap—she's the least of my struggles when it comes to the bedtime routine.

Marlene, however, has her hands covering her head, twirling around, one braid frayed loose, the other one swinging like a rope. I can't even slip the nightgown over her head. "It's time for bed, Marlene. We must follow your parents' rules."

The second week in this house has dragged on even longer than the first, and I assume the third week will be worse. Eventually the days and weeks will never end.

"No! I don't want to go to sleep. The sun is still up," she whines, her words quieter than the conversation between her parents' downstairs. "I can still hear the other children playing on the street. It isn't fair."

She isn't wrong, but I don't make the rules. I just enforce them.

"The sun stays out for longer in the summertime, but it's still the same bedtime as it is all year round," I remind her. "Plus, sleep helps our bodies gain strength, so we'll be stronger tomorrow than we were today."

"Mama and Papa must be very, very strong," she mumbles with a roll of her eyes.

"They sure are," I say, needing to bite my tongue before anything different comes out of my mouth.

With her thoughts swaying from her nightgown to her parents, she drops her arms by her side, allowing me a quick second to pull the silk fabric over her head.

"How about I read you a story before bed? Your choice." I peer across the room at the ornate bookcase with hand-painted flowers along the trim.

Marlene walks past me to the bookshelf, slides one out from the end of the top row and brings it over to me. The front cover rings familiar right away. *The Poisonous Mushroom* book Isla was reading yesterday.

"That's my book. You can't read it," Isla says, snapping upright and slapping the book in her hands shut.

"Mama said I can read it whenever I like," Marlene argues.

"Yes, because you don't know how to read yet."

"How about I tell you a story?" I interrupt their argument.

"But then it won't have pictures," Marlene complains.

"That's what your imagination is for." I tap her bed, and she reluctantly climbs up and settles down.

"I could tell you a story about—" I tap my chin. "A princess, perhaps?"

"One who lives under the floor," she says with a giggle.

"Marlene," Isla scolds her. "That's not nice."

"It's all right. Princesses can live just about anywhere," I say.

"Even behind black iron bars?" Isla mutters.

I lower my voice with a narrow focus on Isla's innocent face. "What do you mean by that?"

"Nothing." Isla lifts her book and leans back into her original position to continue reading.

"Which iron bars are you referring to?" I press.

"The ones that keep us safe from the evil Jewish people. Shouldn't you know this?" Isla raises a brow and snarls her lip, making herself a mirror image of her mother.

I step toward Isla's side of the room and kneel by her bed. "Jewish people are not evil." As the words fall out of my mouth, regret forms as Isla's stare grows wide.

"Yes, they are," Isla argues. "They lie, cheat, and steal. They're mean and cruel—they even murder innocent people."

"Are they going to murder me?" Marlene cries out.

"No, no. That's enough. Not everything you read in a book is true, Isla." I can only imagine the absurdity written in this propagated book I'm clenching between my hands. I heard enough after Isla told me the book was teaching her how to tell the difference between a good Jew and a bad Jew.

"I didn't just read about it," Isla argues. "Mama and Papa say the same."

My blood boils beneath my skin. There were many Jewish girls and boys who lived alongside me in the orphanage. There wasn't a difference between us. I'm not sure how to explain that to a little girl who has clearly been raised to think differently.

"She's right," Marlene says. "Mama and Papa do say the same thing."

The truth bubbles on the tip of my tongue, wanting to tell them what their father really does all day. I don't know if they'd question me after seeing the way he treats their mother. Plus, they have no reason to believe me, of all people.

No. That's not true. I'm being a coward. I want to make them see the world differently, better, through innocent eyes.

That's what I promised myself I'd do in this forced situation. Even Gavriel wouldn't stay silent. I know that much now. I saw the way he looked at the children. He doesn't hold them accountable for what they're being manipulated into thinking. He must believe they can be saved too. This is what I need to be doing.

"Your mama and Papa have to follow certain rules and laws in order to keep you safe, but the truth is..."

"What? What truth?" Isla snaps back.

"Never mind. I wouldn't want to get in trouble with your parents. It's not my place to teach you about this topic."

My sigh is heavy as I wait for Isla's curiosity to peak. "I want to know," she says.

"It's not my place. I would be sent away from here for breaking rules, and—"

"No, you can't leave us!" Marlene cries out. "Please. We want you to stay."

"My parents wouldn't listen to a word I say anyway," Isla says. "I won't tell them we talked about this. I don't want you to leave either."

My chest is lighter, as if I've broken through the outer layer of Isla's steel walls. "Love is stronger than hate. Forgiveness is easier than staying angry. And seeing both sides of a story? That's like reading two books in one—twice the truth, twice the understanding."

"Like a book?" Isla asks. "Two characters who have different stories instead of one being a side character to the other?"

"Exactly," I tell her. She understands. "You see, the Jews can't be monsters, killing, stealing, or lying because they're the ones locked behind those black gates. They're scared and hungry. They want to live. That's all. They don't want your life. They just want their own back. But someone decided to read only one side of the story. And now that's the only one being told."

They're both staring at me as if I've told them the sky isn't blue.

"That's sad," Marlene says. "I wouldn't want to be scared and hungry all the time." If I say any more, she'll be up with nightmares tonight. I think I've said just enough to encourage a moment of understanding to set into their fragile minds.

"How about we talk about something different," I suggest. "Have either of you come up with any names for your new baby brother or sister?"

"We don't want another brother or sister," Isla grumbles.

"Why not? Having siblings must be the most wonderful feeling in the world. Or so I imagine."

"You don't have any sisters or brothers?" Marlene inquires.

"No," I say. "Or not that I'm aware of. I grew up without a mother or father. But I had orphan siblings, and they were lovely."

"I bet they didn't cry all day and night," Isla says.

"Some did. The crying doesn't last forever. And before you know it, they're walking, talking, and might just become your very best friend."

"That won't happen with Flora," Isla says. "Mama says there's something wrong with her."

"And what's that? What's wrong with her?" I'm surprised Frau Schäfer has said something like this in front of the girls. Children repeat everything. Surely, the woman knows at least that much.

"She has a bad tummy," Marlene says.

* * *

An hour was far longer than I expected it would take to get Marlene to sleep. The previous nights, they've both gone to bed right away without a fuss. They must be getting more comfortable with me, which I suppose is good, but will also become more trying, I'm sure.

The stairs to the attic feel steeper and longer. I imagine I won't have much trouble sleeping tonight at least.

It takes a moment for my eyes to adjust to the grimness of the rainy night with dark clouds that stole the entire sky just before the sun set. Thunder rumbles in the distance and rattles the glass of the window.

I reach for the writing desk and scoop my hand into the front pocket of my apron, retrieving a tea candle, a book of matches, a piece of notepaper, an envelope, and a pencil I've managed to scrounge up from around the house. Most of the items were scattered along their formal dining room table, a resting place for papers and junk.

With the candle lit, I lift the chair away from the desk and place it down gently. Julia used to sit on the edge of my cot with a candle just like this one when we had bad thunderstorms. She would hum old hymns to help soothe me. I hated thunder. I still don't care for it. She was always there when I needed her, even if I didn't say so out loud. I miss the sound of her voice, and the way she gently combed her fingers through my hair until I fell asleep.

I write her name at the top of the paper and press my fingers to it as if it will somehow bring me closer to her. She must be so worried with how quickly I was forced to leave and say goodbye two weeks ago. Of course, I don't have much to say that won't make her worry more. I'll be vague, say enough so she can rest knowing I can handle the situation and myself.

An hour has passed since I put the tip of the pencil to the paper, and now I'm humming on and on about the amount of bourbon lacing the poor baby's bottle. The guilt of knowing and doing nothing, or not enough, is beginning to chip away at me.

Frau Schäfer has been diligent in making sure she prepares

most of Flora's bottles before I can, which means Flora doesn't scream or cry much at all, because she's constantly asleep or barely awake. I'm sure she must have realized I was skipping the drops in any bottle I prepared.

I drop the pencil. For a moment, I let myself drift back to the last embrace Julia and I had—the precipice of no turning back to the only life I've ever known. Her words against my ear, a whisper and a reminder that *"God brought us together, and together we shall be,"* she'd said with a tremble of certainty, as if repeating those very words would make them hold true.

I believe them.

Her.

She's all I've ever had.

And being without her—it's as if I left a part of me at the orphanage.

The words in my letter stare back at me. How can I tell Julia about this horrible behavior and not follow it up with a way to stop it? I should be doing more to help Flora. I'm not sure if I've gotten through to Isla at all, and Marlene, I think she listens when I talk. I had higher expectations for myself of what I would do here and it's becoming easier to see how irrelevant my existence is in this house.

Except for Gavriel. He notices me. I notice him. I shouldn't, not here in this death trap of a house. But I can't stop it from happening.

With each interaction we have, something blooms inside of me. Giving him those sandwiches earlier—the way he looked at me in return—as if I was doing more than just giving him someone's scraps of food.

It's one thing to make a difference with these young children, but it's another to feel seen by someone, seen in a way I didn't know anyone might desire.

Julia would worry more if I told her about Gavriel, and worse, what it might take for me to save these children.

I just need to do it. I seal up my letter, shove it under the mattress, then slip my hand into my suitcase to pull out the pajamas I never changed into last night. I need to wash up. The thought of going up and down the steep stairs again sends an ache through my legs.

Even the quiet creaks of the floor are louder than they've been. No matter how hard I try to avoid each worn spot that bends and moans, the attic stairs are the only ones I can make my way around in silence. The rest of the house seems like a minefield sometimes.

The kitchen is dark, the hallway is darker, but the light in the servant washroom casts a glow across half of the bottom floor.

My mind circles around a thought—one I should push far away, but that isn't who I am. I knew my conscience would get the best of me. As quietly as I can, I tiptoe into the kitchen and grab the tincture of chamomile from the counter, then bring it with me into the washroom where I close myself inside.

The medicine cabinet doesn't have much aside from an empty bottle of aspirin, smelling salts, dandelion root, and castor oil. I'm not sure what I was hoping to find, but something more natural than bourbon at least. Without a second thought, I spill the bottle out beneath the faucet. The strong punch of bourbon waters my eyes. I'm sure the bottle will still reek of liquor despite replacing it with water. The color is different too.

I stare up at the bottles once more and grab a hold of the dandelion root, twisting it around to read what it's used for.

Pure vegetable
Remedy for sore muscles, aches and pains

It's natural and honey colored. It will work. At least to keep the bottle from being filled with liquor. One drop of the dandelion oil and I mix the bottle around and replace the dropper.

Hastily, I wash up then press my ear up to the washroom door first, listening for anyone who might have come downstairs while I've been in here, but the house is still silent.

I leave the washroom light on so I can hurry into the kitchen and replace the tincture in its right place, then return to the washroom to shut off the light and head back upstairs, wondering what my future will hold tomorrow. I need to find a way to calm Flora tomorrow. It's the only way this will work.

"What were you doing downstairs?" a small voice asks as I set foot on the first step up to the attic.

Marlene.

"What are you doing out of bed, young lady?" I ask her.

"My tummy hurts again. Mama and Papa's door is stuck. I can't get into their bedroom."

I take her by the hand, leading her to the washroom on the other side of the nursery, but she stops abruptly and vomits all over the hallway floor. The sound and stench funnel around us, gnawing at my stomach.

The master bedroom door, just a few steps from the puddle of bile, flies open and Frau Schäfer struts toward us, one hand covering her mouth, the other holding her robe closed around her nightgown.

"I'll get something to clean up," I say, my focus set on the washroom door.

"What happened, little darling?" Frau Schäfer coos at Marlene as she kneels beside her, an unexpected gesture of compassion. "Mama's here. I'm so sorry."

Marlene wipes her mouth with the back of her hand. "After dinner, I was playing house with my doll. I was the baby this time and I—drank Flora's bottle." My throat tightens as the truth chokes me. "Did I get sick because I'm not a real baby?" she asks, her body trembling. She must have done this while I was cleaning the dishes from their meal. The kitchen prisoner returns to Auschwitz once she's done cooking for the night. At that hour, the cleaning becomes my responsibility until she returns in the morning. The girls were in the family room with their parents after dinner and that must have been where she was playing "house."

Frau Schäfer pulls her close and strokes the side of her cheek. "No, no, my sweetheart, I'm sure you just have a little tummy ache, but you should never drink Flora's milk. Her milk isn't meant for big girls like you. Promise me you won't do that again?" Her gaze shifts to mine with a narrow glint, one I'm sure she expects me to decipher as...*I better not mention a word of this to anyone.*

"I promise," Marlene utters.

Clearly it's not just Flora I need to protect from her mother's evil ways...

FOURTEEN

GAVRIEL

July 28, 1943

The fog is dense, like layers of smoke weaving between the group of us waiting to use the latrine. Half of us look like ghosts, but not the man vomiting on the other side of me. I clench my eyes shut and inhale through my mouth, protecting my stomach from convulsing. But the air is so hot and stale, the sour and sulfuric acidity of bile doesn't budge. It sticks, like my clothes to my skin, the dirt and sweat an adhesive.

The wait is going on for too long this morning, and we'll risk losing our privilege of using the latrine altogether if it takes too much longer. The quaking gong will let us know. A ray of light bleeds over the horizon, slicing through the fog, illuminating my right arm and the puddle of vomit within sight. I've never wished away sunlight until right this very moment.

The walls of the latrine rattle, followed by a succession of thuds. A guard storms between the group, pushing us out of his way to get inside. *He almost stepped in the puddle. What a shame.*

Shouting, cursing, more thuds, and a gunshot.

Then another gunshot. This action plays on repeat daily. *Why bother shouting if you're just going to kill them? Save your breath.*

I keep my focus sealed on the sparse patch of grass beneath my feet, not acknowledging what's happening on the other side of the wall. If I look like I care, I'll be noticed. If I'm noticed, God only knows what comes next.

Adam nudges his shoulder into mine. "You know I saw that girl—the nanny—in the attic with you yesterday. Even all the way down in the yard, I could see the way you were looking at her," he says causally, as if we aren't in the vicinity of where two people were just shot by a guard, and as if me being caught talking to Halina would be acceptable if a kapo or any of the Schäfers were to have seen us.

I need to be more careful.

She needs to be more careful.

All we were doing is talking, but it doesn't matter. I shake my head. "Not now."

I would think the line would have started moving again, but no such luck. The gong is going to ring at any moment and all I can think about is the thought of losing control of my bladder. The ache weighing on the lower half of my body is a type of pain I never could have imagined before being sent here. I never thought I would be in a situation where someone dictated when I use the toilet, never mind telling me—us—we're allowed to go twice in a day.

"El malei rachamim..." the man behind chants a soft prayer in Hebrew for the dead, his words rising and falling like lapping waters. "Shehalach l'olamo..." A quiet sob interrupts the prayer, the man gasping for breaths between each release. "...b'shalom al mishkavo..."

The sound of his broken voice chokes me, making me wonder what his story is—who he's trying so desperately to stay alive for, like I am for my family. The line finally moves, and I step to the side to let the older gentleman go first. I place my hand on his back as he passes, just a small gesture so he knows he's not alone.

Somehow, I managed to make it through the latrine before the gong screamed its command—our notice to line up at the labor barracks. The six of us who work in the SS houses reconnect on the walk toward the front gates. In silence, we pass rows of wooden barracks and bodies lying astray. The crunch of our feet over the wet dirt grows louder every day as each of our sets of legs become heavier, despite our weight loss from starving. We pass a line of newcomers, and today, I can't bear to look at them. The guilt of not warning them of what's ahead becomes a burden that never subsides.

"So..." Adam says as we near the labor barracks.

"So, what?"

"Do you think the nanny is the long-awaited love of your life?" Adam presses.

"Her name is Halina and quit talking about her."

"That's a nice name," he says, as if checking another box.

"She's not the love of my life. I met her two weeks ago. There's no such thing. Trust me, I'd know."

Adam drops his hand on my shoulder. "You said you didn't have a girl or wife back home," he follows. "So how would you know?"

"I don't have a girl or a wife back home. I don't even have a home. There was someone once back when I had a home."

"What happened?" Adam asks, as if he's already regretting the question.

"We had been planning for a future together until her father joined the Polish Gestapo. She didn't even give me a reason why she could never see or speak to me again. She disappeared. I found out about her father after the fact and figured out the rest on my own. I thought I knew her. I thought I loved her. I was just a fool."

"We all get fooled, brother. I think most of us learn after the first time. Unless you're like me...then it takes three or four. But maybe the next woman I meet won't crush my soul. There's still hope for us."

Adam and his optimism...I didn't think I'd become reliant on it, but it's growing on me.

"Gavriel, all I know is, she's a beautiful woman, and some might say a bit feisty with the way she snuck food up to us last week," he says with a heartwarming sigh. "So, if you aren't interested in her, I could use a distraction—maybe one that won't break me."

Adam's talking as if he can march right up to the attic and sweep Halina off her feet and carry her away into the sunset. We're prisoners. We're not even supposed to be speaking to her. But really, I'd fight him for her.

"Neither of us need a distraction. That's how we'd end up dead by nightfall, isn't it?"

The loneliness is dark here. It eats at all of us, gnawing like a parasite until it takes over our every waking thought. This life we're living isn't a theatrical production with a predictable ending. It's real, and there is death. Hope is like a buried treasure that nobody here has the strength to dig up, and anything good just dangles in front of us like a trap.

"We only feel like we're dying today, brother. But it's so we can survive another day."

"We will." I don't say what's running through my mind. It's not fair of me to keep reminding him that it seems as if death is chasing us.

I still remember the night Adam pulled me up from the ground after a kapo nearly broke my nose for taking fifteen seconds too long at the toilets. It was my third night in Auschwitz and the man left me bleeding in the snow between the latrine and our block. I couldn't see straight. Everything was a blur, but Adam was there. I heard his voice, telling me I'd won the boxing championship. He draped his coat over mine and helped me to my feet. It took me a minute to understand his joke. I must have looked like I had been in a boxing ring. I doubt I looked like I won, though.

I never asked him why he helped me that night, and he never told me it was so I could survive another day. We just became immediate friends. Brothers in a way.

The only easy part about being in Auschwitz is knowing that I was the only one of my family sent here. I tell myself that the rest of them have been sent somewhere less brutal, making their chances of survival much greater. Maybe it's just a lie I knowingly tell myself. A year ago, I remember telling my younger brothers, Jozek and Natan, that no one would take us down. I wouldn't let them. I would outsmart any one of those German soldiers. I believed those words. I made them believe those words too. Now, I hope they forget about that conversation, because I was wrong. If it was just two of us in a room, me and a German soldier...only one of us would have a rifle.

Adam and I step into a growing row of others, rain trickling overhead, the hint of sunlight breaking through the clouds gone.

"A moment of happiness isn't a crime. You're still allowed to feel what you want to feel," Adam utters, keeping his voice down as the kapos pace in front of us like bloodhounds.

* * *

I'm drenched by the time I make my way up to the attic of the Schäfers' house. My boots are coated in heavy mud and the rain is plunking against the tarp like falling marbles. I turn into the alcove, a hidden space I've built into the framed beams, and grab the gas lamp used on low-lit days like today.

Before I can move again, frantic steps draw my attention to the open doorway, wondering who is rushing up here. Halina bursts by the expansion and into her room, not pausing before she reaches to her side, yanking the zipper of her dress down. The black fabric slips to ground exposing her porcelain skin and a figure that steals my breath.

I can't...I can't look away.

Where is my head? I spin around, my rapid breaths suffocating me. I shouldn't have been watching. I should have made a sound, so she knew I was there. She should have closed the door...

"Halina, I'm sure you can find something under the bed in the attic. Surely the last nanny left something behind, or perhaps the one before that," Halina mutters, mimicking Frau Schäfer in a curt tone. "That woman doesn't have a shred of compassion left in her veins."

I nudge a wooden plank among the pile of others, just to make my presence known.

She gasps and spins around, grabs the dress from the floor, and clutches it against her chest. "Oh my—you could have said something," she breathes, her cheeks crimson. "I didn't know you were—never mind. Of course you're up here."

I peer toward the open door where she stands half-hidden, her shoulders bare, ribbons of golden hair, loose from her braid, fluttering over her silky skin—beautiful.

"You could have closed the—never mind...Is everything all right?"

She eyes me narrowly. "What do you think?" Her response is raw, but by the look of it, justified.

"Can I get something for you?" I offer, uselessly, glancing around the sawdust covered boards surrounding me.

"Marlene is sick from drinking out of Flora's bourbon-laced bottle. She's been vomiting since last night. I avoided being the target until now. I don't have anything else to wear."

I understand the weight of her struggle. None of us at Auschwitz have more than a layer or two ourselves, and it's usually soiled with the unthinkable. I'll keep that thought to myself.

The door creaks as she disappears again, shuffling beneath the bed. I turn away, giving her privacy, and trying to keep myself occupied while being painfully aware of her presence just steps away.

A quick dash across the hall reclaims my attention, finding her in a female Auschwitz uniform—a blue and white striped dress that swallows her petite frame, the fabric billowing behind her as if hanging from a clothesline.

"I'm sorry for snapping at you. I didn't sleep and I've been cleaning up vomit—"

"I've been snapped at for less."

She fumbles with the shoulders of the uniform, which drape indiscreetly. "What happened to the person last wearing this?" she asks.

"I—" I don't want to tell her.

"Tell me," she says, already knowing the answer, I'm sure. She gestures to the jagged hole and dried blood stain on the back.

"Schäfer threw a bottle at his wife. The nanny stepped between them. They replaced her with someone—someone... like you after that."

"A servant." She bluntly suggests the proper term.

"Right. Servant."

Halina's fingers graze the bloodstain. "Where were the children?"

"I wasn't here yet. Someone from Auschwitz told me what happened."

She turns to face me straight on, her eyes glistening with disdain and sorrow. "How can I walk back down to those girls wearing this?" Her voice breaks as she tugs at the loose fabric on her shoulder. "How can I act as if this is normal?"

"I have an idea." I step in closer but pause for a moment. "May I?"

She gives a faint nod and nips her bottom lip, wary but agreeable as she sweeps her braid over her shoulder, exposing her back. Her trust unravels something inside of me.

I loosen the fabric belt at her waist and gather the extra fabric at the back, retying it snug so the bloodstain vanishes into the fold. "There. No one will see it now."

She turns, her eyes catching mine for a flicker before her lashes dip and her cheeks blush. Then she rises onto her toes and wraps her arms around my neck, her small frame molding to mine as if we were meant to be this way. "Thank you," she whispers, her lips brushing over my ear.

"It's been my pleasure. I assure you."

The moment lingers like a beautiful note, one I wish I could hold on to.

Then a shout in the distance, a reminder of where we are—who we are—brings us back to the dusty attic. "I've seen horrors before, but this place...it's something out of a nightmare. That man, he terrifies me. I don't know what he's capable of. Or, I guess, I do, and that's the worst part."

I pull back just enough to meet her eyes, cupping her arms in my hands. "You've already endured more than most. You're still here. That strength, it matters."

"Is this what it's like there? In Auschwitz?"

I swallow hard, unsure how much truth to give her. "Worse. Much worse. I consider us lucky to be here during the daytime hours."

She drops her gaze as if ashamed. "I'm sorry—of course it is. I—can't believe I once thought I had a hard life just because my parents gave me away. I grew up not knowing where I belonged in this world, and I thought that was pain. "I was foolish to think that way."

"No, I'm the one who should be sorry," I say, the words

aching from the bottom of my heart. "You didn't deserve to grow up that way. The pain we speak of...it isn't comparable." I have a family I know and love. I don't have to question where I came from. I'll always know, no matter how we finally end up.

To not know...That's very different.

She lifts her eyes, finding mine again, but this time with a sense of affinity as if it isn't the pain we're comparing, but instead, the understanding of loneliness.

"I won't let that man hurt those girls," she proclaims. "I must find a way to stop Frau Schäfer from harming her baby."

Terror trickles down my spine at her sentiment. "You can't fight them. That isn't how we survive. We have to find a way to squeeze between the rules without leaving a trace. Really, we can only outsmart them if we never step out of line."

Her eyes grow round with question, almost as if waiting for me to say something more, something different. But there's no other advice to give.

She turns toward the door but hesitates. "Do you have a family? Are you married?"

"I had a family. I hope I still do. Married? No."

A small smile curls into her lips. "I haven't had the chance to live a real life yet. But someday...if we're set free, I want to live without rules, love who I want, and to have something no one can take from me. That's what I'm holding on to. Just a dream."

My chest aches at her words. It aches for her.

"I think that's worth fighting for," I tell her.

FIFTEEN
HALINA

The bloodied uniform slips off my shoulders before I even leave the construction space of the attic. I keep my eyes on Gavriel, plodding backward through the construction space. He stands, framed by raw lumber, his arms folded, stance steady. His sleeves are rolled up, revealing corded forearms, each marked with small cuts and smudges of dirt. Sweat beads along his temple, two drops trailing down the curve of his cheek. My heart pounds, almost recklessly. He's captivating in a way I can't quite explain. Like ancient architecture, weathered by battle, built to endure.

With each step I take down the stairs to where Frau Schäfer and the girls are waiting for me to return, the heavy fabric shifts like a thick potato sack rather than a smock dress. I'm no better or different than any person wearing one of these uniforms every day. Flora's cries grow louder by the second. Frau Schäfer might be wondering why her morning bottle hasn't quieted her down.

"Who was it you were speaking to up there?" Frau Schäfer asks, standing at the bottom of the main stairwell with her arms crossed over her chest.

"I wasn't speaking to anyone. Perhaps you heard me talking to myself," I reply. I don't care what she thinks. I've been awake with Marlene all night, have cleaned up several puddles of vomit, and now must find a way to clean my personal clothes without using anything that belongs to this household.

"That uniform is filthy," she says.

"So are my clothes," I reply.

"Come, Halina," Frau Schäfer says, turning on her heels away from the stairwell. Too many responses percolate on my tongue, words she should hear. Instead, I obediently follow her into the kitchen, spotting the girls at the far end in their small play area, Flora crying from her cradle, her hands gripped along the sides, trying to pull herself up to see what everyone else is doing, and the kitchen prisoner standing guard over the three.

A knot forms in my stomach and my breaths constrict as she reaches for the tincture of chamomile. "Do you know what this is used for?"

"There was no comment with reason in the rule booklet for why I should add chamomile to Flora's bottle. So, no."

"Don't be wise," she retorts.

If I was wise, I'd have an answer, but I'll keep that remark to myself too.

"*Chamomile*," I say, accentuating the word, "*can* help upset stomachs, and may be used as a mild sleep aid."

"Yes, it can," Frau Schäfer replies, raising a brow.

"Though, I'm sure bourbon has a much stronger effect." A flaming heat fills my face, a sensation I want to hide at all costs. Fear should have stopped me from saying such a thing, but giving in to my unease would allow the continuation of hurting an innocent child. My anger speaks louder. She needs to know I'm aware of the secret she and her husband were arguing about to possibly take her down a few notches.

Frau Schäfer grabs my wrist and yanks me out of the

kitchen. "How dare you?" she utters, anger seething with each word.

"How dare I take a whiff of something before pouring it into your baby's bottle?"

"You're not a doctor. You don't have a right to comment on what Flora needs. You are here to follow my orders, not question them."

"A doctor told you to pour bourbon into Flora's bottle? And mask the bourbon by swapping it out in a bottle of chamomile oil?"

I've infuriated her and this may be the moment where I find out that she's the one who shot the last nanny, rather than her husband. Though, something tells me Frau Schäfer doesn't have the ability to pull a trigger. "Correct me if I'm wrong, but you're trying to hide whatever condition Flora might have. Because a pure Aryan baby isn't supposed to have physical delays or apparent unexplainable pain. And she shouldn't be crying the way she does, right? Wasn't it just two years ago the Reich was quietly euthanizing children with medical issues? And sterilizing women who couldn't produce 'perfect' offspring. The Reich stopped euthanizing people for that, right?"

Frau Schäfer's brows snap together with disdain, her face darkening in shades of red, her eyes bulging with shock. Except, everything I said is what the Reich wants anyone under their power to believe and live by. We hide what we can't afford to be exposed.

For four years, the German army, alongside the Führer, has been responsible for rewriting birthrights in Poland and now several other countries. No matter how hard I try to understand how we ended up like this, it will never make sense. Why can't we fight back? Why isn't anyone strong enough to push them away? Did we have the strength in the beginning? Before it became too late? Before we were forced to ration food and accept the demise of Europe?

"I'm not a bad mother," Frau Schäfer seethes through clenched teeth.

"I'm not a doctor, Frau Schäfer, but I believe there could be other options to help Flora rather than potentially causing her long-term health issues, as well as damage to her brain and organs."

"And I suppose you know what that is since you apparently think you're better with children than me?"

Isn't that the reason they wanted help? Not that they were overly concerned with qualifications, which doesn't say much for Frau Schäfer.

"I grew up in an orphanage. I've been around many children and have seen quite a bit."

"Then, what I'm hearing is, you think you can help her?"

Now there's desperation in Frau Schäfer's eyes. She might think I was oblivious to the arguments between her and her husband, but if anything was clear, he expects her to hide whatever pain or delays Flora might be suffering with, and to do so without the help of a physician. She's in a very vulnerable place.

"How long have you been quieting her cries with bourbon?"

"Hush, will you?" she snaps. "The children don't need to know. I don't know...on and off for a couple of months."

"Her body might need time to adjust without...I can try and help her with some exercises I've learned from experience with other children. I can't promise it will help, but it might."

"All right," she says. "Fine. You must know, I won't be able to stop Heinrich—Officer Schäfer—from his agitation if she continues to cry at all hours of the night."

"She's a baby," I remind her. Despite her reasons for crying...babies do cry. But she's perfect, and I swear...I will not let the world erase her.

"She's a pure Aryan child, and we are a part of the Lebensborn program. As you just said yourself, there isn't allowance for any slight imperfection, even now, following the end of the Eugenics program. She should be consolable at the very least."

"Lebensborn program?" I ask, unaware of any such program.

"I've said too much. Never mind that. Flora must stop crying. It's simple."

Frau Schäfer crunches her nose and jerks her head back. "What is that stench?"

"Me." I turn around and pull the fabric from the center to my shoulders, showing her the deep blood stain. "I assume someone died in this?"

She grabs my arm and flings me back around. "You better get one thing straight...You are not in control here. You do not speak to me in the way you have been today. You might think you have something on me for the way I've been feeding my infant but let that uniform be a reminder to you that I owe you nothing. You are replaceable and someone else can fill that uniform just as you are. Now, go handle my child."

She pins me under her stare for a long minute, mostly because I don't jump following her threat. "I'm sorry for the way he makes you feel, and for the fear you must live with."

I close my eyes as I watch her lift the flat of her palm up and out. The sting and clap against my cheek cause bright spots to freckle over my eyes. The pain is temporary, but my words will sit with her.

"Now. Go," she hisses.

I will never judge a mother, but I know the result of bad parenting. Marlene and Isla will remember their mother's behavior, and their father's too. These memories will hang in the backs of their minds like paintings, ones they'll view differently as they age.

Flora, red in the face with tears dampening her cheeks, croaks out another loud cry as the sound vanishes into a raspy breath. "Ma!" she shouts as I lift her up, finding her bottom soaked. It's the first time I've heard her utter a word, and it's a shame Ada doesn't respond to her attempt to speak.

"Did you just say Ma?" I repeat her word with a forced sense of joy. "Ma?"

Flora mimics the movement of my lips but doesn't say the word out loud again. It's something. It's a milestone.

"Isla, could you read your sister a story while I change Flora out of her wet clothes?"

Isla drops the book she's holding and tosses her head back. "Fine," she complies.

"I'm going out. I have errands to run," Frau Schäfer says, her tone pompous and unaffected by our conversation. "Sylvia and Oskar are on guard for the prisoners and will be in and out frequently checking on them." The kapos. I haven't seen Sylvia since the first day I arrived, but Oskar charges in and out of the house frequently. He visits the attic at least six times a day, checking on Gavriel's work. "Girls, stay by Halina's side. There are prisoners in this house, yes?"

Frau Schäfer is out the door within seconds of her last statement.

"Yes, Mama," Marlene grumbles, and Isla takes her by the hand and pulls her toward me as we make our way to the stairwell.

No sooner than I set Flora down and remove her wet clothes and diaper, does the squeal of car brakes ping against the windows. Frau Schäfer must have forgotten something.

I set the new dry cloth beneath Flora and fold in the sides. "Can you say 'ba'?" I ask Flora, exaggerating the movement between my lips. "Ba..."

She smacks her lips together a few times and smiles. "Good try, sweet girl!" I say, tickling her tummy.

"Papa's home," Marlene squeals. "He's come home in the middle of the day again!" My hands turn clammy as heat rises through my spine. With everything I've heard about and from

Officer Schäfer this week, I know well enough that there's no saying what his agenda is or what state of mind he'll be in when he enters the house.

"He has a friend with him," Isla adds. "Another officer, but I don't know him. I thought we knew most of them by now."

"Does your father bring officers home with him often?"

Isla turns from the window and faces me as I pull a fresh romper over Flora's head and try to attach it at the bottom as she's busy trying to roll away from me. Isla's head falls to the side, just a bit, and her eyes narrow as if she wants me to read the thoughts going through her head before she speaks them out loud. "Not very often, but when he does, it's usually because he needs a worker taken out or replaced from the house." She peers over at her sister. "Isn't that right, Marlene?"

Marlene drops her head and nods. "Yes, that's right."

The front door slams open so hard, the walls shudder, the paintings hanging in Flora's bedroom rattling. "Where is she?" Officer Schäfer's voice is paralyzing, biting through the walls as if he's only a few steps away. A breath catches in my lungs, choking me, and all I can do is clutch Flora to my chest as I stiffen in wait.

"Where are you?" his voice booms.

"He must be angry with Mama," Marlene whispers.

Their mama isn't here. I am.

Flora must sense a need for calm among the commotion as she pushes herself upright to sit at attention, staring at the bedroom door. Even the youngest of prey knows when to remain still in the face of their predators.

SIXTEEN

GAVRIEL

From the crevices in the roof rafters, I watched Frau Schäfer bolt out of the house, running in the opposite direction that Officer Schäfer's vehicle just came from with only moments in between. It's too coincidental to believe she happened to disappear before he arrived just by chance...

I place down the wooden panel I was about to secure between two rafters and bolt toward the attic's stairwell, peeking around the corner. Halina's been in Flora's bedroom with the girls following Frau Schäfer's departure. I could hear their muffled voices through the thin floor, but there's nothing but silence from them now.

With doors slamming all around the main floor, my pulse quickens, anticipating what he'll do next. The heavy clomps of his boots grow louder as he returns to the front of the house—to the main stairwell. I hold my breath as he stomps up the first steps of the main stairwell.

Is he looking for Halina? I think of her resolve this morning, telling me she won't allow them to hurt the children or the baby any more...What did she do?

A knot forms in my stomach, thinking about what will

happen when he comes upstairs to find her. Or what will happen if he goes near her—

My heart beats out of my chest, rage building within me. I won't let her suffer the same consequence as the last nanny. I'm going to die sooner or later anyway.

Schäfer's movements come to a sudden halt, pausing as if he's heard or seen something. The floor creaks under his feet, the moment of unease lingering. I clench my fists by my side, trying to control my ragged breaths while scrutinizing the cause of his irate commotion. It's clear he doesn't always need a reason, but he's here with another officer.

"Where is she?" he shouts again.

"Can I assist you?" a meek voice murmurs between the shouts. Sylvia—she shouldn't be speaking to him. It doesn't matter that she's a kapo or only here to be guarding the female prisoners on the streets. The prisoners, kapo or not, do not speak to the officer of the house unless they are directly asked a question.

"Bring her to me," Officer Schäfer demands as he strikes his fist against the wall, the thud reverberating up to the attic.

"Your wife has gone out," Sylvia says. Her overpowering confidence and cruelty along our treks to and from Auschwitz in the mornings and evenings are nothing in comparison to the fear quaking through her voice at this moment. Everyone knows how to be tough until they're confronted by the person above them.

"I'm not looking for my wife," he growls. "You know exactly who I'm speaking about."

I dash down the steps, using the double-sided railing to keep the mass of weight from creaking the wooden boards. I haven't moved this fast in longer than I can remember. A split-second flash of the white and blue striped dress catches my attention as I near Flora's bedroom across from the attic's stairwell, spotting Halina clutching the baby against her chest, and the two girls staring up at her as if they're waiting for her to tell them why they should be afraid of their father downstairs.

I sling myself into the room and lift the door just slightly to avoid a squeak of the hinges as I close us inside. "Are you all right?" I ask.

Halina's eyes are wide open, her face drained of color, her arms shaking.

"I'm fine," she whispers, clearly masking the truth. "You didn't have to come down here."

I lean in and whisper in her ear, so the children don't hear me. "You don't need to be alone here with that man stalking around like a beast."

"If he finds you here..." she argues under her breath. "Who is he looking for?"

I hold my finger up to my lips, trying to listen for what Sylvia is telling him. Halina watches my finger, but her gaze doesn't stop there—it lingers on my lips even after I lower my hand. My chest tightens, equal parts panic and something far more dangerous. I lose track of what Sylvia is saying. All I can think about is the bowed curve of Halina's mouth.

"What is this person's number?" Sylvia presses, her voice growing in volume, shaking me out of my distraction.

"Number?" Halina whispers. "What does that mean?"

Sylvia answers too quickly, faster than me. "Prisoner 2138X. She was brought here to clean the house. You reported her death several weeks ago."

I lift my sleeve to remind her of the tattoo, my number. "We're all numbered. They took away our names."

"Your name," Halina repeats, solemnly. "Why would—"

"Oh yes, her," Sylvia's voice spikes, guilt strangling her voice. "That girl's body was taken away."

None of us saw the body of that woman. We had no choice but to believe Sylvia's word.

"No!" Schäfer barks. "It wasn't. The commandant handed

me a deportation list with her number this morning. And our records didn't match."

"That can't be," Sylvia says.

"My wife and daughters were just complaining about whining pipes in the walls. That happens in houses, yes?"

"Of course. Yes. It does," Sylvia replies.

"There's nothing wrong with my pipes. Is there?" he snaps back.

"I—I—" Sylvia stutters.

Schäfer charges down the hallway toward the foyer, stopping at a narrow door to his right. He slashes it open and yanks the string attached to the bulb dangling from the ceiling. The switch on his flashlight clicks as he descends the uneven cement steps leading to his shallow cellar. The light at the door only carries so far, from what I've seen the one other time the door was open.

"Can I go say hello to my papa?" Marlene asks me, as if I have any say about what happens around here.

"Uh—I don't think that would be a good idea right now. He's busy with work and needs to tend to something here," I whisper.

A hint of desperation glistens across Halina's eyes, as if wondering what my words truly mean, why nothing makes sense right now.

"You mongrel! Disgusting Jew. Scum feeding off rats in my own house!" The vulgar shouts continue booming through the vents.

"Who is Papa shouting at?" Marlene asks quietly.

My core tightens as a body thrashes against what must be a wall. A weak feminine moan follows.

"Take this prisoner out of the house," Schäfer must be commanding the other officer.

"I—I'm not sure. Why don't we why find something to read," Halina suggests to Marlene.

"Don't let them near the window," I whisper to Halina. "And you, I don't want you to look outside either. Can you do that for me?"

"Why—" The look in her eyes, the pain, the understanding, the realization of what happens every second of the day inside of Auschwitz, is harder to see in someone else than to feel for myself.

"Please, spare them, and yourself."

She nods, unsure and grabs my wrist. "You should go back upstairs. I don't want you to be caught here," Halina says.

"You're right. Don't forget..." I point at the window then leave the room, wishing I could protect them from listening to the sounds of what I know will happen outside in a matter of seconds.

I head back up to the attic, returning to the constructed framed walls, I peer out between the rafters, spotting Bea, the prisoner who was brought here to keep the house clean, just before Halina started. She wasn't here long before there was a miscount at an evening line-up. Sylvia claimed Bea died, and her body had been removed. Since none of us saw her body, I considered that she may have tried to escape. I told myself she made it, somehow. It was a slice of hope for the rest of us, I guess.

I didn't notice any sounds, or know she was hiding in the cellar this whole time. Likely starving and slowly dying. I feel sick.

The sound of a pistol clicking into place strikes a nerve before the shot even comes. I swallow hard and clench my eyes shut as a strangled whine weaves between the rafters. I press my fist to my mouth as the crack of the gunshot shatters between the enclave of trees.

I release my held breath and open my eyes. I can't let myself feel it...I hardly knew her. I just know she was one of us. And now she's gone.

"Call for a truck," Schäfer shouts to the other officer.

Desperation is the ability to feed off rats or rubbish if she managed to escape to the cans at night. She would have been better off fleeing in the middle of the night, but she could hardly keep herself upright on her knees to clean the floors here. She knew her days were coming to an end. Her skeletal body lies in the grass, her bones like thin branches. Another one of us, dead.

"No, no, don't go over there!" Halina's muffled words shout with panic.

A screeching squeal pierces through floors. "There's a dead Jew on the grass!" Marlene screams.

"Papa killed her," Isla follows, her words unnaturally calm. "She's a Jew. She was just a bad mushroom, Marlene. A bad one. Remember? Papa is protecting us. He's always going to protect us from the bad Jewish mushrooms."

SEVENTEEN

HALINA

An hour ago, I would have had trouble defining the meaning of fear, especially since I'm certain my worst fear would have always been to grow up without parents or a family. I've had nightmares and woken up drenched in sweat, jumped at eerie sounds in a dark room, and even screamed so loud that all the birds flew out of a tree at once, all because a squirrel ran across my feet while I was walking through the woods alone.

Now—after witnessing the death of a woman...

I don't want to ever see someone die again.

That's true fear. And I didn't protect the children. I wrestled with Marlene and Isla, trying to stop them, but it all happened so quickly and with Flora in my arms, I lost the fight. Officer Schäfer must have heard his daughter's scream, but he didn't come upstairs to check on them. He might not have even known we were upstairs at all.

Julia never would have let me see something like that. She would have just known to keep me away from the window. Somehow. She would still keep me away from the window, even now. I didn't realize how much she must have been protecting me from.

How could I not tell her that I loved her when I left? I barely embraced her. She must think I'm ungrateful, but it's not true. Not at all. I'd do anything to tell her what she truly meant—what she means to me.

I hope I get another chance.

I don't know what to tell them. How do I make this okay? I wish I could ask Julia what I should do right now...if there's any way to make this better. Though, I think I know the answer.

I've kept them in Flora's bedroom. The car has left, and a truck has come and gone, leaving us with the resonance of a dead weight falling against the metal lining in the back of the truck. I squeeze my eyes shut, willing the sound to disappear, but it replays over and over, even after they've taken her away. I stare down at Flora, finding her entranced by the magic of her hands, opening and closing them in front of her eyes. How can someone so innocent live in such a hateful world?

With the return of quiet, Flora begins to cry, turning an angry shade of red. I lower myself onto the circular accent rug in the center of the room and lay Flora on her back. "I know your belly must hurt, sweet girl," I tell her, speaking calmly in gentle tones, despite my racing heart, and the cold shock running through my veins.

"Bea was a nice maid. She made my bed smell like a rose garden," Marlene says. "I didn't know she was a bad Jew though."

I close my eyes and take in a deep breath, knowing anything I say will likely be repeated to her mother and father. Isla's sitting against the wall across from me, next to a tall oak bureau, staring up at the ceiling. She presses her hands against her ears to block out the sound from Flora. I take Flora's little feet in my hands and push on them to bend her knees into her belly, a trick I learned with some of the other babies in the orphanage. Julia taught me how to make them feel better. It also helps strengthen her muscles. I've been working on this a little each day with her. I'm not sure if it's helping much.

A series of heavy footsteps hurries down the stairs on the other side of the bedroom and Gavriel returns. Isla stares at him but this time it's with a question swirling in her eyes.

Marlene turns away from the window and redirects her focus on him too. "Are you a Jew?" she asks. "Everyone who wears the same pajamas as you—they're all Jews, aren't they?" I'm surprised Marlene hasn't said anything to me about the uniform I've adopted this morning. Maybe she knows it's borrowed.

"I don't think it matters much," Gavriel tells her.

"It does," Marlene says, her eyes like round coins, faithful to believing her own words.

"How so?" Gavriel asks, pressing his hands against the door's threshold.

"Jews are bad people," Marlene insists, her words as confident as they were likely taught.

"Who told you that?" Gavriel asks, his calm demeanor a wonder when I'm internally fuming for him.

"Papa did. He says Jews come in and steal everything from the good people, which makes them bad."

"Remember what I told you and your sister? The Jews aren't bad people."

"They have their own story too," Marlene repeats what I had told her. "They're scared, hungry, and want to come out of the gates. Right?"

Gavriel's eyes meet mine, and a flash of surprise flickers between his lashes as if he didn't expect me to go against the lies fed to them by their parents.

"Halina's right," he says. "Bad people come in all different shapes and sizes, just the same as good people. In fact, it's nearly impossible to tell the difference between the two unless they've proven who they are inside. Everyone should have a chance to be seen as someone good before they're called otherwise."

Marlene twists her lips to the side, her eyes still as she considers Gavriel's statement. She'll believe her parents over anyone else. All children are like that, I'm sure.

Even though the girls are more than likely very confused about what to believe after being taught one way for so long, they don't argue with either Gavriel or myself, which comes as a surprise.

"Girls, why don't you both go into your bedroom and find something to do while I try to help your sister with her achy belly."

They leave the room promptly and move into the room next door. Gavriel takes the opportunity to step in closer and squats beside me then reaches over and brushes the hair off my shoulder. It's nothing more than a simple touch, a gesture of reassurance, but my body tenses. "I was worried," he says in a hush.

The warmth of his touch melts through the thick fabric of the uniform, and a flutter blossoms within my chest. I glance at him, and catch myself staring into his eyes, caught in a hold I can't release.

"You knew he was going to kill her just outside of the house?"

"She isn't the first—"

Gavriel's gaze drops between us. "I wanted to spare you and the girls. You don't deserve to see such a sight."

"Neither do you."

"Halina...this is all I see now."

"Well, you shouldn't try to protect me from what you're forced to see every day." I can't look Gavriel in the eyes while I say this because despite the walls I've spent my life building around me, they don't seem to keep this level of fear out. "I can look after myself, and I'm tougher than I look."

Gavriel studies me, and for a moment I question if he'll

argue back. Instead, he offers me a small, sad smile. "Maybe," he says. "But that doesn't mean I don't want to protect you."

Maybe life is easier when there's no one else to worry about. What if I've been the lucky one all this time—never knowing what it is I could lose so easily. But now I think I have a chance of knowing what that would feel like...and I'm terrified to lose it.

Thoughts continue to scatter in my head until one rolls off my tongue. "Did you know about the girl in the cellar? I had been hearing noises, but I wondered if they had a cat or maybe there were mice."

"She disappeared a couple weeks ago. No one knew what happened to her."

I wonder why she hadn't run away. If she made it as far as escaping from the lineup to return to Auschwitz at night, why hide in this cellar of all places? "She almost made it, I suppose."

Gavriel shakes his head. "No one escapes Auschwitz, or the bordering 'restricted zone' within, and lives to talk about it. Trust me. She figured that out after it was too late, I'm sure."

His stare becomes dark and a bit lost. "I'm tired of this—all of it," he says, his voice rising with hostility. "The killing, the terror. The way they poison their own children—their minds filled with horrific sights they'll never forget. Ada should have taken her children with her. She knew. She's a coward."

I can't argue. He's right. She left her children here to witness their father murdering a woman. But Gavriel's words aren't just an expression of frustration. It's something different. The look on his face, the way his hands are clenched into fists by his side, all I see is someone who is prepared to do something about it—this life here. Someone like me...

"I better get back to work," Gavriel says. "If you need anything—sorry, I know you have everything under control."

"I should have just said thank you for trying to protect us from seeing what we did. And for standing up for me to the kapo when I first arrived. I'm not very good at this..."

"Good at what?" Gavriel asks.

"Trusting someone, then showing my gratitude. It's something that's missing inside of me, I guess."

"We're all missing something inside of us. You're not in this alone."

EIGHTEEN
GAVRIEL

Hours have passed since Bea was shot in front of an audience. The house has been eerily silent, though loud with grief. The grief is my own. Something inside of me is breaking, slowly crackling like splintering wood. He's going to kill her, or me. Both of us. Adam and the others too. We're on a list of numbers and names, and too many of the others have been crossed out. A one-sided armed war isn't a war—this is a mutiny. They took everything from us then attacked. For years, I've been following rules, biting my tongue, sacrificing everything to be their living victim, rather than a dead one. And now, they have us—the Jews, and every other minority who doesn't fit within their Aryan race, in a chokehold, helpless, and weak—some begging for death.

My pulse drums within my ears and my temples throb, but rather than take the right turn back upstairs, I continue down the hallway and head down the main stairwell. It's time to stop feeling so helpless.

The house is still quiet. Not even the hiss of a stove or the stream of the faucet from Kasia in the kitchen. With a peek into each room on the main floor, confirming I'm alone, I slip into

Officer Schäfer's office and close the door behind me. I've never been here, not even seen past the bookshelf along the wall, visible at the doorway. The entire room is lined with walnut bookcases encircling a worn Persian rug with a matching walnut desk, a leather smoking chair tucked in, and a single lamp in the corner, hovering over a pen stand and bottle of ink.

The windows are trimmed with heavy burgundy linen, and framed maps, certificates, and awards accent every open space along the wood-paneled walls. Between the two large windows are a row of war medals and Nazi paraphernalia. My throat clenches as I take in a whiff of a potent liquor mixed with tobacco and wood polish. A small grandfather clock sits on a shelf facing his desk, each tick of the second hand, sounds like a tapped key on a typewriter. *Tap, tap, tap, tap...*

I don't have long.

The drawers on either side of his smoking chair have brass handles, perfect canvases for fingerprints. With the bottom hem of my uniform top, I yank open the top drawer and shuffle the stack of papers from side to side. I work my way down the three drawers, finding what I was looking for in the deep bottom one.

I retrieve the pistol with a careful grip, as if it might detonate upon an unlawful touch. I've never used a gun—never had a reason to. Pa never liked hunting much and the pistol he kept for safety was locked away beneath his bed. He showed me how to use it if there was ever a real emergency, and how to check the chambers, but other than that one time, it was never seen by my brothers or me.

"Guns kill," Pa told us. "There's no reason for you to ever lay a finger on one unless you have intentions to kill—God forbid any of you ever should." He didn't know what the world would turn into, and we didn't speak much about that gun after he was forced to turn it in per German law.

As a grown man now, I see his point was: don't do as I'm

doing. He had a gun in case anyone ever threatened his family. He'd kill if it meant protecting us.

My drawers won't hold this up with the string I fight with every morning just to keep these heavy baggy pants around my waist.

I hold the pistol in my right hand, keeping a solid grasp around the grip. The hollow feel within the grip tells me there's no magazine loaded into it. I hold the weapon out in front of me, like my Pa always said, and pull the upper slide backward. As the slide comes back, a round pops out and falls to the floor. *Good thing I checked.* With a glimpse into the barrel, finding no other rounds, I slowly let the slide return to its place. I scoop up the fallen ammo and close the drawer.

"I'm well, how are you this morning, Edith?" Frau Schäfer calls out. Someone must be walking by the house. Her voice is muffled but clear enough that she's likely right outside the front door. But she's home.

I close the drawer with a gentle nudge and head for the hallway.

"Of course. That sounds lovely," she says, ending the impromptu conversation.

I make a run for the stairwell, unable to see her profile in either of the tempered glass windows either side of the front door. Skipping every other step, I clench my grip tighter around the pistol, my muscles and joints burn and ache—a reminder that my body has aged far beyond my twenty-three years. My brain can't keep up. I should have the strength to do what I've always done, but I'm losing too much weight, eating so little and pushing myself through twelve hours of labor each day.

The front door opens just as I turn up the attic stairwell. I stop my trampling motion and soften my steps to avoid making a sound until I'm upstairs in the expansion.

"Girls, your mother is home," Frau Schäfer calls out.

"Mama!" they shout, scampering out of their bedroom.

As if on cue, Flora begins to cry again. Perhaps it isn't a coincidence that Halina can manage to keep her calm when the baby's mother is gone. To think Frau Schäfer's bringing another child into this hostile environment is beyond my comprehension.

I spin around the unfinished space and stop in front of the hidden alcove. I knew this small space would come in handy. I pull open the two panels of wood, hinged on the inside to conceal any breathable space. Then, I loosen one of the shorter wall panels, built the same way as the doors, revealing the small, cubed compartment, perfect for hiding smaller objects, and this pistol.

"Of course, my child is wailing when I walk in through the door. What else would she be doing?" Frau Schäfer shouts.

Footsteps cross through the hallway below me and disappear at the stairwell. Halina must be bringing Frau Schäfer her wailing child.

* * *

"Where are the hounds?" Adam whispers. "We should be halfway back to Auschwitz by now."

"I don't know," I answer. We're standing between the SS-owned homes and the brink of the wooded path that leads back to the camp. The two lines of us, men and women, are facing each other, in formation like we should be. By this time, there is usually a guard or two waiting to escort us, but not even the kapos are here. It's late, and much darker than usual. Something isn't right.

Schäfer is sitting in his parked car just a dozen steps away from our lines. There's no way he would be the one escorting us back to Auschwitz, not through the woods. Another set of headlights flashes down the street, a slow, smooth gliding vehicle—another officer.

"What are they expecting us to do?" Benson utters. It's one of the first times he's walked back with us at the same hour. He's been brought here to cook for one of the other two families and doesn't return to the barracks until midnight some nights.

"They're all watching," Reuben says, holding his soot-covered broom in hand.

"If we don't report back on time, we'll miss roll call," Kasia says. "If we miss the roll call, everyone in the barracks will suffer. Maybe we should just go on our own."

Kasia knows just as well as the rest of us that Bea was killed today after her failed plan to escape, which means we're likely awaiting punishment for Bea's decision. But for what purpose when she's already dead?

I turn over my shoulder, and whisper to Adam, "I did something today..."

He swallows hard, the lump in his throat dry and coarse. "Wh—what's that?"

The officer in the newly arrived vehicle steps out in front of the next house down, and his boots thud against the gravel as he walks like a deadly shadow backlit by his headlights.

"I'll tell you later," I say, quieter than my previous whisper.

Officer Schäfer steps out of his vehicle next but walks into the house. He doesn't acknowledge our existence, which should give me relief. Instead, every muscle tenses as I watch the last slice of sun melt into the horizon. We're in the dark. There are no kapos. One of us is dead. And we're going to miss the roll call.

I should have taken the pistol with me. I don't know how good of a shot I would have, but there's a chance I could have taken them both out, set us all free. Though, a guard in the distance at a checkpoint too close for comfort would pick up the sound. We wouldn't have anywhere to run. We're trapped. That's why Bea likely gave up and stayed where she was in the cellar. We walk between two checkpoints with nowhere else to go.

I don't know who I am, even thinking this way. Never in my life had I imagined hurting another person, but this rage building inside of me, it's taking over every fiber of my being, and each day I continue to survive, seems like a year in passing.

"Someone knew about the girl who was hiding in the cellar," the silhouette of an officer belts out. "Which one of you was it?"

No one in the group opens their mouth to speak. None of us knew. At least, I don't think any of us knew. Maybe there was suspicion of Bea's whereabouts, but nothing more. Anytime a guard or officer tells a group of prisoners one person is guilty of a crime, it's to get someone to confess, even when there's nothing to confess. This is when prisoners turn on each other, hoping to save themselves. The SS likely need someone to blame, someone other than a kapo they trusted.

Adam's breathing harder than he was. We had nothing to do with her plan to disappear and hide in the Schäfer's cellar of all the terrible places.

The officer steps up to me, the toes of his boots touching the toes of mine. "You work in the same house as that rat." She's dead. Name calling isn't necessary.

"I work in the attic, away from any others. Hammering all day, leaves me with a hissing buzz in place of any type of quiet."

The officer steps to his right, in front of Adam. "You. You also work there."

"Yes, but outside, in the garden," Adam says. "I—I haven't a clue what's happening in the house."

In the seconds of the following silence, a shout echoes from the Schäfer house. I fight the urge to whip my head around and convince myself I can see through the walls. What more is there to yell about? He already found and killed the girl in the cellar. Flora wasn't crying when I left twenty minutes ago, and Frau

Schäfer was setting the dinner table—or so I believe due to the clinks of dishes and silverware I overheard.

The front door of the house storms open. "Find it, Ada. Find it now," Schäfer yells, his voice carrying loud as he comes closer.

"Anything?" Schäfer asks the other officer.

"No," the interrogator replies.

"I just sent for a guard. Someone will be here within the next few minutes."

The officers walk several steps behind us, and I do my best to listen in on their conversation. "Has your wife ever—"

The conversation becomes entirely silent.

"What? No. Are you sure?" the other officer asks.

"It was locked," Schäfer says, the rest of his statement seeping into a passing gust of wind.

Locked?

NINETEEN

HALINA

Should I act as though the shouting between Officer Schäfer and his wife wasn't echoing between every wall of the house? Or that I'm not just a few steps away from them both? They can't possibly want their children watching this brutal argument take place in the kitchen when the rest of us are in the small adjacent play area. Isla watches them as if she's holding a magnifying glass, studying their every motion, and mentally recording each word.

"It's clear you were in my office," he hollers again. "Why were you rummaging through my work?"

"I—I wasn't in there, Heinrich," Ada says, her words weak, unsure and withering into doubt. "You must have forgotten to lock it when you came out of there last."

"You must think I'm stupid," he snaps back. "Just two nights after you vehemently shared your concern about me keeping a—"

"Don't—" Ada growls. "Not in front of the children."

"You know exactly what I'm talking about then. Following our discussion and your disdain for me—" he lowers his voice as if it will make a difference when we're all in the same space, "keeping means to protect our family at night, I immediately locked my office door. I haven't been in there since, and now—it's unlocked and—the—"

"Heinrich..." she warns him. "This is absurd. No one is coming after us. You're a lieutenant colonel."

"Ada," he growls. "The Allies invaded Sicily. They bombed Rome. And Mussolini was arrested last week. Do you think it all ends there? Italy could surrender any day. First Mussolini, then the Führer will be next, and when he falls, we all go with him."

Mussolini. Arrested? If dictators are being taken down... what does that mean for the ones standing behind them.

"Did any of you see anyone in my office today? Or were any of you in my office today?" he barks at us, stepping to the side of Ada to be in our clear view.

"No, Papa. We know never to go inside your office," Isla says.

"I don't even know where the key is," Marlene follows.

As if he needs to be reminded that the door would need a key to be unlocked, he drops his hands into his pockets and pulls out the silk lining from each.

He takes several more steps toward us, his stare centering on me as I hold Flora tightly to my chest, patting her back as I've found it comforts her for a bit. "What have you seen? You were here all day, were you not?"

"I didn't see anyone walk inside your office. I haven't seen a key. I certainly didn't go inside, and neither did the girls. I'm afraid I can't be of much help." I'm able to speak with a level of confidence I've possibly stolen from Ada. I'm not sure where I'm pulling this strength from, but I have no reason to sound guilty or afraid to answer him truthfully.

"It must have been one of the prisoners," he grunts, turning around and ambling past Ada. He wraps his hands behind his red neck and weaves his fingers together, his gold ring catching the kitchen's ceiling light.

The thought of the blame shifting to the others cramps my stomach, leaving me with a sense of guilt I couldn't prevent.

"They wouldn't have a key, dear," Ada follows. "Where did you put the key after you locked the door?"

Heinrich doesn't respond. Instead, he begins to pace back and forth between the entrance of the kitchen and his wife.

"Papa, do you want me to help you find the key?" Marlene offers.

"Do you know where it is?" he snaps, coldly.

"No. But I can help look."

"No, no," he said, shooing his hand at her. "You—" he says, pointing at me. "Take them upstairs. At once."

The girls jump up and stand as if at attention before filing through the kitchen, past their parents. I follow, keeping my eyes set ahead just the same.

The moment I turn the corner into the hallway, a harsh slap of flesh against flesh slices through the air. My teeth clamp together, my jaw straining against the tension.

"Where is the key?" he shouts again followed by a hard thud and glass rattling.

"I don't know," Ada cries out. "I would have told you."

I hurry the girls to the stairs as they try to look over their shoulders, a look of concern lining their eyes.

"It must have been one of the prisoners—they might have picked the lock," she rambles.

Adam was outside all day. The woman who slaves in the kitchen doesn't move from the space unless she's instructed to, and I can't imagine she would have the courage to break into his office. If it was Gavriel—what was it he took? Why would he take the risk? I don't want to think about the consequences.

"Why don't we go to your bedroom first so you can change

into your pajamas, then you can help me get your sister ready for bed," I suggest.

Neither argue nor go right into their bedroom where I'm reminded of one of Marlene's vomiting spells that occurred in her bed.

"Oh, Hali..." Marlene says, placing emphasis on the shortened version of my name she's decided upon. "I had a small accident last night," she says, her cheeks burning pink. "I haven't had one in a long time. I didn't mean to. But my bed, it's still wet."

Isla covers her mouth, muffling a giggle. "Isla, that's enough," I scold her before returning my attention to Marlene. "Sweetheart, accidents happen. It's quite all right. Where can I find you a fresh set of bedding? Do you know?"

"Papa would not say it's all right," Isla grumbles.

"He's forgotten what it's like to be five. That's why," I say, my words sterner than intended, though I don't care at the moment. "Where can I find fresh linen?" My question is directed at Isla this time.

"At the end of the hall," she says, pointing in the opposite direction to the stairwell.

I sit Flora down on their round carpet in between their beds. "Could you stay with your sister while I go look for it?"

Marlene plops down beside Flora and takes her little hand into hers. Isla moseys over to her next, but with far less enthusiasm. My muscles tense as I step back out into the hallway. I only came down this way to help Marlene in the washroom last night, but I don't recall spotting any other doors except Heinrich and Ada's bedroom at the end.

Just past the washroom, I notice two inset doors, squarely across from each other. I open the one next to the washroom first, hoping to find the linens. A whiff of mothballs and dust cloud around me and I reach inside to the interior wall searching for a light switch. Reluctantly, my fingers scrape across a button, and I press it, revealing a small room rather than a deep closet.

There's nowhere else to settle my eyes than on the pile of objects mounted across an entire bed. I glance to my right, ensuring no one is watching, then step inside. It takes a minute to understand what I'm seeing, and I'm overcome by a wave of disbelief. Silk scarves and handkerchiefs, handbags, fur muffs, pearl necklaces, silver hair combs, diamond brooches and gold-plated jewelry boxes.

I lower my hand, lifting one of the handkerchiefs. I'm not sure I've ever felt real silk—a cool, soft and smooth texture. This one is embroidered with the initials B.A. and encased by a Star of David on each side. My gaze drifts to a small jewelry box and I open it, finding a small prayer card inside with Hebrew letters. Inside the top lid has the name Sarah engraved. I pull my hands away and cup them over my mouth. These must all be stolen.

A rush of nausea forces me to step back toward the door. I find the light switch and back out, with the doorknob in hand. Without a breath left in my lungs, I clutch my chest and turn around for the other door, terrified of what else I might find.

Stacks of bedding are folded neatly into piles. Thank God. I reach in and take out the smallest stack, hoping it will be the right size for Marlene's bed. With the pile resting in my arms, I notice a bottle labeled blonde liquid hair dye.

I balance the pile of linen in my arms to the side so I can slide the next pile to the left a bit so it's in front of the bottle that seems to be hidden. Of all the things she would potentially hide, I'm not sure why it would be a bottle of hair dye. She must not want anyone to know she's not a natural blonde, or perhaps not a pure blonde-haired, blue-eyed Aryan. I'm surprised she doesn't color Isla and Marlene's hair too.

I hurry back to the girls' room with the bedding, hearing the racket continuing downstairs.

"Are you ill?" Isla asks the moment I step back into the room. "You look like you just vomited too."

"No, of course not. I was just looking for the bedding," I say, my voice sounding full of guilt. Isla will be the first to notice something awry with me too.

"You must have gone into the wrong room and saw all the Jewish jewels Mama's collecting. Someday she's going to pass some of it down to me. It's all so beautiful, isn't it?" Isla asks.

TWENTY

GAVRIEL

Every crunch against thicket, or the snaps of frail twigs, adds tension to the tight muscles in my neck as we near the dark gates of Birkenau. Damp dirt sticks to the soles of my borrowed boots and sweat continues to trickle down the back of my spine even in the night. The closer we get, the thicker the air becomes —a rotten stench, mixed with lingering smoke, and aridity from a looming rainstorm. The sun was out most of the day, but at night—that's when the sky cries the most.

If I've learned anything in the four months I've been a prisoner here, it's that everything can change in a split second without warning or reason. Just the same as there is no reason for being assigned laboring work beyond the gates, versus work on the inside. I have a skill, but so do many others here. I just happened to be noticed.

Before Officer Schäfer conscripted me to work at his house, I saw members of the SS as evil, emotionless, and hollow. I wondered if their hatred for Jewish people has been something they truly feel in their hearts, or if they're too afraid to oppose the dictatorship above them. I wanted to believe that when they went home to their wives and families at night, they became a different person—someone with a heart and emotions, perhaps. I dreamed that one day, they would come to a point where they realize they don't want to be these monsters. But I now think German people only believe what they're told and witness, and all they know of are their victories. There is no truth to be found in propaganda, and until they see through the smog, they'll continue thinking they are the heroes, and the rest of the world are the monsters.

"It doesn't sound like you're even breathing," Adam whispers, dropping his hand on my shoulder as we walk toward our barrack, led by the guard called to escort us back to the prison. We don't know where the kapos went. Oskar or Sylvia—they could be back tomorrow, or we might never see them again. I have no attachment to them, but they are protected prisoners and if they're no longer protected, it means the rest of us are in even more danger than ever before.

"I have a lot on my mind," I reply quietly.

"What were you trying to tell me earlier when we were lining up in front of the Schäfers' house? You said you did something today..."

"I can't tell you yet." I imagine an officer or guard is somewhere in the nearby vicinity, and with the growing darkness, I can't take the chance of saying something I'll regret.

Adam takes in a deep breath and releases the air from his nose, slowly. "Well, now I'll be wondering."

As we turn down the long row of blocks to make our way down to the center where ours is located, the crowds of others spill out onto the carved interconnected paths, returning to their barracks from the direction of Roll Call Square.

"I knew it," Rueben says. "We weren't at roll call, so we won't be eating tonight."

"Hey!" the guard shouts, turning around and stopping us sharp in our steps. No one has said a word since we left the Schäfers' house, including the guard. "Is there a problem?"

No one responds. No one ever will. Neither a guard nor an officer's broad question is ever answered unless we're looking for further consequences. I had already assumed we would miss roll call and our evening meal would be withheld. We're being punished for Bea's decision even though she's already been murdered.

A whistle blows from behind us, grabbing the guard's attention. "Move!" he demands, pointing us toward our barrack, but stays back, answering to the whistle, I assume.

Once out of hearing range, the words spill out of my mouth to Adam. "You know, Schäfer...he beats his wife, and she's with child. He wasn't at all concerned for his daughters witnessing Bea's murder today. Maybe he didn't know the children were home with Halina because they were upstairs and remaining quiet through his tirade in the house, but he didn't bother to check if they were home before putting a bullet through a young woman's head outside their window."

Adam pauses and stares straight ahead, not blinking, maybe digesting my statement. Maybe thinking about his mother and sister.

"He isn't a man. He's a wild animal. What form of decency could you expect from him?" Adam asks. "All we can do is mind our own business and be grateful we're worthy of work, right?"

Are we worthy of work? Or just temporary help?

I'm not certain what he was yelling at his wife about while we were being questioned about Bea outside, before being escorted back here for the night. Though his question to the other officer about whether his wife had done something similar, and talking about something that was locked, has me wondering if he knew someone had been in his office. The door was unlocked and so was the drawer with the pistol. If that's what he was referring to, someone else must have unlocked it first. He might have been referring to something separate and my guilt is eating away at me, but regardless of what he's angry about, he needs someone to blame. Halina is the only other person in that house at night besides his wife.

My anger and rage pulled me into that man's office, and while I don't regret taking his weapon, I should have thought the plan through more first. I don't want Halina being blamed for anything I might have done, or even for something I didn't do. His wife appears to be his sole target, but that's not enough to convince myself he won't go after Halina tonight.

Moments after we step inside the barrack, Benson grabs me by the back of my shirt, Adam, and Rueben too. Benson grabs my hand and shoves his balled-up fist against my palm, crumbling something dry and gritty into my palm. Bread, maybe. It has an oily scent, something that reminds me of Mama's cooking. That world—one that no longer exists for me. My throat tightens at the thought of sitting down at the table to enjoy one of Mama's long-prepared meals after a hard day's work. I'm grateful to Benson for just the brief memory.

He does it twice more for the others, giving Rueben and Adam a portion of the food too. Maybe he figured we'd all be paying a consequence for Bea tonight and he took the risk of swiping some food from the kitchen he works in.

"What is that?" a man shouts from the bunks. "Give it here!" The man clambers out of his narrow bed opening and catapults himself into Adam, swatting at him to give up what's in his hand. I thrust myself between the two of them and grab the man by his bony wrist.

"Take mine and be quiet before you get us all in trouble," I hiss at him, slapping my smashed crumbs into his hand.

The man's eyes well up and all tension subsides. He falls to his knees and licks the crumbs from his hand. Hunger is pain. Pain is part of life, and if I'm living, so be it—I'll go hungry.

I keep walking down between the row of bunks, not wanting to see guilt in Adam's eyes, or Rueben's, or Benson's. A hand grips my shoulder, interrupting my sluggish strides. I turn to face him, finding a boy, maybe sixteen or seventeen. His shaved head, big ears, and rigid nose strike me as familiar.

I study him for a moment, wondering why—how I would know him—where from. "You're a good person. It's hard to tell if there are many left in the world," he says.

He looks like my youngest brother. Not him, but close— same wide-set eyes and narrow chin. He's almost grown into his face, but his innocence is shredding away page by page each day.

"It's a choice we all make. I'm sure you make the right choices everyday too."

I didn't make the right choice today, but I wouldn't say it made me a bad person. Maybe I shouldn't give advice that I can't follow myself.

I crawl into my bunk, and shimmy onto my side, the straw from the thin and warped mattress poking me in too many places. The sour stench of sweat, musk, and mildew strike me as they do every night when I rest my head. As if it's a new smell. It's just worse than it was yesterday. I close my eyes, trying to drown out the sounds of coughing and moaning, and insects chirping near my ear, by envisioning Halina...such a beautiful sight, pure, innocent. Her eyes still cling to hope, but only because she hasn't seen the worst of what's around her.

What if Schäfer blames her for everything no one confessed to? What if he already has? What if...Halina is paying for what I did?

The thought of her disappearing from that house punches at my gut. It's selfish, I know. I don't want her stuck there, but she won't be released to go back to where she came from. As long as she's inside those walls, at least I can keep watch. And keep her close.

TWENTY-ONE

HALINA

It's an hour before midnight and the relentless arguing hasn't ceased for even a moment between Ada and Heinrich. All the thrashing comments are futile and senseless.

I've done everything possible to get the girls to fall asleep, but Flora is screaming in my arms, kicking her legs and squeezing her hands into little fists. Marlene is sitting up against her headboard, hands cupping her ears, and Isla is standing in front of the dressing mirror between their two bureaus. She's tugging on her hair, studying it as if she's looking for something hard to find. I'm still not sure what the argument is even about, but from what I've seen, they fight more than they speak civilly to one another.

I don't know how Julia managed so many of us at the same time. She always seemed so calm, as if nothing bothered her. Even if someone were having a fit, she'd continue brushing or braiding my hair, humming in my ear with a smile I could hear. She'd kiss me on the head and whisper goodnight, then move on to share her love with the next girl. Before she finished with everyone's braids, whoever was having a fit settled down and found their way to bed. I looked at Julia as if she was magical sometimes. I don't have the same magic inside of me, even though she might say I do. The panic shivering through my veins only continues to grow stronger.

"Do you even care that I'm with child? Perhaps a boy who will carry on your name?"

Following Ada's shout, Isla's reflecting stare shifts to the bedroom door.

Flora takes a moment to catch her breath, her lips still pursed into a pout as she sucks in bouts of air. "Shh, shh, it's all right," I coo to her and make my way over to Isla. "Is something wrong?" Everything is wrong. Her parents have been fighting for hours and if it wasn't clear to her before, her father is desperate for a son.

"No," she snaps. "It's unfortunate I wasn't born as a boy."

"That's not true," I tell her. "If the world was made up of only boys, there would be no more children." I realize I might be starting a conversation I don't want to get into at this hour, but it's true. Women are just as important as men despite what anyone thinks or says.

"Papa might be happy without any more children," she says.

"I'm sure that's not true either."

That man hates himself too much to love anyone.

"I want them to stop shouting at each other. I'm tired," she says.

"Another little miracle," Heinrich shouts. "Is that it? I should be thankful we have another child coming into the world when we can't shut up the last one?"

"See?" Isla says.

"You can come up to the attic and stay with me. Would that be all right?"

Isla looks unsure and Marlene is still holding her hands over her ears. I'm not sure Ada or Heinrich would agree to that idea, but they must allow their poor children to sleep.

I reposition Flora, pressing her tummy to my chest as I continue rocking her while walking down the stairwell toward the family room where the battle has been taking place.

My heart pounds, which will upset Flora, so I try to take a deep breath before reaching the bottom of the steps.

Sweat forms on the back of my neck as I approach the archway of the family room.

"What do you want?" Heinrich snaps, slashing his hand through the air toward me.

"Th-the girls are having trouble falling asleep so I was thinking I could bring them up to my bedroom with me. Would that be all right?"

The man's eyes are lit up with wrath, unblinking, a cold ruthless stare. A short glass of liquor is pinched between his grip, sloshing around with every movement. To my right, Ada sits perched on the edge of her upholstered chair, hugging her belly, staring at her husband as if I'm not standing here.

"There are mice and rats up there. Why would I want my children to sleep up there?" Schäfer replies.

I'm not sure if he's speaking literally or figuratively but I choose not to respond and instead wait for a more suitable resolution.

"I'm going to bed," Ada says. "The girls can go to sleep in their beds. I'll take Flora with me." She stands from her chair, struggling as if in pain and takes Flora out of my arms. The cries ensue, but with a greater force. Without acknowledgement of the progression, Ada continues moving without another word, leaving me behind to fend for myself against her husband.

"I asked you if you witnessed someone in my office today," he says, his voice calm, as if unbothered by the last few hours of arguing with his wife. "I didn't ask if *you* were in my office?"

His stare could suck the soul right out of my body. Now he'll accuse me and I'll be the next nanny to be removed from his house.

"No," I say. "I have no reason to go into your office, nor have I been given permission to do so."

Heinrich steps forward, hands in his pockets. "It's the quiet ones I never trust."

"I'm not quiet. I've been doing my job."

He narrows his eyes at me like an animal before it lunges. My breath tightens, but I force my spine straight. I won't let him see me flinch, despite the image of a woman lying dead on his front lawn earlier today.

"Is that right?" he says.

He pulls folded papers from his pocket. My documents. The ones I gave him when he took me as his servant. I didn't think he'd hold on to them all this time, but since he had, I figured he hadn't read them thoroughly.

"These are missing critical information," he says.

"The information doesn't exist," I reply before he can say anything more. "I'm an orphan."

He arches a brow, an expression that calls me a liar without saying the words. "We'll see about that. Report to the prison camp tomorrow morning at ten, sharp. Your name will be on a list. A guard will bring you to me."

"There is nothing to see, or find," I say too quickly. I sound too confident. I should have kept my lips sealed.

A smirk pokes at the left side of his face. "If you're just here to do your job," he says, his smirk fading into the age lines around his mouth, "and you are who you say you are, it won't matter, right?"

I turn around and walk away from the family room, toward the stairs. "What should I do with the children?"

"Do not bring them. Ada can manage to watch over them while you're gone."

He's sending me to Auschwitz. It's a trap. I know it. He's done with my presence in this house. Done with me listening to their arguments. Done with whatever he thinks I've stolen, and the way I stand up to Ada...

The easiest way to get rid of evidence is to...

TWENTY-TWO

HALINA

I spent several hours scrubbing the stench of vomit out of my black dress and apron last night. I can still smell the rot of partially digested food. But I have to change out of the striped prison uniform before showing up at the gates of Auschwitz. Heinrich saw me in that attire last night, didn't question it, didn't even know his daughter was vomiting from drinking the same bourbon-laced milk as his infant.

Ada handed me a map on my way out the door as Marlene was pleading to go with me on my "walk." I could run. I could escape. There's a false feeling of freedom as I walk down the street, but as I turn a corner, I find guard posts, roads blocked, and only one direction free to pass. I might be living in an attic of a house rather than a cell, but there is no way out of this prison town.

The unfamiliar road I'm following by points on the map, reminds me of the time I tried to run away from the orphanage when I was twelve. There were no Nazis here then, just tall trees, unmarked paths and an idea that there could be a life waiting for me somewhere. If I could find my parents, they'd see me and wish they hadn't left me. I didn't consider how I would go about finding these two strangers. I guess I just figured I'd walk past them someday and feel a sense of connection—know it was them, and that they had been looking for me just like I was looking for them. It was such an outlandish thought and dream, one that got me lost in the woods and eventually found by the police who took me back to the orphanage. There was no escaping the life I was destined to live then or now.

A red post box catches my attention at the next corner I'm taking. I was hoping to find one so I could mail my letter to Julia. I pull the sealed envelope from my apron pocket and quickly drop it into the box as I continue walking down the street, doing what I can to avoid extra attention from onlookers in the nearby buildings.

Within view is a wide, brick building the trains travel through. I look down at my map, finding my destination to be in a different spot to the main gate. A train passes, the rumble startlingly loud with a faint murmur of cries beneath the steam whistle. I can't help but watch as the train passes, spotting hands poking out between the wooden slats of the cattle cars.

Bile rises from the depths of my stomach from the overwhelming grief, the sound of pain, and the violent odor of rotting earth mixed with thick smoke. All those stories—the rumors and assumptions. Do these people know where they're being taken? Where they're going to end up?

I should be focused on where I'm going. I could be walking in as unsuspecting as them, just through a different entrance.

The path I'm on runs alongside a tall fence, topped with barbed wire. At first, I avoided looking beyond the fence and into the camp, afraid of what I might see. The truth. People are everywhere, just men from what I can see though. They're all dressed in the blue and white striped uniforms, standing in a line, walking in a line, dragging a wagon, or doing nothing at all except staring back at me. The longer I keep my eyes set on what's happening within, the more I see. People falling to their knees, some crawling, others not moving, face down. I straighten my focus, promising to only look straight ahead rather than at the reality I'm passing. A watch tower looms over my head, making me feel like nothing more than an insect as I pass. Another wooden tower unfurls ahead, but it's short and behind a gate.

The people in front of me have the same badge as the two kapos I saw at the Schäfers' house. They show their forearms as identification, a number that's matched up to the notes in the guard's hand.

I don't have a number but I know Gavriel has one. I step up to the tall guard, his face hidden in the shadow of his low angled cap. "I'm here to see Officer Schäfer. I'm the nanny at his household for his children. My name is Halina Wojic."

The guard watches me in silence for a long moment—a form of intimidation maybe. It's not needed. I don't want to be here. He finally glances down at the papers clipped to his board and flips a few pages then drags his pencil down the center of the page. He turns to his right, presses his fingers beneath his front teeth and whistles to whomever is listening.

"Another guard will take you to him."

A minute doesn't pass before another identically uniformed guard approaches the gated entrance. Without a word, he gestures for me to follow. As if I'm stepping over the ledge of two different worlds, the weight of my body pulls me into the soggy ground, my shoes smacking from the tackiness of the mud. Fumes of burning rubbish assault my nose. There are no prisoners in my path, but I feel them around me. The air is quiet, no birds, or chirping insects, just distant groans, and muffled shouts.

My mouth becomes bone dry—I'm unable to swallow while questioning why I've been told to be here.

A long, narrow one-story building with a harrowing pitched roof is in front of us and a cold sweat climbs up the back of my neck as we approach the foreboding entrance. Damp wood, mildew and musk taint the air, despite the modern appearance of the interior. The floors are unfinished, and the wallpaper pattern is dark and busy. The atmosphere is tense.

Officers and guards stride by me, ignoring my presence as if I'm nothing more than the shadow of the man I'm following. We walk past rooms, bleak with desks with typewriters, chairs, and filing cabinets. A larger room with one long table and many chairs appears to be a meeting space. Then there are closed doors, slimmer than doors to the offices. The corridor appears endless as we continue walking ahead until the guard stops and pivots on his heels to face an open door.

"Officer Schäfer, your enslaved laborer has arrived."

The introduction makes me curl my fingers into fists by my side. I've been many things in my life, but to be referred to as a slave when slavery has long been abolished can only be seen as a purposeful method of intimidation—name calling. Though, I'm not sure what else he could refer to me as, as I'm working against my will.

"Come," Schäfer commands.

He speaks to people as if they're household pets. This man has nothing more than traits of inferiority masked with his ability to make a one-shot kill. The guard steps aside, allowing me to walk inside of Schäfer's barren workspace: a simple oak desk, typewriter, telephone, pen, inkpot, and a leather-bound notepad. Through the windows, rows of identical wooden barracks stretch into a foggy gray horizon. My pulse hammers in every vein as I stare at this man.

He opens a desk drawer, retrieves a folder, and drops it flat on his desk. "Sign these."

"What are they?"

He snickers, an odd sound from the permanent scowl he wears. "I take it you can read?"

I take the folder into my hands and open the flap, finding a short stack of German typed papers. While he continues to stare at me as I struggle to read through all the text and decipher unfamiliar German terms, my focus catches on one line I can clearly make out:

In corroboration to your position serving a lieutenant of the Reich, you agree to any necessary retrieval of birth records, school records, and religious affiliation records.

"Fill these out and sign the communication agreement at the end," he states.

"Now? I'd like time to review them properly."

"These papers do not leave the room. You have ten minutes."

He leans back in his seat and folds his hands behind his neck.

My throat swells and I dip the pen into the ink and begin writing. By the time I reach the last section, my hand is stiff and shaking. It's a rewritten copy of the house rules, a reminder not to speak to any prisoner or other slaves working under his roof. No speaking without permission. And never mention what I've seen or heard. Consequences for not obeying these rules will be at Officer Schäfer's discretion.

He takes the papers from my hand and flips through the pages. "You've missed answers."

A raucous scream drives through the rumbling window. Schäfer doesn't flinch, but I can't stop myself from looking out for the source of noise.

I squint at what I'm seeing outside. "There's a man having a seizure or something of the sort just on the other side of the fence."

"Not a seizure," Schäfer says.

"How do you—he's—"

"He's dead," Schäfer drones. "Those fences have electrical

currents running through them, and some of the—" he clears his throat, "—Jews can't accept their fate in this world and turn to other means of escaping."

If I react, I will be giving him exactly what he wants. I will not react. I didn't want to see another person die. It's been a day. Just a day.

"I gave you everything I have. There's nothing more to find. I tried to explain this to you last night."

"And why is that?"

"I don't know my parents' names."

"You were a ward," he says. "An orphan."

"Yes."

"Perhaps I can help." He taps the pile of papers into alignment. "There are sealed records, protected information—children born out of wedlock, adoptions, that sort of thing. These files are not easily accessed."

My stomach twists into a painful knot. "Unless, what?"

"Unless a person has certain privileges, of course." He means himself, clear by the prideful glow in his greedy eyes.

"That's not something I want to be involved with. And I doubt most others would either," I say.

"You'd be surprised." He taps his fingers against his desk and squints at me. "However, I've noticed there is one matter you haven't kept your distance from..."

TWENTY-THREE
GAVRIEL

I was thrilled to have completed the roof rafters and ceiling panels, but now the sound of Frau Schäfer bellowing at her children in a plea to quieten down fills the air—never mind the poor baby crying. They sent Halina somewhere this morning, on her own, and I don't know where or why. We only crossed paths as I was coming into the house, and we shouldn't be making eye contact with one another. I was relieved to see she was in one piece, then to also see the alcove in the attic was untouched too, but that moment of comfort dissolved when she was sent out on her own. In the time I was around the last nanny, she was never once separated from the children until her last day.

I can't keep myself from glancing out the window every minute, hoping I'll see her returning from wherever she went, but all I see are the kids from down the street chasing a football.

"Excuse me," a small voice utters from behind my back. I almost drop the wooden panels for the window boxing. I spin around, finding the younger of the two older girls—Marlene, the one with big, sad blue eyes and a little nubbin nose. She could be an illustration in a children's storybook with her doll-like features.

"What are you doing up here all alone, sweetheart?"

She cups her hand to the side of her mouth and whispers, "Do you know when Papa will let Hali come back?"

Hali. She's already given Halina a nickname.

"I'm sorry to say, I'm not quite sure where she went this morning. Did your papa send her somewhere?"

Marlene shrugs. "Mama said Hali had business to handle with Papa at work."

In Auschwitz.

My stomach pinches and terror grips me like a vice as I gaze at Marlene's little face.

"Your mama doesn't know you're up here, does she?"

Marlene shakes her head, slowly, unsure if she should be confessing anything to me, I'm sure.

"You don't want to be caught up here talking to me," I tell her. I should be more concerned about what would happen if I was caught talking to her. I'll be the one to get in more trouble than she ever will.

"I just don't want them to hurt Hali. She's the nicest girl we've ever had." Marlene's lips fall into a simper. "They never let us love anyone for long."

It's hard to absorb everything the five-year-old is saying, and take it for what it's worth, but it's been made clear she's seen far more than any other young girl I've ever known, and she knows too much, just the same. "You know, when something worries me, I always ask myself why...and what reasons I have. And if I do that now, I can't think of any reason your parents would have to hurt Hali," I say, more for myself than her.

"Well...Mama is upset with her for hurting Flora. She said, 'That girl has something to prove, and she'll do so at any cost—even Flora's'. But I'm not sure what that means. If anything, Hali has made Flora's belly hurt less."

The only person I've seen hurt around here besides Bea, is

Frau Schäfer. How could she or Marlene think Halina's done anything to Flora? "Do you think Halina hurt Flora?" I ask.

"Her name is Hali. No, I don't think so. Hali has the softest hands, even when she takes my hand. Someone like that can't hurt someone else."

"Marlene! Where are you?" Frau Schäfer shouts.

Marlene's cheeks flush. "Oh..." she squeaks under her breath. "Papa's going to give me a whipping if I get in trouble with Mama."

Her words shred my heart into pieces, just thinking what they might have done to this poor child.

"Tiptoe down the stairs, quiet as a mouse. Then tell her you were looking for a book in your bedroom."

Marlene holds her finger up to her lips and turns for the stairs.

"Marlene Schäfer, you better answer me right now, young lady!"

As soon as Marlene is in the clear, I look out the window again, finding the children still playing with the football, and now their nannies talking on a patch of grass, staring at this house as if there's a secret to tell. What do they know?

TWENTY-FOUR

HALINA

I believe I just signed my life away without a choice or say in the matter. As if perfectly timed, a man took his life as a measure of reason and proof to fear the other side of those gates. Then, Heinrich's statement about the one matter I haven't kept my distance from.

It didn't come as a surprise that he chose not to follow his remark with an explanation—just another tool in his box to coerce with and cause terror. I could easily assume he was speaking about Flora's bottle, and the lack of bourbon no longer tainting the liquid. Or he could suspect my loyalty to Gavriel.

Between each blink and step, I can vividly see the decomposing world of Auschwitz, the gloom and smoke, people struggling to move. How does Gavriel survive there when he's not working himself to the bone at the Schäfers' house? It's far worse than anything I imagined or thought I'd seen from a distance.

A shiver bears down my spine despite the heat radiating from the sun as I turn the last corner onto the street with the three houses owned by the SS. The irony of watching children play in the street, as if life is nothing but ordinary, leads me to unanswerable questions. How will any of them grow up to find a semblance of normalcy? They'll find out who their fathers are and what they do. There's no way of knowing if they'll forgive them or run as far away from here as possible. Most of them are too young to know of a world where they weren't considered to be among the elite.

Celina and Rosalie are huddled beneath a trimmed willow tree, chatting as the children shriek and squeal with the joy of running with freedom of space, fresh air, and full bellies.

"Where are you coming from? Alone too? Goodness," Rosalie says, her words snipped and a bit cool. Jealous, perhaps? Though she wouldn't be if she knew what I was doing and where I've come from, I'm sure.

"An errand," I reply, keeping my response short.

"I've never seen the Schäfers allow their servants to wander off alone without the children," Rosalie continues.

Celina stares at her while she talks, a troubled grimace tugging on her quaint face.

"You should bring the children out to play," Celina adds. "It's a lovely day."

"I'll see what Frau Schäfer has planned. Thank you for the invitation," I offer. Is that what that was? An invitation for someone else's children to play on the street?

I make my way to the front door and hesitate before walking inside, unsure if I've earned the right to act as if I belong here rather than I'm the slave as I was so kindly told. With caution over where I figuratively stand, I knock on the door. Ada will probably be irritated that she's forced to get up from whatever she's doing to let me inside. Either way, I would be wrong.

The kitchen prisoner opens the door, a girl whose name I still don't know. "Frau Schäfer is in the family room," she says, bowing her head at me as if I'm something of more importance than she is.

I step inside and place my hand on her shoulder. "No need to bow," I whisper. "I'm no one important."

"You're not a Jew," she replies with a small shrug.

"What's your name?" I ask just as quietly.

"Kasia, but—" she presses her shirt sleeve up and twists her arm to show me a set of numbers tattooed along her forearm. "This is who I am now."

"You're still Kasia to me," I say, pushing past the ache in my chest—the tears that threaten to burn down my cheeks.

How did we get here? I thought I knew so much, and now I see I knew very little.

Kasia's dimples deepen but she doesn't smile. Instead, she turns and walks back to the kitchen. I follow, but stop in front of the family room, finding Ada perched on the sofa with her stocking covered feet up on the coffee table. She's reading a fashion magazine. I didn't think those existed anymore.

"Oh, good. You're back," she says, her voice monotone. "The older girls are reading in their bedroom, and Flora—she's down for a nap."

"Very well. The other children are outside playing together. I thought I might bring the girls out to join them?"

"I don't care what you do with them," she says, flapping the back of her hand at me. "Leave Flora to sleep, though."

"Of course."

Ada doesn't take her eyes off the magazine and flips to the next page as I continue to stand here. "Might I ask how far along you are in your pregnancy? I'm sure everyone is looking forward to another bundle of joy."

Ada drops her magazine onto her lap and places her hands around her belly as if I've insulted the unborn child. "I should be nearing four months along," she says.

"Any inkling of a gender?" It's best to act as if I didn't pick up on any of their argumentative words from last night.

"It's a boy. I'm quite sure. I'm carrying differently with him than I did with the other three."

"That's wonderful. I'm sure the girls will be thrilled to welcome a baby brother."

"Yes, they will be," she says with an annoyed sigh.

"I'll let you get back to your magazine."

I gather the girls and wait for them to use the toilet and pull on their boots before we can go outside. Isla leaves with a book in hand and Marlene has her hand curled in mine, leaning her head against my arm. "I didn't know when you'd come back," she says as we step out the door.

I close the front door behind us and lead her down the front steps. "I'm back now," I reply.

"Gav was worried too," she says.

"Gav?" I question her.

"The man in the attic."

"Gavriel," I correct her.

"No, I call him Gav." I can't help but snicker a bit. I'm not sure how this little girl has so much personality when she's being raised by the Schäfers.

"He was worried about me?" I ask her.

My heart flinches. How can someone who carries so much pain still find the strength to worry about someone else? And me, of all people. I'm not sure what to make of that but it thaws something icy inside of me, making it harder to convince myself I don't feel safer when I'm around him.

"No one knew where Papa made you go."

I turn over my shoulder and stare up at the construction, finding the gaps between the framing to be covered, leaving the windows to see in and out of now. I catch Gavriel's eye through the open frame. He stops mid-step, moving closer to the window as if pulled by something invisible. "Are you all right?" he mouths.

The sight of him, the worry written along his face, it

unravels me for a second. My breath catches in my throat and my cheeks tingle. He's a prisoner, but he still wants to protect me. The look in his eyes says things I've never believed I had the right to feel.

I nod ever so slightly, hoping to be discreet amid Rosalie and Celina who are likely watching my every step right now.

It appears he was worried. How can he worry about me when he's living in that place?

"Ah, look who's joining us outside to play!" Celina announces to the children.

"I'm not playing," Isla quips. "I have a book to finish reading by tomorrow." I wasn't aware of any deadline for her to finish reading.

"Soak in all the sun this week, young lady," Rosalie follows.

"Is something happening next week?" I ask as I step in toward the other two ladies.

"Of course. School starts back up," Celina says, looking at me with wide eyes as if it's impossible that I didn't know this. "They didn't tell you...? Little Marlene is starting her first day—the poor thing must be all wound up."

I glance over at her as she approaches one of the other little girls around the same age as her. I'm not sure which child belongs to whom yet, but I suppose I should figure that out too. She hasn't said a word about starting school. No one has.

"How does it all work? Do we—take them in the morning, and pick them up? I'm not sure what time or where to go? What do they need?"

Celina and Rosalie give each other a look that makes me feel like more of an outsider than I already am. "We'll help you. Don't worry," Celina says.

I wonder if the two of them are paid to do their jobs? Am I being punished for the accusation of begging and loitering?

"School begins next Wednesday at eight in the morning. It's

just down the road, a ten-minute walk. It's a small schoolhouse for children of—"

Rosalie lets out a soft cough.

Nazis? I'd like to say it out loud.

If it's a school for children of Nazis, that means Marlene's little mind will begin processing the form of corruption next week. Whatever she hasn't already picked up at home, will be burned into her head quickly, I'm sure.

"Do we walk together?" I might be setting myself up to be laughed at with how little I seem to know compared to them.

"Of course," Celina says. "We can walk to pick them up together in the afternoon as well."

"Thank you. That would be wonderful."

"Where's the little angel?" Rosalie asks.

"Taking a nap," I say, feeling uneasy about the way Ada shared that tidbit of information. Flora has not taken a nap in her crib since I've arrived. Unless she's rocked to sleep and shushed for an hour, there hasn't been a hint of rest.

"She got her to go down?" Rosalie continues.

"So she said."

"Hmm," Celina says.

The same thought went through my mind too. I'm sure they're figuring she's been given a helping of bourbon.

"That boy up there, he fancies you, doesn't he?" Rosalie says, looking at the attic window.

"I don't know him. I'm not allowed to converse with anyone in the house."

"Of course," Celina says. "We know that. But let's be honest with each other. Who can truly live like that?"

"I suppose."

"It's a matter of being able to avoid getting caught doing the things we're not supposed to do," Celina whispers.

"You aren't very good at that," Rosalie tells her. "Your voice carries, you know?"

"Oh, and you're as quiet as a butterfly?"

"I suppose I'd be cautious if I was you, in that house too. There's no saying what that SS man will do next. He's far worse than the other two on this street. Ada isn't much better, but she's been brainwashed into submission. She doesn't even know who she once was or where she came from." Celina leans in closer to me. "From what we've heard, she was raised on a farm, working alongside her parents until she was old enough to marry. She has a whole family who's never even been here to visit or meet the children. It's quite odd."

"Everything is odd," Rosalie adds. "We're living in a dark, miserable world that will likely never see the light of day again. We've gone back in time to when women have no voices and citizens have no say above the reigning government. We're nothing and no one, and we may never be someone again."

TWENTY-FIVE
HALINA

August 5, 1943

It's the night before school recommences for the children, and also the first night in a while that the entire family have been in the house together without yelling or shouting. Perhaps it's just the calm before the storm...

Ada walks past me as the girls finish their supper and shoves two pleated dresses against my ribs. "You'll need these for the morning."

"Yes, do they have knapsacks, or school supplies I should prepare? And what about their lunches?"

"You," Ada says, flapping her hand at Kasia. "You have all that, yes?"

With a simple nod, Kasia dries her hand on a rag and shuffles out of the room. It's getting close to the time when she, Gavriel, and Adam leave the house for the night to return to Auschwitz, but she still has a sink full of dishes. And I'm just standing here. I push my sleeves up to my elbows and tend to the sink, avoiding any passing gaze from Ada. I shouldn't need to worry about Heinrich as he's sitting at the table, unengaged, legs crossed, and a newspaper open full spread in front of his face.

With the first dish in hand, I take the wet soapy rag and begin to scrub. Ada shoves her elbow into my side, and I swallow a gasp before looking over at her. Her bulging eyes, scrunched nose and pursed lips sneer at me, telling me all but the word, stop. She's silent about her demand. Another unlikely gesture from her. I figure she would want to put a target on my back and tell her husband to grab the gun.

I won't bother explaining that I was trying to help since I know Kasia will be leaving soon, but there's no purpose. Kasia returns and hands me two brown canvas knapsacks, both weighed down with supplies inside. She cracks open the refrigerator and points to two brown paper bags, each with the girl's names written across the top. She must not be allowed to speak. Though I've heard Gavriel speak to Heinrich.

"Both of you, go wash up and get ready for bed. You need your sleep tonight," Ada tells Isla and Marlene.

It's time for Flora's bottle and I'm glad I don't see one prepared on the counter. I'm quite sure Ada had her way with her while I was gone this morning. She's been far too quiet all afternoon. It sickens me to know what state that poor baby is in.

"Flora cannot stay awake crying all night. Do you understand? You must keep her quiet," Ada says.

"Of course." Another impossible situation I must agree to, but I will not poison her daughter.

The bedtime routine for the girls drawled on for what felt like hours before they both settled down. All three of the girls are quiet and Flora is asleep even without a helping of bourbon in her last bottle.

I make my way up to the attic, my feet throbbing from not sitting down much today, and my shoulders heavy from tension. Inside the room, a folded piece of paper starkly contrasts with the old dark floors. I close the door behind me before picking it up to inspect.

I turn it from side to side, finding nothing written on the front or back, but I can see there's writing inside. My hands tremble as I unfold the note, knowing it could be anything and from anyone given how absurdly this family behaves.

Hali,

Marlene is the only one to call me that since I was a young girl with a handful of friends living with me in the orphanage. I suppose I grew out of the nickname.

I hope you're resting now, after a day that felt longer than most. I found this paper and pencil on your desk and I couldn't help myself. Also, I needed to leave something behind, even if just a few lines. I hope you don't mind.

I'd be lying if I said I wasn't worried. When you were sent out of the house last week, I didn't know what might have happened to you. Admittedly, I kept glancing out the window, listening for your footsteps along the gravel, hoping I'd see you making your way toward the front door.

Needless to say, I was relieved when you returned, and from what I could see, physically unscathed, I hope. But you've been quiet since then and our paths have barely crossed even though we're under the same roof.

It's incredible how quickly someone's distance can make the entire world feel out of place...

I overheard the girls talking about starting school tomor-row. I started working here just a few days before they were released for their summer break. From what I noticed, Ada likes to take that time to run errands. If you find the house too quiet or your thoughts are too loud, maybe you could come visit me. Only if you'd like to, of course.

Sleep well tonight, Halina.
I'm thinking of you.
Gavriel

The note sends a warm flutter to my heart, an unexpected warmth. He's kind. Thoughtful. And it occurs to me that I've never lived in a time where I was allowed to see the people around me as anything but a sibling sharing the life of an orphan, or now, older, as children I care for.

Connections with others have never been a part of my life, not with how frequently people come and go. And if I leave my heart unguarded, I know pain will inevitably find me. On the other hand, I don't remember the last time I allowed myself to risk a chance of pain. Maybe pain is the consequence of something wonderful. Could that be?

I press the note to my heart just long enough to feel the weight of each written letter. I've been quiet around him, so I don't chance him getting in trouble, or myself for that matter. I signed a paper. A foolish paper. Allowing someone to dictate more of my life. I'm tired of the rules. I hate being afraid. I want to feel something. I want to live. I want to be me.

I slip the note beneath my mattress, tucking in the corners with a gentle touch. A smile tingles at the edges of my lips before I can stop it.

I sweep away the dander from the bed quilt that's accumulated throughout the day. The ceiling must be covered in dust, but aside from the slope in the corner, I have no way of reaching the top panels.

Within seconds of dropping down on the lumpy mattress, the silence stews and I'm convincing myself the house is making noises when I know that's not what I'm hearing.

Flora slept all day. I shouldn't expect her to be asleep all night too.

Part of me knew I wouldn't get a chance to change out of my clothes.

I whisk down the steps and rush into Flora's room to scoop her up before her cries grow any louder.

"I know there may be mice and rats upstairs, but I'll keep you safe from them," I hush as I carry her upstairs.

Once closed in my room, I sway side to side with her, finding her cry softening but not stopping completely. "What if I tell you a story?" I whisper to her. "Would you like that?"

As if she understood, she takes a breath and coos a response.

"Is that so? Do you understand what I'm saying?" I ask, gently poking her little nose.

Another coo and a touch of a smile this time.

"Very well. I have just the thing!" I sing softly.

I kneel beside the bed and pull down my old folktale book from the nightstand. I can't remember any of the stories now. Julia used to read them to me until I was old enough to read on my own, but I suppose I lost interest in children's tales at an early age.

I twist around and take a seat on the edge of my bed, cradling Flora in the crook of my arm. "Which story shall we read?"

Flora slaps the first page and grunts. "I don't think you'll find the copyright page too interesting," I tell her.

She slaps every page I open. "How about, *The Frog Princess?*"

I jump right in without checking to see how many pages the story is, but after the sixth page, not only are my eyes starting to close but Flora has fallen asleep. I gently place her down on the bed, careful not to disturb her.

The book falls off my lap, slapping against the wooden floor and I nearly shout at myself for being so careless. Thankfully, Flora remains asleep. I lean down and pick it up, grabbing it by the back cover. I shut the book and place it down beside me and curl Flora into my arms, so she doesn't roll off the bed.

Despite nearly falling asleep moments ago, all I can do now is listen to Flora's long, deep breaths, and stare at the side of my book, glowing from the moonlight peeking in through the window. I never noticed the pages didn't align before. The pages must be warped. But I've always been so careful with it, so I don't know how that could have happened. I flip the book open to the end, where the last page doesn't meet with the back hard cover. It's warped—the thick paper coating beneath the bound canvas covering.

Staring at the slightly raised center, I notice the beveling is in the shape of a perfect rectangle. I sweep my fingers over it again, finding a distinct edge on each side. Along the bottom as I find both corners, the protrusion budges upward. Something's behind the paper lining.

I pick at the canvas, seeing if the glue will come loose easily and it does. The fold is so tight around the edges that it must have been holding the back flap together. Even the lining is loose. I slide a finger between the back panel and the lining and catch the corner of what must be a folded piece of paper. It takes me a minute to fidget my finger in the right position to pinch the paper enough to slide it to the open edge, but once it's free, I'm dumbfounded to find another piece of paper worn and soft, old, but untouched.

What is this? My fingers tremble unsteadily as I try to carefully unfold the paper, scared to tear whatever it is. Once it's unfolded completely, I find crisp penmanship, perfect lettering —the hand of a calligrapher maybe—of a letter made out to:

My Sweet Halina

TWENTY-SIX

HALINA

My body deflates on the bed, and I can't figure out how to make my eyes keep reading past "My Sweet Halina—"

There's two pieces of paper that were folded in together and I desperately flip each paper over, in search of a signature. Then I find it...

With all my love to you,

Your mama
(Nora Belle Wojic)

The papers flutter to my lap as my eyes fill with tears. I haven't read any other words. All I see is a blur of script in soft brown ink, each loop of a letter elegant but purposeful—like she was trying to define herself through the ever curling sweep of her pen. I don't know what she has to say or how I didn't know this note was folded into the seams of the book. Why now? She couldn't have known when I'd find this. My questions are endless, which is why I'm struggling to lift the papers back up. What if there are no answers?

My entire life...I've just wanted to know who they are, what they looked like—why...

I shove my hand back into the book's torn seam, searching for anything else, a photograph, anything, but the note is alone.

I turn the pages back over and lift them up, my hand unsteady as I try to keep the pages still enough to read.

Nora Belle Wojic, I repeat in my head.

With a long, tired blink, I resettle my focus on the top of the page and push through the salutation:

My Sweet Halina,

I hadn't planned to write you a letter, not before you ever took your first breath. But a heaviness inside of me, something I can't explain told me I should. My parents, your bubbie and grandpa, God rest their souls, used to tell me that when great life events are imminent, we gain a sense of clarity. I see now that must be true.

The doctor tells me you're a girl, by the way I'm carrying you, and he also said you are quite spirited, so much, you keep me awake many times with all your little kicks. Sometimes I press my hands to my belly and whisper to you as if you're already here. I cannot yet see your face, but I know I love you more than I ever thought I could love anyone.

If this letter finds its way into your hands, it means the worst of my fears were in fact a premonition. You may not yet understand what this means. If you're young, I ask you to tuck this away. One day, when you are older and the world makes more sense, read it then. And you will understand.

Your father and I never wed. We spoke of it, the idea of exchanging vows during a small ceremony, nothing grand, but the idea was always talk for another day. Then, I took ill with what I thought was a passing sickness, which turned out to be you.

There in a small medical office, your father and I seated side by side, the doctor asked about our religious affiliations. Of course, with great pride, I told him that I am Jewish.

Your father stood as if he'd been struck with a mallet. He hadn't known. I hadn't been to a temple in some time, not since your bubbie and grandpa passed. But when I learned that I was to become a mother, I promised I would return to the temple, reconnect with tradition to do right by our faith, for you—for us.

Your father changed in an instant. His silence was deafening. Like too many men who returned from the war, he carried grief and blame within his heart. He believed the lies and whispers that trickled down our city streets that our people, the Jews, were to blame for the nation's loss.

From that day on, he turned against me. I became his enemy. He demanded I rid myself of you. I would not. Could not. I already loved you with everything I had. You were already a part of me, and I would do anything to protect you.

He grew violent. First with words. Then with hands. He tried to force my decision through fear, bruises, and threats. I've begged him to leave and told him I would raise you alone. We would be fine. But he told me...no Jewish child, would live to carry his name.

I've been hiding at night, slipping from place to place, watching over my shoulder for him. I've saved what little money I could for a train ticket to get away from here. But I fear I'm running out of time. He's much faster than a weary, swollen woman.

This is the part I've been dreading: If he finds me again, I don't know what he'll do. He may try to rid us both before you're given the chance to draw your first breath. But if by a miracle, you enter this world and survive without me, you must find someone kind and show them this letter.

Even if your father puts on a gentler face, I don't trust he will remain that way. He's hurt me far too many times. Men like him do not change. Ever.

You are Jewish. And that means you come from a line of people who were born in bondage before being led to freedom. We were taught to show compassion and kindness, to offer bread to the hungry, and never let cruelty slip into our hearts. That is who we are—that is what runs through your veins. It is sacred, and unbreakable. Be proud of it.

As I write this, I picture you with my smile, dimples, your small hand curled around my finger. I pray with all that I have that I will live to see you laugh, to braid your hair, and teach you the Shema prayer. But if I cannot...let these words be my voice when you need it.

I pray this letter remains tucked inside your folktale book, never needing to be read. But if you are holding this letter in your hands, you must know...

You were a dream I prayed would come true.

I protected you with everything I had.

You were always and will always be loved by me.

With all my love to you,

Your mama

(Nora Belle Wojic)

The Third day of May, Nineteen-Twenty-One

I brush my finger across the date beneath her signature. I was born just one week later according to the paper pinned to my baby blanket. My body trembles with fury. Tears burn behind my eyelids—tears I've refused to let fall since I was little.

Yesterday, I was an invisible nobody. An orphan. A mishap. Today—today, I'm the daughter of a woman who fought to protect me. And I'm still here. Alive and breathing. That must mean something, mustn't it?

My hands shake so violently the bed frame rattles against the wall. I squeeze my hands together to stop myself, but the tremor moves into my legs. I can't stop shaking.

I carefully slide off the side of the bed, onto the floor so I won't wake Flora. I fold myself into my knees, the pressure against my chest not doing enough to suppress this ache. It hurts too much. I've never felt this type of pain. I'm not sure what it is —if other people feel like this when...their lives were ruined before they could form a memory.

Who is this man—my father?

What did he do to her?

She didn't say his name in the letter.

This letter has been with me my entire life. Hidden and out of sight. The truth was tucked in beside me every night.

She loved me. My mother loved me.

She loved me.

And my father hated me.

Because I'm Jewish.

Because I'm like her.

I'm Jewish.

And I'm working for the Nazis.

Serving them. Feeding their children.

My stomach heaves, and my hand flies up to my mouth. I hold my breath and close my eyes, my body swaying back and forth. Back and forth. *Why? Why did it have to be this way?*

I fold the papers back up, as tightly as they were, following the original creases, and pull myself up onto the bed to slip the note back into the seam of the book. I shove the book back into the interior pocket of my suitcase and button the flap.

No one has ever searched for my mother's name. Will Heinrich have access to papers that Julia didn't? Could that happen?

"You look like a Jew." His voice bounces around in my head, the memory of those words he spoke to me the day he found me along the edge of the woods.

I have to get out of here before they realize the truth.

Out of this house.

Out of this prison.

What if I can't? What if it's too late?

I scoop Flora into my arms, careful not to move her around much. She's still very much asleep and I need to get her back to her crib while I figure out how I'm going to escape a life behind those tall iron bars of Auschwitz.

The beat in my chest is erratic, like fists pounding the head of a drum as I steady myself to amble down the stairs, then keeping my arms from shaking as I lower Flora into her crib. A cold chill snakes up my spine and I manage to return to my room without causing a stir. I'm still trying to picture my mother writing these words without a foggy hint as to what she looked like. Do I look like a horrible Jew hating person or do I look like a woman who would give up everything for a baby she never met?

What am I made up of?

What part of him is in me?

Is it the chill I've learned to use as battle armor?

Or the sharp use of tongue I sometimes can't control.

What if I've been the one keeping him a part of me all this time? I don't want it. I don't want him to be a part of me.

Julia will know what to do. I have to get to her. They can't keep me here. I am not their servant. I will never be their slave. They don't own me.

I don't think...

How can someone hate an unborn child? Where does that kind of hatred come from?

I thought I knew who I was.

Doesn't everyone by this age?
Not me. I don't know anything about myself.
I'm a stranger in my own body.
And I can't think of a lonelier, worse feeling.

TWENTY-SEVEN
GAVRIEL

August 6, 1943

The Schäfer house is ordinarily boisterous in the mornings when I arrive, despite the early hour, but this morning holds a larger atmosphere of chaos. Frau Schäfer is fully dressed, in thick soled heels that pound against the wooden floors.

"There's no time for this," Officer Schäfer scolds his wife. "My answer is final."

"I've had this appointment for months," she replies.

"The house cannot and will not be left unattended. Do I make myself clear?"

Frau Schäfer stops short in her heavy pace. "I didn't agree to this," she says.

"And I didn't agree to the revolt that partially destroyed the Treblinka extermination camp four days ago. People escaped. And worse, the Red Army managed to reclaim control over Orel after two years in our holding. This has all happened in a matter of four days, Ada. How long before we have an exodus at Auschwitz?"

Well, I certainly didn't agree to becoming their prisoner

slave. But I know well enough my sarcasm and lack of humor will not be appreciated or tolerated here. Still, the thought of a revolt resulting in the destruction of Treblinka means there's a chance for us in Auschwitz. Or...liberation, perhaps—if the Soviets are advancing this fast...maybe, we'll live long enough to see it.

"I don't understand a word of what you're saying," Frau Schäfer complains. "What does Treblinka or the Soviet Union have to do with us?"

"For God's sake, Ada. If there's a revolt at the Treblinka concentration camp, and the Soviets are reclaiming territory, it means the tide is turning. Do you think we're immune? We're sitting next to Auschwitz with prisoners working under our roof. It only takes one slip, an unsupervised hour, and they could sabotage us. We cannot leave our home and children unguarded."

My knees complain as I climb the stairs, aching more today than yesterday and the day before that. Pa never let my brothers or me work on an empty stomach and made sure we had plenty of water. He warned us of repercussions for not taking care of our bodies when under constant duress. "Comes with the territory," he would say. "A builder's body is made of strong muscles and healthy bones. It's your most important tool so protect it." Thankfully, Mama took pride in making sure her men were always well fed, which made her job difficult when we were put on strict rations at the start of the war. Even then, she came up with inventive ways to keep our plates full and would sit at the other end of the table, marveling at the way we would scrape up every morsel. We used to joke that we showed our love through the giving and taking of food in our home. Mama put her whole heart into everything she prepared for us. That's what it meant, and I see that now.

At the top of the stairwell, I find Halina holding out an unbuttoned sweater for Marlene to shove her arms through, but

Marlene appears to be more interested in making her skirt spin around her body as she twirls away from Halina.

"We're going to be late for your first day if you don't put your sweater on," she says firmly, but in a hushed voice.

Isla is leaning against the wall, her knapsack in hand, staring mindlessly at the abstract portrait hanging on the wall across from her. I sniffle, for no other reason than to garner Halina's attention briefly.

She peers over her shoulder at me, and a small smile pokes at her lips. "I can't talk now," she mouths.

At least, I think that's what she said. We've spoken in front of the children before, making me question if something has changed. If something has happened to her...

I hold my hand out, palm up and gesture the act of writing a note with my other hand gripped around an invisible pencil. I mouth the words, "Did you get my note?"

She nods and smiles again, a more heartfelt smile this time— also, somehow with more pain too. I continue up the attic stairs, taking each step slowly in response to the pain in my legs, yanking harder on the banister than I probably should. The creaks along the walls match the weight of my heavy feet along the worn stairs.

"The two of you need to go downstairs and take your lunches from the kitchen. I'm going to grab my sweater. I'll meet you down there in a moment," Halina tells the girls, her tone firmer than before.

I'm just about to verify the safekeeping of Officer Schäfer's pistol in my alcove when I hear footsteps treading quickly up the stairs.

She already said she can't talk now. I won't bother her. I'm sure she has enough on her mind, with taking the girls to school for their first day. I can only imagine what that place looks like —a special school for children of the SS. There must be swastikas painted in every corner of that building with rules for abiding hatred toward all kinds with the exception of their kind.

I busy myself by the pile of electrical wiring to install for the requested light fixtures and switch, untangling the used materials Schäfer left for me.

A coarse scuffle pricks at my ears, and I turn around, finding Halina, pale and with loose strands of her braid falling over her tense posture. "Thank you for your note," she says, her words spilling out as if she's running out of time. She peers over her shoulder toward the doorway before turning back toward me to speak. "I need to be more careful here. Heinrich forced me to sign papers yesterday, agreeing I won't speak to any of the other...any of the—"

"I'm a prisoner. I know," I tell her.

"I don't know if everyone is forced to sign a paper or if it's just me, but—I've been desperate to speak to you. I hope there will be time after I bring the children to school."

I push myself up to my feet, unable to mask the groan scraping against my throat as I do.

Halina presses her hand to her chest. "Are you hurt?"

"Are you?" I retort. I stood to ask her the same question. What could she be desperate to speak to me about?

She shakes her head. "No, I'm not. Not at all. I—my life as I knew it, I—don't know...it wasn't what I thought...I'm not just a poor Polish orphan. I couldn't have imagined that label—one I greatly despised—wasn't just about how little or how much I had. It was hiding the truth of who I am. Who I've always been." She lifts her hands from her chest, bringing them to her face. "I'm sorry. I don't even know what I'm saying."

I reach out and take her wrist, tugging her hand from her face. "Whatever it is...you can talk to me." I sweep my thumb gently across her warm cheek.

"I—I'm not allowed to..." her voice squeaks through a whisper. "But if Ada and Heinrich find out who I really am, I'd only be allowed to talk to you. I know it makes no sense, but I'll explain more later. I must get them to school."

I don't understand what she means. She's speaking in circles but is obviously perplexed about whatever is bothering her. "Sure, of course. I'll be here."

"You don't look well," she says with a tired sigh. "Are you sick?"

I shake my head. "I'll be fine."

"You're hungry," she tells me.

At Auschwitz, we are all hungry. "Please, don't worry about me."

"I'll just get your friend Adam some food then, yes?" My bottom lip falls, not expecting her quip of a remark. "That's what I thought. I'll find you both something."

I didn't realize I was still holding on to her wrist until her gaze falls to our linked arms. I release my hold and nearly fall backward as she swings her arms around my neck and presses her cheek to my chest. "I've never needed someone before. I've always been able to take the world on myself, but—" No one has been this close to me in so long that I've forgotten when it's like to be desired. An embrace, the warmth, a connection, a moment where grief can't cut through my chest.

I debate whether it's all right to reciprocate, but my arms find their way around her before I've made up my mind. "Everyone needs someone," I say, interrupting her.

TWENTY-EIGHT

HALINA

I hate to feel surprised to find Rosalie and Celina waiting for me as they said they would this morning. It's been hard to figure the two of them out. I'm not sure if they're actual friends or simple acquaintances forced to spend time together for the sake of the children.

Flora is already complaining about the bumpy ride in her baby carriage, which I'm sure will turn into hard cries at any moment, but maybe the forward motion will settle her down first. Celina and Rosalie both have carriages too, but theirs are designed for children a bit older than Flora.

"Are the girls nervous for their first day?" Celina asks as she turns off the residential street.

"They didn't say so. They seemed eager to get ready this morning."

"Good. It does appear that most of the children are quite excited to return. Except for these little ones," Celina says, shuffling her fingers through the little boy's white-blonde hair in her carriage, then moving her hand to the girl, who's a bit older, walking beside her. "Halbert and Lisbet aren't old enough for school yet, and they're a bit sad to know their sister and brother get to have all the fun."

The little girl in Rosalie's carriage lets out a stern yelp, grabbing the outside white bars of the carriage, twisting around to see Rosalie with a scowl. "I don't go!"

"You are not going to school, Hilde. You're only three. They won't even take you in yet, so there's nothing to worry about." Rosalie sweeps her head to the side, giving us a giant eye roll. "This one is not like the others. She would love nothing more than to be the only child with all the attention."

"Isn't that what all children want?" Celina asks with a chuckle.

No. Not at all. I keep my answer to myself, knowing most people don't see life through the same lens as me.

"How old are the four children who are going to school?" I ask them both.

"Greta is ten, and Claude is seven," Rosalie answers first.

"And Konrad is nine, and Erika is five," Celina follows. "Konrad is almost ready to enlist himself into the army," she says with a phony grin. "Nine going on eighteen."

"Don't be rude," Konrad says. "Mother and Father don't appreciate your tone when you speak like that, yes?"

"Why do you care so much?" Claude asks him, from a younger point of view and a different family.

"Because...you should too, Claude. We'll both be men of the house sooner than you realize."

The conversation between them and the words spewing from Heinrich's mouth this week have a gut-clenching grip on my stomach.

The schoolhouse appears just over the hill in the near distance, marking its territory with a blood red flag and the iconic Nazi symbol. I've almost forgotten what this town once looked like before it became cloaked in these waving symbols of death. The Nazis don't want anyone to ever forget, even for a moment, who is always watching over us.

"They can sense fear," Rosalie speaks quietly.

"Who?" But I'm staring right at the who...The Nazi guards at the small school building's entrance.

"Rosalie and I have concluded that they aren't worth much to the higher ranks if they've been placed on duty at the school, which makes them meaner, more miserable. Don't make eye contact and you'll be fine," Celina adds.

As if there are no Nazi guards standing before us, all the children, except Marlene, run for the open school door with hardly a whisper of a goodbye. Marlene turns to face me, walking backwards. "Will I be all right?"

I stop pushing the carriage, knowing I'm on borrowed time as Flora is wide awake and yet, peaceful, for the moment. "School is wonderful. You're going to love it, and you'll make lots of friends. You'll become smarter every single day. It's quite an amazing experience." I was lost in thought about my school days, feeling like a common child among others, rather than an orphan in a home for lonely children. Marlene is walking into a Nazi supervised school riddled with an education designed by the Reich.

Marlene wraps her arms around my waist and gives me a tight squeeze. "Will you be right here after school?"

"You can count on it," I say, placing my hand on her head. "Go on."

"Halt!" a guard shouts as Marlene approaches the door on her own. She stops short, dust kicking up behind her patent-leather shoes. She turns to face the guard, straightens her shoulders and holds her arm out like an angled sword. "Heil Hitler," she says meekly.

Rosalie and Celina turn their carriages around, their backs facing the school yard. I do the same, feeling a tug at my heart after watching Marlene become the newest victim to this race.

There's so much I want to say—such anger running through my veins, and I wonder what Rosalie and Celina feel. Are they used to this life so much so that it doesn't bother them to see what these children are subjected to?

A minute passes as we continue walking away from the school when Celina releases a heavy sigh. "That's all there is to say," she complains.

Rosalie's lips pinch tightly together as if she's holding something in her mouth. "We were real people before...this. Like you, I'm sure." The words are uttered from her mouth, but her lips hardly move. We're alone on a road, lined with thick forests, but I know better than to assume we're safe to speak freely anywhere.

"What was your life like before?" I press, keeping my voice down to match her subtlety.

"Well, I was a midwife, but the family I worked for before being brought here, offered me more than I could ever ask for if I agreed to stay with them as a nursemaid for their son. The Silbergs were the most loving and warm family, treating me as if I was one of them. They were one of the last wealthy Jewish families to be torn out of their homes in the Małopolska region, giving us more time together than most had. However, when their time was up, everything happened so fast. They were there one minute and gone the next." Rosalie's cheeks burn red and her eyes well. "When the Gestapo came for the family, they questioned who I was in relation to them, then told me I wasn't allowed to go where they were going. I stood there, outside of their house, debating how I could help the Silbergs, but before I could do anything, I was approached by SS Officer Weyman, and told where I would be going next."

"I'm so sorry," I offer. "A midwife—and a nursemaid—I can see why you might have been sought after, but you deserve better than this life."

"They all want more Aryan babies. That's for certain,"

Rosalie says with a sigh. "It seems they have a reason for choosing who will be a 'good' fit to work for their families. But I'm not sure any of us want to know the truth."

Celina releases a hand from her carriage and pats Rosalie's back. It's hard to believe there's any real reason we were chosen. Heinrich certainly knew nothing about me and if he did, I don't think I would have been on a list of candidates.

"Celina's story is far more fascinating than mine," Rosalie says, sniffling and pressing the top of her hand against her nose.

"Well, that might take way more time to explain than we have, and I want to know your story—where you came from too," Celina says, her focus set on me.

I'm sure my story doesn't compare in the slightest. "I think it might have been Heinrich's mistake," I say flatly.

The two of them burst into laughter, a sound of trapped joviality finally breaking free.

"Oh gosh, I like you," Celina says. "You're quite funny."

My story. How can I tell them my story when all the pages were torn out last night?

"I worked at the orphanage I grew up in. One of the little girls was as defiant as they come, ran straight out the front door, through the woods, and onto the road with guard posts. That's when Officer Schäfer pulled up in his car. I forced the little girl to go back—before it was too late for her too. I didn't want him to know about the orphanage or where she came from."

"Oh my."

A cool morning breeze whips around us, blowing Flora's blanket out of her pinched grip. The familiar sound of despair places a bookmark in the conversation between Rosalie, Celina, and me, and I welcome the opportunity to focus on something different. I scoop Flora out of the carriage and wrap her up snugly in her blanket and prop her up on my chest, leaving my free arm to push the carriage. "Brrr," I mumble to her. "Brr, brr, brr. It's chilly, isn't it?"

"B-b-b-b," Flora mimics the b sound and smiles proudly.

"Good job. Brr!"

"B-b-b-b," she says again.

The other two older babies begin whining when they notice Flora receiving more attention, leaving us without another moment of quiet among us.

"I need to run a couple of errands at the marketplace square for Frau Weyman," Rosalie says.

"I can join you," Celina offers. "Frau Drexel won't be back home until later in the day."

"Marketplace square?" I inquire, wondering if I'll be sent on errands at some point too.

"It's just up the road a bit. There are shops and vendors. Most of the SS families collect their supplies there," Rosalie says.

Good to know.

"I should head back to the house," I say with a sigh. "I'm not sure I've earned such freedom yet, or if I ever will."

Celina scoffs and flaps her hand toward me. "Trust me... when it's convenient for the officer's wife, you'll earn your so-called-freedom."

"Well, enjoy the rest of your day." *Is that even possible?* I give them a quick wave before heading in the other direction.

An unusual silence fills the house, making me wonder what I'm arriving back to. I overheard Ada and Heinrich arguing over her leaving for an appointment this morning. He told her she wasn't allowed to leave. I pass the family room, finding nothing more than a sofa with worn round divots from overuse. The kitchen is empty as well. Not even Kasia is here. There's no sound of hammering from above, either. There's always the sound of hammering. Gavriel does nothing but hammer all day long from the moment he arrives until he leaves at night. I peek out into the back; the large yard being tended to by Adam. He wouldn't be here alone.

"What is this?" a man shouts. His voice makes me jump back away from the window and frightens Flora out of her momentary calmness. "There are weeds. Weeds are a waste of living space—like Jews. We remove the Jews. And we remove the weeds." With another quick peek outside, I watch a man in a prisoner uniform with one of those kapo arm bands charging toward Adam. I can't watch what happens next.

Has this kapo already been inside and inspected Gavriel's work too? Has Gavriel been hurt? I hurry to the stairs, making my way up to the second floor and do a quick sweep down the hallway to check for any signs of Ada. Even her bedroom door has been left cracked open, which hasn't happened since I've been here. I glance in, finding the mundane decorated space empty.

There's only silence as I climb the stairs toward the attic. Carrying Flora in my arms and the rush of movement adds to the heat, making it hard to catch my breath. I poke my head into the construction area, searching for Gavriel. A pit in my stomach tightens as I pass each corner, confirming he's not here.

What's happened?

"Oh, God!" His cry is guttural.

TWENTY-NINE

GAVRIEL

Flora screams over Halina's gasp as my heart dislodges from my throat.

"You scared—" she begins to say, exasperated.

"You? I thought you were—" I swallow the last of my words as I step out of the alcove.

"I didn't know there was an alcove," Halina says, peering around me to get a better look.

"You still know nothing about an alcove," I say, pointedly. "But do you want to see inside? It's not quite a closet."

This little nook wasn't always here, at least not like this. It was just a hollow gap around the chimney situated between Halina's room and the new expansion. It isn't livable space. I added a couple of shelves, reinforced the beams, and disguised the hatch with a seamless clamp. It was nothing but a wall before and looks like nothing but a wall now. The Schäfers will never notice.

Hali looks a bit hesitant as I would expect but her curiosity is stronger as she makes her way past me, stepping into the alcove.

"I didn't expect—it's cozy, like a small hideout of sorts."

"You never know when one of us might need a few minutes to disappear from this house. A few minutes can mean everything."

"You're brilliant," I whisper. "I'm impressed." She sweeps her hand along the lower shelf. "I've always wanted a hiding spot where the world can't find me, just a place to go to when I need to think. There was never any privacy in the orphanage when I was growing up."

"Well, this little place can be our secret," I tell her, catching her captivating stare, holding it within mine. My heart gallops into my throat, sensations reviving from a life long ago, stronger than I can remember. There's something between us, more than something, and if I stand here like this staring at her much longer, I might crumble. "I should get back to doing what I'm supposed to be doing, but if you want to revel in the hidden spot until a certain tiny human starts crying, you're welcome to." I gently pinch Flora's nose. "Isn't that right, little princess?" Flora shocks us both when an adorable little smile perks up her cheeks. "Well, let me guess. You would like your own little hiding spot too, young lady?" Flora releases a hearty giggle—a sound I've never heard from her before. I was wondering why I hadn't heard such a beautiful little sound from her since I was sure babies found their laughter earlier on. I brush my knuckle along her cheek. "See, no reason to be sad. I'll be happy to make you laugh whenever you want."

"That's the first time I've heard her giggle," Hali says, a smile growing across her cheeks too.

"What happened to you last night?" I ask, knowing our moments together end as abruptly as they begin. There was something incredibly distressing behind the words she used this morning.

She hoists Flora up higher on her chest, resting her arm

beneath Flora's bottom. "Oh, it was just a typical evening—like any other evening really, loud, spewing with rage, and tyranny," I say with a roll of my eyes. "Aside from that, I found a letter in the seam of a book that was left on the doorstep with me. It was from my mother." She narrows her eyes, but stares past me. "Mother. That word doesn't sound right on my tongue."

"You said you didn't know anything about your parents before, right?" I follow.

"Well, it turns out my father is no better than a modern day Nazi, beat my mother while she was pregnant with me, and she was planning to run away with me after I was born and live out our fairy-tale life, but this just-in-case letter was only meant to end up in my hands if the worst happened to her."

My pulse throbs in my head as I dissect her words, trying to make sense of the story. "What do you think happened to your mother?" I ask.

Hali shrugs. "I'm not sure if she died, or was murdered, or if she's alive, but the letter was only meant for my eyes if she was gone."

"Did she say why your father was so spiteful?" I'm not following. I must have missed something.

"He blamed the Jews for losing the Great War. In the letter, my mother said he didn't want to bring a Jewish child into the world, so he tried to solve the—" she points to herself. "—the problem before it happened."

"Wait..." I whisper. "Did you just find out you were Jewish last night?" Is that what she's trying to say? It must be. That is what she said, but if she knew prior to this and—she wouldn't be here as a servant. She *can't* be here as a servant.

Hali's small, upturned nose scrunches and her chin trembles. "I'm so scared," she whispers.

With a gentle motion, I wrap my hands around Flora and lift her off Hali's chest and place her on mine. I take Hali's hand

and tug her out of the alcove and around the corner to cross the shallow corridor into her room. I lower Flora onto the bed and notice a small teddy bear leaning against the thin pillow. "Is this okay for her to hold?" I ask Hali.

She nods with a small, broken smile, fighting through the tears she won't release. I hand Flora the small bear and ruffle the matted fur against her chin. She coos and grasps at the bear to inspect it. With Flora entertained for a moment, I engulf Hali's delicate and petite hands in my battered and beat up grip, then squeeze gently to claim her attention.

"Look at me," I tell her, angling my head down to catch her gaze in return. The gloss of her stare captures the sunlight and casts reflections of the window within her pretty hazel eyes. "This group of Germans—the Nazis—they don't see people as Jews, or by the color of their skin, if they're rich, or poor, handicapped, old, or young. It's the difference between the rest of the world and them. They are the ones who don't want to feel inferior to others—to so many others. This is why they put their efforts toward creating a society where only their kind belong. Anger and hatred are blossoms of a jealous root, and anyone who needs to prove their power is a weak person with nothing to show. That is who we're surrounded by."

"The reason doesn't matter. We have nothing to fight back with," Hali says.

"If everyone who isn't a part of this force says that, what will become of the rest of this world at the end of this war? Because I'll tell you something...I will not give up. My brothers, Jozek and Natan, and our parents, they're out there somewhere and I will do whatever it takes to see them again. And you—your mother obviously survived long enough to give you a chance at life. Therefore, you must take it and not give up. If anything, now you fight harder—fight like she fought for you."

"How do you stay so optimistic when—I saw the inside of Auschwitz...I saw the way you're living, and the way people would rather die than take another breath of the death filled air."

"I believe we are a part of history in the making, and maybe—maybe eighty years from now, long after this war has ended, people will see a bigger picture—they'll see it isn't one act of heroism that stops evil, but rather a culmination of bravery and camaraderie that succeeds. There are more of us than them—not just Jewish people—the good people of this world. We just need time for everyone to pull together."

This is what I tell myself before I fall asleep each night, hoping I will wake up still believing there's enough time left for it to all be true.

She's gazing at me as if I'm a painting hanging in a museum, one with many possible meanings. "If Heinrich finds out I'm Jewish, I'll be turned in. They'll likely kill me because that's what they're doing to more than half of the Jewish people who arrive at Auschwitz, isn't it? That's what the stream of smoke is in the sky? People would speculate on the outside the restricted zone. The smokestacks are hard to ignore on a clear day, even in the surrounding towns. The rumors were too frightening to be something made up just for the sake of gossip. If I die before I've had a chance to live, I won't be a part of history. It will be as if I never existed, just like my father hoped."

"He's not going to find out," I say urgently, without thinking about the validity of her concern. He could find out. Maybe there are papers she doesn't know about. Everything she said—it isn't wrong, except that one thing...I pull her into me and release her hands in exchange for her warm cheeks, as I stretch my fingers out to weave around her ears and into her silky hair. "You exist, Hali. You exist here with me at this moment. No one can change that."

She gasps a quiet inhale and peers up at me from beneath her lashes. My pulse stammers, fast and hard, relentless as I lean in and kiss her. She rests her hand on my chest, her fingers grasping at the fabric, scratching at my skin. I need air, but I'd rather go without if it means staying here like this for however many more seconds the world allows.

A searing pain slices through my stomach, crippling my upper body as I release Halina and cower into my ribcage.

"What is it?" she cries out. "Did I do something? Are you hurt?"

Black dots form in front of my eyes and the pain forces me to my knees. Halina follows, yanking at my shirt to find a source for the pain she can't see on the outside. "You're pale, Gav. Oh my—I told you I'd bring you food, and I—When's the last time you ate?"

"Hali, I can't remember—I, this—isn't your fa—" I can hardly breathe through the pain, let alone complete a sentence.

She shoves her shoulder beneath my arm and tries to help me to my feet but struggles. I can't move. My muscles won't release their contraction.

"Okay, stay here," she says, panicking.

"I have no choice," I utter, knowing I would normally laugh at my own demise.

She snatches Flora and the teddy bear off the bed and scurries down the stairs, then the next set too. That kapo is here, in or just outside the house somewhere, he's been in to check on me three times this morning and I'm due for another visit soon.

Either I'm becoming delirious, or Halina's managed to make it all the way down both flights of stairs, and across the house, and back up here within seconds. I pray it's her when the door opens.

"Here, Kasia made sandwiches for the entire week for the girls. I'll make another so they don't see one is missing. Eat this." She struggles with Flora held in one arm as she lowers herself to her knees with a wax-paper-wrapped sandwich and an entire pitcher of water, setting them on the ground beside her.

"That kapo—he's going to be back," I choke out.

Halina sets Flora down beside me and presses my shoulders back so I'm leaning against the side of her bed. She grabs the pitcher and lifts it to my mouth. "Drink," she demands.

A door slams beneath us, sucking the oxygen out of the room. Halina places the pitcher down and jumps up, rushing out of the room. Two seconds merely pass before the hammer thumps against—something. It won't stop him. He'll still come up here. The hammering stops for a second, and just before it starts again, another door slams. Again, the hammer stops and Halina rushes back into the room. "He was just passing through the house. He's in the front yard," she says breathlessly, while grabbing the sandwich and tearing the paper off.

Minutes of fear-filled silence come and go while I try to swallow as much of the sandwich without pausing to chew much. She lifts the pitcher of water back up to my lips after I've swallowed the last bite, and I drink as much as I can, feeling a slight relief of pain in my stomach.

"How's the pain?" she asks, a flash of concern flickering through her eyes.

"What pain?"

Halina drops her head to the side. "Very funny."

She lifts Flora to settle her on the bed before offering me her hand to help me up. I think she might have forgotten she wasn't able to move me just a minute ago, but despite that, even if she can't lift me, the effort means everything. I manage to get back on my feet and Hali touches her cool hands to my cheeks.

"I shouldn't have Flora up here. You shouldn't be in this room," she says.

"I don't want to be anywhere else," I tell her.

She grabs my arms, clawing at them as if trying not to lose her grip, then rises onto her toes to kiss me once more—a kiss no longer than a blink, but a second worth remembering for eternity. Then she shoves me out the door.

Flora releases a shrill cry, loud enough to give away her

presence up in the attic to anyone inside or outside the house. Halina scoops her up, snatches the pitcher of water, and the wax-paper-wrapper then hurries down the stairs. The timing couldn't be worse. The sound of the front door swinging open coincides with her footsteps hitting the bottom landing, her arms filled with food and water remnants, and no explanation...

THIRTY

HALINA

Flora weighed heavily in my arms as I was storming down the hallway of the main floor toward the kitchen to return the pitcher of water, when the front door swung open. Instinct spun me around, leaving me face to face with the man I saw shouting at Adam outside earlier. The rules between these prisoners who are called kapos and the prisoners themselves are foggy. I'm not supposed to speak to the prisoners. I wonder what the rule will be when I become one of them.

Does he see the guilt on my face, the worry in my eyes, or the heaviness of my breath. Does it matter? He's scrutinizing me with his dark stare in a way I don't think he should. Perhaps like a bumble bee, if I stay very still and ignore his presence, he'll continue along his way. If not, I suspect there will be questions.

My brain is in a fog until Flora's burst of tears reignites. "Let's go have that warm bath, sweet girl, shall we?"

"In a drinking water pitcher?" the kapo says. His words snake around my throat and squeeze.

"I can't find a different one," I utter, brushing past the man to return up to the bedroom floor.

"Is there a problem here?" Ada's voice yanks me to a stop before climbing up another step.

"No, Frau Schäfer," the kapo says, removing his striped cap and bowing to her.

I hurry up the stairway, telling myself it was only the kapo she was questioning.

"Halina, what are you doing with the pitcher of water?" Ada follows, again stopping me from making it up any further stairs.

"I was going to give Flora a bath." With the wrong pitcher of water. The proper one is in the washroom upstairs, where it's kept.

"I see," she says with a sigh. "Except you are aware that is not the pitcher we use for bath water, yes?"

I wouldn't know what pitcher of water is used for bath water because you haven't given me any instructions aside from poisoning your daughter, the hours to wake up and go to sleep, and to act as though the Jewish people working in this house don't exist. It's becoming exceedingly difficult to keep my thoughts to myself.

"I didn't know," I say, simply, lying, acting as stupid as she sees me. I'm aware of the bath pitcher in the washroom.

"Yes. There is one beneath the sink pedestal in the upstairs washroom. What have you been using all this time?"

"This..." I say, peering back at the glass pitcher. "I didn't know there were separate ones for various uses, but I understand now." I tread back down the few steps and twist around the banister toward the kitchen to replace the water pitcher.

"Halina," Ada says, stopping me once more. "Has there been any trouble while I've been gone? Anything I need to report to Officer Schäfer?" Ada's voice continues to drone, but her words are blunt and accusatory as she shifts her focus back to the kapo.

"No, Frau Schäfer. Everything is in order here." I'm surprised he didn't make mention of Adam's indiscretion in the backyard.

"Good," she says.

I replace the pitcher on the counter and make a note to dispose of the wax paper in my apron pocket somewhere Ada won't notice.

The kapo leaves through the servant door in the back, likely to go back to scrutinizing Adam, and Ada is shuffling through envelopes in front of the decorative wall table beneath the stairs.

Just before I pass, she stretches her arm out to the side, an envelope pinched between her fingers. "Take this," she says. "Then burn it." I swallow hard while reaching to take it from her, immediately spotting my own handwriting on the front of the envelope, as well as the envelope sliced open at the top. "The next time you decide to send a letter to this Julia person, I strongly suggest you refrain from speaking a word about my family. Given that you've signed papers agreeing to the confidentiality of all matters within this household, I would think you'd be more cautious before trying to deceive us."

I can't think of a word to say. I won't apologize, but I did break her rule. Just as Gavriel is explaining our intelligence versus theirs, I make a mistake that could cost me my safety within this servant job. The invisible noose around my neck tightens more and more each day I'm here. "I understand." I'm not sure my words will be enough, not this time.

She turns to stare at me, her blue eyes cold with spite. "Do you, really?" A cold numbing pain shoots through my chest and my knees threaten to give out. But I'm holding Flora in my arms. I can't fall. "Are there any other rules you might be breaking that I should know about before my husband finds out?"

"No, Frau Schäfer." Every word that comes out of my mouth is a lie.

And I believe every word that comes out of her mouth is a lie as well. How different are the two of us? I recall what Rosalie said about her past, growing up on a farm before her life was taken control of by Heinrich.

"I'll likely be out of line for asking this question, but...are you all right?"

Her expression grows stale and frozen, taken aback by my question. "I beg your pardon?" She clutches her chest, her polished fingernails pressing against the silk fabric.

"Your husband—he isn't very kind to you. It's none of my business, of course, but from one woman to another, you don't deserve to be—"

She takes a blunt step toward me and lowers her voice. "It's the nature of this life I've committed myself—" She wrenches her hand around the side of her neck and closes her eyes tightly, loose skin folding along her lids. "You know what, enough," she snaps. "Who gave you the right to comment on my marriage? Do you have any idea how hard my husband works? And for this country no less?"

There's a fine line between enraging Ada and planting a small nuisance of an idea in her fragile head. "I'm sure you work just as hard here in the house, raising your three, soon to be four, children. You're quite literally creating life right this very moment and still carrying on with the household errands. It's no easy feat. In fact, some say a mother's job is the hardest of all the jobs in the world. But of course, men are typically too selfish to admit this fact out loud."

The momentary pause of silence is enough to tell me that she's considering my words.

"What is your point, Halina? Surely, you must have one."

"My point—you deserve respect and appreciation, even from a man who holds a rank and title."

She doesn't deserve much of anything, but no one should be a victim to their own spouse—not even her. Ada continues to stare at me, and I can't decipher her next thought or response but I'm holding her child so she must be taking that into consideration. "You think because you found a way to keep Flora from crying as much, you're entitled to speak down to me?"

"Not at all. As I said, I'm speaking to you, woman to woman."

"I am a woman. You, however—" she says, holding her tongue at the end.

You have no idea who I am, but despite that, I know I'm better than you.

I walk past her and head upstairs. "By the way, your hairdo looks lovely, Frau Schäfer." It appears she's opted for a professional hair-dye treatment rather than using the box of hair peroxide she's hiding in the linen closet.

* * *

While settling Flora into her carriage for our walk back to the schoolhouse, a motion in the upstairs attic window catches my attention. Gavriel peers out for a brief second, only to smile down at us before backing away. His small gesture sends a flutter of joy through me as I recall our moments together this morning—how unexpected yet desired it all was. His comfort was something I couldn't have asked for, yet he gave it to me without question. It's almost as if he understands me more than I understand myself.

I've set out to be a strong woman, knowing I have nothing to fall back on, and that seemed to be enough until last night. No matter which way I look at myself, the German Reich won't see me any differently than any other Jewish woman they aim their hatred toward. If my birth records show the truth, they don't care who I thought I was before. I will be what I am.

There is a ticking clock hanging above my head now and there's no saying how long I might or might not have before Officer Schäfer finds out who I really am.

I've complied with his threats for the sake of my well-being, also knowing most other Polish women have been sent to forced labor in some capacity. Remaining complicit is as dangerous as the alternative.

"I hope the little princess allowed you a moment of quiet this afternoon," Celina says as I approach her and Rosalie near the weeping willow tree between the houses they work in.

"I think this little girl desires calmness in her life. Until there is commotion around her, she's quite happy," I say.

"The houses are very loud with so many children and—and the aggressiveness of the men," Rosalie adds.

"I want more biscuits!" Halbert shouts from Celina's carriage.

"I too," Hilde shouts from Rosalie's carriage.

Celina hands both children half of a small biscuit to nibble on as we begin our ascent to the Nazi school. "Oy, they're both *meshugana*—sorry, absurd," Celina mumbles, translating automatically.

Rosalie clears her throat, and I catch her elbow Celina in the ribs, shooting her a meaningful look. "I know some Yiddish too," I say cautiously.

Both ladies stare at me as if I just admitted something I shouldn't. "I don't know much Yiddish," Rosalie says quickly. "Only a few words. It's more of a—"

Now Celina makes a sound to break the silence. "It's nothing. Did you learn it at school, or—"

I try to remember back to when I learned some key phrases. I'm not fluent by any means, but I grew up hearing it often. "The other children in the orphanage spoke it, mixed in with their Polish. I just picked up on it over time."

"We shouldn't be speaking about this," Rosalie says, peeking around in each direction.

"About Yiddish?" I ask.

"Yes," she says. "Someone is always listening. A spoken word of Yiddish is as dangerous as walking around the 'restricted zone' with a Jewish yellow star badge." Her warning thrusts into my gut as if someone had shoved me backward.

THIRTY-ONE
GAVRIEL

With the electrical work only taking up the day yesterday, I'll be starting on the interior wall and ceiling panels. The lumber was delivered at some point overnight and it took me a few hours to shuttle it all up the two flights of stairs. If I were working alongside Pa and my brothers, we'd be looking at finishing up the job in the next week or two, but not on my own. Still, I can't stop myself from wondering what will happen to me once the attic is complete. Officer Schäfer hasn't said anything about more work. They'll just be done with me unless one of the other houses on the street has something to utilize me for. I try to keep my focus on the current day, so I don't fall into a dark web of thoughts.

Trying to find boards the same size has been impossible, leaving me to saw them down. I won't have any strength left for the day if I can't even get through a quarter of the boards I need to trim.

The saw is flimsy and I'm waiting for it to crack. This man wants all this work done, with tools that have seen their day. I guess it'll just be another cause for the length of time it takes—a delay in whatever they'll do with me later.

By mid-morning, the circulation within the room is stale

and sweat is dripping from every limb, acting like a glue between the fabric of my uniform and my skin but it's almost easier without the heavy material swaying around, and I've got a good system working. Kind of. Measure, mark, measure, saw, and curse. Then repeat. The boards aren't just different sizes, they're also warped, and some are swollen from the moisture and heat. Each one gives me a fight, causing the blade to catch every few seconds, which gnaws at the aching joints in my wrist. I'm going to feel this for weeks.

When I need to catch my breath, I stop, dry my hands off on my pants, clean the sweat from my face, listen in for any new activity downstairs to consider how long it will be before the kapo returns to check on me. I don't think anyone is home. Halina must be making her way back from dropping the girls off at school. Frau Schäfer left minutes after Halina, and Kasia doesn't arrive until after noon now. The new kapo must just stand outside watching Adam break his back all day.

I grab the next board, center it between the makeshift trestles and press down a bit harder on this piece, wanting to get through it before it takes my remaining energy. My pulse ignites the harder the faster I yank and shove the saw. It's not the right way, but it's just the way it works right now.

"Gavriel, when you rush, mistakes happen," Pa would always tell me. It wasn't that I was in a rush. I just thought it would be best to get the job done faster. Everyone likes a quick and efficient worker. Pa disagreed. He'd disagree now too.

With that thought in mind, the saw catches and the board slips—and in the next second, blistering flames shoot through my hand.

"Shiii—!"

The pain is instant, and searing, rooting from the base of my thumb. "No. No. No." I stare at it, the blood pooling up too quickly, too red. It's bad, deep. I've seen worse, but not on myself. Pa wouldn't have injuries on his watch. That's why he told us speed should never be on our minds.

I sink down against a support beam and wrap the hem of my uniform jacket around the wound and squeeze. It isn't the pain that's making me sweat through this—though it's there and it's real—it's the thought of how I'm going to treat the wound that's bringing me to my knees.

My pulse thumps between my ears, the heat rises, hotter, more oppressive, and the pounding—my pulse—I think—but it grows louder. Or maybe it isn't my pulse.

Footsteps?

No. Not now. Not footsteps.

It's going to be the kapo. He can't see this. He'll insist on replacing me with someone else, leaving me without work and possibly a functioning hand—it will be the end for me.

I try to push myself up, but the blood rushes away from my head and all I can do is fall into the beam. "Gav, my friend, you all right? I heard you shout," Adam says, huffing his words, nervously checking over his shoulder. "The jerk is out front— the kapo. He'll be returning any minute. You're bleeding." Adam trudges across the wooden planks, stopping just in front of me, kneeling. "What happened?"

"Saw slipped," I mumble. "I'll be all right." I'm not sure that I will be. I can't get myself up to my feet right now.

"Oh, God...I'll see if I can find some medical supplies. Keep pressure on it, my friend."

My pulse is quivering and burning through the wound. I need to get up.

I rock forward until I can get onto my knees and use the leverage of the beam to stand up straight. The blood has seeped through my uniform and is covering my other hand too.

A scream from Flora distracts my apprehension, followed by another pounding of footsteps. Maybe Adam's found something.

"Are you hurt?" Halina barges into the room without a child in sight, which explains the shrill cry from the floor below. "Adam said you need help. The kapo was on his way to the yard. He had to go back out there. Oh goodness," she says, spotting all the blood. "I'll go find a clean rag and bandages. Rubbing alcohol, too."

"Stop, Hali, stop, you—you can't take that stuff—they'll know. Someone will get in trouble for it. We can't do that."

"You're hurt," she argues. "I won't just leave you like this. Can I see the wound?" I release the pressure from my hand and pull it out from beneath my top, finding the skin gaping open. "You need sutures. You need a hospital."

"I can't. Please, Hali—I'll be fine. I can't go to the hospital. They don't treat Jews. The infirmary might help or might get rid of me. You have to understand what I'm saying."

"I'm getting something to wrap it up. Then I'll find you medical supplies."

"Hali," I say again, my voice weaker this time.

She leaves, an echo of her steps thudding down to the next floor. A door opens and closes, but it doesn't sound like the front door. Her heavy breaths are louder than her steps as she returns, carrying a folded bed sheet. She wastes no time in tearing the fabric into strips, using her teeth when she can't break through the stitching.

"Here we are," she says, her voice calm, soothing, and I'm not sure how. She wraps my hand as if she's done this a hundred times before, making small knots when the fabric ends to connect it to another thin piece. "Is that too tight?"

"No," I utter.

"I'll find my way to the marketplace square. The other nannies mentioned going there for supplies. Frau Schäfer won't be back until after noon. I'll be back before then. If the Kapo comes up, just try and keep your hand hidden."

"Do you have money?"

She shakes her head. "Don't worry."

"I am worried. You're putting yourself in danger and there may not be medical supplies anywhere in the nearby vicinity. Trust me."

"This time, trust me," she says, peering at me with a flare of pain in her eyes. "Tuck in your top. It'll hide most of the blood." She presses her cool hand to my cheek and kisses me, the gentleness of her lips contrasting the wild panic so clearly rushing through her.

THIRTY-TWO

HALINA

Gavriel needs a doctor. Without proper care, there are too many risks, and I saw where he lives—how filthy the place is—it's a breeding ground for disease. Without his hand, he can't work. If he can't work, he's of no use…It's easier to tell someone else not to worry, but that isn't what I feel inside.

Before grabbing Flora, who's screaming at the top of her lungs, I shove my way into the Jewish jewel room. "Forgive me, God. Forgive me. It's out of compassion." I spot a gold watch and shove it into my pocket. I take a golden brooch too, just in case. I take Flora back out of her crib and run downstairs, out the front door and place her back into her carriage before I take off in what will likely be the wrong direction.

"Where are you off to?" Rosalie's voice follows me. I stop, finding her sitting beneath the willow tree where Hilde, the youngest of the children she cares for, plays with blocks.

"I—ah—" I glance over my shoulder back to the Schäfer house. "I have to run to the marketplace square."

"She sent you on an errand there?"

"No, not exactly. Do you think you could point me in the right direction?"

"I'll grab the carriage and come with you," she says, drawing up the hem of her dress to stand. "Frau Weyman won't be home until later this afternoon, after school."

"Are you sure? I don't want you to—"

"Nonsense. I've been here long enough," she drones with a sigh. "She doesn't question where I take the children. We can't ever go far anyway."

I notice a subtle flare in her eyes, maybe a blend of rebellion and contempt. Or she's been doing this long enough that she's had time to accept this way of life. She has a good point. Still, I want to be home before Ada. If I can find medical supplies. I don't want her to see that I've managed to acquire them. She knows I have no money.

Rosalie is quick about getting Hilde seated in the carriage, leaving the quilt and blocks beneath the tree. "What's the emergency?" Rosalie asks once we've left the street.

I struggle to find the words, unsure how she'll react. "The man working in the attic—" I begin.

"The one who fancies you," she coos quietly.

My cheeks burn in response. The thought of Gavriel noticeably admiring me is both terrifying and palpitating. No one should know. And yet, I'd love to shout it out to the world. No one has ever looked at me the way he does, and what is there to look at? I'm a servant. "Uh, yes, well, he's gotten hurt quite badly and there's nothing in the house I can take without the Schäfers noticing it's gone. I managed to find him a clean sheet to wrap the wound, but—"

"How will you buy anything? Do you have money?"

I study Rosalie for a long minute, debating how I'll respond. "No, I don't, but—" Rosalie's eyes dart from side to side, likely worried to find out about my solution. I keep my voice down when I say, "Frau Schäfer has a room full of..."

"Jewish jewels," Rosalie replies in a matching whisper. There isn't a speck of shock written along her face. If anything, her expression tells me this is old news. It would be easy to assume the madam of her household has a similar room. She takes in a short breath and nods. "Good thinking. There's a place where we can trade those down an alleyway in the marketplace. I've seen it before while running errands."

We walk in unison down the rubble roads surrounded by rural pastures with overgrown shrubs and a peppering of old houses scattered in no particular order. Each façade a tan brown, or peach with red beaver-tail tiled shingles. Some of the houses look abandoned, others, occupied or taken over. Posters dangle from sidewalk posts, warning Polish citizens they're forbidden. In their own country.

The road veers into a wooden clearing between old, scattered trees, grass matted beneath overgrown weeds, and a path lined with rotting wooden fences that flounder with each gust of wind. The carriage wheels grind along, the sizzle whirring around us. "To think I used to love walking along small dirt paths. When I was a little girl my mother would take me berry picking every Sunday. It was my favorite time of the week. Then, when I grew older, I found nature to be a door to serenity. It all seems like it was in a different lifetime now," Rosalie says.

"Paths through the woods like this have always made me think there's a source of freedom on the other side. It's a place to run with hope of finding that place."

"It's a great place to hide," she adds.

"Is that right?" I press. "Was *hiding* part of the serenity you were seeking?"

"At one time," she says with a quiet sigh. "Until we became separated."

"We?" I ask, gently, wondering what memories she's surviving.

Rosalie flutters her eyes closed for a second and a smile touches her lips but fades just as quickly. "It's just me here in this horrid place, thankfully, but I'd like to think we'll find each other again someday." She shakes away the thought. "I've gotten carried away. Goodness. The bridge is just around the next bend. We aren't far now."

She's in pain. There's nothing worse than being alone and hurt.

The bridge sprawls out into the distance, the far end being swallowed by a patch of fog. The red cement walls scream of Reich territory, and I find myself squeezing the push-bar of the carriage tighter than before.

"We should slow down once we enter the square," Rosalie says. Her thoughts must match mine. It's clear by the people passing us how few Poles are left in this area. The distinct sound of German chatter echoes off the walls. The sense of comfort displayed by others, living their life as if there's nothing to fear or worry about, makes me wonder if they're in denial, or if they simply don't care about all the Polish citizens who have been displaced from the only place they've ever known as home.

I've been to this marketplace before when it was open to the public and not caged inside this restricted zone. It's been a while since, but Julia used to take us on the weekends to watch street performers. The wide-open square is outlined with rows of pastel-colored buildings, but everything looks different now. Even the signs on storefronts are unfamiliar. The people—they aren't Poles, made obvious by the volume of their German chatter, the forgotten sound of laughter, and the sight of children weaving their bicycles between the groomed trees. It's as if there is no war here, but to the Reich, this is just the sight of victory in the making.

"Come this way," Rosalie utters, taking a casual turn down a narrow cobblestone street. It's dark and musky, fog lingering from earlier this morning. The crisp sound of our footsteps follows closely behind us as we make our way down a couple blocks before turning onto another narrow street.

"Where we go?" Hilde grabs onto the side of the carriage and looks around the dreary street.

"We're just making a quick stop, little love," Rosalie says. "There. That man will take the jewels." She nudges her head toward a ragged looking man with wooden crates stacked up in front of him.

Despite the damp, cool air between these buildings, I'm growing warmer by the second, fearing this won't work. My hand shakes as I slip my fingers into my pocket and retrieve the watch and brooch. "How much for these?" I ask in German.

The man with an oily beard, heavy eyelids, and scruffy eyebrows, scoops up the items and brings them to his lap where he inspects them with a magnifying glass, his eyes flickering toward the corner once every few seconds.

A pigeon swoops by us, cooing as its feathers flap against the air.

"Birdy," Hilde shouts.

"Hush," Rosalie tells her.

"Fifty Zloty," he mumbles in Polish rather than German as he continues to stare at the watch. "Or thirty in Reichsmarks. Unless you're in need of a sack of potatoes and a pack of cigarettes. Your choice."

German Reichsmarks are worth almost four times more than Polish Zloty, but I'll be using this money in the pharmacy, likely being run by Germans now. If the collector doesn't assume I'm German, it could be cause for concern. A Polish woman wouldn't be walking around with Reichsmarks, and if she is, it could be a sign of theft. But the Zloty isn't desired here anymore and won't be enough to get what I need for Gavriel. It's a risk either way.

"Thirty Reichsmarks," I tell the man.

His eyebrows rise, a look of surprise before reaching into his deep pocket and carefully pulling out a small wad of Reichs-marks to count in the shadow within his overcoat. The man glances at Flora then back at me. "You didn't get this from me, you hear?"

"Yes."

Between a vacant bakery and a cobbler with a line of people standing outside the door, holding pairs of worn shoes, is the pharmacy. There's no window, just a narrow door, uninviting, and questionably unlocked.

"The carriages won't fit inside the doorway," Rosalie says, close to my ear. "I'll stay out here with the children."

Before this walk, I might have questioned if I could call this woman a friend, having not known her long. But I see now, we're the same in many ways. We just took different paths to get here.

I must be taking too long to answer as she reaches out and takes my hand. "I know what you're thinking, as you should, but you can trust me. We're both unwelcome in this city."

A small smile lifts my lips and I check Flora, finding her surprisingly asleep. "I'll go as quickly as I can."

"Not too quickly. Be confident. You have a right to be in there," she whispers.

No, I don't, even less of a right than she does. It's difficult to walk around, now knowing I'm Jewish and living as if I'm not. If I hadn't found that letter, I might not have known for years or longer. I could have a false sense of confidence, not knowing, or the truth might be written on my face now. I'm not sure.

I wrap my hand around the sun-warmed rusted door handle and push open the blue painted wooden door, the creak so loud I consider how many people have turned around to look at me walking inside.

With no windows, the inside is dimly lit by a few hanging lights. Tall wooden cabinets create a thin maze within the cramped space. Each cabinet is covered with smudged glass panes and each shallow shelf holds paper-labeled brown bottles. Nothing looks new. Even the names written on labels are wearing away. The air is thick with mold and mildew, or maybe old herbs, and the floor creaks with every step I take. In the back of the shop is a counter with a middle-aged man in a brown wool vest worn over a white buttoned shirt, the sleeves neatly folded up to his elbows. A woman in rags, hair in disarray, leans over the counter toward the man, speaking quietly as she slides a scrap of paper closer toward herself and simultaneously presses a small stack of coins away from her. The man places a bottle on the counter from a shelf beneath and she snags it quickly, dropping it in her coat pocket, then turns around and hurries out the door.

"Can I help you with something?" he asks me in German. Though the sound is garbled by the rolling carts and wagons outside the door, I can tell German isn't his mother tongue. I belong here, I tell myself, wishing my inner thoughts were more convincing...

"Yes, I'm looking for supplies to dress and disinfect a wound," I say, making my way up to the counter.

"You'll need iodine, bandages, gauze, and painkillers? Is there any sign of infection?"

"No, not yet."

The man locks eyes with me, as if he's waiting for me to give him more information. Or maybe he's wondering if I'm good for the products I'm requesting. I reach down into my apron pocket and shuffle the Reichsmarks between my fingers and place them on the counter. The man's eyes light up when he sees the Reichsmarks then studies me once again, likely piecing together the sound of my bad German accent while carrying their currency.

"Whatever thirty Reichsmarks can get me."

"Yes, of course. Come this way," he says, peering past me toward the front door.

I follow him along the back side of the store until we reach a door in the farthest corner. He pushes inside then pulls a string dangling from the ceiling to illuminate the storage closet he's stepped into. He swipes items from the shelves and reaches behind him for a paper bag that he hollows out before dropping the items inside. "This should be enough to treat a moderate wound."

I hand him the money and he drops it into his pocket while handing me the paper bag. "Thank you," I utter before turning around and making a quick exit.

Rosalie turns to face me as I step outside, her eyes wide with curiosity.

"I got what I need."

"Thank goodness."

Our brief conversation has caught the interest of a Gestapo standing nearby but behind Rosalie and I didn't notice him when I walked inside the shop. He studies the bag in my hand then shifts his gaze to the carriage. I tighten my grip on the paper bag and press Flora's stroller forward over the cobblestone. "Let's go."

Just as we turn the corner to the next block, the hairs on my arm rise. The sound of boots closing in behind us...I hold my breath. Waiting.

"You, ladies, wait there." The voice slings around my throat like a lasso.

"Speak German. Don't show your fear," Rosalie whispers.

"No fear. I'm not afraid." It's a lie.

"Officer, have we done something wrong?" Rosalie asks, her German far more fluent than mine.

He studies us and the children, stalling, my nerves fraying. "Where are you off to?"

"Back to our servants' quarters," Rosalie replies without pause. "We're running errands for the madams."

"Identification," he demands, staring past us as if he's lost interest and found something more important to focus on.

"The paper from the booklet, stating who you serve, will do," Rosalie whispers.

The breathy words catch the officer's attention, his eyes narrow with daggers as if I've cursed at him. "I'm new to the role," I mumble, trying to hide my poor German.

"I'm responsible for training her," Rosalie adds, handing him her paper. He scans it and returns it just as hastily.

My hand quivers as I dip my fingers into my apron pocket, retrieving the paper I slipped inside the day I set foot in the Schäfer house. With a long inhale, I struggle to steady my hand as I hand the paper over to the officer. He doesn't hesitate to take it from my pinched fingers, scans the information and stares as if puzzled by what he's reading.

THIRTY-THREE

HALINA

While the officer dragged us through a storm of panic and suspicion, it was several minutes before he confessed to recognizing Officer Schäfer's name but couldn't seem to recall where from. I don't think he knew the name at all. They seem to find pleasure in making us squirm. A shrug of his shoulders marked the end of his scrutiny before leaving us to make our way back to the houses.

Flora and I slip back inside the Schäfer residence, and I freeze, straining my ears over my pounding heart. The house is quiet except for the high-pitched whine from a moving saw blade upstairs. I stop by Flora's bedroom before going up to the attic and take the blanket draped over the side of her crib, knowing I'll need to set her down upstairs while I tend to Gavriel's wound.

I'm out of breath by the time I find Gavriel, and he's pale, struggling to push and pull the saw, and blood is seeping through the sheet-made bandage. I drop the blanket from my grip and kneel to settle Flora in the center. I pull open the paper bag and sift through the items, finding everything but the iodine —the one thing I fear he will need more than all the rest.

"No, no. He said he was giving me iodine. He made a show of giving me what he had."

"Maybe he didn't have any," Gavriel says.

"He's the one who listed it when I said I needed to treat a wound."

"I'm sure whatever you got will be enough."

"No, you need an antiseptic to prevent an infection. If that becomes infected—" I shouldn't be saying this all out loud. The last thing I want to do is panic him, but I'd been so relieved, thinking I had everything that would help him, and now I realize I am missing the one thing that will help him. I slap the paper bag shut and utter a growl. No iodine. How could a pharmacist leave out the most critical thing?

"Hali," he says, reaching his uninjured hand out to me. "Please, don't worry about me. This is more than I could have asked for—this is unimaginable, really. I wouldn't have thought any of this would be available at all around here."

"I'll find you an antiseptic," I tell him. "When's the last time the kapo was up here?"

Gavriel closes his eyes for a long second. "Uh—may—maybe a half hour ago."

I want to clean up the wound before I go on a hunt for antiseptic, but I can't leave it exposed, and I don't want to waste bandaging. "How's the pain?"

"I'll manage," he says, swallowing his words. He's not being honest. He's toughing it out and that won't do him any good right now.

"There's aspirin in the bag. It will help."

A small smile pinches at his lips. "More than you know."

"I'll be right back."

"Be careful," Gavriel says in a raspy whisper. His eyes don't leave mine, making me wonder if there's something else he wants to say, something hiding within the pain he's masking.

"I always am."

I lift Flora from the ground and take the blanket too, then hurry back down the stairs. I go into the washroom first and search through the medicine cabinet, which doesn't have much. The linen closet is next, knowing there was hair dye hidden behind the bedding. Flora tugs on my fraying braid and squeals.

"Shh," I tell her with a smile, hoping she picks up on my cheerfulness rather than nerves.

There's nothing else in here. I spin around, debating on the room of Jewish jewels or Ada and Heinrich's bedroom. I should doubt that there's antiseptic among the pile of stolen items, but with it being a hard commodity to come by, there's a chance.

I fix my gaze on the door to their bedroom, my stomach knotting, a voice in my head telling me no—a voice I have to ignore. I reach for the doorknob and step inside. The bureau is clean apart from a porcelain backed hairbrush, a handheld mirror and a small wooden jewelry box. Then I spot an ornate wooden vanity in the farthest corner. With a tall oval mirror carved with details of scrollwork and floral accents attached at the back of the tabletop, it's hoisted on top of outwardly curved bronze legs that bow in toward the feet. A worn floral-patterned upholstered bench with matching legs and a wooden frame is tucked in beneath the adjoining drawers. I doubt there's iodine in her vanity.

Still, I make my way over, peeking out the window to ensure there's no sight of anyone approaching the house from the front. The coast is still clear, but there's no saying for how long. Hastily, I open the drawers one at a time, finding combs, makeup, nail polish, hairpins, and a door key...

A door key. Heinrich's office door perhaps? I wouldn't put it past her.

I open the next row of shallow drawers, finding a stack of old photographs resting on top of a doctor's script, dated from a few years ago. I pinch the corner of the script and pull it out just a bit more, finding the medical office to be a women's clinic. I pull the script out to see what she was given.

Dr. Franz Rosenbaum
Tychy Women's Clinic
Tychy, Poland

—*Private and Confidential*—
Patient: Frau Ada Schäfer
Date: 17 April 1942

Rx_______
Luminal (Phenobarbital)
15 mg tablets

Summary: To alleviate symptoms of chronic insomnia and hormonal imbalance caused by Neurasthenia Nervosa. The patient reports restlessness and stress regarding failed concep-tion. Recommend quiet rest and avoidance of stimulants. Consider marital support.

Instructions: Take 1 tablet nightly before sleep for ten days.
Refills: 1 (by practitioner)
Signature: F. Rosenbaum

My hand trembles as I hold the paper, repeating the date: 17 April 1942 in my head. The words blur for a second as my mind tries to make sense of this. I shouldn't read more—but my fingers move before my thoughts steady. I reach down to replace the script beneath the photographs, tucking it neatly back into place. My stare lingers. It shouldn't. I've seen too much already.

A second paper by the same medical office—the top left corner is peeking out from below other papers.

No.

No. *Just leave it.*

Close the drawer. There's no hint of first aid in this mess.

I can't. I need to know...I slide out the letterhead typed paper from the pile and unfold it the rest of the way to read what's written.

Dr. Franz Rosenbaum
Obstetrics & Gynecology
Tychy Women's Clinic
Tychy, Poland

Patient: Frau Ada Schäfer

CONFIDENTIAL CLINICAL FINDINGS

Date of Examination: 28 August 1942

Fertility Evaluation – Results:
After several consultations and a comprehensive reproductive evaluation, Frau Ada Schäfer, thirty-two years of age, has been diagnosed with Secondary Infertility. The patient has previously carried two pregnancies to full term, a daughter born in 1933, and a second daughter born in 1938 without complications prior to delivery. Despite consistent attempts over the previous two years, conception has not occurred.

Suspected Causes:
Clinical infection post-delivery following the birth of the patient's second daughter. Scar tissue formation is likely the cause.

Recommendations:
No current intervention recommended due to health risks.

Physician's Note:
Frau Ada Schäfer shows moderate signs of emotional distress regarding these findings, particularly due to her husband's desire for more children. Marital counseling is recommended if available.

Dr. Franz Rosenbaum
12 March 1942

My blood runs cold as I question the reality of this diagnosis —of secondary infertility. This makes very little sense. Maybe the letter isn't even real? My stomach snarls and a surge of nausea seeps through me. Serves me right for snooping.

I shove the letter back where it belongs, and whip open the other drawer in search of iodine. A small metal box with a red cross on the lid grabs my attention immediately. I reach down and pull out the box, prying it open with my one free hand. Small, yellowed boxes labeled with a variety of first aid supplies, silver tubes of ointment, a small bottle of rubbing alcohol and a matching size amber bottle of iodine. Thank goodness. I grab the iodine, close the box and place it back into the drawer. My mind spins erratically. I just need to get back upstairs to Gavriel and put the rest of this dizzying information to the side until he's on the mend.

He's still so pale when I return and still trying to saw through his stack of wood. I wish he could stop. He shouldn't be putting any pressure on his injured hand. It'll only make it worse. "I found iodine."

"I don't want to know how or where," he says, his shoulders falling forward with worry.

"Never mind that. Unwrap the sheet bandage."

Once again, I plop the blanket down on the ground and place Flora on it, silently pleading with her to remain calm for just a bit longer.

As Gavriel unravels the bandaging, I see the wound has stopped bleeding thankfully. I grab the bottle of iodine from my pocket, untwist the cap, take his hand and— "Hold your breath and close your eyes," I tell him.

"I'm fine," he says.

I shake my head and tip the bottle over the open wound. "Don't squeeze a muscle in that hand or arm," I warn him, knowing that regardless of him saying he's fine, he's likely in excruciating burning pain.

"You're very bossy," he says, his voice croaking.

"Only when necessary," I reply, trying to maintain my placid demeanor, but I feel the blush rise anyway. He's watching me too closely. It's as if he sees more in me than I could ever hide.

I hold his hand out in front of him. The iodine needs to dry before I can bandage him back up. It never occurred to me how many different roles Julia had to take on as the head of the orphanage but whenever she was fixing up an injury, she would speak the process out loud. I'm not sure if it was just the way she worked or if she was trying to teach us how to follow her lead if necessary someday, but I suppose it worked.

We must be running out of time. I'm sure either the kapo or Ada will be returning at any moment now. With a damp cloth, I clean away the excess, the brown stain seeping down the sides of his hand and into the sawdust beneath us.

I dig back into the bag and grab the gauze and bandaging, moving faster now, knowing this is the last step. He'll be on his path to recovery at least. With the final wrap of the bandage, I smooth the cotton around his wrist, tucking the end into a fold. But my hands don't leave him right away. I feel the heat of his skin from beneath the bandage. He's staring at me, and for a second—I feel something unexplainable—something right. I didn't know that was possible. Not here, like this. "There," I say with a sigh.

He doesn't respond, so I look up at him, finding his eyes welling with tears. "Not even my ma would bandage me up that well." He tries to laugh, but his voice catches in his throat. "Actually..." He sounds nervous now. "She might even throw a little dirt in the wound and tell me to toughen up."

"I don't think she would say that to you now. I think she'd be proud of how strong you've become," I tell him. "Besides, I don't think anyone should have to be this tough." I wonder what my mother would say to me if I was hurt...Will I ever know?

"Where did you find the iodine?"

"Their bedroom."

Gavriel's eyes widen with horror as fear takes the place of the tears. "You were in their bedroom?"

"It's a treasure trove in there," I utter, thinking about the script and letter I read. The thought pulls my attention down to Flora, who's munching on the blanket like a hungry little bear, her knees tucked in beneath her and her hands pressed to the floor as she rocks forward and back like she's ready to hop away.

"She's certainly gaining some strength," Gavriel says with a chuckle.

"She is...Flora's almost a year old. Isn't that right, little princess?" I would like to think nothing makes much sense right now, but I'm afraid that's not quite true.

"You knew that, didn't you?" Gavriel asks.

"Well, yes, but according to a paper I came across while in her vanity, Ada was diagnosed with secondary infertility about sixteen or seventeen months ago," I say, trying to count the months out in my head.

A moment passes, both of us lost in thought. Me counting while he stares past me to the window. "Wait...no. That can't be right," Gavriel says.

"What do you mean?"

He closes his eyes and shakes his head, as silent words form on his tongue. "If...Flora is just about a year old—" He pauses again. "That would mean she received that letter when she was three or four months pregnant already. Surely a doctor would know whether she was pregnant versus suffering from infertility." Gavriel is clearly better with numbers than me, confirming my suspicion.

Is Flora a prisoner here too?

THIRTY-FOUR

GAVRIEL

Boom.

A rumbling thunderclap shakes me out of focus, and I come to realize I didn't complete even a third of what I should have today. It won't go unnoticed. Just as soon as I've swept up the sawdust and stashed away the brown paper bag with the remaining medical supplies away in the alcove, someone is blowing a whistle outside. We should still have another half hour before we're supposed to head back to Birkenau, but I thought it was odd that the kapo hasn't been up here in a few hours. I'm sure I'm about to find out why.

The sky is orange and gray, cloudy, with heavy drizzle, but it's daytime. There's still light and we've never returned to Birkenau in the daylight. I tuck the jacket of my uniform into my pants and pull the drawstring as tightly as I can to conceal the blood stains. I compress my fingers around the bandage, feeling a swelling burn and pull along the edges of the wound, but I need to keep my hand tucked into my sleeve as much as I can. Injuries are a sign of liability and first-aid supplies could be a sign of theft—both cause for punishment while working beneath an SS officer.

The house is as noisy as normal with Officer Schäfer home, Frau Schäfer, and all three children. The sound of bickering grows louder the closer I move to the main floor, and it's bickering between Isla and Marlene as well as the usual husband and wife spatting. One would think they would all look around and see how much worse their lives could be and appreciate the luxury of having a home and food on the table, but they're incapable of seeing the truth—all of them, except Halina.

I pass the kitchen, finding the four family members seated at the table and Halina standing complacently in front of the countertop, bouncing Flora on her hip while watching the family as if they're putting on a production. Her gaze sweeps to the side, spotting me, her eyes soft with concern. She chews on her bottom lip and I'm not sure she's aware because Frau Schäfer's seat faces her direction.

"Goodbye!" Marlene shouts.

I speed up, avoiding any trouble. Marlene shouldn't be speaking to me.

The racket of a chair scraping against the wooden floor stings my ears as I reach for the servant's entrance. "What have I told you?" Officer Schäfer scolds Marlene.

"She says hello and goodbye to everyone she passes," Frau Schäfer says. "She doesn't know the difference."

"Well, I know he's a Jew," Marlene mumbles. And with that, I close the door behind me.

As warm bread sits before them, ignored for the chance to have the last word, the bickering ensues as I amble around the side of the house to the meeting place for all prisoners. Adam, Benson, Rueben, and Kasia are already in their appropriate lines, but there are still a couple others missing from the other two houses.

Up next to Adam, I settle into the line and release a heavy breath. "How's the hand?"

"Not good," I reply. "You in one piece?"

Adam holds his hands out to inspect, flips them over then back. "Guess so," he says. I nudge my shoulder into his.

"What would a day be without a dose of your humor?"

He stretches an exaggerated yawn. "Bor-ing," he utters, long and low like a ship's horn in the fog. "While on the topic...Kapo Blockhead is back." Oskar. The man without a soul. "Sylvia is back too," he says.

I figured they'd been let go and killed. That's what happens when someone doesn't return to their position.

When Oskar steps into sight, a shiver runs down my spine, finding him battered and bruised almost beyond recognition. I can't imagine what they've done to him, or still, why they've sent him back. Is it to show us what our fate will be?

"Someone here—someone who works in the Schäfer house is responsible for a missing key, stolen food, and other objects I won't mention. One of you will confess before we leave this property," Oskar grunts.

My breaths shorten and numbness spreads through my veins. I could be accused of all but the key. Though I didn't personally take anything, I also didn't deny it when presented to me. Halina replaced the sandwich, and the other food was set to be thrown away. The pistol and ammo from Officer Schäfer's desk...it's still in their house, just in the alcove. I don't think they would have waited so long had they known about the pistol. What did I do? Why was I so stupid?

No one speaks up and if anyone were to, it should be me. If there's no confession, will they just remove all the carefully selected help they've assigned to these houses? I can't see them doing that, but I've seen far worse for much less. Any long-lasting prisoner at Auschwitz knows to keep quiet. There's a better chance of a lesser punishment if a person confesses.

"I'll say it again!" Oskar shouts. "Someone will fess up to these crimes before we leave."

I know what this is...they're reacting to what happened in

Treblinka with the prisoners revolting against the guards. This is what Schäfer was fighting with his wife about when he told her she needed to stay home all day and keep an eye on the house. Except it was the kapos he was worried about trusting. Now, it's the kapo blaming the prisoners.

"We know better than to take anything from the officer's house. Not one of us has a death wish," Adam says, his words brave, but his voice wavering as he holds his hands up in plea.

Oskar tilts his head to the side and steps in toward Adam. I should elbow him. Tell him to shut up and not say anything else. He knows better. We both do.

"You think you're pretty smart, don't you?" Oskar asks Adam.

"No, I'm not smart. I'm nothing," Adam says, his bravery gone.

"That's for sure. If you weren't such a screwball, you'd have gotten rid of the evidence you're lying about."

No. There's no evidence. He didn't do anything. He wouldn't.

I'm peering at Adam from the side of my eye, watching the lump in his throat bob up and down. He's nervous. He should be. I am too.

Oskar reaches into his pocket and pulls out a wax sandwich wrapper, a key, and a diamond bracelet. "These were found at the bottom of the tin watering can you use daily."

"No, no...I didn't—" Adam cowers, his denial more of a plea. His knuckles tighten by his side. Sweat trickles down the back of my neck as Oskar takes another step closer to him. He grabs Adam by the collar, pulling him off his balance. "No one else uses that water tin."

"I—I didn't steal," Adam utters with only a squeak of sound left in his voice. I don't know this side of Adam. He's so full of hope, it's made him fearless. I've never met a person like that. And now...now what?

A door opens and closes behind us and quiet footsteps sponge through the grass.

Shuffle, shuffle, shuffle.

All I can see is the look on Kasia's face, her eyes bulging, her bottom lip drooping. I have to say something, or do something... But I'm in a chokehold of terror. My silence is appalling. I can't just stand here. If they—if he does something to Adam, that will be on me. It will. "Please don't," I mutter. Adam turns his head toward me and I catch the look in his eyes, the emptiness, the unknown, the fear...I've seen that expression before.

* * *

"We shouldn't have been so confident we'll find food somewhere," I say to Jozek and Natan. "There's nothing in sight." Nothing but hungry Jews, some slumped against walls, others lying on the ground, curled into their coats along damp cobblestone.

"There must be something. We've only been in the ghetto for two days. We just need to find where the vendors hide," Jozek says, pausing to peek into a dark shop window. "Nothing."

"There's probably some type of black market under a building," Natan adds. "We'll need to ask around."

"If we ask the wrong person, we're done for," I say.

"I can read people. Leave it to me," Natan replies.

He can't read people. He just believes everyone likes him until they sneer.

We barely make it past the darkened, closed theater when two Gestapo officers step out from around the corner, blocking our path.

The dim orange light of dusk washes over their pale faces, sharpening their stone-like expressions. "Papers," one snaps at us.

What's the purpose of asking for papers when we're already caged inside a ghetto? They've already determined we're not worthy of freedom.

I instinctively move in front of Jozek and Natan, but Jozek grabs my shoulder and steps beside me. His grip trembles. "We have our papers," he says, reaching into his pocket.

"We're just getting some fresh air," Natan says, flashing the kind of smile he thinks can change their mind.

"No work permits?" the shorter of the two officers asks, glancing at our papers without reading them. He already knows we don't have them.

I look at Natan, ready to stop him, silently pleading with him to stay quiet. If I could elbow him, I would, but they would see.

"That's quite a funny story, actually," Natan says.

There's no story.

The officer grabs Natan by the collar and slams him against the wall. His body hits like a hollow pumpkin, the thud sickening. The sound of Natan's breath whooshing from within his chest, steals the wind from mine.

The officer draws his pistol and presses it to Natan's head. My heart cracks, my stomach coils. A fire ignites in my chest.

"We'll get them right away, officer," I say, holding my hands up in surrender. A plea. It's all I can offer.

Natan's pupils are the size of a gun barrel, wide and black with terror—a kind of terror I've never seen on my brother's face. Or anyone's face.

* * *

That look in Natan's eyes...is now in Adam's.

Click-clack. A metal slide moving forward and backward before...

Snap.

The chamber is loaded.

Click-tick.

Click.

Boom.

A startling explosive bang, then a high-pitched ringing zings through my ears.

Adam isn't as fortunate as Natan was that night.

My vision darkens and blurs, feeling the world spin around me, shake me around and thrust me off my feet. The sound doesn't stop...it just echoes in my head and strangles the air out of my lungs. A scream warbles and I don't know if it's mine or someone else's. I can't open my eyes...I don't want to.

THIRTY-FIVE
GAVRIEL

No. Adam. You're all right. You have to be. We're in this together, remember?

I can't move. As if I'm stuck inside a nightmare, one that burns through every limb of my body.

A click...then *boom*. The sound continues to float around me like a falling leaf, too soft for what it's caused.

I can't breathe in or out. I press my fists into my chest as if searching for my lungs. There's no sound. Not really. Something inside of me tears like paper ripped down the center, jagged and destroyed. Unmendable.

He said we were getting out of here. I should have believed him.

He should have been right.

This isn't real. It can't be. We've made it so far.

He would have said we were close to the end.

I can't go through this again. Losing my brothers, now Adam. I can't—

A boot to my ribs, sending me flying backward. "Get up!" Oskar shouts. "Get up, or you're next! There will continue to be a *next* until we find the person responsible for the stolen items."

He must think he looks like a hero to Schäfer. A Jew holding the Nazis' prey hostage for the ease of his hunting. An innocent man who had nothing but hope in everything he did. Blood gushes out of the back of his head as I clamber to my feet, my knees weak, my hand throbbing, a cold sweat steaming from my skin within the unwavering summer heat.

"You and you, take the body," Oskar says, pointing at me and Rueben. His words are muffled beneath the unrelenting ringing in my ears, but I understand what he's said.

Rueben and Benson look the way I must look, empty with shock despite knowing there's nothing shocking about this moment. I move to Adam's head and scoop my hands beneath his arms, waiting for Rueben to have a hold of his feet. He hardly weighs enough to be considered a grown man.

Adam's eyes are still open, holding on to the last second of realization that his life was ending. Everything inside of me shatters as I remember conversations of what he planned to do with his life. He spoke as if nothing could happen to him— nothing would happen to him. It was as if he knew he would walk back out of those gates unscathed, but he was wrong. Or, he was right, I suppose, but he'll be brought back in through the gates so his remains can be burnt into disintegration, undoing his existence. And for what? A threat to whoever is killed among us next?

"I wish we had survived this day together," I whisper. I know he didn't do what they accused him of. This is what they do when they're looking for a reason to get rid of someone. He shouldn't be dead. I shouldn't be carrying his lifeless body as the wound on my hand stretches with each step. Warm blood seeps around the bandage at my thumb and all I can think is that I could be next. But I can't let that happen.

Rueben's eyes are filled with tears and his chin trembles as he sucks in his cheeks, likely biting the insides like I am.

"What is wrong with your hand?" Oskar shouts at me.

"Nothing," I reply. I can prove it's nothing by continuing to carry my friend back to Auschwitz despite the pain writhing through my hand and arm.

"Doesn't look like nothing to me. Looks like your thumb has been gnawed off by a dog." He can't see my thumb, wrapped in the bloody bandage. I want to call him an idiot for suggesting I was bitten by a dog when I've been sawing all day.

"Where'd the bandage come from?" He's a traitor of the worst kind; a man who helps kill the innocent to keep his own name off a list. I hope he lives a long life—long enough to remember the face of every person who he helped disappear.

"There were a few in the toolkit in the attic," I say, sounding as if it shouldn't come as a surprise even though I came up with this answer earlier in case questioned. Regardless, injuries are common in construction. He doesn't need to know about the iodine or alcohol.

"It's a nick from the saw. I'm fine."

Oskar glares at me for a long moment, not with concern, but with judgment as if he's filing this acknowledgement away for a later time. "You'll go to the infirmary when we return. They'll decide." The silence that follows his statement can either be deadly or a mere escape from death. I don't know which of the two.

The walk is a blur. The gates to Auschwitz are darker than night, and just as we cross the threshold into hell, Oskar yanks me out of the line and throws me to the ground, pain radiating through my arm upon impact. The impact against my back knocks the wind out of my lungs and flickers of light flash in front of my eyes.

"Get up!" the scream bellows in German, the echo ringing between my ears.

A flash of Adam's face with a bullet hole in his head is all I can see. A friend who became as close as a person can get to a brother. Gone without warning. Someone grabs my collar and drags me, nearly strangling the life out of me. The backs of my boots catch on every rock and pit in the gravel. I can't talk. I can't ask questions. I don't know where they're taking me. I just want air to breathe.

Is someone taking me to the infirmary? Or does this have something to do with Adam? The decision seemed to be pre-planned. They needed someone to help carry Adam's body back. Now they're going to get rid of me too. I did take food. I did know Bea was missing, but I didn't know where she was. I took a weapon too. I know too much.

It doesn't matter what I did or didn't do. They don't need a real reason here. They only need fear. And right now, it's clear they're fearful of us becoming traitors like the ones of Treblinka. I'll never know why Adam was the spark that set them off, but by the dark entrance I'm being dragged into, I have a feeling I'm their next example.

A metal door opens. Then another. The temperature rises. The air becomes wet, sticky, and reeks of death. I can't see anything around me or make out where I am. It's so dark. Finally, I'm back on my feet for less than a second before two hands shove against my ribcage, pushing me into a group of people. Another metal door slams. This time in my face. I can't move. There are too many people around me.

"Don't even try to sit," someone grumbles. "You'll be dead within the hour. Welcome to a new form of hell—the prison inside of the prison."

THIRTY-SIX

HALINA

The tension between Ada and Heinrich has been palpable since he arrived home from his hours at Auschwitz, but as usual she's ushered her husband to the dinner table, with what appears to be hope that food would resolve his irrational anger.

Despite a mouthful of food, he's still demanding answers from Ada.

"Have you found the key to my office?" he growls.

"I already told you I hadn't. We'll find it, though," she assures him.

"And your private study, did you find out why that room was unlocked as well?"

"I told you I must have forgotten to lock it the last time I walked out," she says, trying to keep her voice calm, unafflicted by his growing rage.

"This is nonsense, Ada. You know very well those prisoners are stealing from us. Do you know what will happen if my commandant finds out that I allowed that to happen here in my own home?"

"Heinrich, you're being irrational. You're hungry, that's all. No one is stealing from us, dear," she argues as if he's being foolish. They deserve to be stolen from. I don't see what's so absurd about his assumptions, but I find it interesting that she's evading his accusations.

Heinrich scoffs and smirks then shoves himself away from the kitchen table. "Forget it." Heinrich drops his fork to his plate, the metal pinging against the hanging light. "I'll handle this myself, to cover for your indiscretions."

Handle this…What does he mean?

Heinrich storms out the door, into the yard. Ada's hand touches her lips, her eyes wide and unblinking. I can read the cues, the signs, the premonition.

There are claws around my neck, nails piercing through my skin, and fire breathing down my spine.

A gunshot.

Gavriel. He just passed through the kitchen.

My breath stops. I can't move. I can't even blink.

The house is trembling, the blast still shivering through the walls and my bones.

Who did Heinrich see? Who is he accusing? My mind spins like the blades of a windmill in a storm. I can't hold onto one solid thought. Except— *Please, not Gavriel.* Please, not him.

I strain to listen. For anything, a voice, a cry, a call for help. But there's nothing. Just stark silence as if the world is covered in a heavy blanket. It's the kind of silence that follows death.

Ice veils my heart and my hands press against my chest, needing to replace the warmth inside of me.

Mere minutes pass before Heinrich returns, his face patchy with red blemishes as he grips the back edge of the kitchen table chair, yanks it out further and sits back down before dragging its legs across the floor. Ada says nothing, she just stares down at her uneaten food. Isla and Marlene stare at their father with question and wonder but dare not ask what just happened.

Heinrich takes another few bites of his dinner then swipes for his napkin and holds it over his mouth, staring through his wife's head. Then he twists in his seat and looks in my direction. "Did you witness any of the prisoners in rooms they shouldn't be in?"

I shake my head violently. "No, Herr."

"And you? Have you been in any rooms aside from the children's, the washroom, and the kitchen?"

Again, I shake my head. "No. I read the rules."

"You agreed to the rules," he corrects me. "And by the way, I received confirmation today that your birth records were in fact located. I should have them in my possession soon. Perhaps we can find out who your parents are, together."

As if I'm not already on the verge of falling ill with their baby in my arms, Heinrich takes a shot at me, not with a bullet, but a threat that will ultimately bring me down. My religious affiliation will be on those papers if they're complete.

"Her parents?" Ada questions Heinrich.

"She has no parents. Didn't you know that? No confirmation on anything, really. I can't have a stranger working with our children in our house."

"Halina has proven to be trustworthy and good with the children," Ada mutters. "We need the help."

"What you mean to say is, she's trustworthy enough for you to go on a freedom spree in the mornings to run your unnecessary errands?"

I can't believe she just defended me to him. Why would she do that? It's clear no one who works in this house means anything to anyone.

But the people working in this house mean something to each other...The image of Gavriel falling to the ground following the gunshot is all I can see. My heart plunges deep into the pit of my stomach. He was just right outside.

Ada clunks her glass down on the table, a hollow thud rumbles through the air. "I can't sit at this table with you for another moment." She pushes her chair back, stands and storms out of the kitchen. The commotion sets Flora off, her cries rising despite my steady rocking. My joints lock like rusted hinges, and worse, my stomach cramps with terror at the thought of what just took place outside.

Heinrich dabs his face with the linen napkin on his lap, then dumps it on his place. "Papa...don't leave us too," Marlene whines, reading his gestures like a picture in a storybook.

"I forgot something important at work. I have to go retrieve it. Finish your dinner," he says.

When the front door slams shut following Heinrich's exit, I move to the table and take the girls' napkin-covered dishes to the sink. "Why—why—uh—" I clear my throat, trying to loosen the sensation of being strangled. "Go find something to keep you busy over there," I say, pointing to their play nook. "I—I need to bring your sister upstairs. I think she has a wet bottom."

I need to see if Gavriel is all right. How will I know?

"Is Papa going to come back?"

We should all hope he doesn't, but a child wouldn't understand. Not his child.

"Yes, I'm sure he'll be back. No need to worry now."

I rush upstairs to Isla and Marlene's bedroom, then to the window, wondering if there's anything outside to see—a body, as I fear the most. The sun is nearly set, but I don't see anything in the place where they line up every night. That doesn't mean anything.

With an unsettling weight on my shoulders, I make my way across the hall into Flora's nursery and pull the blanket from the side of Flora's crib and flutter it out to the side so it feathers to the ground where I can set her down before preparing a fresh nappy and pajamas for her. After sorting through her top drawer and finding her pajamas, I turn to the closet for the cloth diapers, but notice Flora is no longer on the blanket. I gasp and drop to my knees to look beneath the beds, making no mistake that she is not on the floor of this bedroom anymore.

I run out into the hallway and spot her on hands and knees, crawling away as if she's been crawling for months. I didn't realize babies just figured out how to crawl and take off. I hurry after her, getting my hands on her just as she's about to move in through the cracked opening to Ada's bedroom.

The moment I have her in my arms, I glance through the cracked door.

And I freeze...

Ada stands before her vanity mirror, clutching a bundle of linen collected at the center of her waist. She's pulling at it while adjusting straps beneath the back of her blouse. My breath hitches in my throat when realization strikes...it's not her stomach. It's fabric, wrapped in nylon. A false belly.

She isn't pregnant—she's only pretending to be.

"Ma!" Flora shrieks. I jump out of sight from the partially opened door.

"Halina?" Ada says.

My breaths stagger and catch in my throat as I stop short in the hallway and will myself to turn back around in front of her bedroom door. "Yes, Frau Schäfer. I'm sorry to disturb you. Flora's learned to crawl, and well—"

"How long were you standing at my door?"

She opens the door more, and stands in front of me, her eyes wide, face pale.

I shouldn't confess to standing there long enough to see what I did, though maybe she ought to know.

"Not long. I had just scooped Flora up to bring her back to her room."

"You're lying. I can read it all over your face."

Yes. I am lying. What choice do I have?

"What would you like me to say?" I ask, keeping my tone meek to spare myself any additional grief. Not like I'm facing any positive situation coming up here, but I wasn't looking for trouble tonight, not while wondering who was killed just outside the walls of this house a half hour ago.

"Nothing," she says, her voice wavering.

"Ma!" Flora shouts again, reaching her arms out to Ada.

My eyes narrow and not for the reason of trying to intimidate her, but because alarms are sounding in my head the longer I look at her, then down at Flora, and back at her. The papers I read today...the secondary infertility...it's real. Flora must not be hers either, just as Gavriel and I were thinking. She has made a baby a prisoner of this house. *Where is her mother?*

Ada doesn't move a muscle. It's as if her feet are glued to the ground. My feet are becoming numb the longer I stand here waiting to see how she's going to handle me—my awareness of her secretive life. She can get rid of me before Heinrich does. I might have just run out of my last thread of hope.

"Heinrich doesn't know," she says, her words quiet, but pointed.

What doesn't Heinrich know? Which part of what lie? Does he know Flora must not belong to them? How can someone get away with this? More importantly, how is it that I've managed to mistakenly witness her adjusting a fake stuffed belly strapped to her midsection, but her husband who shares a room with her doesn't know?

"What do you mean?" I press, afraid of what her reaction will be.

"He thinks I'm pregnant." Her lips purse as if she's bitten into a lemon. "If he finds out I'm not..." Her stare widens and loses focus. "You don't know what he's capable of." *Unfortunately, I do. It's all I can think about at the moment. What he might have just done to Gavriel.* "I have no one left. No family to run to. No friends who are truly friends. Just him, and our daughters that he would try and take away from me."

"Flora isn't even a year old," I say, my brows knitting

together with accusation rather than question. "Why would he expect you to be pregnant again already?"

"He wants a son now, and has...proven to me that he will do whatever it takes to make that happen." Her eyes well and her cheeks pucker. "I wanted him to stop. He was hurting me. I became his property, an object, no longer his wife."

She was looking for a quick solution to protect herself, but all she's done is corner herself where she'll never get away.

"He wants another baby, so you're pretending to be pregnant. How has he not noticed?"

"What is there to notice? There's nothing real between us. He thinks I'm pregnant, and that's all he wanted. We share a bed, but he hasn't looked at me or touched me since I told him I conceived."

"He will be expecting the birth of this baby in a few months. Then what?"

"You're right," she says in a breath. "I just don't have the ability to fix this overnight."

She must mean she can't find an innocent baby to call her own in one night. That must be her solution. Nausea reels in, and a cold sweat layers across my skin as I curl Flora tighter into my chest. How could anyone do something like this? To Flora?

"Are you going to tell him what you saw?" she asks, sniffling through her words.

It wouldn't matter if I tell him because as soon as he finds out I'm Jewish, nothing else will matter. "I'm expected to continue living here as a slave to you, taking care of your children for free, eating slop while you feast on warmly prepared meals every night in front of me, and protect your secret from your husband?" Your husband who just murdered another innocent person outside of his house. Possibly...Gavriel. The thought pierces through my chest like a sharp blade.

"I don't expect anything from you. I simply want to know what you plan to do."

I think back on the words in my mother's letter about the way my father treated her. I wouldn't wish that on anyone. I also wouldn't wish my lonely childhood on anyone.

Flora.

She doesn't deserve this orphaned life without knowing who she is or where she came from. There's no greater cause of loneliness. No one should have to go through that.

I think fast, wondering how I can spin this to my advantage. Wondering if this is my chance to get what I so desperately need. Freedom...

"I won't tell Heinrich your secrets, but in return you owe me. You're going to need to find a way to let me go. Not just me, but the man who has been dying of starvation and exhaustion while building your attic expansion—that is, if he isn't the one your husband just murdered outside tonight," I say, my final words sticking like molasses to my tongue. Another image of Gavriel being shot passes through my mind, his body falling to the ground, lifeless. *Please tell me it wasn't him.*

"I don't know who was—" she says with a break in her voice. "All right, I agree to your terms. But I need time. Nothing can change too fast. If I do anything rash, he'll suspect something."

"I don't have long, Ada," I say. It might be too late for Gavriel. Too late to learn I've secured something of a promise for our freedom. He may never find out. How can I live with that?

THIRTY-SEVEN

HALINA

I didn't sleep, not even for a second. My mind is numb yet racing with disjointed thoughts of the gunshot and finding Ada adjusting a fake pregnant belly beneath her dress. It felt deliberate, as if she wanted to be discovered. But why? Everything that happens in this house seems premeditated and poorly planned, too much to be a reality. Or perhaps I'm just realizing the world I've truly been living within—how much worse it is than I even thought, if possible.

I've been a nobody since the day I was born, not the best at anything, but not the worst. Smart, but not brilliant. Agile, but never graceful. A façade of strength with a fragile core. And now I'm here—accused of begging on the street, threatened with an arrest or become a slave here in this house. I'm being forced to stand in the grim shadows of the most inhuman beings on the face of this earth, tending to children who don't know they're being poisoned by lies. Acting like I don't feel the tension snaking through the walls of this house.

How did I get here? And why is my mind and soul in ruins just thinking about Gavriel? Plenty of boys came and went from the orphanage but not one of them caught my eye or sparked my interest because I suppose I looked at each of them as brothers. In school, I was avoided, stared at, forgotten. Because I came from a place without a name, not a home like most of the others.

Gavriel is the first person who ever looked at me and saw more than just a stray thread clinging to the first thing I could latch onto. I've never had anything to keep me grounded until he offered me a peephole of hope that maybe my entire life doesn't have to be centered around loneliness. I could be a part of something with another person, fit into someone's life as if I'm supposed to be there. It happened fast, but naturally, as if our connection is some unworldly plan, written in the stars. Our fate, though, we'll be kept from it as if we're undeserving, unworthy, and untitled. Even if that bullet took someone else last night, it's hard to avoid the thought that it's only a matter of time before it will take one of us.

There is no escape here, despite the bargain I've made with Ada. She might let me go, find a way to make it happen, but how far will I get before I'm caught again—as a Polish woman without proper identification on my person.

That isn't who I am though. If I were to give up hope, I'm not sure I would have made it this far in life. Every day of my life has been filled with pain and questions, wondering who I am and why I was left on a doorstep. Now, I have an inkling of an answer, but still no further information on if and why I was abandoned. It's as if there isn't a possibility of being whole in any capacity.

It will be the same with Gavriel. If he was... murdered last night it'll be the second time in my short life that I've had a chance to feel whole with someone, only for it to be taken away before it had a chance to become something more. It would feel worse than mere rejection and exist as a reminder why I should never let my guard down for anyone, ever, because I should learn to depend on myself, and only myself. Maybe that's God's plan for me—to live a life of solitude, protected by some inner strength I've yet to find.

Part of me wants to stay in bed, fake an illness, and tell Ada to handle her own children today. My imagination can be quite a tease sometimes. Though, I question what would happen if I stayed up here and never went downstairs today. Will she give her husband an excuse as to why I'm not downstairs, hurry him off to work then let me do as I please, just to keep me quiet?

I glance up toward the window, finding the moon still high in the sky. There won't be a hint of sunlight for at least another hour. I flick on the gas lamp on the nightstand and roll forward to reach into my suitcase beneath the bed, pulling out the folk-tale book that holds the truth of my life within its seams.

I flip through the pages, wondering if anyone ever read me these stories and why I don't remember any of them. I wonder if my mother had planned to read them all to me, maybe one before bed each night, teaching me about the world in the form of surrealism. I would have liked that.

At the very center of the book, the pages stop wavering, one sits slightly bowed on each side and I trace my finger along the water-color illustration of a dog, cat, and mouse all staring at each other.

A long time ago...

A dog sought out the king, asking for written permission to protect dogs from being mistreated by humans. The king agreed, granted the dog his request with a signature and handed back the paper. The dog knew he would need to keep this paper safe, so he turned to a clever cat he knew for assistance.

The cat quickly agreed to help, perhaps too quickly, and found a spot, hiding it in the eaves of its owner's house.

But it wasn't long before the dog catchers were on the prowl again.

The dog returned to the cat for the important paper. The cat went into the eaves of its owner's house, finding the decree nibbled to shreds by the mouse.

Angered, the dog began to chase the cat. The cat, in turn, chased the mouse.

Ever since that day, dogs chase cats, and cats chase mice.

And the king's signed paper was never to be seen again.

This was the story Gavriel told the girls the first day I was here. It seemed like an innocent way to distract them for a moment. But reading it now, I can't stop thinking about what it truly means.

We're the dogs, desperate for protection, hoping something as feeble as a promise can save us. The cat, like Ada...who isn't helping anyone due to loyalty, but instead, guilt or fear of being exposed. And Heinrich? He's the mouse, quietly destroying, chewing through the remains of decency. The king is just an illusion of justice offering a promise never meant to last. Even a king would be powerless in the face of the Reich's false promises.

Is that what Gavriel was thinking too? It can't be. I refuse to believe it. There must be something deeper I'm not understanding. Why would he have told the girls this tale?

None of the prisoners arrived this morning.

I look out the window, straining to see around the bend to the path they take to and from Auschwitz, but there's no one in sight.

Gavriel isn't returning. Neither is Adam, or Kasia.

Heinrich has already left. The girls are scooping up mouthfuls of oatmeal that Ada prepared for them, and she's now pacing around in circles holding Flora, cooing at her, poking her nose and smiling. Nothing is right.

"You look ill," Ada says to me, brushing by, her words vacant of any true hint of care.

"The people who had been working in this house—" I say, peering at the sink where Kasia should be. "They're human beings like you and me. They have families and purposes, a future and a past, but it's as if you don't see that, do you?" I wouldn't have spoken to Ada this way yesterday, but now I know her secret.

"I don't tell my husband who to remove from this house," she replies simply.

"Mama, that isn't really true, is it? Remember the last nanny you didn't like?" Isla infers, tilting her head to the side with perplexity in her eyes.

"Isla, that isn't what happened. I'll remind you again to keep your nose out of places it doesn't belong."

"Or you'll lose it!" Marlene shouts with a cackle.

Ada's lying, and Isla knows it. She reports back to her husband. She chooses to treat them as if they're something less than human—less than most animals too.

"Who did he—ki—" I stop myself from completing my question with respect to the girls, but surely, she notices the desperation leaking out over my words.

"Do you truly think that's a question I would ask him?" she replies. "You can't be serious." I figure a man like Heinrich would take pride in his kills, brag about them.

I can't help but look at her as if she's just grown a second head. "My heart is hemorrhaging with torment because of your husband." Because I'm not like you who claims to have not one but two beating hearts in their body, I'd like to say.

"I'm not told where or when people come and go," she says with a careless shrug.

"Is the builder coming back?" Marlene asks.

"What did I tell you about the people who work in this house, young lady?" Ada scolds her daughter.

"To act as if they're ghosts," Marlene utters.

I step in front of Ada as she's ambling toward me again. "I need to know if he's alive," I whisper.

"There's no way I can promise to find that out," she says, her voice pitched an octave higher than usual. I glare at her for a long minute until my stomach knots from disgust and nausea. It's likely the only honest thing she's said to me all morning.

Chasing the cat won't fix anything.

THIRTY-EIGHT

HALINA

August 20, 1943

The heaviness in my chest has yet to subside. Each morning, I wake up with a dwindling amount of hope that Gavriel will return to continue working on the unfinished attic expansion— if he's alive. Am I foolish to believe it wasn't him who was shot?

"*Worry is a symptom of love,*" Julia would say to us.

She's right.

There hasn't been a word mentioned about any of the prisoners between Heinrich and Ada. I've listened as well as possible. Not only do I know nothing about Gavriel's state, Adam and Kasia's too, as none of them have returned in the last two weeks, but I imagine Heinrich will have my birth records in his hands any day now, if he doesn't already.

The walls might as well be closing in on me.

While making my way down the rickety steps to the second floor, I tie a second knot around the ribbons of my apron, finding that the fabric is beginning to overlap along my back. I can't complain about the lack of food, knowing how much worse it is a short walk from here, but Ada leaves me with scraps for meals that don't come close to filling up my shrunken stomach. When I touch my cheeks, I feel the harsh line of bones. Even my eyes look larger because of the sunken spots above my cheeks. I'm a frightening sight in the mirror so I avoid my reflection at all costs now.

"Kasia, this isn't warm enough," a scold bellows from the kitchen.

Kasia? She's been gone since that night...Not one of them had returned. She's back, though.

I hurry toward the kitchen, my pulse thumping, a knot in my stomach.

The thought of passing by Gavriel in the hall like we had most mornings shoots a tremble through my limbs. But the disappointment of an empty hallway steals the glimmer of hope. I'm scared to look outside and possibly spot Adam, which is a terrible thought. I don't want anything to have happened to him either. But Gavriel...

If I see Adam, I'll know the likelihood of who took the bullet. My hand rests on my chest as I walk into the kitchen, my jagged fingernails pinch into my flesh as I try to compose myself.

Ada is slowly pulling a chair out from the kitchen table for herself and when she turns to the side, I notice the bump in her belly has grown overnight. A noticeable change.

"Oh, Frau Schäfer, allow me to help you. You must be growing uncomfortable. Just look at you..." I say, taking the chair from her hand and pulling it out quicker. Pregnant women aren't made of glass, and that's how she's acting.

"Yes, yes, I seem to have popped overnight," she says, and her words almost sound believable, but I know the truth.

"It's a boy," Marlene says, bouncing up and down on her knees at the table. "I've already guessed."

"Is it?" I question her. "How do you know?" Because I'm willing to bet, the baby is a small stuffed pillow.

"I just do," she says with a proud smile.

"She does have a curious sense of intuition," Ada follows. The urge to roll my eyes and sigh is strong.

I spot Flora in her cradle in the girls' play area and turn for the bottles to prepare her breakfast. "Flora should be moving onto solid foods," I say as I grab the powdered milk.

"She doesn't have an interest," Ada says. "Plus, it could be dangerous with her delays."

She hasn't offered her solid food in the time I've been here, and Flora drinks down her bottle in a matter of minutes. I'm hard pressed to believe she would have no interest in solid food, and I'm not sure it would have a negative effect on her delays. If anything, the solids might help her sensitive stomach.

"I gave her some potatoes the other day and she liked them," Isla says, as if it's not a big deal.

"Why in the world would you do something like that? What if she had choked? She could die, Isla. How many times have I told you never to put anything near the baby's mouth?"

Isla doesn't reply and her face doesn't flinch. She's becoming one of them. Emotionless, heartless, and unaffected. Isla, at ten, has seen people die. She might think it's a normal part of life—to witness someone take their last breath.

Knowing Kasia is just a few footsteps away from me and I can't ask her the only question on my lips is draining me of all my patience.

Sylvia, the female kapo, walks in through the servant door and stops just before entryway of the kitchen, staring at Kasia while she cleans the pots and pans used to make breakfast. I try not to make it obvious when I glance at the kapo, but she must know what I so desperately want to know too. I'm so close to the answer and yet, I could stand here like this all day between these people and never find out. All I know is, if he was all right, he would be here.

Instead, there is an invisible wall breaking up this room

between Kasia and Sylvia and the rest of us. I shake up the bottle for Flora and make my way over to her cradle, finding her asleep. She shouldn't be asleep at this hour. Or, she hasn't been asleep at this hour until this week. Ada must be giving her an extra bottle in the middle of the night, one she makes up specially. I lean over her and gently place my hand on her chest, having a hard time deciphering if it's moving up and down. I close my eyes for a brief second and release my breath when I feel her chest move.

"I'll let her sleep," I say. "She's been awfully tired at such an early hour this week."

No response, as expected.

Isla finishes her breakfast, drops her spoon on the table, shoves her chair out and takes her books out of the kitchen to get ready for school.

"Fix Marlene's hair. It looks like...a rat's nest," Ada says, gaping at me, making it obvious she's comparing Marlene's hair to mine as she glowers at my disheveled braid. I haven't been able to take very good care of myself here with the limited resources I have access to in the house.

Marlene isn't finished with her oatmeal but places her spoon in the bowl. "I'll go get my hairbrush and ribbons," she says, her words quiet, her eyes pained as she heads upstairs.

Ada pushes her chair out from the table, stands, and checks a thin golden watch I've never seen on her wrist before. I can take a guess at where it came from. "I have somewhere to be this morning. I'll go say my goodbyes to the girls now."

I want to ask her if she's heading to the doctor for a prenatal check-up but instead, the words burn my tongue. I've gone back and forth shifting my blame from her to Heinrich on this horrific decision. He has no idea she's not pregnant, but she's made up the story to keep him in the dark so she doesn't appear worthless to him. He wants children and she can't bear any more. I don't understand the worth in staying with a man like

Heinrich. She'd be better off without him. Regardless, I likely won't be here when he finds out the truth, and I'll forever wonder how her lie turns out for her.

The moment Ada's feet touch the stairwell, I turn toward Kasia but stop myself from making the mistake of speaking to her in front of Sylvia, who's still staring at her like a hungry snake. I decide to go back to Flora's cradle and sit with her so I'm not standing on the brink of their invisible wall.

I watch Flora's eyes glide up and down beneath her thin eyelids. "I hope you're dreaming about something sweet," I whisper, sweeping the back of my hand down her cheek.

The open and close of a door startles Flora awake, her blue eyes flashing open. Her lips form an upside-down *u* and those pretty little eyes well with tears before I can scoop her up into my arms.

I rock her from side to side, moving around in a circle that reveals Sylvia has left. Kasia is alone in the kitchen. I continue rocking Flora gently, taking long strides toward Kasia.

"Kasia," I call out in a breath.

Her head turns sharply, her eyes finding mine as mine find bruises and cuts all over her face that I couldn't see when she had her back turned toward us. She looks as if she's been beaten multiple times, with some of the bruises yellowing. "Are you all right?" It's not the first question I want to ask her but it's the first one I must ask.

She shakes her head and sniffles.

"Can I do anything for you?"

She shakes her head again, more fervently this time, her fear palpable.

"Kasia, who was killed that last night you were here?" The question sounds like a puff of steam exhausting from a tired iron.

She swallows hard, as if it's a struggle then presses her hand to her throat. Her eyes close then clench shut. She swipes her hand at her nose and sniffles again. "We were all punished," she utters, "but—"

"Halina," Ada calls from the stairwell. In response, I step away from Kasia, terrified of getting either of us into trouble for speaking, which would be my fault, just as whoever got killed two weeks ago was likely because of something I did too. "I need you to handle Marlene's hair. Now."

"Yes, Frau Schäfer," I call out. "Coming now."

Her heavy heels ascend the staircase, leaving me with another moment to extract the answer from Kasia.

"Please tell me," I whisper.

Kasia stares out the arched opening of the kitchen, her eyes unfocused as if she's replaying the scene in her head. Her bottom lip falls then she directs her focus on me, staring for a long second—one I don't have. One, she doesn't have either.

"It was the man who works—"

The servant door swings back open, Sylvia returning with a storm brewing on her face. I hold Flora close to my chest and bounce her gently. "Come on, sweetheart," I say, making it sound as though I was only handling Flora rather than pleading with Kasia for one simple answer.

"Snap to it. You have laundry to do," Sylvia shouts at Kasia.

THIRTY-NINE
GAVRIEL

A muffled shout ending with "X3742," rings in my ears. X3742. X3742...

A bolt clinks; too much clinking. Metal grinding against rusty metal, a high-pitched screech drilling into my head. A hand grabs the collar of my shirt and yanks me forward, a reminder of the first night I was blindly thrown in here for a crime still unknown.

I stare through the darkness, making out less than an outline of a figure in front of me. "Jozek? Is that you? My brother... you're here? Is Natan here too?" My voice is cracked and phlegmy, but he must know it's me. Am I really here?

* * *

"Shh, just a little longer," Jozek whispers. "Silly baby Natan will never find us here. He's a-a-afraid of the cellar." Even as the oldest of us three at nearly thirteen, I don't like it down here very much either. No one should. The creaks from upstairs sound like ghouls dragging their feet across the wooden boards, and it smells like sweat. I think I might be the one sweating though.

Jozek laughs, the sneaky laugh he makes when we're doing something we shouldn't be. He and Natan begged me to play hide-and-seek. I should have known better. It always ends with someone getting into trouble.

"Maybe we should spare him from this place. He's only eight. I know a spot outside where we can hide. It's a great hiding place," I say, trying to convince Jozek to play fairly.

"Come on, Gav, you're not talking about Pa's toolshed that hardly any of us can fit inside, are you?" Yes. There aren't many places to hide when we've spent entire summers doing nothing but hiding and seeking.

"Jozek," I say, using the deeper voice I've suddenly developed. "Let's be fair."

"Your fairness will rub off on me someday I suppose. But it's lame. It is. Come on, quick before he counts to a hundred."

* * *

The memory of the cellar in my childhood home fades. The tender nostalgia of my brothers pales. I'm left with only the ripe stench of rot and sewage and the clatter of metal slabs.

"Shut up," a man barks, his syllables spewing spit on my face. "Or I'll put you back in there." A gloved hand tightens around my wrist and a handheld light blinds me despite the stark darkness surrounding me. "Move it, trash." A fist jabs between my shoulder bones, shoving me forward, forcing me to stumble, then jerks backward. The fist drops but another grasp of my wrist follows, pulling me until my feet hit a barrier. "Up!" The shouting continues, right in my ear. With every bit of strength I can muster, I lift my left foot, my toe hitting the barrier twice more before finding a flat surface of the stairs. I try to look behind me from over my shoulder, wondering if it really was Jozek I thought I saw. There's no one behind me though. The others are still in the cell, the door now closed again.

My limbs cramp with each movement and nerves tremor through me, a warning I might collapse before I reach the top of the uneven steps I'm navigating. A light much brighter than the one that just assaulted my eyes, bears over me so heavily I can't keep my eyes open as I move closer.

How long had I been down there? Am I alive or dead? I've promised myself I'll stay upright, not give in. Visions of Halina, her smile, the small moments of joy she's given me, the craving for her has been worse than for food. I need her warmth even after I've likely sweat every bit of water out of my body. She must be wondering if I'm dead too.

A warm draft of air washes over my face, leaving me with the stench of waste, mildew, and decay. The breeze chokes me, drawing out a dry painful cough that heaves my body forward. Again, I try to open my eyes, but the daylight burns, aches, weighs more than I can withstand.

My clothes drag underfoot, damp, soiled, and gaping at my waist.

Another flash of Adam's face whips through my mind, the shock within his wide eyes as I lifted him from the ground. I didn't do enough to save him. My mind is like a broken carousel, life spinning around me with no way to make it stop.

The gravel kicks up and slips into the gaping sides of my boots, adding more pain to each step. The camp sounds different, more buzzing from the electric wired fences and fewer cries of pain. A siren rings in the distance but I'm not sure from what direction. Prisoners limp by or carry themselves past as if their only job is to keep themselves upright, and they stare at me as they do. I'm the vision of a consequence. A consequence that had no cause. I'm sure the sight of me is reason enough for no one to step out of line. I catch a stare, holding on to it as if the world is moving slowly around us, a conversation full of questions pooling in the man's eyes. Can he read the answers in mine?

Maybe the dirt is the same, the wooden buildings are just as dark, the people still sick and weak. It's me who's different, the sun burning my eyes, the air cooler than the inside of the cell, the burning ash less acidic than the bile inside.

A whistle in the distance repeats over and over, striking a sensitive nerve in my ear, causing a pain to shoot down my neck. Dogs bark too, one at a time, as if they're conversing.

The hand still around my forearm releases, but not without swinging me forward into the side of a building. "Latrines. Five minutes," the growling voice says.

I squint through my swollen eyes and lift my hand in front of my face to block out the sun as I drag my feet toward the opening of the latrine. The wooden walls envelop me as my head wobbles like a puppet hanging from a string. A man is sprawled out on the ground in front of me, alone. No one else is in here at this hour, whatever hour it is. It's not dark, and the sun isn't rising or setting. At least, I don't think so.

I grab the rim of the trough, feeling a searing burn in my hand, forgetting about the wound that's still masked by the original bandaging. I don't know if I've been healing or if the wound has grown. I've had no means to see anything or care for myself in any way. The pain isn't a good sign after the many days that have passed since the injury. I switch hands and twist around, hovering over the man and pressing against the aching joints in my legs to reach my fingers to the man's neck. His cold neck.

His neck without a hint of a pulse. Someone just left him here. Dead.

My stomach quavers from hunger and nausea, and the thoughts compiling in my head. I need his pants. I won't be able to work in mine. I won't be able to work at all right now.

How can I consider something so awful? Taking away a man's dignity when he's already lost his life. I pull myself back up and crank the water nozzle adhered to the pipe, tilting my head below the weak stream of warm water. My head grows heavier as the stream runs over the sides of my face, useless as watering a dead plant in the middle of a desert. A groan escapes my throat, and my eyes roll back into my head as I imagine being home, soaking in a tub—a thought so far gone, I've almost forgotten the sensation. I gulp in the water, mouthfuls at a time, as much as possible before the nausea becomes unbearable. With a few splashes of water on my face, neck, and chest, I glance back down at the dead man.

"I'm sorry. I wish I knew your name, so I could politely ask if it would be all right if I borrowed your pants?"

Please God, forgive me.

* * *

I was hoping today was a Sunday, the one day we don't work, but it's not, or so I should assume since I'm being led down the familiar path to the SS residences. I still don't know why I was locked up. I'll never know. The others locked in there with me said they likely needed to blame someone or people for something and I was one of them. No crime is necessary to end up in a cell. What was the purpose if they're keeping me alive?

It doesn't make sense. I don't know what I've done wrong, if I did anything wrong, that they know of.

Will Halina still be there?

Will she recognize the mess of a man I've surely become?

My face is swollen—I can feel it with every blink and breath. The top of my uniform reeks of manure and it's falling off my shoulders. Who would want me in their house?

"You better pull yourself together before stepping back into that house. Officer Schäfer expects the completion of his attic expansion by the end of the month," a kapo tells me, a man I've never seen before. I should just be glad it's not Oskar, that bastard. "That's in ten days."

How should one pull themself together after being locked

in a dark prison cell with God only knows how many others, but enough that no one could sit or lie on the ground? We leaned on each other for support, and the support came from the outer layer of people next to the walls. We fought over scraps of food like rats in a sewer and water was dumped over us as if we were a fire they were trying to put out. No toilet. No light. Just daily beatings. Pain, hunger, and images of people dying.

What if they got rid of Halina while I was gone? I would never see her again. Then again, even if we do see each other once more, I'm almost sure it will be a temporary encounter. This is likely just a continuation of my punishment.

I wish I had gotten a chance to spend more time with her, live a real day with her. As if the persecution against innocent people isn't horrible enough, I ache for what could have been if life had been normal, even a semblance of normal. Though, perhaps we would never have met then...

We step off the path surrounded by the woods, over the very spot where Adam's body had fallen. I clench my fists in silent agony. We walk around the back of the house toward the servant door, over the stone patio with pockets of puddles. I struggle to step over one, nearly losing my balance that still isn't right yet. I catch my reflection in the swirling water, finding a disfigurement of a person, wondering if it's me that's disfigured or an illusion from the water.

"Go on inside," the kapo says.

Why is he being so much kinder to me than Oskar was? Is he real? Or am I seeing him like I thought I saw my brothers. If Halina's here and she walks past me, I guess I'll have my answer. Maybe I'm stuck somewhere in between living and hell.

I step inside and glance into the kitchen, toward the oversized clock on the wall, marking the day at ten in the morning. Kasia isn't in the kitchen, and I don't know what's become of her. Did she suffer the same punishment as me? I hope not.

The stairs are painful and higher than I recall, and I use my good hand to do the heavy lifting along the banister. A momentary sense of relief washes over me when I reach the bedroom floor but then I remember the awful stairwell to the attic and how much more painful those will be.

"And so, they were married, and they lived happily ever after. The end."

Hali? I glance around making sure no one else is around before limping toward Flora's bedroom and poking my head inside.

She's still here. Or am I imagining this?

"Hali?" I call out in a whisper.

I watch her playing with a stuffed bear, moving it from side to side as Flora rocks back and forth between her knees and hands. But she doesn't turn toward the door—toward me. I don't know if my voice came out at all...

FORTY

HALINA

It's been two weeks since I heard Gavriel's voice, but it drifts through my mind like a feather dancing along a breeze. I hear him when I'm falling asleep at night and sometimes right when I wake up, and I'm with him in my dreams most nights too. Except, I always wake up to the painful reminder that a dream is just an illusion devised by the hungers of my heart and mind. I've never thought about anyone so much, so distractingly, so frantically in my life. I've known nothing other than learning to live without love, but that was before I knew what it felt like.

Flora's resting on her tummy in the center of her room, reaching toward me with a groan. "Come on, sweet girl, come get the teddy bear," I coo at her, bouncing the bear next to me, encouraging her to push herself up on her knees to crawl again. But she's staring at the doorway, a small droplet of drool forming on her bottom lip, her eyes wide, and a gleeful sound of what sounds like a "hi" from her sudden interest in trying out words.

I sling my focus toward the bedroom door, and an icy chill trickles down my spine. Are my eyes deceiving me? I push myself up from my twisted posture, needing to move in closer, to see if this is real. If *he's* real.

I've been hearing his voice. I could be seeing things now too.

But this sight, it's too hard to imagine. It's heartbreaking.

I bite the inside of my cheek to keep myself from reacting.

"Gav..." I utter, his name a question in my throat.

What did they do to him? It's as if they just wanted to keep him alive but with only a few last ragged breaths to sustain him. The sight of him holds me hostage. Every fiber of muscle and fat has depleted, leaving his skin draping over his bones. He clenches his hands by his side, a tremble quaking through both fists. A dirt covered bandage is still wrapped around his hand, almost as if it's part of his skin now. His shirt clings to his hollowed chest, his cheeks cave inward, and he's covered in dirt, only the mere whites of his eyes being the source of light coming from his body. He tries to stand up straight but grabs a hold of the wall.

I don't want him to see what I'm thinking, the shred of my heart tearing deeper into my core. He needs strength from me, not sorrow. I can hardly take in a full breath as my lungs constrict. The last time I saw him, he was tired and hungry, but he was whole—he was all right. His hand was wounded, but he was fighting through this battle like a warrior. This isn't the same man.

I push myself up, my legs unsteady, numb as I move toward him. "My God," I utter, gently pulling him into the room—to me, feeling the heaviness of his frail body. I wrap my arms around him, holding him so tightly, I'm not sure either of us can breathe. "I thought—I was sure you—" I gasp for air, the relief and pain swelling into one overwhelming sensation.

"I know," he replies. "I'm still alive, somehow, and—" he takes a few short breaths. "I didn't think you'd still be here. I didn't think I'd ever see you again."

"What happened?" It's a short question with an answer I might not be prepared to handle.

His eyelids blink so slowly, I'm not sure he has the energy to explain. "They—uh—they put me in a cell, underground, with nothing, not a place to move, or sit. It happened after Adam was shot, after we arrived back at the camp."

"Adam," I say, realizing it was him. He was shot. I heard his death.

My stomach aches and my knees strain against my weight, trying to offer support. For Adam. For him.

He closes his eyes and keeps them closed for a long moment as if he's trying to recall memories. "I was interrogated about Adam and the other prisoners who work in the Schäfer house, then forced to agree to things that didn't actually happen. They told me I was a traitor, but I wasn't. I don't think. I don't understand what that means. I'm a Jew. How can I be a traitor?"

His words are slurring and I'm not sure he's going to be able to stay on his feet much longer. I'm not sure how he even made it here like this. "All right, hush," I tell him, brushing my fingers across his stubbled cheek. "You've been through too much. It's too much."

It's too much. I feel sick. I might get sick.

I reach for breaths that have escaped me, trying to anchor myself in this moment, remember what I'm doing, who I am, and why I'm here.

Flora.

I check on her, finding she's sitting upright, holding the teddy bear, staring at us. "Can I help you up the stairs?"

"No. I—I'll get up there," he says, his words saying one thing and his body saying another.

"Well, I'll—I'm going to find food and wet rags."

Gavriel nods his head weakly. "You can't steal anything from the house. They'll kill us like they did Adam, and I don't think he even took anything."

It was me. I'm the one who has been taking things for the sake of keeping Gavriel alive. "That's why they killed Adam?"

"It's my fault," he utters.

"No. It's mine. It's all mine. You can't take this blame. I will tell them it was me, so they know how wrong they've been in punishing you."

"No," Gavriel growls.

Flora peeps out a quiet cry.

"It's okay, princess," he whispers. "I'm not mad. See?" He tries to smile but his bruised face is swollen in too many areas beneath the hollowed caves of his cheeks.

"I won't argue with you, but don't argue with me either. I will not stand by and watch you—" My throat tightens, and hot tears burn the backs of my eyes, a sensation so foreign to me.

"I'd rather starve to death than chance something happening to you," he argues. "I don't want you to go through that." The sound of his voice fades before his last word.

The thought of Ada's guilty demeanor and the fear in her eyes after catching her with her fake pregnant belly...the strength I garnered in that moment...I need it all back now.

"Ada is going to help us escape. I'm going to get you out of here. I am."

The confusion weighs over his eyes, his bottom lip hanging. "What? How—"

I nod sharply. "It's-it's true," I utter, my words stumbling. "Two weeks ago, the last night you were here, I caught her." The memory of her adjusting her fake belly nauseates me still.

"Caught her?" he says before swallowing hard.

"Yes. Her pregnancy is fake. It's an impossible situation, something she couldn't lie her way out of. In return, she agreed to let us go. She said it would take some time, and I haven't pushed her because all I could think of was you—whether you were still alive. If I'd see you again. How I could find you. Then I'd assume the worst and the cycle would start all over again.

But you're here now, you're alive—and I'm collecting on her agreement."

Gavriel blinks slowly, transfixed with confusion. "Fake?" he repeats, clenching his eyes as if struggling to think. "The-the... secondary infertility diagnosis, it was true..." He peers over at Flora as the scattered pieces fall into place. "And Flora..."

I nod, a grimace tugging at my chin, aching. "She's been lying to everyone," I confirm. "The dates from the doctor's letter and Flora's age don't line up, and neither does the rest of the uncovered information. Heinrich has no idea, and if he finds out, she's finished. She's going to give me what I want. What we need. Or—or I'll—I'll ruin her."

"I don't..." Gavriel's stare is unbreakable against mine. I'm not sure he's taken much of a breath in the time I've been speaking. It's a lot to take in.

"Go upstairs. If you need help, I will help you up there. Otherwise, I will go gather what I need to help you get better. Then we are getting out of this place, together. Do you understand?" Each word is pushed through clenched teeth, my eyes are wide with the fiery anger writhing through me, failing to understand how anyone could treat someone as innocent as this man the way they have.

Gavriel's eyes squint and his chin trembles. "Yes," he whispers.

I feather my fingertips to his cheek, worried about causing him any pain. "I'm here with you. You'll be all right. I promise."

"I'm scared," he says through a weak breath. "What if she's setting a trap? I don't know why they even sent me back here. What good am I now?" He looks down at his failing body and shakes his head.

I don't trust Ada. But I can't waste a chance to escape. "If it's a trap, I'll make sure we aren't caught. We're going to get through this. Together." I feel the promise deep in my chest, but I know the risks involved too.

He reaches for my shoulder and wraps his arm limply around my neck, struggling to pull me in closer. I'm careful as I touch the side of my face to his chest and loosely loop my arms around his waist. His heart is beating so hard against his ribcage, I can feel it inside of me. I need to be here, with him, like this, in his arms, he in mine. We're supposed to be together as one. I can feel it in every bone in my body.

I don't know when I began to feel so much passion and longing for this man, but it happened somewhere between the rush of risks, the way he coos at Flora, and his relentless faith in me. I couldn't have planned for this, not in a million years, but here we are. In the impossible. The two of us.

He presses a kiss to the top of my head and takes in a long inhale. "You're the one who saves me—how lucky am I?"

Left in a state of shock after Gavriel limps down the hallway toward the attic's staircase, I'm numb all over. I've never seen someone so brittle and battered, and to imagine the pain he must be enduring...I should have found a way to help him sooner or at least be more careful about how I helped him. I replaced the sandwich. I doubt she'd even noticed the gold watch and brooch was missing, not with how many items she's stolen.

My guilt has been eating at me, the entire time he's been gone. I need to make sure this plan goes off without a hitch.

I hold Flora closer to my chest, her heartbeat calm, peaceful and unknowing of the ugly world around her. With a quick glance out of Flora's bedroom window, I make sure Ada isn't anywhere in sight. She doesn't come back to the house until after the girls come home from the school, despite the continued arguments between her and Heinrich about leaving the house unattended.

Since the revelation between Ada and me, I've been stashing non-perishable food away in my suitcase little by little each day. There wasn't a plan yet—not without knowing what had happened or what was happening with Gavriel. I just knew I had to be ready for whatever came next. No one else has been here but me. Not one of them returned until today. Not even the kapos. I was the only one she could blame for stolen food, which wouldn't help her.

However, as many days have passed without a word about our agreement, I fear I might need more bargaining power at this point. More proof. Something to seal the fate of this agreed escape.

"We're going to take a little trip into Mama and Papa's bedroom," I whisper to Flora.

"Ma!" she shouts.

"Shh," I hush her.

I go right for Ada's vanity, my footsteps restrained but determined as I make my way across her pristine polished floor. A tremor jolts through my hand as I pull open the top drawer on the left, and the movement awakens the remnants of her expensive perfume, still lingering from earlier in the morning, blunt and rosy. I suppose roses can mask any façade. I shuffle through the top papers quickly, my fingertips skimming through the small pile of photographs on top until I find it—the prescription, and secondary infertility diagnoses papers.

A floorboard creaks in the hallway and my veins fill with ice and stone. I shouldn't be afraid of this woman. I shouldn't have to be. What if it's someone else, though?

With nowhere to run, I wait for another sound, but there's only silence to follow. I fold the papers in half and shove them into the pocket of my apron, hoist Flora higher up on my hip and make a run for the door.

No one is in the hallway. I'm not sure what I heard.

With only a moment of hesitation, I yank open the closet door and grab a few folded rags. In the washroom, I soak two of them in water, wring them out, and head for the attic stairs. As we reach the top step, Flora's chin lifts from my shoulder and I twist to see what's captured her attention. A look of confusion tugs at her blonde brows and she lifts her hand over my shoulder. "Ma-ma." My pulse hammers. I turn, half-expecting to see Ada, but the hallway is still. It's empty and just as silent, but Flora's tiny hand is still pointing.

Whoever saw me or is watching me from afar—I don't care anymore. I'm done being patient. I need to get Gavriel out of here before it's too late.

FORTY-ONE
GAVRIEL

This isn't going to work. My legs can hardly hold my body upright. I'm staring at the saw, still wondering what reason they had to send me back here. Is it so they can say I died of natural causes? Why would they care? They don't. It's clear. My knees refuse to straighten, and I move closer to the wall so I don't collapse in the middle of the unfinished floor. I try to lower myself down with ease, but still lose my ability to control my weight, or lack thereof, I suppose.

Halina bursts in through the opening of the room, coming from her bedroom. Her arms are full with Flora, food, rags, and papers. I've come to realize when Halina becomes nervous, she overthinks, overdoes it, and jumps in headfirst.

"What is all of that?" I ask, my words garbled from the ache in my jaw. I don't remember the last time I was beaten but it wasn't long ago. I can feel that.

She doesn't respond. Instead, she searches around the wooden enclosure intently for something...

"Where's the bag of first aid supplies?"

"In the alcove," I murmur, trying to lift my arm to point

toward the corner on my right. "There in the hidden closet on the left side."

Her eyebrows stitch together, confused as I didn't show her the small hidden closet. At least, I don't think I did.

She places the rags and food down next to me, a not-so-perfect portrait for Officer Schäfer or Frau Schäfer to walk in and find me with.

Halina keeps Flora in her arms and searches the corner for the seam in the wall. She finds it rather quickly, slides her hand down to the floor and curls her fingers beneath the cracked opening, dislodging the plank door. She moves inside and stares to her left, at a blank canvas of a wall for anyone who doesn't know I placed a small closet within the wall. It takes her a minute but again, she finds the seam fast and has the square door open within a few seconds.

The crinkle of the bag grows louder as she backs away and closes the panel, and the alcove panel too and makes her way to my side, lowers to her knees and plops Flora in my lap. "I'm going to pretend as if I didn't see a stolen pistol with a round of ammo in your hidden closet, but only for now. We might need it soon."

My eyes open wide, forgetting I had put Officer Schäfer's pistol in there. Of all the things the prisoners have been blamed for stealing, he never mentioned the weapon again. "I forgot I—"

"I was sure Ada was hiding it, waiting for the right moment. I believe she has the key to his office sitting right on her dresser. It was just one of many things I saw in her room."

The overload of information makes me dizzy. Flora is on my lap, but I can't do much else than rest my head back against the wall.

The sound of a can cranking open followed by a whiff of something salty with a pungent tang and a faint scent of spices hits my nose. My stomach lurches with rage as if it's grown claws that are scraping along my insides.

I twist my head to the side, watching her bend the tin top into a curved scoop before handing it to me. "Be careful. I have nothing to smooth the edges of the tin with," she says.

Flora twists herself around and presses her hands to my stomach, watching me as I try to get the first bite into my mouth. She must catch a whiff of the canned meat because she reaches up toward Gavriel's chin.

"Oh, Flora, you just had applesauce an hour ago," Halina tells her. "Don't be rude, little lady."

I get the first scoop into my mouth and my nerve endings go wild, pinching and smarting, but when the sensation subsides the taste is the most wonderful thing. I feel it travel down my throat. A frenzy takes over and my mind tells me to be careful, but I'm starving. The only thing I'm careful about is not slicing my tongue with the tin.

"All right, let's just give your stomach a rest for a minute. You can't afford to get sick," Halina tells me, taking the can from my hand. I don't release my grip at first, like some kind of mad animal, but then I find her eyes, her soft gaze, and I let go.

She takes one of the rags and gently presses it to my cheek, wiping away whatever grime has settled into my skin. My eyes close, searching for heaven in response to her touch.

"I dreamed about you, even with my eyes open."

The motion of the damp rag slows and her knuckles feather across my cheek. "You don't have to dream now. I'm here."

I reopen my eyes, finding her gazing at me with wonder. "You might need to pinch me then."

She leans in and gently touches her lips to mine, our noses glide side by side, and I grasp her waist, needing something to hold on to as a frenzy of nerves fizzles within me. My lips begin to tingle after a short moment and she pulls back, staring up at me from beneath her dark lashes. My heart might leap right out of my body. Between heaven and hell, I'm lost here with her.

"I need to check on your wound now," she whispers, her breath fluttering against my cheek. "I'll be quick." I allow my head to rest back against the wall, the weakness of everything burdening my strength.

A tingling sensation covers every spot of my exposed skin and when I look at my good hand, the one branded with my inked number, I realize I haven't been able to make out the number clearly in at least a month. My skin is clean.

Halina has my other hand resting in hers as she's unpeeling the first layer of the bandage. It isn't long before she stops— before my skin pulls. "It's bad. Isn't it?" I ask, my voice sounding a bit stronger.

"No. You'll be fine." If I hadn't spent time studying the varying inflections in her voice when she talks to me, I might believe her. She's worried. Her voice goes up higher in tone when she's worried while saying everything will be all right. She takes another damp rag and begins to sponge the last layer of bandaging over my skin, pressing with a little pressure. "What are your brothers' names? I realized I had never asked you."

"Jozek..."

She's trying to distract me as she peels the bandage away from the wound it's adhered to. The burn radiates up my arm and I press my head back into the wall and close my eyes. "You have two brothers, silly," she says.

"And," I say, swallowing hard, "Natan."

"Who was the troublemaker of you three? I'm guessing it wasn't you, being the oldest."

I huff a small laugh. "Natan. Always in good fun, but never a dull moment. A prankster always looking for his next dangerous adventure and a way to make everyone laugh."

I swallow again, trying to ignore the pain searing through

my entire arm now. "Natan wanted to be like Jozek for a while, but announced he was funnier and better looking than Jozek by the time he turned thirteen. The two of them are hard workers, loving, and care too much about too much. They were my greatest friends, the best brothers." Hearing myself speak about them as if they only belong in the past brings a knot to my throat. Before I was taken from the rest of them, I never pictured a day in my life without them. I wish they were here. But, also, I don't. I hope they're just somewhere safe.

"So they're just like you," Halina says with a smile I can hear.

Air hits the flesh around my wound, then the wound itself. "How's the wound?"

"It'll heal completely. You'll be fine," she says with no higher pitched inflection, which I'm grateful for.

She saturates the wound in disinfectant then unravels clean bandaging from the leftover roll. Once the bandage is secure, she drops the supplies back into the paper bag, rolls up the top, sets it to the side and hands the can of meat back to me and moves Flora from my lap to hers. Before I scoop another bite out, I find Halina's beautiful stare, the kindness emanating from every part of her. "I've never been in love before. Was always too busy for that. Maybe I just thought I was too busy. If you had come around, I would have dropped everything to occupy myself with only you."

"Gav," she utters.

"Weeks, a month, whatever it's been here and there, feels like an entire lifetime. A day is like a year. It does. And if it were true, it would mean I've been falling in love with you for years. I'm nothing special, and have nothing to offer you, but love—I can give you an endless amount of that."

"Is it the canned meat?" she asks, holding back a smile.

"What else could it be?" I tease her. "Hali, I thought about giving up too many times these last couple of weeks. I fought to keep myself alive because I needed to find my way back to you somehow. And now that I'm here, I'll never let you go. I need you, and I've never needed anyone or anything—until now."

"I've always needed someone," she says, her gaze falling to the floor between us. "I just didn't know how much. I tried to convince myself it wasn't you who was shot and killed, but I was drowning in doubt, day after day, while still trying to hold onto a sliver of hope." Halina takes a shallow breath as her gaze rises back to mine. "Even my heart swells and pounds, flutters ripple through my chest and stomach, and my cheeks grow hot whenever I'm near you. Love never existed for me. But these feelings—this twist of fate...It must be love."

Halina wraps her arm around Flora and shimmies closer to me, her back against the wall, her shoulder touching mine. I lift my arm and lower my hand to her leg and lean my head gently to the side of hers.

Flora takes the opportunity to scoot off Halina's lap then climbs back up on mine, crinkling whatever papers are in her apron pocket. The little wanderer is intrigued and shoves her hand into the pocket and whips a small pile of folded papers out and holds them in the air like a trophy.

Halina takes them from her hand before she scrunches them up. "What are those?" I ask, returning my attention to the can of meat.

"Proof," she says. "Our ticket out of this place."

"You really think it's enough? Will it work?" I ask.

"I hope so." She flattens out the papers and folds them back up neatly, an index card slipping out from the center. It floats to the ground like a feather, landing face up on my outstretched legs. "Oh, I don't know what that is. I didn't see that when I grabbed the other two papers."

I drop the tin scoop into the can and lift the card to get a closer look. "It's a prisoner intake card," I say, studying it further.

ABRAMOWICZ, BETTINA.

Born 03.01.1919 – Katowice, Poland

Polish | Widowed | Mother | Jewish

Accompanied Children:

Flora Abramowicz (Two weeks old on arrival)

Transport RS-239/xx|Arr. Auschwitz: 14.09.1942

Assigned No. 4562—(Bettina)

Infant, Flora: blonde hair, blue eyes — placed in medical quarantine, unnumbered.

Noted: Mother restrained at intake due to distress

[KONZENTRATIONSLAGER AUSCHWITZ]

I place the can down at my side, my eyes blurring over the typed information.

"What is it?" Halina asks. "May I see?"

I pinch my lips together and stare down at Flora, still plucking at the pocket of Halina's apron. "This is Flora's mother," I whisper, pressing the card to my heart. "Bettina Abramowicz. She came with a two-week-old daughter—Flora. Then they were separated. It's all here in black and white. Flora isn't the Schäfers' child, Hali. She was stolen. And Ada kept the proof." The picture of the woman on the top left—she has Flora's eyes and heart-shaped lips.

FORTY-TWO
HALINA

"You know, when you've lived in this house for as long as I have, you know which stairs creak and which don't," Ada says, clomping heavily into the unfinished attic room.

Her appearance in the doorway has grabbed a hold of my heart and is choking me with it. Why am I afraid? Why does she think she has something on me when I'm the one who can ruin her entire life with less than a few words?

"Ada," I say, keeping my voice calm, unaffected. "What are you doing up here?" She might be looking for Flora, her stolen child. Stolen. This poor baby girl. Her mother might still be alive and she's without her. She's been without her all this time. Ada is cold and unloving, or does a good job of appearing that way, and all a baby needs is unconditional love. Maybe that's why she's done nothing more than cry, until recently anyway.

"Why do you have my daughter up here with a—" she stares at Gavriel and age lines pucker across her forehead, the sides of her mouth sag as if an uncontrolled reflex. "Good God, what happened to you?"

Her daughter. My God. She's lost all her marbles if she still thinks I could believe Flora belongs to her.

And then to act as though she's clueless about what happened to Gavriel...She knows he's been gone for two weeks. What does she think happened to him?

"Your husband," Gavriel replies. "He had a hand."

Ada knows what Heinrich does. A look of surprise won't do her any good. She spots the empty can of food next to him and panic is still driving through me. I'm playing a dangerous game with her and she could change everything in a matter of seconds in ways I can't imagine.

"I took that can of food, so if you need to shoot someone, shoot me," I say, directly, staring her right in the eyes. If there's anything I've learned throughout my life, it's to make direct eye contact with whoever I'm afraid of. It will take a sliver of their strength away, not much, but enough to make me feel like I have some control.

"Shoot you," she scoffs. "I don't handle weapons, dear. That's my husband's job."

"Well, tell him to shoot me then. Either way, my blood will be on your hands."

"Halina," Gavriel grumbles.

"I should have figured there was something going on between the two of you—I'm not sure what you see in him, or what you see in—her," she says glaring at me.

"Ada, let's stop the games. I need to pick up the girls from school, and while I'm gone, I need you to come up with a definitive escape plan. A real plan. Not a maybe-later plan."

Ada's voice strains. "I told you...I'm working on it. These things take time."

I glance at her fake protruding belly. "Do they? Because you're running out of time."

I step in closer. "If you're worried about your husband finding out the truth about your pregnancy, you'll be far more concerned if he finds out the child you've been parading around as your perfect Aryan daughter was stolen from a

Jewish woman in Auschwitz. You've been drugging her. Hiding her delays and pains while dressing her in pretty outfits. Flora is a Jewish child, Ada. A Jewish child stolen from the camp. Imagine what your husband would do if he knew."

The color drains from her face.

"I'm already going to hell, Halina," she says hoarsely. "Nothing you say or do will change that. It's too late for you to weasel your way under my skin. I know what I am, what I've become, and who I sleep beside every night." She straightens her posture and narrows her eyes. "But I still decide how this ends. Not you. Besides, we're hosting a dinner in the back tonight. It would be impossible to make this work while so many people are here," she says.

"That's not my problem," I reply, the heat and rage taking over, speaking for me.

"And for your information, Flora is not stolen," she says, her voice catching in her throat. "Can't you see the resemblance between us?" She's faltering, and she knows it's over.

"Unless you bleached this child's head like your own, then no. I don't see it. What about Isla and Marlene, both of whom have dark hair like you and your husband? Wouldn't you prefer a resemblance to the children you did birth?"

"Children can have different hair colors," she snaps. "Surely you know basic science." Her defense is weak, and she knows it.

"Jewish children can have blonde hair too," I add. "Surely you must know a little something about genetics. Plus, I have proof of everything you've done."

Ada's eyes bulge, and her bottom lip trembles. She has no words left to fight with. The cracks in her façade are beginning to show. The lie about her pregnancy was one thing but stealing a Jewish child to call her own...that's a death sentence, and she knows it.

"I should've kept my doors locked," she mutters. "Heinrich

was right. I've let too much in." Her stare sharpens, the tremble subsiding.

I don't know if I've pushed her too far or if I'll actually see the light of day again after today, but I won't let this woman do to me or Flora what her husband is doing to her—what my father did to my mother, or what the Reich are doing to my people.

My breaths quicken as I realize I could be putting Gavriel in more danger despite him not speaking. "Look, growing up as an orphan, I learned how to read people at an early age—it was a form of survival for me. I can read you, Ada. You were raised properly and had a nice life and made some wrong choices that have gotten you here. Your marriage has dissolved into nothing more than ash. You're afraid of your husband but can't fathom the thought of giving up the life he provides you. You have no one. You're all alone. You yourself said it—you're stuck, and I'm sorry for you, and those beautiful little girls. There is goodness still left inside of them, and it must have come from you."

The smile lines at Ada's lips sink even deeper and her chin trembles. "There is?" she whispers.

"Yes. There's still time to make things right for them. They have a mother. Be their mother—perhaps the mother you have or had."

"Have," she utters beneath her breath.

I nod. "Will you allow us to escape tonight?"

"Yes," she says. "Yes, but there's something I need to handle first."

A cutting chill slithers down my back.

"Handle?" I ask, the words biting at my stomach.

"Yes." Ada turns around and leaves the space, her heels catching on uneven boards on the way out. A sniffle follows her down the stairs.

My chest nearly collapses in on me and I press my hands to my thighs to hold myself up and take a deep breath.

"I've never seen anything so brilliant in my entire life," Gavriel whispers. "I will never forget the bravery—the strength, the courage—I just witnessed, never in all the days of this life I have left."

"I could have gotten us killed. I don't know when to stop sometimes. My anger—I'm so angry, Gavriel. For what you've been through, and Flora. The others who work under the same conditions on this street. Every person in that prison, and in this continent. I can't control it..."

"Stop. I'm a firm believer of dying by trying. It isn't worth it if you don't fight."

"While I'm going to get the girls, I need you to keep that pistol on you, just in case...We can't trust her. She's living in turmoil and desperation, and God only knows what she must handle before tonight. So please, will you keep the gun on you?"

He glances toward the alcove and nods slowly, unsurely. I don't know how he'll have the strength to get away tonight, but I'm not sure he has another day left in him in these conditions.

"We need a plan. A good one," he says. "That woman can only help us get so far, and Flora—"

"We need to take her with us," I finish what I assume to be his thought.

He nods, agreeing, then reaches over to Flora, placing his hand gently on her back. "You don't know where your real Mama is, do you, sweetheart?" he utters to her, his head tilting to the side with a pained look of regret.

I rest my hand on his knee. "I've been thinking about this relentlessly since you left, and even before I knew for sure that Flora didn't belong here, this need to protect her..." I press my fist into the ache in my chest. "I can't ignore it."

"Flora needs to be part of our plan. Without a doubt," Gavriel says without a moment's hesitation.

"We must try to find her mother. Flora doesn't belong here.

If we can't find her mother, I'll take care of her. I'll make sure she always has a home. I won't let anything happen to her."

A glimmer of shock warps along Gavriel's dreary expression. He swallows against his dry throat and nods. "The poor thing. Her mother—from Auschwitz, she must be—"

"What?" I press. "Must be what?"

Gavriel's bottom lip quivers and he closes his eyes for a short second before shaking whatever thought is clawing through him. "Nothing—she—she just must be worried sick. That's all. But I won't let anything happen to her, or you. And as for a home—if a home is what you want, what you need, I promise to make sure you have one. I'll build it with my own two hands. You deserve that. I'll make sure you have a home."

"You'd build me a home?" I lose track of the urgency in our moments, baffled by a promise that no one should ever promise another person. He's hardly able to stand upright. He's starving and weak, and on the verge of—No, I can't think that way. We have to make it through this. It's a chance.

"A perfect home with a barn and a swing, a front porch. Whatever your heart desires," he says, making it sound as if it's no harder than handing me a freshly plucked dandelion.

A chance is all we need.

And a home is the one thing I've always dreamed of.

"I think I have a plan to go along with Ada's..." I say.

FORTY-THREE
HALINA

I'm already out of breath from my racing pulse and I haven't made it to the weeping willow tree where Rosalie and Celina are waiting for me to go pick up the children from school. The wheels of the carriage crackle over the gravel as I approach the others, and they're watching me as if waiting for me to tell them something. Maybe it's my guilt, knowing I have a chance to leave, and they don't.

"You're paler than a bedsheet," Celina says. "Are you all right?"

I shake my head and swallow hard. Neither of them pushes me for an answer, knowing we're too close to the SS houses and need to move away from the street before I say any more.

"What's happening?" Rosalie asks as we turn onto the road lined by just trees.

"I'm not sure where to start," I say, my words phlegmy and sticking to my throat. "There's something I haven't told you."

"Well, you're making me nervous now," Rosalie says.

"What is it? You can trust us," Celina adds.

What if they don't trust me after I tell them what's about to happen? I'm leaving them behind. We all know it's each person for themselves in a time of war, but it doesn't diminish the fact that I've always been a person who helps others. Without certain life connections, like a family, it's easier to put other people first and worry less about myself—or so I've come to realize.

"I found myself in an impossible predicament with Frau Schäfer. Before I go on, you should know her life choices and current situation is not one I believe she planned for but rather ended up within. And while I won't defend or forgive her actions, I do believe the woman is scared for her life and the life of her children."

Celina stops walking, stops pushing the carriage. "What predicament? What happened?" Rosalie stops as well and turns to face me, waiting for me to go on.

"Frau Schäfer is not actually pregnant. It's an act, for everyone around her, including her husband and children. I walked in on her adjusting the fake belly she's had tied around her mid-section."

By the look of their paling faces, I assume the three of us must look similar now. "Dear God. For what reason would she do something like that?" Celina asks.

"I don't know much about the officers you live with or the relationships between them and their wives, but Officer Schäfer is brutal, aggressive, irate, and cruel to his family. From what I gather, he wants as many children as possible to support the Aryan ideology, specifically a boy now, but Frau Schäfer suffered from secondary infertility after Marlene's birth due to complications post-delivery. I think—no, I know—Flora was taken from a Jewish mother at Auschwitz."

Both Rosalie and Celina slowly drop their gazes to Flora, despondence settling into their expressions. Rosalie lifts her hand to her mouth and Celina presses her palm to her chest.

"What—I'm afraid to know what you're planning to do..." Celina utters.

"I made an agreement with Frau Schäfer," I say, peering over my shoulder to make sure no one is coming up behind us. "With Gavriel returning in his dire state today, I'm not sure he'll make it another night in the prison." His trembling hands, the bruises. He's so weak and frail from starving and torture—the grim look in his eyes is etched in my mind like bleeding ink on paper. "I must act swiftly. I told her that she needs to find a way for us to escape tonight. If not, I threatened to inform her husband of all the lies she's hiding. It would ruin her life."

"Are you mad?" Rosalie asks. "You can't make a threat like that to the wife of an SS officer. She'll find a way to have you killed before you could even open your mouth to Officer Schäfer. What were you thinking? And the officers' dinner party is tonight, being hosted in the Schäfers' backyard. We're all supposed to be there, working."

Celina reaches her hand out and places it on my shoulder. "Oh, sweetheart," she says.

"Ada is a weak, battered woman. She knows how to growl but I'm not sure she has teeth sharp enough to bite. And, I don't have a choice. This plan might be Gavriel's only chance of survival, and not just his, but mine too...Officer Schäfer has been eagerly searching for my birth records and appears to have acquired them. Once he gets his hands on them, he'll find out I'm a born Jew, something I didn't know myself until a few weeks ago."

"You're Jewish?" Celina whispers.

"Yes, I am," I tell her, pressing a smile into the corners of my lips. I've never wanted anything more: to finally know who I am and where I came from. Now I do.

Celina's hand is still clutched around my shoulder and her grip tightens. She opens her mouth to speak but hesitates or stumbles on the words forming on her tongue. "I'm—" she says, pausing to clear her throat. Her nails pinch my flesh a bit before she continues speaking. "I'm Jewish too," she finally says, her eyes bulging with fear as if I might judge her. Whatever reaction she sees on my face, it's nothing more than shock. "But I've done things to hide any traces of the truth...forged papers, an erased past—no history. I'm me in the moment, and that's all I can be."

"We need to continue walking or we'll be late for the children," Rosalie says, her voice strained and her eyes wide.

The three of us continue in silence, behind the quiet mutter of Celina's two young ones.

"How did you end up here of all places?" I ask Celina.

"I was in the process of joining a convent to solidify the masking of my identity—sinful, I know. Upon entering the convent as a postulant, my lack of knowledge of the Catholic faith, despite my desperate attempt to learn all I could in a short period, became obvious to the others, and I was shortly thereafter released from the convent. The mother was kind enough to let me go in private, but it turned out SS Officer Drexel happened to be standing nearby in the church gardens—close enough to overhear my somber release. Needless to say, I didn't have much say in what took place after that. I'm just grateful the truth about my Jewish faith is still unknown to them. I'm sure I would have been sent directly to Auschwitz rather than given a labor position at his home."

I rest my hand on Celina's back. "We all do what we can to survive."

"Our lives aren't so much different from each other's," Rosalie adds. "We try to find hope in the grimmest of places, never knowing how we'll end up, but it's all we can do to get by, right?"

"I'm sure neither of you will think fondly of me if I manage to get away. If I could take you with me—"

"Don't think like that," Celina says. "We're all in a save-who-you-can situation, and sometimes it's only ourselves, and sometimes another person who needs help becomes lucky in the process, but we all need to find our way, and you shouldn't feel remorseful about that."

This isn't who I am. I will always feel remorse if I live long enough to have such a feeling. "I do hope someday we'll find each other again but in different circumstances, God willing," I say.

"We can all pray for such a day," Rosalie says, kindness and warmth emanating from her eyes. "You're a good soul, Halina. Never forget that."

I don't think the guilt will subside and I'm sure once the two of them have a chance to mull over this conversation more, they might feel differently about me. It isn't fair that they need to remain here as servants. Though I shouldn't think that way until I see the light of day on the other side of what might or might not come to be.

"If you are taking Gavriel with you, what do you suppose will happen to Benson, Rueben, and Kasia, the three other Auschwitz prisoners still working in our homes?" I'm sure they've come to know Benson and Rueben like I have Gavriel as each of them come and go from duties within the houses they work in.

This thought has already crossed my mind after what I witnessed with Bea and Adam. "Keeping them safe will be part of my bargain with Frau Schäfer," I tell them, praying my plan will work. The stakes are high, and I feel like I'm walking across a minefield.

With the last reveal of my fragile plan, we approach the school, guarded by Nazis, surrounded by blood red flags, and the dark world the children are being transitioned into daily. As if on cue, Flora begins to cry. It isn't a cry of hunger, it's the kind of cry I don't think she has a real reason for, or maybe because something is broken inside of her. I understand her pain.

I lift her out of her carriage and prop her up on my hip. She places the side of her head to my chest and clutches the fabric of my dress within her tiny grip, gasping for relief and air between her stuttering sobs.

The children spill out of the school, not with thrill or delight, but in a strict marching line that branches out once they're through the guarded gates. It's been days since Marlene has greeted me with a smile, but she still wraps her arms around my waist and gives me a quiet embrace. Isla takes the carriage from my hand and turns it around to begin the walk home.

"How was school today?" I ask.

"Fine," Isla says.

"I don't like school," Marlene says.

"No one does, stupid," Konrad adds, tossing his knapsack at Celina's feet.

"He's becoming his father," Celina whispers. "How charming."

"Isla, wait a moment, please," I say, turning around to face Konrad. "You're going to lose your knapsack and get yourself into trouble later. I don't think that's a very wise idea," I say, folding my arms over my chest.

"She'll take it," Konrad says, pointing at Celina.

"Her hands are already full, as I'm sure you can see. I'm afraid if you don't take it, it will remain where it is."

Celina looks like she might become ill, but she needs to set some boundaries. This child will grow into a man and act much worse than he is now.

The blonde-haired boy who is about a year away from being my height sneers at me with apparent anger. I stare back, telling myself he's still a child. If I can spare Celina the trouble of caring for a Nazi in training, I will.

The stare between me and this rude child breaks and he swats his hand for the shoulder strap of his bag and trudges off ahead of the rest of us.

"No one has ever spoken to him that way," Celina whispers.

"These children are being taught to hate when we were all born to love. There is still a chance for them," I say. I must believe that. If I don't, there might be no hope for the future of humanity.

FORTY-FOUR

HALINA

Upon arriving back at the Schäfer residence with the children, I see there are a couple of vehicles parked out in front of the house. Neither of the cars belong to Heinrich, leaving me to wonder who I'll find inside, and for what reason. My chest burns, knowing Gavriel is in there, and wondering what business Ada had to tend to, and if this is the result.

"Who's here?" Marlene asks. "Are we having friends over?"

"Some of the people your father works with," I answer flatly.

Sweat beads on the back of my neck as I settle the carriage by the front of the house and make my way to the door. Marlene races ahead of me and flies into the house with curiosity. Isla is dragging her knapsack on the grass behind me, moping in my shadow. I turn to wait for her to walk in ahead of me, spotting drivers inside the cars, both staring out the windshield in waiting.

I step inside, finding several people moving back and forth between the kitchen and the servant entrance. Ada storms out of the kitchen, taking a hard left in our direction, greeting her children with weak hugs and kisses on each cheek. "How was school, my darlings?"

Marlene begins to chatter but Ada's mind is elsewhere as she stares at me with an undecipherable thought she must think I can read from her mind.

"What is it?" I whisper.

She grabs my arm and pulls me into the family room—the forbidden space to anyone but family. "You and—him," she says, peering up at the ceiling as if Gavriel is directly above her rather than on the other side of the house and in the attic, "will have the chance to—" She shifts, preparing to explain her undoing. "Go...at eight p.m. tonight during the commandant's speech. I can't do anything for you at any of the checkpoints. This is all I can offer."

"Gavriel will have to return to Auschwitz before eight," I tell her, delaying my thought on how in the world we will make it through a guarded checkpoint.

"I've arranged for him and the others to stay until the dinner is over—to serve where needed." Gavriel can hardly stand, but I understand the options are limited. "He's already been informed."

Ada takes Flora from my arms and holds her against her chest with her fingers splayed across her back as if she's holding a fragile piece of a glass—not in the way she normally holds onto Flora. A subconscious goodbye for the one she'll never have, perhaps. Flora should be her in mother's arms, not Ada's. "The girls need to be dressed appropriately tonight for their brief appearances."

This is her grand solution—or so she claims. All I can do is pretend to believe her. To trust that tonight isn't a carefully crafted trap I'll walk into. I turn toward the staircase, gathering the girls with a wave of my hand.

"Wait," Ada says.

I pause, turning back.

Ada takes a linen wrapped square package and hands it to me then pats the top with a silent finality. "That boy can't be seen in that uniform. I have some clothes that should fit him," she says, a tremor taking a hold of her body. "I do hope you understand the kind of wrath I'll face after you've gone missing."

I glance down at the bundle of clothes, realizing I hadn't thought about Gavriel's tell-all uniform. "You might consider marking an end to his vengeance. It's your life—you should have a say in how you live it." It pains me to offer heartfelt advice to a woman who clearly thinks she's better than the rest of us, but I believe there is good in everybody, even if it's been overshadowed with years of manipulation and hatred. The only way for her to end the evil is to stop taking part, but that takes a form of courage she doesn't have.

Ada scoffs and rolls her eyes up toward the ceiling. "You must think I'm a fool who married for status...Well—I was, but since then, believe me, Halina, I have tried to put an end to my situation here." She hisses like a snake and shakes her head. "I should have taken the gun from Heinrich's office when I had the chance, but it turned out my inner conscience is still alive, somehow, and I remembered who I am—who I was. That's the real pity of my story."

* * *

Marlene and Isla are settled for the moment, taking a rest before a long night, giving me time to see to other loose ends before getting them prepared for the dinner. I've even managed to set Flora down for a nap in her crib, something she doesn't normally cooperate with. Ada's words are playing repeatedly, the shock in her confession surreal, unfortunate, and yet, all too understandable. Everything in life has a consequence and she knows this just as well as the rest of us.

I make my way upstairs before I lose the chance to check on Gavriel and find him slouched over two wooden saddles with a plank overlapping both. He has the saw locked in a slight wedge of the wood, sweating, straining, shaking to get the saw to move.

"I have clothes for you to change into," I whisper, drawing nearer to him. His complexion is still pale and waxy. He's on his feet though.

"How?"

"Ada gave them to me."

"How can we trust her?" Gavriel asks, staring at the linen wrapped bundle.

"We can't. We won't. But you need these clothes."

He acknowledges my words but doesn't respond. I don't know if he's managed to get any physical work done today, but if he has, I'm sure that took the remainder of whatever strength he had left. He needed that to make it through the night. The kapo though...if he finds Gavriel sitting rather than working, he wouldn't make it until tonight.

"Everything is all set for tonight. We're going to follow through with our plan at eight p.m. Ada told me she's arranged for all prisoners to stay throughout the duration of the dinner party. They might assign you tasks, but just before eight, you'll need to come back up here and change into these clothes then meet me at the bottom of the attic's stairway. I'll be waiting with Flora. Do you think you have the strength for this?"

"Yes, I will do my part. I won't let you down, Hali."

I stare into his tired eyes, still glimmering with a hint of hope.

"You couldn't possibly let me down, no matter what you do or don't do," I tell him, placing a gentle kiss on his cheek. "I have to write a letter to the commandant then prepare the girls for an appearance tonight. Will you be all right for a bit longer?"

"A letter to the commandant? You say this as if you're

joining him for tea too. What do you mean?" Gavriel's eyes speak of amusement, confusion, and concern, all at once.

"You can trust me," I tell him, using the same words he offered me when I arrived.

"I do. With all my heart."

* * *

Downstairs, the air is steeped with mouthwatering aromas spilling out of the kitchen, fatty juices from a roast, fresh bread, pastries, dressed up potatoes—it's like a dream I won't be taking part in. I'm sure Gavriel can smell it all up in the attic too, just more torture for the starving.

Chatter is bouncing between all the walls, between hired help, slave servants like me, and prisoner laborers like Gavriel. No one here is of the same labeled class, yet we all entered this world the same way. It will never make sense to me. The closer we get to the start of the dinner party, the more nervous I become.

"We need more linen tablecloths, Halina," Ada shouts from the corridor between the kitchen and the servant door. I should have known she would find a way to assign me work rather than taking care of her children. I move into the hallway to make my way to the washroom where the laundered table linen is stacked and pass Benson on the way, holding a tray of cooking utensils, and Rueben carrying pillars of candles out into the back yard. I've only seen the two of them from a distance, never officially meeting them, but they appear to be in the same battered condition as Gavriel, maybe just not as bruised as he currently is.

Just as I turn the corner, I nearly collide with Heinrich. I didn't know he was home, or when he got here. Only I'm startled. He isn't. Nothing fazes him. "Just the person I was looking for," he says, his voice low, quiet amid the hustle and bustle around us. He lifts a brown envelope, the flap already open, and waves it in the air in front of my face.

"What can I do for you, Officer Schäfer," I say, showing the man a form of respect he doesn't deserve.

"If I had known the importance of the paperwork I was waiting on with regard to you, I might have asked the couriers to expedite the handling process." My papers. My lungs stop moving. My chest threatens to cave in, and I can't catch my breath. "This is quite an oversight, isn't it?"

"I'm—I'm not sure what you mean," I reply, sounding as if I already know what he's talking about, which I believe I do.

He puckers the opening of the envelope and shuffles the papers around inside, looking into the dark hole before reaching in then slowly revealing my demise. An angry heat singes through every limb of my body as he unfolds the documents and holds them out in front of his face.

"Halina Wojic," he reads. "Daughter of Nora Belle Wojic. No known father listed. Jewish by birth."

Pain slices through my temples and the room begins to wobble as if I'm a spinning top, though I haven't moved an eyelid. He must be able to hear how hard I'm breathing. He's taking pleasure in this moment while I die inside. Heinrich folds the papers back up and slides them into his coat pocket like it's nothing more than a paper napkin.

"Well, you've hidden yourself well. But I'm sure you know it's only a matter of time before every one of you is found. That's our job—and we do it well." He steps in closer to me, uncomfortably close, his breath stale of nicotine and hard liquor. "You'll do whatever Frau Schäfer has assigned to you for work tonight," he utters under his breath. "We'll handle this after dinner. This will be your final night in this house, as I'm sure you can guess."

Words don't come to me, not like they have when I've been wrongly brave too many times in the presence of this family.

Has he already told Ada what he's found out about me? Will she call off our agreement now knowing I'm even more inferior than she thought hours ago? Even if I told Heinrich all her secrets, he wouldn't believe me now. Germans of the Reich think all Jews are liars. They've made that clear.

No. They hardly speak unless it's for argument's sake. He'll tell her after he "handles me" as he said. But not if I get out of here first. I have to keep focused. Gavriel and I—we have a plan. It's our only plan. Our only chance...

Heinrich walks off, out into the back yard where people are filing in from the side gate.

Flora releases a timely shriek, informing me she's awoken from her nap. She slept longer than I expected, which gives me hope that she'll be content as I showcase her, Isla and Marlene around the party as if they're prize-winning ponies on display. Only so the high-ranking officers' wives can comment on how precious they are.

I collect the children, double checking their appearance, and present them outside. Each of my strides, casual, calm, unafflicted—as if I don't plan to escape this nightmare before the night's over.

After we've made our full stride around each table, we end at the elite table in the center, the name cards carrying the commandant's title, his wife, son, and daughter, along with a couple of foreign dignitaries. Another round of compliments are gifted to Isla and Marlene, both of whom respond with a curtsy. And Flora is content, pulling at my braid and ignoring the fuss around us somehow.

"All right, ladies, it's time to go inside now," I tell the girls. Isla and Marlene curtsy once more as smiles draw from cheek to cheek. I spot Celina and Rosalie waltzing around the children they care for, both with a side-eye on me.

The commandant and his family stand from their seats, smile at us and walk toward the crowd. I reach into my apron pocket and retrieve the letter I wrote earlier today and place it beneath his folded napkin. It's hardly a full page of writing, but it should be enough to convey the message, marked as concern.

There's only a very fine line between the enemy and their uniform, decorated with medals and rank insignia. The line is their integrity—frail and insecure. Abuses of power result in a violation of German civil code. Isla and Marlene's schoolbooks cover these laws in incredible detail. They must be important.

A child born to a Jewish mother in Auschwitz who was stolen by a member of the SS for personal gain, thus compromising Aryan loyalty for the sole purpose of portraying a "good family." Heinrich Schäfer not only physically abuses his wife but emotionally abuses his daughters and poisons the stolen infant by lacing her bottle with bourbon to keep her asleep all day. The commandant should know that the Reich is unknowingly supporting this behavior toward a woman and her children. Heinrich gives SS officers the poorest look while representing the most elite and superior race of thugs. In an honest world, no one would be surprised. But in this world, even where the death of innocent people is condoned, it isn't considered acceptable to treat fellow Aryans this way.

I usher the children inside, knowing every second matters right now.

"Right, upstairs girls, so you can get ready for bed," I say, following in their footsteps.

* * *

It's 8:00 *p.m.* Now or never.

The girls are in their room, tucked in, unaware. I wanted to wish them both well as it pains me to leave them, but I can't risk them thinking my words are a goodbye. They are. Gavriel is waiting by the attic's stairwell, and I walk into Flora's room and scoop her up into my arms, but the moment I do, she begins to cry. Not her fussy cry, but her broken-hearted one that cracks through her lungs. I rock her, hum in a whisper, and shush. Nothing works.

She must sense my panic. I'm sweating, breathing heavily. She must feel my heart galloping against her. Her cries grow louder, and she's arching away from me, her arms reaching behind her—toward him.

Gavriel steps forward, his eyes never leaving mine as he cradles her into his arms. "I'll take her."

"Gav—" I utter, "you need your strength."

But the second she's settled in his arms, she stops. As if Gavriel is the only one who still makes sense to her within this horror.

I understand the feeling.

"Come on," he says. "It's past eight."

I nod, swallowing against my fear. "You go first," I whisper urgently. "Take her now, out the front door."

Gavriel hesitates. "But you—"

"I'll follow. I need to make sure the girls stay in bed. I'll cover your exit. If they get up and see us all leaving, they'll scream. We'll be done." Gavriel and Flora have been through enough. I need to make sure they can make it out of here.

He doesn't look like he's going to agree with this plan, so I lower my voice and press the truth... "She's quiet with you. She'll be safe with you. You can get farther if no one spots you. Just don't stop. Don't look back."

Gavriel studies me, his eyes speaking a million different thoughts all at once. But then he nods, just slightly.

He disappears down the stairwell and my limbs begin to tremble, but I force myself to turn back for Isla and Marlene's bedroom to make sure they're in bed and stay in bed while Gavriel makes his way across the front lawn with Flora.

They're not in bed. They're standing at the window. "Girls, you should be in bed," I say, trying to keep my voice calm. I hurry to their sides to escort them away from the window before it's too late.

The moment I wrap my arms around their shoulders and tug them away from the window, Isla shrieks.

"He's taking her! The Jew has Flora!" her voice slices through the air and there's no saying how far her words will carry.

FORTY-FIVE

GAVRIEL

I should have waited for her. Where is she? I must keep moving. Her plan was to meet at the first wooded opening on the path back to Auschwitz. I know she was trying to protect me, but she might be the one who needs to be protected and I'm out here with a baby I've now stolen.

As soon as we make it to the border of the wooded path, I spin around to watch the front door, waiting for it to fly open. But it doesn't.

"Whatever you do—keep running. Do not stop and come back for me. I'll be fine," she said. I agreed. Why would I agree? It's not fine.

"Ma!" Flora cries out.

Oh God. "No, no, darling. I know you're confused," I say, breathlessly. "We're going to try and find your real mama, as soon as possible." If ever possible, I should say. If the war ever ends. If people are set free from the prisons. If, if, if. Guilt eats at me as I realize I shouldn't offer her this hope, even if she doesn't understand what I'm saying. I can't imagine her mother is still alive in Auschwitz.

Maybe we'll witness a miracle someday. Just for her.

God, please spare this innocent little girl.

I hold Flora so tightly within my arms, praying I don't trip on a root. I can't see a thing at this hour and there's no kapo with a light, thankfully, but at the same time—what if I can't find the opening within the trees?

What if I can't breathe? Why does everything in my body feel like it's on fire?

God, please, let me get out of here. Please.

A rustle of leaves catches me by the neck, and I stop moving, not sure if I should be silent or call out to what I pray to be Halina.

"Hali?" I whisper.

Nothing. Not a rustle of leaves.

Then, a squeal as something swoops over my head. A bat. It must be a bat. "It's all right. Just a little creature playing in the woods. Let's keep moving," I whisper to Flora. I think I might need to listen to my words of reassurance more than she does.

FORTY-SIX

HALINA

"Where is he taking her?" Isla screams. She's been screaming for five minutes. I've been trying to get her to stop, praying no one from outside hears. I've considered just leaving her here screaming but she will absolutely go out back and find her parents, as well as the rest of the officers here. I have to find a way to reason with her so I can leave.

"Listen to me, please just listen to me for a moment. I know you don't like me. I understand. I do."

"I hoped you would stay with us," Marlene utters, her eyes filling with tears. "But now you're going to leave us like all the others, right?"

"All the others have been killed by Papa," Isla says, begrudgingly, to her.

"Is he going to kill Hali too?" Marlene asks, holding her small hands to her lips.

"Girls," I say, interrupting them. "Listen to me. Try to remember what I'm about to say because it's important..." Isla isn't shouting at least, and Marlene is staring at me, waiting to know what I have to say. "War does something to people, and I know neither of you probably know much about the world before the war, but people are different now, and when the war is over, people will change again."

"But Papa will always have to know he killed people," Isla says. "He wants to be like Hitler. I don't like Hitler. I don't like school or saluting to him. I don't like hating people." A tear falls from her eye and she swallows hard, trying to regain her strength and composure—something a ten-year-old shouldn't have to maintain.

"You both have your entire lives ahead of you and you get to be whoever you want to be. Hitler doesn't need to say that. The war won't last forever." I hope and pray. "The world wants it to be over. We all do."

"What about Flora? That Jew—" Isla says, stopping herself for a moment. "The man, Gavriel, took Flora."

"Why do you think that is?" I ask, taking her hand in mine.

Isla drops her gaze to the ground. "She's not really our sister, is she?"

I let my eyes do the talking because I think this answer would be better off coming from Ada. "Why would you think such a thing?"

Isla shrugs. "Mama never loved her the way she loves us. Flora doesn't look like us. And, she's been sick, as Mama says, but she never took her to a doctor. She always takes us to a doctor if we're sick."

Isla is too smart for her own good. I watch the thoughts spinning through her eyes, trying to make sense of something that will likely never make any sense to her. "There are reasons for all things in life, some of which we may never understand. But you're right, Flora does need to see a doctor. It's important that she does, right?"

Isla gawks at me. "Yes, yes, it's important. Is Gavriel bringing her to the hospital now? Is that where he's taking her?" Isla asks.

"Yes. I'm going with him to take her to the hospital to see a doctor so she can get better. It's the right thing to do."

"Will you bring her back after she's better?" Marlene asks.

"She's not our sister," Isla adds. "Did Mama steal her from someone?"

My throat becomes too dry to continue this conversation. "I don't have that answer, but what I do know...it's important to be a good person and make decisions that help others. Never hurt them. That's all I want to do."

"You helped me," Marlene says, a lopsided grin curving into her dimpled cheek.

"I did? How so?"

She shrugs but steps forward and wraps her arms around me. "I don't know, but I'll miss you a lot."

Isla wraps an arm around me, a half embrace, but I'll take it. "I'll miss you too, Hali. I hope you stay safe. I hope Flora gets better, so she isn't—"

"Isn't what, sweetheart?" I ask gently.

"Sent to the place where all the other sick children seem to go. The place they don't come back from."

"I'm sure it only seems that way," I say, lying, unsure who I'm protecting but something remains of their innocence, at least.

Her words sent a shiver down my spine, recalling the Kinder-Euthanasie program the Reich was running until two years ago. The program was publicly declared over, two years ago, but even after that, Julia and the other housemothers at the orphanage said we had to protect disabled and sick children at all costs because the program still ran in secrecy. I tried to convince myself it was only a rumor and we were just taking extra precautions.

"I don't think that happens anymore." My words don't sound true.

"It does. Papa told Mama so. That's why they didn't bring Flora to a doctor," Isla adds.

I curl my hands into fists until my knuckles ache. Nausea spikes through me. This shouldn't come as a shock. I know what's happening in Auschwitz. It must be part of their push for the superior Aryan race—healthy, perfect Aryans with one ideology. There's only one way to do this—brainwash, kill, and manipulate, but like everything else, it must be done covertly.

"I'm going to do whatever I can to make sure she gets well. I promise. And remember, you are strong young ladies with your whole lives ahead of you. Do something wonderful with it."

Isla and Marlene stand stiffly, as if rooted to the spot. A tear falls from one of Marlene's glossy eyes—rolling down the length of her cheek until it drops to the wooden floor. Isla clutches the fabric of her nightgown, her cheeks flushed. Neither says another word. They just watch me walk away from them. They don't know how much it hurts to leave them behind.

I make it out the front door and to the mouth of the woods, deeper and deeper, unable to see anything by the time I'm a minute deep between the trees. Gavriel said there's a clearing a quarter of the way along the path, a place where even a cloud-covered moon offers a flicker of light. He said all we have to do is keep walking and we'll find it. I hope it's that easy to spot on my own.

The path is roped with moss covered roots, perfect for tripping or hurting an ankle. I'm moving as fast as I can without running. The leaves swish and swash over and over like thick paper being shuffled together into a pile of disarray, the sound mild but loud enough to cover any other noise I might pick up around me.

When the leaves stop rustling for a moment, I stop, close my eyes and try to listen for a sound. Any sound.

Finally.

The baby's desperate cry travels on a gust of wind, whipping around me as I forge through the darkness along the narrow path, running as fast as I dare. The thicket of trees presses in on me, their low-hanging branches like clawed arms with gnarly fingers catching on the fabric of my uniform. The ground is warped with bowing roots, threatening to trip me with every step, and the night tightens around me as I press on, only focusing on moving forward.

For a moment I stop, just to catch my breath, bending forward, hands on my knees, ears straining for the baby's next cry. Except, the next gust of wind travels alone. I gasp for air, my lungs burning, my pulse thrumming. I can't afford to stop.

My legs grow heavier as I trudge on, the trees thinning until a sliver of moonlight spills across the ground, exaggerating every shadow but guiding me toward our meeting spot. Broken twigs and damp, matted leaves litter the dirt, and the air clings to the scent of late summer rain.

A whimper ripples through the air and my breath stutters as a piercing cry follows, drawing me to the next tree where Gavriel waits, shrouded in his loosely fitted clothing, gently rocking the sweet, innocent baby girl in his arms.

"Shh," I whisper through my panting, touching her chest, trying to calm her down. When she hears my voice up close, her cries falter as she grasps onto a strand of my hair between her tiny fingers. Her tired giggle bounces between the trees, but her delight will be short-lived.

"We have to go," Gavriel says, his scratchy whisper catching in his throat.

"Here, I'll take her," I say, reaching my arms out.

"Not yet. I've already had a minute to catch my breath. You haven't."

Behind us, raging shouts fire out in the distance and dogs are barking. They know.

I follow Gavriel through the clearing and onto another uneven dirt path as the little baby in his arms let's out a relentless wail. Is she hungry? Hurt? Tired? Or does she sense the danger we'll face if we don't make it out of the woods quickly?

The trees end abruptly, spitting us out onto the road, our breaths heavy with exertion and worry. My foot presses into the gravel, and I hesitate...just for a second. Gavriel doesn't. He pushes forward into the sweep of spotlights.

Just beyond the trees to our right, the barbed wire surrounding Auschwitz hums with electricity, a sound I'm familiar with. The existence is a warning of the grave consequences we'll face if we're caught.

"Stay under the branches to the side of the road," Gavriel says, still charging forward.

To our right, the barbed-wire fence enclosing Auschwitz cuts across the horizon like a jagged scar. We're not inside the death camp itself, but we're close enough to make out the faint cries from within. Still, we're trapped within German seized land, an SS-controlled zone.

The checkpoint ahead isn't an exit from the main Auschwitz compound, but from the so-called "Area of Interest," a tightly patrolled forty-square-kilometer restricted zone meant to protect the secrets of SS homes, camp-run factories, and the regime's lethal order. Beyond it, where I come from, Polish civilians still scurry about. If we can just make it past this checkpoint, we might find somewhere safer than here.

This was the first gate I crossed when I was brought here, where I let go of the hope of ever seeing the Vistula River again. Nothing says the "end" like an SS guard with a rifle slung under his arm. Gavriel slows... then stops. I nearly bump into him before he turns to face me, his gaze catching mine in the dark. "Here," he says, his voice low and raspy. "It's best if you take her now."

As I take the sweet baby girl back into my arms, her cries turn into more of a weak whimper, and as we walk, she finally takes a deep breath and sighs, falling quiet. I keep my eyes on the road, avoiding the deep, jagged holes, making sure I don't trip. There's too much to fear all at once.

"What if this doesn't work?" I don't expect him to answer. The question is weighing heavily on us both.

But he stares into my eyes, "We can't think that way. It's our only option—it will work."

Each step closer to the freedom lying beyond this last blockade is endless, especially now that the guard's flashlight is gliding our way.

The damp rubble beneath my feet crackles and pops and the fog hanging in the air begins to suffocate me. My heart pounds painfully. "Papers," the guard demands. "Where are you coming from and what is your destination?"

We stop just in front of him, his eyes concealed by the rim of his cap. "We've been on the compound visiting family, the Schäfers—you must know them. We were to attend their dinner party tonight, but our baby's illness has taken a turn for the worse. She needs a doctor. She's very sick. If we don't get her there—"

"Papers," he snaps, interrupting me.

My throat tightens and my focus falls to the rusty gate, framed by sandbags and stacked wooden crates. A smeared red streak near the latch...is that paint or blood?

"There's no time for papers," Gavriel says, his German accent impeccable. "Our daughter...she won't survive another hour. She needs help right away."

No one comes and goes easily from the occupied villages surrounding Auschwitz. The entire area is heavily barricaded by guards even though the only people who live within this "restricted zone" are working members of the Reich, domestic servants, and beyond them, the prisoners.

This little girl so obviously senses every emotion surrounding her, explaining the return of her piercing cry. I hold her tighter but don't rock her in my arms like I normally would. I don't hush her either. It's important that she continues to cry now.

"What is the baby ill with?" the guard asks with haste, shining his flashlight onto her sensitive eyes, lingering on her flushed skin. He stumbles back a step. "Typhus," he utters, as if the word itself is infectious.

All the guards are afraid of this disease. As they should be.

"There's a rash—on her belly. The fever...spiked just an hour ago. She's already had one seizure. We're sure it's typhus," Gavriel explains.

I gasp a shuddered breath as a sob relents. "You must understand," I cry out. "Feel her head—how hot she is..." I hold her out toward him, my arms shaking.

He won't touch her. The risk of typhus isn't worth it to him. *Please God, keep us safe right now.*

The guard takes another step backward. "Go on," he snaps, tearing a handkerchief from his pocket to press against his nose. "If you return without a doctor's note..." He doesn't finish his statement, but the implication is clear.

His grip tightens on the gate lever. He's letting us go. But then his jaw clenches, and as if someone has whispered a warning in his ear, he appears to reconsider. The flashlight angles toward our faces, blinding us. "Show me your forearms."

"Wh—what do you mean?" I ask. "Why must you see our arms?" My acting isn't believable—nor is my naivete.

He's looking for tattooed numbers from Auschwitz. The tattooed numbers all the prisoners within the barbed-wire fences have...the tattooed numbers we shouldn't have if we're truly just visiting family here on the compound.

"Show me, or you don't pass."

I move first, praying he will let us go when he doesn't see a number on my arm. Gavriel's will give us away.

With a jerky movement, I struggle with Flora in my arms, wishing I could tell her to let out a cough for the sake of our story. I pull my sleeve up to my elbow, showing my pale fore-arm. She can't cough, but I can. With the phlegm coating my throat from running through the damp air, I'm able to muster a barking cough I can't cover without a free hand. My timing is planned for when the guard steps in closer with his hand-held light to check my arm.

He jumps backward and recenters his handkerchief over his nose and mouth. "Go, go," he mumbles, opening the metal gate.

I take Gavriel's hand in mine and run, my heart beating so hard it's cold despite how hot I am from panic.

We continue running down the side of the street until we're out of sight from the checkpoint. "I know where we are now," I tell Gavriel.

"You do?"

"Follow me." Back into the woods, but down an unmarked path I could navigate blindly.

FORTY-SEVEN

HALINA

Gavriel keeps a hand on my back as we continue through the darkness into a circular dirt opening with a church buried in the shadows of the old trees lining the back side of the building. Behind a set of tall bushes is a concealed narrow door, the main door left unused for years since the church had a congregation.

I thrash my fist against the wooden frame, stern knocks with urgency, not the sound of a bullish Nazi going for intimidation.

I press my ear to the door, listening for a hint of sound from within. What if the Nazis finally got to the church, raided it and forced everyone out. We kept waiting for it to happen, but we told ourselves we were too deep in the woods and the building looked to be in too much disrepair for them to want anything to do with the old church. The inside has been maintained, but we've let the outside become part of nature with its tangled vines and overgrown weeds and brush.

"Where are we?" Gavriel asks, still trying to catch his breath.

Flora groans.

I knock once again and listen through the door, this time hearing the floorboards creaking. The clunky locks clatter and the door squeals as it parts from the threshold, just enough for two eyes to peer over the chain-link lock. "It's me, Halina," I whisper.

The door is pulled closed, and the chain released before the dark opening invites us in. I take Gavriel's hand and guide him inside, knowing they won't light a lamp or a candle until the door is securely closed and locked again.

Once the chain is replaced, a scrape of a lantern from a table and the flickering of the dial echo around us before the entryway is illuminated.

The light glows against Julia's face, full of shock and terror. "Halina," she whispers. "It's really you. You've come back. You're alive and safe?" She throws her arms arm around me, the lamp bouncing off my back.

Then I wrap my arms around her. With every bit of strength left in my body. For every hug I should have given her before. "It's me. I'm sorry. I'm so sorry. I love you. I love you so much. It's all I've wanted to tell you since I had to leave. I love you, Julia."

Julia sniffles against my ear, her fingertips pressing into my shoulder. "Thank God. Thank you, God. I've been praying for you every day. I was so afraid when I didn't hear from you. I've been fearing the worst," she says through a sniffle and choked cry. "My sweet girl. I know, love. I never questioned it from you. All I cared about was you surviving."

"I'm alive," I utter, loosening my hold around her. "And this is Gavriel and Flora."

"Oh my," Julia says, holding the lamp toward Gavriel. "You poor dear." She places her palm on his face. "I'll heat some soup for you."

Julia reaches out with a hint of hesitation toward Flora. "Hello, beautiful girl," she murmurs.

"She was stolen from her mother at Auschwitz," I tell Julia. "She's been through too much in her short life." Flora doesn't fuss when Julia's hands wrap around her body, which brings a small smile to my face. Julia has always had an angelic way with children. They flock to her.

"Go find yourself some clean clothes and wash up. I'll look after this sweet baby girl while you do."

"Come on," I say to Gavriel, taking his hand.

"Is this where you—"

"This is my home," I say.

Once settled, and washed up, I bring Gavriel downstairs to the kitchen where Julia is using her favorite wooden spoon to stir the contents of a large pot on the wood-burning cast iron stove from the late eighteen hundreds. Flora is in a highchair that's been used by hundreds of children over the years, comfortable and content as could be.

"Will you be staying with us?" Julia asks, a plea of hope brightening her tired eyes.

"I don't think it's safe for us to stay long. My birth records were uncovered by the Reich," I say, staring down at my fidgeting fingers as I pull at a hangnail.

"I gathered all the available documents," Julia says, her expression grief-stricken. "I'm sure the Reich has access to files I never would have been allowed to see—especially ones kept sealed for the protection of a mother and child. An SS officer would have the authority to demand access to those."

I nod, understanding and believing her words. "I found a note from my mother in the seam of my folktale book too. It turns out I'm Jewish."

"As am I," Gavriel adds. "And Flora too."

"It's best we aren't here to cause you or the children any trouble in the future," I say.

"A note?" Julia asks as if she didn't hear anything else we said. Her wide-eyed stare screams with worry.

A note I will keep for the rest of my life. I reach into my pocket and pull it out, handing it to her to read. Julia takes a moment to read it, seemingly troubled while absorbing each written word. Her eyes fill with tears as she folds the paper back up.

"Your mother loved you with all her heart, Halina. That much is clear through her words." But I still don't know why I was given away. I may never know. Julia's breath catches in her throat before pulling out a handkerchief from her pocket. She dabs her nose. "You know I will still keep you safe here, don't you?"

"I can't keep you or the other children safe if we are here," I tell her. "It's my turn to watch over you now."

Julia nods and turns back for the soup pot, taking the wooden spoon from the side of the stove to mix the broth again. "Very well," she says softly. "At first light, I'll take you to a friend of mine, a priest near the train junction. He'll help you get papers. Tickets. A way south," Julia says while staring through the swirling broth. "One of the other housemothers can watch over the children while I'm gone."

Julia takes in a gasping breath and holds it for a long pause, then she opens her mouth to speak but only the air of a whisper comes out. "We'll need to be quick. There has been heavy German police activity due to recent partisan displays of resistance near the tracks."

My stomach knots, a pain followed by a sour spell. "How dangerous is it?" I don't want to put her in danger. I want her to be safe here, and she's only safe here if she isn't hiding undocumented Jews.

"If everything goes according to plan, it won't be something you have to worry about."

But I am worried, and terrified for us all, still.

FORTY-EIGHT
GAVRIEL

A bed. A real bed with a mattress still filled with stuffing, and linens that hint lavender soap. And Halina folded into me like she belongs nowhere else. With her silky hair spilled across my neck and her leg looped over mine, I didn't allow myself to move. I wanted to stay like that and listen to her breaths, slow and warm like the lapping water of a calm lake. It was all so perfect, I couldn't sleep, not while considering how many ways I could let her and Flora fall.

As I've come to learn, repeatedly, perfection doesn't last—not here, or anywhere during this war. Darkness gives way to dawn long before I'm ready, and with it comes the weight of what lies ahead for us.

The sky is still more shadow than light, a bruised violet pool with a blush of dusky pink streaks along the horizon. It's later than my usual waking hour to prepare for a day's worth of labor. Soon the fog will settle in and cling to the ground as if it doesn't want to be pulled back into the clouds.

Halina's hand is in mine and Julia is smitten with Flora, perched on her hip. The silence of the morning has kept us quiet, but as buildings grow closer, her grip tightens. "Are you doing all right?" I ask.

"Of course," she says, her eyebrows furrowing. She's fibbing. I know that look now. I pull her toward my side and lift her hand to my lips, kissing her knuckles.

"Not much longer, we're almost there," Julia says, tightening her black shawl around her head and shoulders.

The priest, Julia's friend, agreed to help us. He said to return by dawn, and he would have the forged papers, the travel documents, and train tickets prepared for us. All we have to do is give him an hour before returning to the stairwell beneath the bell tower of the church—quietly.

At the top of the hill we're walking, I see the chapel we visited earlier this morning, grateful it's in sight. We're so close, I can feel the papers in my hand. I have Flora wrapped in my arms, holding her tightly as I've learned she likes it most. Julia has Halina's hand wrapped in hers. I can see the love she must have given Halina when she needed it the most. It warms my soul to watch, distracting me from the pain in my leg, an injury I've been forced to ignore. It happened during an interrogation in front of the prison cell. I was thrown to the ground and kicked too many times to count. I'm surprised I don't have more injuries aside from bruising and lacerations. It's not important right now though. I've put the pain out of my mind as best I can these last couple of days. I must keep going.

My stomach lurches at the sound of footsteps growing from behind us. Heavy boots, moving fast.

Julia stops so suddenly I nearly crash into her back, but she turns around and steps to my side quickly. I'm not sure what she's doing. "Keep walking. Don't stop," she utters without moving her lips.

"Halt!"

Gestapo. Julia said there have been less around at this hour in the morning. That's why we came so early.

Despite what Julia said, I stop, grabbing a hold of Halina's hand, squeezing tightly. Flora jerks her head up, looking around over my shoulder.

"It's just me. I'm coming from the chapel," Julia says, her voice slicing through the thick air.

"Papers," the demand bounces off the stone wall to our right.

Julia has papers. We don't. That's why she said to keep walking. I yank Halina's hand. "We need to keep moving. She'll catch up."

"Well, I don't have my papers with me," Julia says, her voice calm and unconcerned. She does have her papers. I watched her place the folded booklet into her pocket just as we were leaving this morning. "You see, I was delivering food to the church for the service this morning. There's supposed to be a lovely sermon. Will you be joining us?"

Halina hesitates with each step, the guilt eating away at me the farther we walk from her. The broken gate is just ahead of us on our right, now. We have no choice but to walk through. I clutch Flora tighter. Her head nuzzles beneath my chin as she releases a heavy tired sigh.

The voices of Gestapo rise in the close distance, just on the other side of the short stone wall. Julia's voice rises next. The argument ensues as we reach the bell tower and slip in through the unlocked door, the priest waiting for us, a lantern in one hand, and our documents in the other. In the glow of the lantern, his eyes are stark-wide with fear. "Where is Julia?"

"There's no time," Halina rasps with a sniffle. "She—she's protecting us at the moment."

The priest shoves the papers into Halina's hands. "You must go now then. Right away. Platform three. Southbound cargo. The train won't stop completely, but it will slow down enough. Do you understand?" he asks, speaking so quickly I'm trying to absorb his distinct directions.

"Yes," Halina says. "I understand."

The priest holds his hand out to me, and I release one grip from around Flora to take his hand, feeling an object pressed between our hands. "For the baby," he says. "Run, and may God bless you always." I unclasp my fingers, finding a wooden cross in my hand, close my fingers back over it and slip back out of the bell tower's door.

My pulse hammers through my veins as we make our way closer to the broken gate, noticing the yelling has ceased and the Gestapo are gone, but it isn't until we step back out onto the street that we find Julia's body, outlined in blood.

Her shawl torn, her body still.

FORTY-NINE

HALINA

I fall to my knees at Julia's side, pressing my cheek to her chest. "Please...no," I whimper. "I still need you." My heart bleeds like hot acidic rain, burning through every limb. As if a knife has pierced my lung, my breaths fall short. Tears burn the backs of my eyes. "This is my fault. It's my fault."

Gavriel's hand rests on my shoulder. I know we can't stay here. I know who's lurking around the next corner, but I don't know what to do. "Hali, my God, I—I'm so—I'm sorry. I—"

I lift my head from Julia's chest, not knowing how to let her go. "Don't apologize," I say, my voice cracking. "It isn't your fault." It's mine.

I cradle Julia's limp hand in both of mine. The one that brushed my hair and bandaged up scrapes. The one that would hold mine when I was sad or afraid. The thought of leaving her here...how could I? What kind of world is this where she takes me in after birth and then...I leave her on a road after death?

"What would she tell you to do?" Gavriel says, his words shaky and unsure.

"She—" I gasp for air. "She'd tell me...she'd tell me to keep Flora safe." More stunted breaths, my chest caving in. "To keep myself, us, safe." She devoted her life to protecting others. I hope she knows her efforts were never in vain.

"I'll keep you safe, but we aren't safe here," Gavriel murmurs.

I squeeze my eyes shut and press a kiss to her cool cheek. "God brought us together, and together we shall be," I whisper in her ear. "I'm sorry I can't take you with me."

A train whistles. A haunting chime smothered in the thick air. Distant, but close.

"We have to—" Gavriel begins to say, his words hesitant, but full of worry.

I nod, a slight gesture I can barely muster. "I know." I don't want him to feel the weight of telling me to leave her. I rise, my legs shaking at my knees, and curl into Gavriel's outstretched arm. Each step away from her is like a fight against gravity. I peer over my shoulder once more, knowing I'll never forget this feeling, leaving her on a blood-soaked street beneath the ghostly fog.

* * *

The train didn't stop. Not for us, not for grief, not for goodbyes, and not for the body I left behind.

My knees are still damp from the ground, holding me hostage in that moment—an impossible forever goodbye.

Like the chug of the train, my heart stammers and weakens me to the core. We've been quiet so long, sitting in the darkness of the cargo car with the morning light chasing us through the open back door as we leave another part of our lives behind. Flora is curled up within the sling of my dress, between my knees, my sweater covering her as a blanket as she sleeps soundly. Gavriel's hand is locked around mine, grasping me as if he needs to hold on to me so I don't slip away.

Flora stretches her arms out over her head. I study her with solace as she curls into a more comfortable position on her side. Her tiny movements reel in all my thoughts to a focus of just one...

Is it my turn now?

Am I strong enough to protect her?

Will I find her mother?

Gavriel lifts my hand to his lips, resting them there for a moment.

The track curves.

A new direction.

Sunlight spills over us, cloaking us in its golden rays, warm and embracing.

Julia raised me, even when I wasn't hers. I know now, I was never unwanted, but instead chosen. She somehow prepared me for this moment without knowing how our lives would unfold, and I know I will be more than what this war has made of me. I'll be what she believed I could be.

Flora needs me. I chose her...and will do everything in my power to be who she needs, even if it's just the person who returns her to her mother. She will always know who she is, and that she is loved.

I'll be her Julia.

EPILOGUE

GAVRIEL

Spring 1947
The Polish Countryside

The meadows outside the window sway with the gentle breeze, dancing to a silent orchestra as they wave at the sky. The tall grass is a different shade of green from what I remember as a child, but when the sun blankets the earth, the golden hue returns, chasing away the cold. Ma would love it here—fresh air, birdsong, and insects trilling. Pa would be looking for scrap wood to build something—an addition to our house, a barn, and a swing for Flora. A swing big enough for him and Flora to share.

I built our house from the ground up. A place to call home, somewhere to raise a family, to share love and memories, an heirloom to pass on to the next generations. A way to keep me alive long after I'm gone. Pa said that's what we were doing for people when we were building houses, but I have nothing left from him, nothing to hold onto. Nothing but his words and our memories. So I built this place. Made it perfect just like he would. Even added a barn and a tree swing.

Pa would be proud. I'm proud. And our family business is back up and running. Sometimes, I imagine Pa, Jozek, and Natan working alongside me, cracking jokes or wise comments, and I feel like we've gone back in time for just a moment. I'm carrying this business forward—keeping it alive just as I once promised to do.

Halina's sitting at the kitchen table, her arms wound around Flora, who's coloring another masterpiece of the grass, sun, and sky—half on paper, half on the table. Her legs dangle over Halina's lap, her braids down her sides as two golden ropes with tight little curls framing her face. With a daily dose of endless, worldly questions mixed in with contagious giggles, I believe this little girl owns a sense of peace and safety. I gave them their first homes. Watching what it looks like from the inside paints a different picture of what I had always thought I was giving others when building their houses. I only ever saw it from the outside and imagined the inside. The inside...it's warm, rich with scents of fresh bread and biscuits. The sunlight brightens up each room. It's us. Our home together. Our new life.

Flora takes her drawing and twists around on Halina's lap and pats her belly before flipping the paper upside down and backward. Then she whispers, "Do you like my picture, baby? I'll teach you how to color lots of pictures soon too," she croons. With a hand cupped around the side of her mouth to make her conversation a little more private, Flora continues. "I'm your big sister. So, I can teach you everything."

Halina and I exchange a glance, a smile meeting a smile.

Flora's cries, delays, pains—the ones that once felt unending, were all connected symptoms to an infant's unsettled stomach. No doctor was able to give us an official name for what was wrong but told us we should wait and be patient. That she'd grow out of it as her digestion matured. And she did.

I turn for the sink to prepare the potatoes for our dinner, my hands still moving in a careful regiment of stiff, quick movements, no noise, no pausing—a remaining scar of prison life.

Someone was always watching. Waiting for us to trip. *Sometimes I question if the walls have eyes. If the Nazis can still see us—still want to steal our happiness.*

Daily, I must remind myself that the war is over. We're safe. But the memories...they'll never go away.

The reminders will never stop.

A letter arrived yesterday without a return address. A name isn't needed. The words say it all. Halina read it first then left it face down on the counter without a word.

Heinrich Schäfer—tried and convicted. Hanged.
Thank you for saving us too, Halina.
–Ada

Halina watched as I read the short letter after she did. I read the one line several times, waiting to feel something...

I didn't feel anger, or triumph, or closure. Just nothing.

No one knows how they will survive when leaving loved ones behind. Will they fall to pieces with broken hearts, grief stronger than the will to breathe, tears that could drown us in our sorrow?

Halina and I have forged our own way through grief together. We've learned how to let sorrow move through us like ocean waves—lifting us, dropping us, then lifting us up again. We know we won't drown if we just let it pass.

Heinrich Schäfer was buried in our minds long before he faced a trial. We hoped the confession Halina wrote—the one she slipped beneath the commandant's napkin during the dinner party, would be enough. The proof of taking another woman's child, truths of his abuse to his wife, the way he tormented his children, and stole treasured goods from Jews at Auschwitz, is what was punishable, even from the view of a high-ranking Nazi. The murders—Adam, included—we had to wait for justice on those.

Ada likely got away with the crimes she committed. That was Halina's hope—that Isla and Marlene might have a chance at a life untouched by the blood on their father's hands. Knowing what I do about Auschwitz, I also believe Ada unknowingly saved Flora's life. Most children did not survive that place.

There was no letter from my family. No notice to say my parents were shot and killed while stepping out of a cattle car, or that both of my brothers were worked to death then burned to ash. No ceremonies of remembrance, and no stone to kneel beside. Just a list of names among thousands, tucked in an archive. But I found them. And they will be with me forever, wherever I go.

Flora jumps off Halina's lap and runs to my side with her drawing. "Look, Pa! You have to see my picture too!"

I dry my hands on a dishrag then take the paper in my hands and admire her drawing. It's different from the series of sunshine and flowers she's been focused on this week. Today, there's three lopsided figures lined up with smiles and their hands joined...

"A dog," I say, pointing at the first animal, "a cat, and..." There's a little gray blob with a long arm and I'm not sure—

"A mouse, Pa. It's a mouse. It has a little pink nose," she says with a squeak. "Can't you see?" *A dog, cat, and mouse. Of course.* "They're friends."

"This—this is wonderful—absolutely beautiful, sweetheart," I say, my heart swelling with joy and pride. "I think you know what we need to do now."

"Tape it up!" she shrieks, jumping up and down as blonde curls pop out of her braids. I press a kiss to her forehead and hang the paper with the others on the wall—our makeshift gallery of Flora's hope.

From the time we made it to Slovakia to moving back to Poland last year, Halina was relentless in her search for Flora's mother. Countless aid stations and archive offices, waiting with bated breaths as clerks flipped through records. Halina left our contact information and the name of Flora's mother on a note for every person who helped us, until we were handed a transport list to Auschwitz with Flora's mother's name among others, and an x marked in the box to label her as deceased.

The understanding of what Flora's future would look like morphed from the initial shock of let down to a quick rebound and an endeavor to raise her right, especially for Halina after living her life not raised by her own parents.

"We can give her love. All the love in the world to make sure she always holds on to a connection with her mother. We won't ever let her down," Halina had said, holding Flora tightly to her chest as we left that last archive office.

Halina is still sitting at the table, scribbling something now as a smile pokes against her dimples. "Mischief. That's all I see on your face," I tell her. That's not all I see, though. I see the woman who saved me when I couldn't save myself.

I walk up behind Halina, finding her drawing stick-figure people, four of them, one man, one woman, a little girl with braids, and a baby, all holding hands.

"It's almost like our very own folktale."

"It's real," Halina says. "We're real." She reaches for my hand and places it over her swollen belly, placing hers beside mine, our matching gold bands. "But it sure seems like a miracle."

It's been almost a year since we exchanged our vows in a quiet ceremony outside, under the blue sky and heaven where our loved ones were witnesses. Flora wore a wreath of daisies and stood between us. I told my girls the one important thing I hope they never forget. "You can trust me. To be yours. Forever."

"Did you feel that?" she asks, her eyes glowing with excitement.

My pulse flickers as I realize what I just felt. "Did our baby just kick?" My words catch in my throat.

"It must be your touch," she says.

Our baby. I'll have a part of my past within my future. A gift. A blessing. For all of us.

I help her out of her chair and pull her into her arms just as Flora's arms loop around our legs. As the sunlight spills in through the window, illuminating us within its golden stripes, it's clear, that light has taken over the darkness.

A gentle knock on the front door startles us from our quiet moment. "Who's that?" Flora asks, releasing her grip and racing toward the door.

Halina stiffens. Her hand lifts to her belly. I see the concern in her eyes before she says a word.

Neither of us were expecting anyone and the unexpected stirs inside of me as we follow Flora. "Wait over there please," I tell our curious little girl, pointing to the space behind the door.

"But who is it?" she presses.

I scoot Flora to my right and open the door.

A woman stands before us, middle-aged, light brown hair pulled back at the nape of her neck. Her eyes...tired, but also full of hope.

"Can we help you?" Halina asks before I have the chance. She steps closer to the woman, studying her as if she can't make out what or who she's looking at.

The woman holds out a piece of paper, her hand unsteady. Halina takes it, unfolding it hastily. I can only make out the header: Registry of Names.

"Is there someone you're looking for?" I ask her, wondering why she's struggling to speak.

She swallows hard then stares directly at Halina. "I'm looking for you," the woman utters.

"Me?" Halina whispers.

"Halina Wojic," the woman says.

"Yes, I'm—I'm...she."

"I've been looking for you for a very long time. I've traveled through many paths, between what seemed like every tree in this country in search of you. Your father locked down your records and documents—it was impossible. Until I was liberated from Auschwitz. That's when I found your name in a registry of survivors. I wasn't sure—I didn't..."

Halina's eyes fill with tears as she lifts her hands to her heart. "Are you—are you my mother?" Her last word is spoken in a breath.

The woman nods, a slow, timid gesture. A tear skates down her cheek as she searches between Halina's eyes and her stomach. "You were a dream I prayed would come true. Even when they told me you'd been taken by your father. Even when I thought I couldn't believe in miracles ever again."

Halina touches her fingers to her mouth, a sob murmuring in her throat. "Mama," Halina utters.

Flora presses between myself and Halina, then tugs on her sleeve and pinches my hand. "This is my mama and pa," she says with pride. Then she tickles Halina's belly. "And that's my baby. But you can come inside too. Do you want to?"

I open the door wider, heart in my throat.

"I'd like that," the woman whispers. "I've been waiting a lifetime."

Halina steps aside and reaches for her mother's hand, a gesture that speaks of an unbroken bond, unlinked and lost for far too long. But now, together again, a generation later. At the beginning of a fresh start.

There was once a girl who didn't know she had a story...

Because she was the story.

The beginning. The middle. And the end.

I was just lucky enough to be written into the pages.

A LETTER FROM SHARI

Dear reader,

I'm grateful you chose to read *The Nanny Outside the Gates*. There's nothing more fulfilling than sharing my books with readers from all over the world. If you would like to keep up to date with all my latest releases, just sign up at the following link. Your email address will never be shared, and you can unsubscribe at any time.

www.bookouture.com/shari-j-ryan

This novel is a work of fiction, but most importantly, developed from truth. The world of this story, set within the "Restricted Zone" (the most common German term used for this area), was a residential area outside of the Auschwitz gates where families of several SS officers resided. Other names for this area were: Interessengebiet Auschwitz ("Area of Interest Auschwitz"), Sperrgebiet ("Restricted Area"), Schutzgebiet ("Protected Area"), SS-Siedlungsgebiet ("SS Settlement Area").

Quiet residential lives existed just steps away from Auschwitz, patrolled by their own. The horrors that unfolded within this zone were unfathomable and real. Through extensive historical research, survivor accounts, and archival records, I've sought to honor the experiences of those who endured the Holocaust, as well as expose the secret lives of the privileged officers of the Reich. Halina and Gavriel's stories were constructed from true accounts of survivors who endured similar circumstances.

To respect the identities and stories of the victims, I've made the mindful choice not to assign any fictional prisoner a known historical number. You may notice that the prisoner identification numbers in this book include an "X" to signify that these are fictional creations, not tied to any real person who perished or survived. This is my way of acknowledging the weight of those numbers while still sharing a story grounded with the raw truth.

Writing books like this one is both an act of commemoration and personal reckoning. My grandmother and great-grandmother survived the Holocaust. My great-grandfather and great-uncle did not. One perished in Dachau, the other was murdered in Auschwitz. I carry their memories, and the legacy of my family's survival in my heart. These stories are my way of linking to the past—to give a voice to those who were suppressed and hope to those who still search for pieces of themselves in history. Like me.

If you enjoyed reading *The Nanny Outside the Gates*, I would be grateful if you could write a review. Since the feedback from readers benefits me as a writer, I would love to know what you think, and it makes such a difference helping new readers to discover one of my books for the first time.

There's no greater enjoyment than hearing from my readers —you can get in touch on my Facebook page, through X, Goodreads, or my website.

Thank you for reading!

Shari

KEEP IN TOUCH WITH SHARI

www.sharijryan.com

 facebook.com/authorsharijryan
 x.com/sharijryan

ACKNOWLEDGMENTS

Writing *The Nanny Outside the Gates* was an incredible journey of learning and unraveling new points of view I hadn't discovered before. As I spent many days and nights writing, deleting, and rewriting these words, I'm grateful to have gotten to a place where I can call the story complete.

Thankful to the incredible team at Bookouture for continuing to believe in my words. Growing alongside you as a writer has been one of the great joys of my career.

To Lucy, my brilliant editor, your sharp eye for details and thoughtful guidance brought this book to life in ways I couldn't have imagined. It's an honor to work with you, and I'm already excited for the next book.

Linda, your unwavering support, gentle honesty, and cheerleading spirit have lifted me through the hard moments. I value our friendship more than I can say.

To Tracey, Gabby, Elaine, and Gosia—you've been my sounding boards, safe space, and my encouragement on the days I needed it most. Thank you for always being there.

A heartfelt thank you to the ARC readers, bloggers, influencers, and passionate readers who pour so much love into the publishing community. Your voices make such a difference, and I'm infinitely grateful.

To my sister, Lori—you've always believed in me, and that means the world. Thank you for always being my first reader and best little sister in the world.

To my family—Mom, Dad, Mark, and Ev—thank you for

standing by me through every deadline, and every draft. Your love means everything to me.

Bryce and Brayden—each book I write feels like a time-marker, and I don't know how I've been writing and publishing since you were both babies, but now you're both bigger than me, becoming amazing young men. I have never and could never ask for the amount of support you offer me. You are my life, my reason, my purpose. I'm here to support *you* in all your dreams. That's *my* job. But, to know you're proud of me...I keep that gift in my pocket and will always carry it with me.

Josh—after all these years, you're still my rock. Your unwavering faith in everything I do has given me wings to fly, and I hope you never forget that all these books have a beginning, middle, and end because you dared me to do what I dreamed of doing. I love you with all my heart.

PUBLISHING TEAM

Turning a manuscript into a book requires the efforts of many people. The publishing team at Bookouture would like to acknowledge everyone who contributed to this publication.

Audio
Alba Proko
Sinead O'Connor
Melissa Tran

Commercial
Lauren Morrissette
Hannah Richmond
Imogen Allport

Cover design
Eileen Carey

Data and analysis
Mark Alder
Mohamed Bussuri

Editorial
Lucy Frederick
Hannah Wilson

Copyeditor
Shirley Khan

Proofreader
Tom Feltham

Marketing
Alex Crow
Melanie Price
Occy Carr
Cíara Rosney
Martyna Młynarska

Operations and distribution
Marina Valles
Stephanie Straub
Joe Morris

Production
Hannah Snetsinger
Mandy Kullar
Nadia Michael
Charlotte Hegley

Publicity
Kim Nash
Noelle Holten
Jess Readett
Sarah Hardy

Rights and contracts
Peta Nightingale
Richard King
Saidah Graham

Dear Reader,

We'd love your attention for one more page to tell you about the crisis in children's reading, and what we can all do.

Studies have shown that reading for fun is the **single biggest predictor of a child's future life chances** – more than family circumstance, parents' educational background or income. It improves academic results, mental health, wealth, communication skills, ambition and happiness.

The number of children reading for fun is in rapid decline. Young people have a lot of competition for their time, and a worryingly high number do not have a single book at home.

Hachette works extensively with schools, libraries and literacy charities, but here are some ways we can all raise more readers:

- Reading to children for just 10 minutes a day makes a difference
- Don't give up if children aren't regular readers – there will be books for them!

- Visit bookshops and libraries to get recommendations
- Encourage them to listen to audiobooks
- Support school libraries
- Give books as gifts

There's a lot more information about how to encourage children to read on our websites: **www.RaisingReaders.co.uk** and **www.JoinRaisingReaders.com**.

Thank you for reading.